After surviving their own haunting experience with the supernatural, these paranormal investigators are ready to beat ghosts at their own game.

GHOST TOWN

MEET THE TEAM:

Amber Lozier is the most sensitive member of the group. For years, she suffered from sleep deprivation, depression, and nightmares until she finally confronted the spirits that terrorized her. Now her vivid, often sinister, dreams verge on the psychic, allowing her to subconsciously work out problems and gain insights that prove valuable to her investigations.

Drew Pearson is a psychologist who has been trying to find logical explanations for seemingly supernatural phenomena since he was a teenager. His intuition helps people deal with frightening and sometimes violent supernatural manifestations, and his expertise helps determine the emotional causes of their trauma.

Trevor Ward is a writer who specializes in travel guides to haunted places. Since the terrifying night they spent together at Lowry House fifteen years ago, he's been trying to convince Amber and Drew to help him write a book about their experience. His connections, wealth of knowledge about paranormal topics, and research skills are important assets to the team.

CALGARY PUBLIC LIBRARY

NOV - - 2012

GHOST TOWN

JASON HAWES AND **GRANT WILSON**
with **TIM WAGGONER**

G

Gallery Books

New York   London   Toronto   Sydney   New Delhi

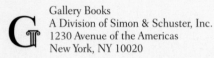

Gallery Books
A Division of Simon & Schuster, Inc.
1230 Avenue of the Americas
New York, NY 10020

This book is a work of fiction. Names, characters, places, and incidents either are products of the authors' imagination or are used fictitiously. Any resemblance to actual events or locales or persons, living or dead, is entirely coincidental.

Copyright © 2012 by Jason Hawes and Grant Wilson

All rights reserved, including the right to reproduce this book or portions thereof in any form whatsoever. For information address Gallery Books Subsidiary Rights Department, 1230 Avenue of the Americas, New York, NY 10020

First Gallery Books trade paperback edition October 2012

GALLERY BOOKS and colophon are registered trademarks of Simon & Schuster, Inc.

For information about special discounts for bulk purchases, please contact Simon & Schuster Special Sales at 1-866-506-1949 or business@simonandschuster.com.

The Simon & Schuster Speakers Bureau can bring authors to your live event. For more information or to book an event contact the Simon & Schuster Speakers Bureau at 1-866-248-3049 or visit our website at www.simonspeakers.com.

Designed by Jacquelynne Hudson

Manufactured in the United States of America

10   9   8   7   6   5   4   3   2   1

Library of Congress Cataloging-in-Publication Data
Hawes, Jason.
    Ghost town : a novel / Jason Hawes and Grant Wilson, with Tim Waggoner.—1st Gallery Books trade paperback ed.
       p. cm.
    I. Wilson, Grant. II. Waggoner, Tim. III. Title.
    PS3608.A8828G47 2012
    813'.6—dc23   2012008973

ISBN 978-1-4516-1382-7
ISBN 978-1-4516-1384-1 (ebook)

I have dedicated the last twenty-five years of my life trying to find the answers of what lies beyond this realm, this life and this world. I plan on spending the next twenty-five years doing the same.
I dedicate this book to all those who have stood beside me during my life's journey. The investigators that make up the T.A.P.S. family and other groups around the world. The inventors who have dedicated so much time in making equipment for us. Those who came before us and those who will carry the torch long after we are gone. To all those who have helped me create and expand this thing of ours that started in the basement of my house. Eventually, we will all find our answers, in this world or the next!

—*Jason*

I dedicate this book to those who have gone before us into the unknown: the people who lived a full life and passed through the veil. Thank you for trying to reach us. It has indeed made my life much more interesting and full. I hope to meet you all some day, and laugh and learn together.

—*Grant*

To Ramsey Campbell, who, without knowing it, taught me how to write a scary story.

—*Tim*

GHOST TOWN

ONE

"...**just feel** the energy, you know?"

Tonya Jackson ignored the man's comment. She finished scanning his books—*Spectral Encounters, A Grimoire for the Beginning Warlock,* and, most ridiculous of all, *Pets from Beyond: True Stories of Animal Ghosts.* When she was finished, she slid the trade paperbacks into a plastic bag and then looked up, making sure to keep her expression neutral. The last thing she wanted to do was encourage him.

"That'll be twenty-nine ninety-five."

The man went on as if he hadn't heard her. "I mean, the whole town just *oozes* psychic energy!" He turned to the girl on his left. "Am I right?"

The girl shrugged. She seemed far more interested in the gum she was chewing than in what her companion was talking about. Tonya didn't blame her.

The man was in his forties, short, with a prominent belly but stick-thin arms and legs. His unkempt beard was mostly gray, but he still had threads of black in his hair, which he wore in a ponytail bound by a leather thong. He wore a tan coverall with his last name sewn over the left breast—Donner—and the *Ghostbusters* logo sewn on the back. At least he wasn't wearing a fake proton pack, Tonya thought. The girl was around her age, Tonya guessed, somewhere in her mid- to late twenties. She was a good head taller than her companion and thin almost to the point of looking malnourished. Her black hair was short and wild, as if she hadn't combed it in weeks. Despite the fact that it was late October and chilly outside, the girl had on a black minidress that left her shoulders and arms bare, the better to display the tribal tattoos on her back and chest. *The sacrifices we make for fashion,* Tonya thought.

Instead of reaching for his wallet to pay for his books, the man glanced down at the counter, and his gaze fell on a stack of brochures sitting next to the register. He picked one up and opened it.

"Esotericon? What's that?"

Tonya fought to hold in a sigh. She *loathed* chatty customers—especially weird ones. She had a sociology test the next morning, and she needed to be going over her notes. She didn't have time to waste on this geek. Besides, she was getting a creepy-old-man vibe off him. He was at least fifteen years older than the girl he was with, maybe more. But Jenn had left her in charge of the store that night, and she was always telling Tonya that she needed to work a little harder on her "customer relations."

She forced a smile as she answered. "It's a conference on the paranormal that's held every year in conjunction with the town's Halloween celebration."

"You mean Dead Days?" the girl asked, sounding bored.

Tonya couldn't stop her sigh this time. "That's right."

The man leaned forward and lowered his voice almost to a whisper. "Is it true what they say? Is Exeter really the most haunted town in America?"

"It's just a slogan to bring in tourists. That'll be twenty-nine ninety-five for the books, sir."

He didn't take the hint. "But you live here, right? You must have experienced some pretty strange things."

I'm experiencing something pretty damned strange right now, she thought. "I didn't grow up around here. I just take classes at the college. Twenty-nine ninety-five, please." She said the price more slowly this time, hoping he would finally take the hint. Normally, she preferred it when the store wasn't busy so she could text on her phone, surf the Net, or—if absolutely necessary—study. But now she wished there were some other customers there, so she would have a convenient excuse to end this annoying conversation. There were plenty of people strolling by on the sidewalk outside, many of them wearing costumes, but except for the two standing in front of her, it seemed no one was interested in coming inside to browse Forgotten Lore's stock of new and used books.

The man was undeterred by Tonya's response. He leaned forward a bit more, his eyes narrowing, mouth forming a conspiratorial smile. "Yeah, but you *work* in a paranormal bookstore. You must hear all kinds of stories . . ."

She hated October in Exeter. Tourism was the town's primary industry, and Exeter's reputation as a paranormal hot spot drew visitors year-round. But October brought a whole different level of crazy. People thronged the town, drawn by the twin attractions of the weeklong Halloween celebration called Dead Days and Esotericon, a conference that featured everyone from reputable scientists to what the con organizers generously referred to as "enthusiastic amateurs."

"You know what kind of stories I hear? Pathetic spook fantasies from morons like you who actually believe in all this shit." She waved her hand in a gesture meant to take in the entire bookstore.

The man looked shocked, but his companion laughed. "What a rude bitch," she said, almost approvingly, and then she took the man's arm and steered him away from the counter. "C'mon, Donner. Let's go see what other weirdness we can find."

The man gave Tonya a dirty look over his shoulder as they departed, his books left abandoned on the counter.

When they were gone, Tonya let out another sigh. She had tried, she really had, but she had never been one to suffer fools lightly, and working there, fools were pretty much the only customers she got. The store's sections said it all: Ghosts, UFOs, Magik (with a "k," of course), Alternative Spirituality, Psychic Phenomena, Cryptozoology . . . At least Jenn didn't actually believe in any of this paranormal crap. To her, it was an interesting hobby, something amusing to think about and engage her imagination, but that was all. Tonya didn't understand Jenn's point of view—all of this stuff seemed like a monumental waste of time to her—but if Jenn wanted to have a little fun while she made money off the deluded idiots who came in there, more power to her, as far as Tonya was concerned. Still, she looked forward to finishing her course work at Tri-County Community College so she could head off to Purdue, where she planned to major in high-school science education, leaving Exeter—and the loonies it attracted—behind for good.

Tonya pulled her cell phone from the back pocket of her jeans to check the time. Nine forty-two. Normally, Jenn closed the store at seven on weeknights, but she kept the store open until ten during Dead Days. Tonya knew she should be a good girl and keep the place open until closing time, especially since she had blown that last sale. But a few of her friends were getting together to watch movies. Just like Tonya, her friends hated Dead Days, so every year, they held an "Anti-Dead" party, where they watched anything but horror movies. Last year, they had watched comedies, but this year, they planned to watch what Tonya called weepers, dramas that left you in tears by the end. The party had started at nine, and she didn't want to miss any more of it than she had to. But she *should* be a good worker bee—

Her phone let out a few notes of her current favorite pop song to announce the arrival of a text message. It was from her roommate, Isobel: "Get ur butt ovr here, grl! Weve alrdy gon thru a boxa tissues!!!"

A second later, another text came in, this one from Julia: "And a pint of Cherry Garcia!"

Tonya's fingers flew across the keyboard. "BRT!" she texted. *Be right there!*

She slid the phone back into her pocket and hurried to the front door. She locked it and flipped the Open sign to Closed. She felt a little guilty for locking up early, but she told herself that there was only fifteen minutes or so left until closing time, and the chances that anyone was going to come in and make a purchase were slim to none. Rationalization firmly in place, she reshelved the books Mr. Ghostbuster had abandoned, cashed out the register, and made a quick pass through the shop, straightening and tidying just enough so that it would pass muster with Jenn.

Forgotten Lore was located in an old two-story house on the southern end of Sycamore Street, the town's main business strip. Most of the buildings there housed funky little shops that sold art, crafts, or antiques, all of them at least tangentially related to the occult. The buildings were older than dirt, and Forgotten Lore's was, at least according to Jenn, the oldest of the lot. It stank of moldering wood and—thanks to all the books—decaying paper, and Tonya had to load up on allergy medicine before every shift. Even then, her eyes watered, and the back of her throat itched whenever she was there. Jenn didn't overdo the décor, something Tonya was exceedingly grateful for. Too many of the Sycamore Shops, as they were known locally, indulged in what Tonya thought of as horror drag. Color schemes of black and red, crystal balls resting on ornate metal stands, candles shaped like brooding skulls, and fake ravens with plastic feet wired to their perches. And the shopkeepers were just as bad, dressing like morticians or cut-rate carnival fortune-tellers. Jenn always dressed like a normal person, usually wearing a blouse and nice jeans, although she did have a regrettable tendency to wear large, gaudy earrings. Jenn let Tonya dress however she wished, as long her clothing wasn't inappropriate for work—which meant leaving her Skeptics Society T-shirt at home. This night she wore jeans and a bright tie-dyed T-shirt to counter all the black the tourists wore. The shirt was a couple of sizes too large for her. She liked her clothes roomy in general, but not because she wanted to cloak her body. She had a nice shape and a more than generous bosom, but she didn't like wearing form-fitting clothing, especially at work. The last thing she wanted to do was attract any of the nutjobs who shopped there.

Tonya glanced at a small display table by the front door. A number of books were stacked there, with cheesy titles such as *Taverns of Terror* and *Insidious Inns,* a few sitting propped up the better to show their covers. A small sign enclosed in a clear plastic holder announced that the books' author, Trevor Ward, would be signing at Esotericon the next day. From what Tonya understood, this Trevor guy was a former boyfriend of Jenn's. So maybe she was more into the paranormal than she let on. Or maybe she just had a soft spot for ex-lovers.

Not that Jenn's feelings for Trevor had kept her from setting up a larger display for another writer attending Esotericon. Arthur Carrington, who was also signing the next day, was so famous that even Tonya knew who he was. His books had lurid titles such as *The Horror of Mount Pleasant, Darkness Within and Without,* and *Shattered Innocence: The Haunting of Sarah McKenzie.* Tonya had never read any of his stuff, but a lot of the kids she had known back in high school had devoured his books. From what Jenn had told her, Carrington was in town not only for the conference but also to film a documentary about Exeter. That would be good publicity for the town, Tonya supposed, but it would probably draw even more weirdos.

Tonya had to admit this was a decent job, though, weirdos and all. Jenn was a nice woman and a fair boss, and working there sure beat the hell out of sweating through stressful shifts as a fast-food wage slave, as too many of her friends did. And to be honest, most of the time, working at the store wasn't too bad. Things just got weird during Dead Days, that's all. But she knew the antidote to that: watching sad movies and enjoying Ben & Jerry's ice cream—assuming the other girls hadn't eaten it all before she got there.

Tonya started toward the rear of the store. Jenn had the place rigged so that all the lights in the building could be controlled by a main switch by the back entrance, something Tonya really appreciated. Although she viewed herself as a strict rationalist, she sometimes got a little creeped out when working alone. And while she would never admit it to anyone, the idea of having to go from room to room turning off all the lights before she could leave did not appeal.

She was walking past the register when she heard a soft thump behind her. The sound made her jump, and she spun around to see what had made it. She scanned the store, heart pumping in her ears, but she saw nothing. She let out a shaky breath and forced a smile. *Just your imagination,* she told herself.

Then she saw the book lying on the floor.

She had heard the expression about the hairs on the back of your neck standing up, but until that moment, she had never experienced the sensation. But she did then, and accompanying it was an almost overwhelming feeling that she should forget about the book, turn around, and get the hell out of the store as fast as she could. She almost did, too, went so far as to slide her left foot to the side and begin pivoting her body to turn. But she stopped herself. A book had fallen off the shelf, that was all.

She walked over to the book and knelt down to pick it up. But she froze with her hand inches away from the cover. It was one of the books the middle-aged creeper in the *Ghostbusters* outfit had left behind: *Spectral Encounters*.

She had been in too much of a hurry when reshelving it, and it had slipped and fallen to the floor, that's all. No big mystery. Still, it took her a few seconds to work up the courage to touch the book, and when she did, she half expected to find it suffused with an unearthly cold. But it felt normal. She smiled and shook her head.

She had been working at Forgotten Lore too long. Maybe the next day, she should give Jenn her two weeks' notice and start looking around for another job. Something on campus, maybe.

She picked up the book, replaced it on the shelf, and made sure it was firmly in place before turning and walking away. This time, when she walked by the cash register, she heard *two* thumps. She stopped, adrenaline surging through her chest, and she began to shake.

She turned around and saw that two more books had fallen off the shelves. She didn't have to walk over to them to know their titles: *A Grimoire for the Beginning Warlock* and *Pets from Beyond*. The other two books Mr. Ghostbuster had left.

Tonya gritted her teeth and balled her hands into fists as she attempted to make herself stop trembling. *I won't run,* she thought. *I won't!*

Music drifted from her cell phone as another text message arrived, the sound startling her and making her let out a little bleat of fear. It was just one of the girls wondering what was taking her so long, she told herself—and probably asking her to stop off on the way and pick up more ice cream. She slipped her phone out of her back pocket and checked the message.

"Yes, you should run. Now."

There was no sender indicated.

Before she could react, books burst off shelves throughout the store, but instead of falling to the floor, they circled through the air, as if caught in a swirling windstorm. Tonya gaped in shocked disbelief as she found herself at the center of a maelstrom of flying books, their covers open and spread out like wings. *This can't be real,* she told herself. She was having some sort of hallucination, maybe a stroke. No, she was too young for that. Maybe it was an elaborate practical joke. Dead Days pranks were common in Exeter this time of year, although she had never heard of one this complex. Maybe the town's business leaders faked paranormal events in order to boost tourism. But she couldn't see Jenn going along with something like that, and even if for some reason Jenn had set it up, what good would it do to have it happen so close to closing time? Even if Tonya hadn't locked up early, there probably wouldn't be any customers there. Who else but her would see the flying books?

Jenn couldn't be responsible for this. But who . . . ? Then it came to her. There was a film crew in town, working on some kind of documentary about Exeter. They'd probably set this up, most likely as a "dramatic re-creation" of some supposedly true paranormal event. They'd probably put hidden cameras in the store so they could capture her unrehearsed reaction to their idiotic special-effects show. It was a shitty thing to do, but . . . Then she realized. There were no strings or wires holding the books aloft. Some kind of hologram, maybe? The books looked solid enough, but with the right technology, you could make anything seem real these days. Of course, why someone would spend a ton of money installing holographic projectors in a rinky-dink bookstore—and where they'd conceal the damned things—was beyond her. But that wasn't important right then. What *was* important was proving that it wasn't real.

Slowly, she extended a shaking hand forward into the whirling mass of books.

For a moment, nothing happened, and Tonya congratulated herself on exposing the flying books as fakes. But then a hardback edition of Montague Summer's *The Vampire: His Kith and Kin,* slammed into the back of her hand, and she cried out in surprise as much as pain. She cradled her throbbing hand to her chest, and without thinking, she took a step back from the mass of books streaking in front of her. Unfortunately, this put her directly in the path of those books flying behind her, and bright light flashed behind her eyes as a pair of volumes smacked into the sides of her head.

She fell to the wooden floor, but despite the fierce pounding in her head, she managed to pull herself onto her hands and knees. She wanted to stand, wanted to run for the back door, and she tried. But her head hurt too much, she was too dizzy, and instead, she slumped onto her side. Books continued swirling around her, drawing closer with each pass they made. She covered her head with her hands, curled into a ball, and squeezed her eyes shut.

She heard a woman's voice then. Not Jenn. Someone she didn't recognize. It spoke a single word.

"Stop."

Books began pelting her then—paperbacks and hardbacks— each one slamming into her over and over, striking and then darting away, only to dip back down and strike again. They continued smashing into her long after she was dead.

TWO

"No appetite this morning?"

Amber Lozier gave Trevor Ward a questioning frown, and he nodded toward her plate. Trevor and Drew Pearson had both finished their breakfasts, but she had barely touched her scrambled eggs and wheat toast, although she was working on her third cup of coffee.

Drew answered for her. "Bad dreams." He reached under the table and gave her hand a gentle squeeze.

"Really?" Trevor sounded intrigued. "Regular bad dreams or, you know . . ." He leaned forward and lowered his voice. "*Dreams?*"

The three of them were sitting in the dining room of Eternal Sleep Bed and Breakfast. Like those of so many businesses in Exeter, its name was designed to appeal to tourists drawn by the town's reputation as a paranormal hot spot. Amber was thankful that its interior didn't match its name. The house looked perfectly normal inside, which suited her just fine. Not that she would have been bothered by spooky décor, but given the sort of dreams she often had, the last thing she needed was any more fuel for the darker side of her imagination.

"Not everything is a paranormal experience," she said. "Sometimes a dream is just a dream." She paused. "Still, it *was* weird."

Drew and Trevor gave her a look, and despite herself, she laughed.

"OK, my dreams usually are weird, but this one was stranger than most. It was about books."

"Books?" Trevor sounded disappointed. "Doesn't sound all that weird to me."

"They were flying, their covers spread out like wings. Dozens of them were circling around me."

Trevor grinned. "I read somewhere that any dream that has flying in it is really about sex." He looked at Drew. "Is that true?"

"That was Freud's interpretation, but dreams are far too complex for simple diagnoses like that. Besides, wait until you hear the rest of it."

Amber continued. "The books started attacking, slamming into me over and over. It was one of the most painful and terrifying things I've ever experienced. I wanted to run away, but no matter how hard I tried, I couldn't. The books knocked me to the floor, and I couldn't get up. They just kept hitting me over and over until everything went black."

No one spoke for a moment after Amber finished. Finally, Trevor said, "You're right. That *is* weird."

"There was something else." She frowned as she tried to remember. "Right before everything went black, I heard a voice. A woman's voice, I think. I can't remember what she said, though."

"The voice might not have said anything," Drew pointed out. "It was just a dream. And even if the voice did say something intelligible, I doubt it was some cryptic message, full of meaning."

Trevor scowled. "I thought what we experienced at the Lowry House had cured you of being such a skeptical buzzkill, Drew."

Drew smiled. "Just because I'm now willing to consider paranormal explanations for strange events doesn't mean I think every bad dream is prophetic."

"But to dismiss the possibility out of hand . . ."

Amber reached out and patted Trevor's arm to calm him.

"Don't mind Drew. He's a bit ambivalent about being here this weekend."

Trevor looked at his friend. "Oh?"

Drew took a sip of coffee before speaking. Amber had been dating him long enough to know he did it to stall for a few seconds so he could gather his thoughts.

"I took yesterday off work so I could drive down here. When my supervisor asked why I wanted Friday off, I told her it was because I was presenting at a conference. She asked what conference."

"Let me guess," Trevor said. "She was less than thrilled to hear that you were presenting at an event called Esotericon."

"Her exact words were, 'Are you out of your mind?'" Drew took another sip of coffee. "She wanted to deny my leave request, but I had too many vacation days saved up. She did, however, tell me that if I persist in associating with 'pseudo-scientists and charlatans,' she would have to 'reevaluate my relationship' with the hospital."

Trevor had set up the presentation with the conference organizers several weeks ago, and he had invited Drew and Amber to join him. They were to talk about their experiences with the Lowry House, not least because Trevor wanted to do some prepublicity for the book he had written about what the three of them had gone through there, both as teens and as adults.

"I'm sorry about that," Trevor said. "If I'd known it would cause you trouble at work, I wouldn't have asked you to present with me today."

"Don't worry about it," Drew said. "Dr. Flaxman has had it in for me ever since I was hired. She's the stereotype of the cold, unemotional clinician who views human beings as barely one step above lab rats. We've never gotten along, and ever since she was promoted to director of the ward I work on, she's been looking for an excuse to fire me."

"Maybe so," Trevor said, "but that doesn't mean you have to give in to her."

"That's what *I* told him," Amber said. She turned to Drew. "See? Trevor agrees with me."

Trevor held up his hands. "Whoa! Hold up there! I'm thrilled that the two of you are an item, but I don't want to get sucked into playing relationship referee for you guys. Just think of me as Switzerland: I don't take sides."

Amber laughed, and Drew smiled.

"We'll do our best to respect your neutrality," Drew said. "But I wasn't about to let Dr. Flaxman bully me. That sort of behavior shouldn't be rewarded." He finished his last sip of coffee and put the cup down on the table.

Amber had never met Connie Flaxman, but from what Drew had told her, the woman was, to put it bluntly, an ice-cold bitch. Drew was warm and caring, and he would do whatever it took to help his patients. Not only was he Flaxman's polar opposite, but he was a far better psychologist, beloved by both patients and the other staff. No wonder Flaxman had it in for him. At least, that's how Amber saw it. She knew she wasn't exactly the most objective person when it came to Drew.

He continued. "Besides, after what we went through back home, I'm more open to . . . expanding my horizons. I figure Esotericon is a good first step in that direction."

Home was Ash Creek, Ohio, where the three of them had met and become friends in high school. They had discovered that they had a mutual interest in paranormal phenomena, especially the idea that it might be possible to discover proof of the existence of life after death. They had begun conducting amateur investigations of sites around town that were rumored to be haunted. They had experienced some interesting things, but nothing had prepared them for investigating the most haunted place in town: the Lowry House. What had happened there when they were younger had so traumatized them that they had suppressed the memory for fifteen years. They had returned in early September, ostensibly for their fifteenth high-school reunion but really to confront their past and banish the demons—some psychological, some literal—that had been plaguing them. In the end, they had succeeded and regained their memories but at a high price: the death of a fourth member of their teenage group, Greg Daniels.

"I'm surprised you haven't written any books about Exeter," Amber said to Trevor.

"I did a few articles on it, back when I was dating Jenn. After we broke up . . . well, I didn't get back to town much, you know?"

Trevor tried to sound matter-of-fact, but Amber could detect sadness in his tone. She wanted to say something to comfort him, but she decided it was best to let the matter go without comment. Coming back to Exeter had to be difficult enough for Trevor. No need to stir up old feelings any more than necessary.

Trevor Ward was of medium height and a bit overweight, with thinning brown hair. He usually had a smile on his face, and he exuded boyish charm and enthusiasm—especially when it came to anything related to the paranormal.

In contrast, Drew Pearson was taller, thinner, and more handsome. But then, Amber might be just a bit biased in his favor, considering that they had become lovers a couple of months ago. He had soft brown eyes and light brown hair that always looked a bit tousled, no matter how many times he brushed it. Although outwardly he seemed more reserved than Trevor, he was a deeply caring person, and it was one of the qualities she loved most about him. When he listened to you, he really *listened*, focusing his entire attention on what you were saying as if it truly mattered. And to him, it did.

The last couple of months had been good for Amber. She and Drew still lived in different cities—she in Zephyr, Ohio, he in Chicago—but they saw each other as often as they could. It wasn't an exaggeration to say that her life had been a mess before they got together. She had suffered sleep disorders, migraines, and depression, and she had been on disability for several years. All of her troubles had stemmed from the trauma she, Drew, and Trevor had suffered the night the Lowry House burned down. The buried memories of that night had affected each of them in different ways. Trevor had gone to college, gotten a degree in journalism, and begun writing nonfiction books and articles on the paranormal. Drew had abandoned his interest in the paranormal and become a psychologist who specialized in working with people who had suffered severe trauma. And Amber . . . well, she had barely been able to keep herself together, enduring a series of low-paying menial jobs, a series of lousy boyfriends, and more than her fair share of health and emotional problems.

But that all changed when the three of them returned to Ash Creek to confront their past. The memories they had regained were sometimes hard to deal with, but knowing was better than not knowing, as far as Amber was concerned. Best of all, she and Drew had finally admitted their feelings for each other and had been dating ever since. Amber was off most of her prescription meds, and while she still had bad dreams from time to time, in general she slept better than she had since she was a teenager. Her skin had more color, and she had put on some weight. Not too much, but she no longer looked anorexic. Her shoulder-length blond hair was now shiny and healthy, and when she saw herself in the mirror these days, she liked the woman looking back at her.

"Am I dressed OK?" Amber asked. "I've never presented at a conference before, let alone attended one. I have no idea what people wear."

She had tried on a couple of different outfits that morning and had finally settled on a comfortable long-sleeved purple blouse, tan pants, and black shoes. She had decided to forgo earrings as too dressy, and she had used a light touch with her makeup. Drew had told her she looked fine before they came down to meet Trevor for breakfast, but she still wasn't certain.

Drew wore jeans, running shoes, and a navy-blue sweater over a white dress shirt. Even when he was working, he tended to dress on the casual side. He thought it put patients more at ease. Trevor wore a brown suit jacket over a white shirt—no tie, though—with blue slacks and black shoes. Maybe it was just his journalism background, or maybe he wanted to offset his boyishness, but when he worked, he tended to dress in a professional manner.

"It's been a few years since I attended Esotericon," Trevor said, "but in my experience, people dress in all kinds of ways. Attendees and presenters both range from casual to professional to . . ." He paused. "*Interesting* is the word, I guess."

Amber frowned. "I'm not sure what you mean."

Drew smiled. "He's trying not to say that there's a significant kook contingent at this conference."

"I am not!" Trevor thought about it for a moment, then shrugged. "Well, maybe I am. But that's part of what makes Esotericon so much fun."

"You're not making me any less nervous." She glanced at Drew. "And neither are you. Both of you might be used to presenting at conferences, but I didn't go to college. I've never even held a professional-level job, unless you count waitressing as a profession. I'm still not sure what we're supposed to *do*."

"We don't have to do all that much," Trevor said. "We're free to wander around the conference and attend whatever sessions sound interesting. But the only event we're scheduled for is our presentation. I'll show some pictures, and then we'll answer questions. Nothing to it."

"Maybe for you two," Amber said. "Drew talks to people all the time in his job, and you interview people for a living. Plus, you enjoy being in the spotlight. But the last time I spoke in front of a crowd was during Mr. Vagedes's speech class back in high school. And you guys remember how *that* turned out."

Both Drew and Trevor fought smiles.

She had managed to get through less than a fifth of her speech—which had been on the merits of good nutrition—when she'd had to flee the classroom. She had barely made it to the restroom before throwing up.

Drew took hold of her hand again, and this time he held it tight. "You'll be fine. We'll both be there, and you won't have to talk any more than you want to."

"Besides, you know me," Trevor said. "I'll probably end up doing most of the talking if you two don't shut me up."

Amber smiled. Drew and Trevor had their own methods of trying to reassure her—Drew with emotional support, Trevor with humor—and together they never failed to make her feel better. Sometimes she wished the events the three of them had experienced at the Lowry House—both when they were teenagers and a couple of months ago—hadn't happened. But one good thing had come out of it: the three of them had bonded more deeply than ever.

"As part of the presentation, I'm going to be giving a preview of my new book. I still haven't decided on a final title yet. Right now, I'm leaning toward *Dark Legacy,* but my agent likes *Among Shadows.* The manuscript is with my editor right now, and I'm waiting for her to weigh in on the title. But the book's not in production yet, so there's still time to make any changes you two might want."

Amber and Drew exchanged a look. They kept their expressions neutral, but Amber wasn't surprised when Trevor wasn't fooled. He knew them both too well.

"You didn't read it, did you? I sent you both copies via e-mail last week." He sounded more hurt than angry. "And don't tell me you've been too busy to read it yet. I dedicated the damned thing to the two of you . . ." His voice softened. "And to Greg."

Amber knew how much this book meant to Trevor. He'd wanted to write about the Lowry House for years, but it was only after they had regained their memories that he had started working on the book in earnest. Once he had begun, it was as if a dam had burst, and the words poured out of him in a torrent. He'd finished the first draft of the manuscript in less than a month. Both his agent and his editor were excited by the book and thought it could be a huge boost to his career.

"It's not that we don't want to read it," Drew said. "It's just that it's too soon. For you, writing about the Lowry House was cathartic. But for us . . ."

"We're not ready to relive all that," Amber said. "It's going to be hard enough talking about it today at the conference. But to read about it in detail . . ."

Trevor didn't look mollified, but he said, "I guess I can understand that."

"There's nothing worse than waiting for feedback on a new book, eh?"

The three of them turned toward the man who had spoken. He stood in the entrance of the dining room, leaning against the wall, arms crossed, and smiling. He looked almost as if he were posing for a picture, or as if he were an actor who had just stepped onto a stage. He was a tall, lean man in his early sixties, with thick white hair that looked professionally styled and a neatly trimmed white goatee. His smile was wide, displaying teeth so white and even that Amber had trouble believing they were real. His eyes were a bright, startling blue, and they projected a good-humored intelligence, along with a hint of shrewd calculation, as if the man were sizing up the three of them. He wore a gray suit and a blue tie with small white blobs on it that Amber at first thought were oblong polka dots but soon realized were cartoonish ghosts.

"Pardon me for eavesdropping, but I couldn't help overhearing." His voice was a rich baritone, and again, Amber was put in mind of a stage actor, though a bit of a melodramatic one. "If I wasn't such a late sleeper, I would've been down to breakfast in time to join your conversation from the start. I'll just go tell our hostess that I'm up and famished, then I'll be back to commiserate about writerly woes." He gave them a last smile and a wink before walking off in the direction of the kitchen.

"What an odd man," Amber said.

"Seems a bit of a narcissist," Drew put in.

"That's Arthur Carrington," Trevor said. "I knew he was going to be attending Esotericon, but I had no idea he was staying here."

"The name's familiar," Amber said. "Didn't we use to read his books when we were in high school?"

Drew nodded. "He wrote about supposedly true cases of para-normal encounters. If I remember right, they were long on ghostly atmosphere but short on scientific evidence."

"I remember now," Amber said. "They were good, spooky fun. You could always count on them to send a chill rippling down your back. He had a show on cable back then, too, didn't he? I forget what it was called."

"*Beyond Explanation*," Trevor said. "I have the entire series on DVD."

"Guess you're a fan, huh?" Amber said.

Trevor scowled. "Not exactly."

Before Amber could ask what he meant, Carrington returned to the dining room and took a seat at the table. The table had room for six. Amber sat at one end, with Drew on her right and Trevor on her left, and Carrington took the chair at the other end.

"One of the things I most like about bed-and-breakfasts is the conviviality of dining with fellow guests," Carrington said. "I've been lodging here for a week now, and with the exception of the owners, you're the first people I've had the opportunity to chat with."

A fiftyish woman, short and on the plump side, entered the din-ing room then, carrying a plate of eggs, sausage links, and toast in one hand and a cup of coffee in the other. She set the meal on the table in front of Carrington with a smile.

"Thank you so much, Vivian," he said. "As usual, it smells deli-cious."

The woman beamed as if he had just paid her the highest of

compliments. Her gaze lingered on him for a moment before she looked toward Amber, Drew, and Trevor.

"How are you folks doing?" she asked. "Can I get you anything else? More coffee, maybe?"

Amber glanced at her coffee cup. It was only a quarter full, and she considered asking Vivian to top it off, but she had already had too much, and she was nervous enough as it was.

"I think we're fine," Drew said. "But thank you."

Vivian nodded. She gathered Drew's and Trevor's empty plates but left Amber's mostly untouched breakfast. She gave Carrington a parting smile before heading back to the kitchen.

Carrington took a sip of coffee and made a face.

"That woman has no idea how to brew a decent cup of coffee. Still, she means well." He put his cup down and turned his attention to Amber, Drew, and Trevor. "So . . . introductions, yes? I'll begin. I'm—"

"Arthur Carrington," Trevor said. "We're familiar with your work."

Carrington frowned at Trevor, as if he didn't like anyone drawing attention away from him, even for a moment. But his smile returned. "Ah! Well, then, I assume you must be in town for the conference." He nodded toward Trevor. "From what I overheard earlier, I take it that you're a writer. Might I have heard of anything you've done?"

On the surface, Carrington's question seemed innocent enough, but Amber detected a snide undercurrent, as if he expected to have never heard of Trevor. Carrington's attitude irritated her, and she found herself leaping to Trevor's defense.

"He's Trevor Ward. His books are really great, and today he's going to preview his latest one at the conference."

Trevor gave her a thank-you smile, but Carrington's reaction took her by surprise.

"Trevor Ward! Of course! We've met before, haven't we? A few years back, right here at Esotericon, if I remember right. You were dating that charming woman who runs the Forgotten Lore bookstore, Jenn . . . Rinaldi, I believe. Are you two still together?"

"Afraid not," Trevor said.

"Pity. But then, the course of true love has never run smooth, has it? My three ex-wives can testify to that!" He laughed. "Well, Trevor, how about you introduce me to your friends?"

But before Trevor could say anything, they heard the front door bang open, and a woman's voice called out, "Arthur? Are you up yet?"

An African-American woman rushed into the dining room. She was in her late thirties, her red-dyed hair so short it was almost a buzz cut. She wore horn-rimmed glasses—what Amber thought of as hipster glasses—and a small diamond nose stud. She was tall and thin and wore an open jeans jacket over a T-shirt with the words "Ghost Town" on the front.

She fixed Carrington with a disapproving look. "Did you leave your cell turned off again? I've been trying to call you for the last fifteen minutes!"

Carrington gave her a thin smile. "This is Erin Gilman, a talented documentarian and, as you can see, a somewhat impatient woman. Erin, this is Trevor Ward, a fellow scribe, and his two friends . . . ?"

Amber and Drew said their names, but Erin didn't acknowledge them. She kept her attention focused on Carrington.

"Arthur, we need to go. There's been a—" She glanced at Amber and the others. "Something's come up that's altered our shooting schedule, and we need to, uh, get moving so we don't lose the morning light."

"There's no need to play things so close to the vest, my dear. It's not as if we're doing an exposé revealing sensitive government secrets, now, is it? We're making a simple little film about a town that trades on its reputation for paranormal occurrences in order to attract tourists. Surely, whatever has *come up* can wait until after I've finished my breakfast."

And then, as if he were a child determined to make a point to his mother, he took a forkful of scrambled eggs, put them into his mouth, and began chewing.

Erin glared at Carrington, and from the way things had gone between them so far, Amber had the impression that she did that a lot. "There was a murder here in town last night. A weird one."

Carrington swallowed his eggs and put his fork down. He wiped his mouth with a napkin, then rose from the table.

"My apologies for rushing off like this, but it's unprofessional to keep one's director waiting." Carrington gave them a parting smile before he turned and started to follow Erin out of the dining room.

A cold emptiness opened in the pit of Amber's stomach.

"Where?" she asked. And although she didn't say the word very loudly, something about her tone made both Carrington and Erin pause.

Carrington gave Erin a look, and then, almost grudgingly, she said, "The Forgotten Lore bookstore."

She and Arthur hurried off, and the front door slammed.

"Jenn," Trevor said in a stunned voice.

Drew gave Amber a thoughtful look. "Your dream."

She nodded. Then the three of them leaped up from the table and rushed out of the dining room.

Mitch Sagers was half-dozing in his car when the VW Bug screeched to a halt in front of the Eternal Sleep Bed and Breakfast. He watched the driver hop out and run inside. She was a black chick, not bad-looking, but he didn't like her fake red hair. He didn't know why she was in such a hurry, and truth was, he didn't much care. But he was glad that *something* had happened to wake him up. He had been sitting across the street in the driver's seat of his Chevy Impala for more than—he glanced at his watch—twelve hours now, and the woman's arrival was the first interesting thing that had happened in all that time.

He yawned and stretched, groaning as his muscles protested. His neck was especially stiff that morning, and he whipped his head from right to left to pop the vertebrae. He felt as much as heard the crack, and the stiffness eased. His tongue felt as dry and rough as sandpaper, and his breath was sour from all the coffee he'd had the night before. Empty drive-thru coffee cups, four in all, littered the passenger-side floor, along with several crumpled sacks from fast-food joints. Acid churned in his stomach, and a small burp rose up, bringing with it a burning sensation at the back of his throat.

At first, the idea of doing a stakeout had sounded kind of cool to Mitch, as if he were a character in a cop show or something, keeping an eye on a dangerous suspect. But the reality was anything but glamorous. Not only did his body ache and his stomach hurt, but he felt a headache coming on, and he had to take a piss so bad he thought his bladder might explode. He wished he had thought to bring along several empty liter bottles to pee into, like truckers did when they didn't want to take the time to pull into a rest stop. But then, he hadn't really planned out his trip to the freak show that was Exeter, Indiana. It had just kind of happened.

A few moments later, the black chick came back out, accompanied by an old guy in a gray suit. She ran to her car and started it up, but the old man took his time getting into the vehicle, almost as if he were moving slowly on purpose just to piss her off. Once he was inside, the woman put the car in gear and hit the gas, and the VW peeled away from the curb and roared off down the street.

Despite its name, the Eternal Sleep Bed and Breakfast looked normal enough from the outside—if you didn't count the sign in the yard shaped like a small black coffin, the business's name painted on it in wavy white letters. Mitch figured the sign was supposed to look half-spooky and half-cute, but he thought it just looked all-stupid. The building was an older one, high and narrow, two stories, painted white, with green shutters, a black roof, and a couple of small spires that made it look a little like a castle. The attic had probably been made into extra rooms. At least, that's the way he would have done it. Not that he had ever stayed at a bed-and-breakfast before. Nicest place he had ever stayed at was a Motel 6. But then, he didn't make the kind of money Amber's new boyfriend did. A goddamned psychologist. It figured she would hook up with a shrink. She needed therapy bad enough—not that she could afford it. Maybe Doctor Love was taking his fee out in trade. Mitch could picture her underneath him, naked, sweaty, and writhing. They would screw like rabid weasels, and just before she came, the doc would glance at the clock on the nightstand, pull out of her, and say, "I'm sorry. Your hour is up."

Mitch ground his teeth together at the thought of Amber having sex with that guy . . . what had she said his name was? Drew something. It wasn't so much that he wanted her as that he didn't want anyone else to have her, although in Mitch's mind, they amounted to the same thing.

He and Amber had "dated" for a couple of months last year. They had met in line at the BMV when they had gone to renew their driver's licenses. He hadn't been all that attracted to her— she had been too pale and skinny, and her hair needed washing— but he'd had nothing better to do, so he had turned on the charm and started chatting with her. He remembered what his daddy had always said: "You never know what you're going to catch when you cast your line. But if you don't put your hook in the water, you damn sure won't catch anything." She had been reluctant to respond to him at first, but he had taken that as a challenge and persisted. Once they had discovered that they had the same birthday, she had thawed a little, and by the time they were both done and leaving with their new licenses, she had agreed to have dinner with him.

He had decided that she was pretty enough, in a sickly sort of way, but what he liked most about her was the sense of vulnerability she projected. In some men, that would have triggered a protective instinct. But for Mitch, it triggered an instinct of a far different kind. It told him that Amber was prey.

"Never show weakness," his daddy always said, and he had backed up his words with action. If Mitch had acted weak in even the slightest way, Daddy punished him, usually by delivering a good pounding with his fists. But sometimes Daddy's punishments had been more . . . creative. Mitch didn't mind, at least not anymore. Those punishments had made him the man he was today. Made him strong.

What they'd had couldn't be called a relationship. Mitch would show up at her place whenever he didn't have anything better to do. He figured he had a good thing going, but then, one day, she said something to piss him off—he couldn't remember what—and he had hit her. Not hard, just enough to let her know he meant it. He thought maybe she would cry or maybe even apologize. A lot of women said "I'm sorry" after you gave them a good smack.

But Amber hadn't said anything. The next night, Mitch had pounded on her door until his fist ached, but she hadn't answered. He knew she was home—she only went out when she had to. So he had continued pounding on the door for a solid five minutes before finally giving up. He had called and texted her numerous times after that but still with no reply. He had decided to try showing up on her doorstep again, but this time, there had been an envelope with his name written on it taped to the door. The message inside was simple, clear, and direct: "Mitch, I don't want to see you anymore. Don't come back. Don't call me. If you try to contact me in any way again, I'll call the police."

She hadn't signed it. Mitch had taken that as a personal affront. He'd kicked in the door and rushed inside Amber's apartment, but to his surprise, she wasn't there. She didn't have a lot of stuff, but he knocked over what little furniture she did have, broke her bathroom mirror, and threw a few framed pictures to the floor. It made him feel a little better, but not much.

He had considered staying there and waiting for her to come home. *Then* he would show her what he thought about her goddamned unsigned letter. And he might have, too. But he remembered something else his daddy used to say: "A man's got to control his temper if he doesn't want his temper to control him."

He had told himself that Amber wasn't worth getting upset about. Getting too worked up over anything was a sign of weakness, and Mitch was determined to stay strong. So he had swallowed his anger, left Amber's apartment, and done his best to put her out of his mind.

But then, a couple of weeks ago, he had gone to Target to pick up a new pair of work boots, and he saw Amber working in the women's department. He almost hadn't recognized her. She had been wearing a red shirt, a name tag, and tan pants, just like the other workers, but more than that, she looked different. Healthier. She had put on some weight, and she wasn't as pale as he remembered. But more than that, she exuded a calm confidence unlike the Amber he had known.

He almost hadn't gone over to talk to her, but he figured, what the hell? Might as well cast his line.

At first, Amber had been startled to see him, but she had quickly recovered and chatted with him for several minutes. She hadn't treated him like a friend, exactly, but she hadn't acted as if he was a monster, either. She told him she was working at Target part-time—she had started only a few weeks before—and that she was dating a great guy, a psychologist named Drew Pearson. Mitch hadn't known what to say. He mumbled that he was still working for the same landscaping company and that he was there to buy new boots. Amber told him where the work boots were located in the store, and he thanked her. She gave him a parting smile and returned her attention to straightening a row of blouses hanging on a display.

Not knowing what else to do, he had headed off in search of boots. But halfway there, he had turned around and left the store, making sure to avoid the section where Amber was working.

Seeing Amber had disturbed him on a deep level, but it took him a couple of days to figure out why. He eventually realized that it was because she hadn't been afraid of him. What was worse, she had seemed *strong*. Much stronger than she had been before. Maybe even stronger than he was. He should have asserted his dominance in the store, should have put her in her place. But he hadn't. He had just listened to her talk and had done nothing. He had been *weak*. If Daddy had still been alive, he would have beaten Mitch bloody for being that weak, and in front of a woman he used to screw, for godsakes!

Mitch had wanted to rush over to Amber's apartment, kick down the door again, and show her just how goddamned strong he could be. But he had told himself to control his temper. He needed to play this cool. Revenge as a cold dish and all that. So he had started watching Amber, parking at Target and outside the building where she lived. He hadn't been sure what he was waiting for, but he figured he would know it when he saw it. And then, the day before, it had happened. Amber had left her building and headed to her car, carrying a couple of suitcases. And when she had driven away, Mitch had followed her.

Three hours later, he had passed a sign welcoming him to Exeter, Indiana, the Most Haunted Town in America. Not long after that, he had parked across the street from the Eternal Sleep Bed and Breakfast, and—with the exception of a few quick runs to pick up coffee and fast food—that's where he had been ever since.

He focused his gaze on the B&B's front door and wished Amber would hurry the hell up and *do* something.

A moment later, his wish was granted, when Amber and two men came out and hurried toward a Prius parked in front of the B&B. Mitch had never seen either of the men before, but he had no trouble identifying the tall, good-looking one as Amber's new boyfriend. He opened the front passenger door for her, and once she was in the car, he closed it and got into the backseat. The other man hopped behind the wheel and started the Prius, and they took off in the same direction the black woman and the old man had gone. Mitch started his Impala, pulled away from the curb, did a quick turnaround in the B&B's driveway, and followed them. He planned to continue keeping a close eye on Amber and waiting for an opportunity to get her alone. He had spent the whole night thinking up ways to teach her that Mitch Sagers wasn't someone you ignored, and he couldn't wait to try them out.

As he drove, he caught a glimpse of a dark shape in his peripheral vision, almost as if someone was sitting next to him on the passenger seat. He turned to look, and for an instant, he had the impression of a woman with ivory-pale skin and long night-black hair, wearing a dress that seemed woven from the deepest of shadows. She gazed at him with unblinking ebony eyes, their surfaces as hard and shiny as polished obsidian.

Then she was gone.

Mitch stared at the empty space where she'd been sitting a second before. He felt an impulse to reach over and wave his hand through the air where she had been sitting, as if to make certain that she really was gone. But he resisted. He told himself that she had been a hallucination brought on by a combination of almost no sleep and being in this freaky town. That's all. He wasn't reluctant to touch the space where she had been because he feared he would find the air above the passenger seat colder than in the rest of the Impala, wasn't afraid that by touching the air he would somehow be touching *her*. There *was* no her.

He faced forward, gripped the steering wheel more tightly, and kept his gaze fixed on the road. And if he occasionally saw a dark flickering out of the corner of his eye, he ignored it.

THREE

"She'll be OK," Amber said.

"You don't know that," Trevor snapped.

But then again, he told himself, maybe she did. Of the three of them, Amber was the most psychically sensitive. Even Drew had come around to acknowledging that her dreams were often more than just dreams. But he couldn't allow himself to clutch at straws. One of the dangers of investigating the paranormal was that if you weren't careful, you started to believe in just about anything—especially if it gave you hope when you most needed it. You began looking for favorable signs from the spirit world, seeking insight into the future, consulting psychics, tarot readers, crystal-ball gazers . . . anything or anyone that could provide reassurance that things would be all right in the end.

Amber reached over and gave his hand a squeeze, and Drew leaned forward and put a hand on his shoulder. He was grateful for his friends' calming presence, and he drew strength from them.

The Eternal Rest B&B—and wasn't that a name that suddenly no longer seemed amusing—was located in one of Exeter's nicer residential neighborhoods. The houses there were older, dating from the first half of the twentieth century, but they had been well maintained, and many had been recently renovated. A steady influx of tourist dollars had kept the town economically healthy, even as other areas of the country had been struggling over the last few years. Trees lined the streets, their autumn leaves only just beginning to fall. They drifted down, red, orange,

brown, and yellow, the colors rich and vibrant, like an oil painting brought to life. On any other morning, Trevor might have
found the falling leaves beautiful, but today they only reminded
him of winter's approach. Death was still death, even when it
was pretty.

"They're out early," Drew said.

At first, Trevor didn't know what he was talking about, but then
he glanced at the sidewalk and saw a quartet of people in costume heading toward the center of town. Two men, two women,
barely out of their teenage years, all four garbed in black Victo-
rian fashion—the men in suits and top hats, the women in long
dresses—white makeup on their faces and black circles painted
around their eyes.

"The fun never stops during Dead Days," Trevor said. "As the
day goes by, more and more of them will hit the streets, until by
tonight's parade, the town will be so filled with people in costume
that it'll be almost impossible to get around."

They fell into silence then, and Trevor kept driving, resisting the
urge to jam the accelerator to the floor. The last thing he needed to
do was wreck his Prius.

Exeter wasn't large, and it took only a few minutes for them to
reach downtown. He saw the police cars first, three of them, parked
in front of Forgotten Lore, along with a blue-and-white paramedic
van. A small crowd had gathered on the sidewalk, some of them in
costume but most dressed normally. Employees from the various
businesses nearby, Trevor guessed. The onlookers stood well back
from the bookstore, talking among themselves and craning their
necks to get a better look at what was happening. Although Exeter
didn't have its own TV station, the Dead Days festival always drew
a significant media presence, and a pair of news vans had pulled
up to the curb as close to the bookstore as they could get, their
reporters already outside on the sidewalk, microphones in hand,
cameramen pointing video equipment at their solemn faces. One

reporter was male, one female. Both were young, well groomed, and dressed professionally. Two junior reporters who had been assigned to do lifestyle segments on an eccentric town and who couldn't believe their luck that a juicy murder story had fallen into their laps. Despite the serious expressions on their faces, Trevor could see the excitement gleaming in the reporters' eyes as he drove past.

He was forced to park at the end of the block, only a few spaces away from Erin Gilman's VW. She and Carrington stood not far from the TV reporters, Erin filming the scene with a small hand-held video camera, Carrington standing close by, waiting for his turn to go on camera. Trevor felt a wave of anger at them both. They were nothing but a pair of opportunistic leeches feeding off a local tragedy in order to add a tawdry touch of sensationalism to their so-called documentary.

He turned off the engine and for a moment just sat there.

"Trevor?" Amber said.

He took in a deep breath and then let it out. "I'm OK. Let's go."

The three of them got out of the car and began heading toward Forgotten Lore, Amber on his right, Drew on his left. He tried not to picture Jenn lying on the floor of the bookstore, her body bloodied and battered, as in Amber's dream. As a writer, his imagination was his most-prized asset, but it could also be his greatest weakness. As hard as he tried, he couldn't keep from imagining worst-case scenarios, and the images running through his mind right then were horrific indeed.

As they drew near the bookstore, it became harder for him to catch his breath, and he felt a surge of panic. He was surprised by the intensity of his reaction. He didn't want Jenn to be dead, of course, but they had broken up a while ago, and although they had remained friends, he hadn't had much contact with her over the last couple years. An e-mail now and then, an occasional phone call to check in and catch up. But the way he felt now—nausea roiling in his stomach, heart thundering in his ears—you would have thought he was still in love with her. But the idea was ridiculous. She was over him, and he was *definitely* over—

She walked out of the bookstore, accompanied by one of Exeter's finest, a tissue clutched in her hand, eyes and nose red from crying. She stared straight ahead, her expression blank, and the officer kept one hand on her elbow, as if she needed his guidance to walk. Trevor couldn't help feeling a wave of relief so strong that it nearly knocked him down. She was alive, and despite the obvious trauma she had suffered, she had never looked more beautiful to him.

She was half-Korean, on her mother's side, with long, silken black hair and creamy skin. She was taller than Trevor—almost as tall as the police officer who accompanied her—and model-thin. She wore a dark blue cardigan open over a T-shirt with an image of Toulouse-Lautrec's *Chat Noir* on it, along with a black skirt, black flats, and a cloth replica of an iris blossom pinned into her hair. The shirt was classic Jenn: the black cat at once both a nod to Exeter's spooky reputation and a stylish, playful mockery of it.

He started walking faster when he saw her, and she turned her head in his direction, as if she sensed his presence. At first, she stared at him with dull, uncomprehending eyes, not seeming to recognize him. But then her gaze cleared, and she moved away from the police officer and ran toward him. Trevor rushed past Carrington and Erin to meet her, and she threw herself into his arms and sobbed. He held her tight, leaned his head against hers, and breathed in the familiar smell of cherry-blossom shampoo and herbal body wash. It was like coming home.

Drew and Amber joined them just as the two reporters moved in like hungry jackals starving for fresh meat, cameramen close on their heels.

"Ms. Rinaldi, can you tell us what happened?" the male, a young African-American, asked.

The woman reporter—an anorexic-looking blonde—shouldered her competitor aside and shoved her microphone toward Jenn. "Is it true that one of your employees was murdered last night?"

Undeterred, the man fired off another question. "Do you feel this tragedy is connected to the Dead Days celebration?"

The blonde raised her voice, as if by doing so, she might goad Jenn into responding. "Rumor has it your employee was killed by being bludgeoned to death with books. Is this true, and if so, how do you, as a bookseller, feel about that?"

Trevor was appalled. He might not have been a news reporter, but he *had* been a journalism major in college, and he despised it when so-called professionals displayed this sort of callous disregard for someone's feelings. But before he could say anything, Jenn lifted her head and glared at the reporters through her tears.

"A woman died in my store last night! How the fuck do you *think* I feel?"

Both reporters still possessed enough basic humanity to look chastened by Jenn's words but only for an instant.

"Did you actually see the body?"

"Do the police have any leads?"

Trevor released Jenn and stepped forward to tell the reporters what they could do with their microphones, but Amber caught hold of his arm and stopped him. Drew stepped in front of Trevor and Jenn, gave the reporters a warm smile, and held out a pair of business cards.

"Hi! I'm Dr. Drew Pearson. I'm a psychologist, and my specialty is helping trauma victims." He paused, still smiling, still holding out his hand.

The reporters looked at him, looked at each other, and then—as if they had no idea what else to do—they each took one of Drew's cards.

"I'd be happy to provide some background information for your viewers. In fact, I recently read an article in the journal *Psycholog-*

ical Trauma which I think might be quite illuminating in this case. It was written by Austin and Wells, who have a well-regarded joint practice in Phoenix, and the article details their work with survivors of severe automobile accidents. Now, I'll grant you, at first, the correlation between those cases and this one isn't immediately apparent, but if you'll bear with me, I think you'll come to see that—"

The reporters—whose eyes had glazed over before Drew had gotten halfway through his spiel—mumbled thanks and turned their attention to the police officer who had escorted Jenn out of the bookstore. He was a sixtyish man with thick white hair and a bushy mustache. He was tall and beefy and had a bit of a belly. But he still looked in good shape, more like a former football player than the cliché of a doughnut-gobbling, gone-to-seed small-town cop. As the reporters and their cameramen approached him, he squared his shoulders, put on a professionally neutral expression, and prepared for their assault.

Good, Trevor thought. *Let him deal with those vultures.* It was part of his job, after all.

"A most impressive performance. If you can't dazzle them with logic, baffle them with bullshit, eh?"

Carrington walked up to them, smiling. Erin was right behind him, video camera down at her side. As hot as she had been to get Carrington there while the police investigation was going on, Trevor was surprised she wasn't filming Jenn. Maybe she had more common decency than those reporters. Or maybe, since she was making a documentary, she wanted to be careful not to upset Jenn. She would need her to sign a release form in order to use any footage of her—and Jenn wouldn't sign if Erin seemed to be trying to exploit her grief. Trevor didn't care where Erin's consideration originated, he was just grateful for it.

Drew turned to Carrington. "Sometimes pedanticism is mightier than the sword."

Carrington smiled at Drew before stepping forward and taking Jenn's hands in his own. A serious expression came over his face as he spoke.

"Ms. Rinaldi, I'm *so* sorry to hear of your loss. Was it the young woman who worked for you? Her name escapes me at the moment . . ."

"Tonya," Jenn said. Her voice was rough from crying, but she managed to hold back her tears. "I live above the shop, but last night, I was helping to get the Exhibition Hall ready for Esotericon, so I took a room at the hotel. Tonya was supposed to close by herself, and I told her to call or text me before she left to let me know everything was OK. When she didn't contact me, I figured she just forgot. She was scheduled to work again today since I'm supposed to sell books at the conference, but I came in this morning to pick up some more stock. Your books, Arthur—and yours, Trevor. But when I went inside . . ."

She trailed off, and a lone tear trickled down her cheek.

"I think it would be better if we continued this conversation somewhere else," Drew said. "Have the police already questioned you?" When she nodded, he said, "Good. I'll check and see if they need you to stay any longer." Drew looked at Amber. Silent communication passed between then, and she nodded. She stepped close to Jenn as Drew walked over to speak to the officer. The reporters were still grilling him, but when they saw Drew coming, they wrapped up their questions and moved off. Trevor was certain they would return to interrogate the officer further once Drew left.

Amber gave Jenn a sympathetic smile. "Hi. I'm Amber Lozier, one of Trevor's friends."

Jenn brushed away the tear on her cheek and gave Amber a weak smile. "Yes. You were with him in high school when . . ." She glanced at Carrington and Erin and fell silent.

"That's right. Is there a place where we could go sit down and have a cup of coffee?"

"There's Burial Grounds. It's just down the street."

Trevor wished there was a place they could go that didn't have death as part of its theme, but in Exeter, businesses like that were hard to come by. Back when they had been dating, he had taken Jenn to Burial Grounds many times, and he hoped the coffee shop's familiarity would help calm her.

"Sounds good," Amber said.

Drew returned. "At first, the chief was a little reluctant to let you leave, but when I told him it was my professional opinion that it would be best for you to get some distance from the store, he relented. He said he'd contact you if he needs to speak with you further."

Jenn nodded, her gaze unfocused, and Trevor wondered if she had really heard Drew's words.

The four of them started walking down the street, Carrington and Erin tagging along behind. Trevor wasn't thrilled about that—especially since he feared they were only interested in exploiting Jenn for their film—but he didn't want to make an issue of it, given Jenn's fragile emotional state. The less conflict right now, the better.

As they walked, she leaned against him, and without thinking about it, he slipped an arm around her shoulder. Despite the circumstances, it felt good to be close to her again.

Mitch wasn't able to find a parking space near the bookstore, so he parked the next block over, got out of his Impala, and walked to the store. Once there, he joined the crowd of rubberneckers, but unlike them, he didn't watch the reporters or try to catch a glimpse inside the building. He kept his gaze fastened on Amber. He didn't know what had happened—only that whatever it was had been important enough to draw the cops and the media like flies to rotting garbage—and he didn't really care. All that mattered to him was keeping Amber in sight.

He stayed toward the back of the crowd in case she looked in his direction, but he needn't have bothered. All of her attention was focused on the Asian bitch with the fake flower in her hair. She looked pretty damned upset, and Amber radiated concern for her, as did her precious Drew. But neither of them looked as concerned as their overweight friend, the guy who had driven them there in his candy-ass Prius. Mitch figured he had something going on with the Asian—or at least wanted to get something going. Mitch didn't blame him. She was hot. Maybe when he was finished with Amber, he might track her down, see if he couldn't get a little of that for himself.

After talking for a bit, the four of them were joined by the black woman and the old man who had left the bed-and-breakfast before them, and they all headed down the sidewalk—luckily, in the opposite direction from Mitch. He waited a moment to allow them to get enough of a head start before he followed. As Amber walked, she reached out to take Drew's hand, and the sight of them acting like a couple of lovesick teenagers turned Mitch's stomach. He was looking forward to getting her alone so he could remind her of what it was like to be touched by a real man.

From the corner of his eye, he had the impression of a black-garbed figure walking beside him, but he didn't turn to look. He sensed that it was the sort of thing you couldn't see if you altered your perspective too much. Like a funhouse mirror: change where you were standing, and the image altered. Or maybe this was more like looking at an eclipse: stare at it directly, and you risked damaging your vision. He remembered the woman he had imagined sitting next to him in his car back at the B&B. He especially remembered her eyes. They had been so black . . . so cold. He continued to believe that she had been nothing but a hallucination, though. *This* woman—and it was a woman, he knew that—walking next to him now was probably just one of the many costumed loonies wandering around town this weekend, that's all. But he still didn't turn to look at her.

He thought he heard a whispering voice then, its words as soft as leaves rustling in the autumn breeze. He couldn't make out what the voice was saying, not clearly, but he somehow still understood its meaning.

"I know what you want, and I can help you get it. But first, you'll have to help me."

There *was* no voice, he knew that. It was all in his head, nothing more than a product of stress and sleep deprivation. Still, he whispered back.

"I'm listening."

Drew was glad to see that the interior of Burial Grounds looked like a typical coffee shop. More funky than corporate, a college hole-in-the-wall hangout instead of the anonymous ubiquity of a Starbucks. The items on the menu had spooky-cute names such as Mocha Monster, Hemlock Tea, and Java of the Living Dead, but otherwise the place had few visual associations with death—which was exactly what Jenn needed right then.

They had to push two tables together to accommodate them all, and Drew figured they were lucky to find anywhere to sit, considering the Dead Days celebration was in full swing. He assumed that word about Tonya's murder had spread quickly, and a number of Burial Grounds' patrons had left to go check out the scene, leaving the place only half full. Death was a powerful lure for many people—it both fascinated and repelled in equal measure. More so, he suspected, for those who were already attracted to Exeter because of its morbid reputation.

Amber asked Jenn what she would like to drink, but she didn't answer. She sat expressionless, staring at the tabletop. Trevor answered for her.

"Just coffee, with cream and two sugars." He glanced at Amber and in a softer voice added, "Better make it decaf."

Jenn didn't contradict him, so Amber nodded and turned to Carrington and Erin. "Would either of you like anything?"

Both demurred, so Amber went over to the counter to order. Instrumental guitar music played softly over the shop's speakers, a smooth jazz piece that was the audio equivalent of a tranquilizer. Drew approved. The most important thing was to try to keep Jenn calm.

No one spoke until Amber returned with four coffees. She put Jenn's down on the table in front of her and gave Drew and Trevor theirs before sitting down with hers and taking off the lid. She hated drinking anything too hot. They didn't need coffee, not after the amount they'd had at breakfast, but Drew guessed that Amber hadn't wanted Jenn to feel singled out. He might be a trained psychologist, but Amber had a deep sensitivity to people's needs and emotions that no amount of training in the world could provide.

The seven of them sat quietly for several moments, until Jenn reached out, picked up her coffee with both hands, and took a sip. She sat holding the cup, as if trying to draw on its warmth for strength.

"I suppose this is the part where I tell you what happened."

"Only if you want to," Drew said.

Erin opened her mouth as if she might protest. No doubt, she wanted to hear every gory detail and get it all down on film if she could, but Carrington put a hand on her arm to stop her. She gave him a frustrated look, but she didn't say anything. Drew was surprised. Carrington didn't strike him as the caring type. Maybe Drew had misjudged him. Or maybe Carrington simply didn't want his director's eagerness to keep Jenn from telling her story.

"I already told you most of it." She took another sip of coffee. "When I went inside the store, I saw books scattered everywhere.

Not a single one was left on the shelves. My first thought was that we'd had an earthquake or something overnight. Ridiculous, right? This is hardly earthquake country. But I couldn't think of anything else that would've knocked the books around like that. Next I noticed the blood. I didn't realize that's what it was at first. Tonya had been dead for a while, and the blood had . . . had . . ."

She fought to control her shaking hands as she took another sip of coffee.

"Dried," she finished. "It was brownish red, not bright red, like in the movies." She gave them a weak smile. "Movie blood always stays red, doesn't it? No matter how much time has passed since it was spilled." She turned to Erin. "I guess it looks better on the screen that way, huh?"

"I, uh, guess so." Erin shot Drew a look, but he kept his attention focused on Jenn. He wasn't worried about her going off on a tangent. Unfocused thinking was a normal result of trauma.

"The blood covered dozens of books, but the majority of it was centered on a mound in the middle of the floor. I didn't know what it was, at least not consciously, but I began to feel nauseated as I made my way into the store. I stepped carefully through the scattered books as I made my way toward the mound. When I got there, I crouched down and reached out to start moving books—I guess I'd figured out there was something hidden beneath the mound—but before I touched any, I saw a patch of pink peeking through a space between two books. I didn't recognize what it was at first. Maybe I didn't want to. I stretched my index finger toward it, and when I touched it . . . You know how they always say that dead people are cold? Tonya's fingers weren't warm, but they weren't cold, either. They felt like uneaten chicken wings someone had tossed in the trash. Just meat and bone."

Another sip of coffee. Her hands didn't shake as much this time, which Drew took as a good sign.

"I didn't scream, didn't jerk my hand away from Tonya's fingers. I kept touching them for several minutes—at least, it seemed that long—not really thinking or feeling anything. And then I heard myself speak. I said, 'You shouldn't be touching anything.' I stood up, picked my way back through the books to the door, stepped out onto the sidewalk, and called the police on my cell."

She took another long sip of her coffee and finished it off. Drew, Amber, and Trevor hadn't touched theirs.

"It only took a couple of minutes for the police to arrive. Chief Hoffman came himself. I went to high school with his daughter. Small-town life, you know? Some paramedics showed up, too, although I don't know why, since there was nothing they could do for Tonya. Standard procedure, I guess. The county coroner arrived not long after that. The chief started to question me outside the store, but when those two reporters showed up, he pulled me inside and shut the door. He was just trying to protect me, but I couldn't stand being in there while the police and the coroner examined Tonya's body. So he took me outside again, and that's when I saw you." She paused. "I still don't believe it. I mean, I just spoke with Tonya yesterday. And to die in such a horrible way . . ."

Jenn seemed calmer now that she'd told her story. Not relaxed, by any means, but she had taken the first steps toward dealing with the trauma: allowing herself to begin processing the emotions she'd experienced. She seemed like a strong person, and although at this stage it was difficult to make any predictions, Drew thought that with time and counseling, she would be fine.

Erin had remained silent while Jenn spoke, but she couldn't hold back any longer. "How did she die?"

Both Trevor and Amber gave her a dirty look for asking such a blunt question, but Erin ignored them. Her attention remained firmly fixed on Jenn.

"Chief Hoffman said it looked like she'd been hit by books. A lot of them."

Drew looked at Amber. She had gone pale upon hearing Jenn's words, and he put his hand on her leg and squeezed gently. She smiled at him to show she was grateful for the gesture, but he could tell by her expression that she hadn't been reassured. He didn't blame her. If he found it eerie that the circumstances of Tonya's death so closely echoed Amber's nightmare, how much worse would it be for her? Not so long ago, he would have thought the similarity to be nothing more than coincidence. And while he supposed that remained a possibility, he doubted it. He might not understand the nature of Amber's psychic gifts, let alone the extent of them, but he had seen them in action too many times to discount them.

Trevor gave Drew an "I told you so" smile, and Drew nodded back.

"I don't suppose you have security cameras in your store," Erin said, not bothering to hide the eagerness in her voice. Drew imagined she hoped to get her hands on footage of the murder to use in her film.

"No," Jenn said. "It's just a small-town bookstore, you know? Unless you're an occult bibliophile, there's nothing worth stealing, and I don't keep a lot of cash on the premises."

Carrington jumped in then. "Do the police have any idea who's responsible?"

"No," Jenn said. "Chief Hoffman said Tonya had been texting with some of her friends before . . . before it happened. She was supposed to go home after she closed, but when she didn't show up, they didn't worry about it. Tonya had an on-again, off-again relationship with an ex-boyfriend, and they figured she'd changed her plans and gone out with him. And before you ask, the chief checked, and the boyfriend's got a solid alibi. The chief then asked me if Tonya had any enemies. Isn't that ridiculous? A young girl going to community college in a small Indiana town. What kind of 'enemies' would she have? It's not like she's some kind of criminal mastermind. The chief didn't say anything, but I had the impression that he thinks some nutjob who came to town for Dead Days is responsible. Most of the people who visit Exeter are normal enough, and they come here to enjoy a bit of harmless, spooky fun. Some are more serious about the paranormal, but even the most ardent true believers still have a majority of their marbles." She glanced at Trevor and gave him a small smile. "Although some have more than others. But every once in a while, a person comes into the store and gives off an 'I'm a little more crazy than the average bear' vibe. I figure Tonya was killed by someone like that."

"There might be another explanation," Trevor said. He sounded hesitant, as if he were speaking against his better judgment.

Anger clouded Jenn's face. "Don't you start, Trevor! Tonya was killed by some lunatic, not by some kind of ghost!"

Amber frowned. "I don't understand. Your store—"

"Is a fun business," Jenn said. "And that's all. I don't judge my customers, but for me, the paranormal is just a game, a way to indulge my imagination. I don't take any of it seriously."

Drew and Amber looked at Trevor.

He sighed. "As you might've guessed, we've had this argument before." He turned back to Jenn. "But it's different this time. Amber—"

"Will be happy to get you another cup of coffee, if you like." Amber smiled, but she gave Trevor a look that said she wanted him to cool it.

Drew agreed. It was not the time or place to try to convince Jenn that not only did the paranormal exist, but it was also somehow tied in with her employee's death.

Trevor might not have understood why Amber wanted him to shut up, but he got the message and remained silent.

"Thanks, but I don't want any more coffee," Jenn said. "I have to pee bad enough as it is."

"Let's go, then," Amber said. "I could do with a pit stop myself."

She rose from the table and waited for Jenn to do the same. She wobbled a bit as she stood, but she seemed steady enough on her feet.

"I suppose I'll continue the time-honored tradition of women going to the restroom in packs." Erin got up to join them.

Drew figured she didn't want to miss any bathroom talk that might occur about Tonya's murder. If Amber's eyes had been capable of emitting laser beams, they would've cut straight through Erin. But if the woman noticed Amber's disapproval, she didn't react to it. Drew doubted she cared one way or another what people thought of her, just as long as she got what she wanted.

The women moved away from the table, Amber staying close to Jenn in case she needed a steadying hand. When they were gone, Carrington said, "That was quite a story, wasn't it? And to think we were there filming a segment yesterday, only hours before the poor girl was murdered."

Trevor pounced on the statement like a cat eager to catch a mouse before it scurried away. "You were? What was it about?"

"Nothing earthshaking, I assure you. Erin's been filming background on the town's various attractions over the last week. The Ancient Spirits bar, the Beyond the Veil Museum, and so forth. Important enough for the project, I suppose, but dull work. Erin insists on my being there to offer a quote or two about each place, which I dutifully provide, but the rest of the time, I'm standing around watching Erin and her crew work."

"She has a crew?" Drew asked. "I had the impression she films alone."

"It's a minimal crew: one camera operator, one sound person, one lighting-slash-makeup person. Occasionally, Erin will film on her own if she doesn't have time to get the crew together, like this morning. But that's rare. It's quite a shoestring operation over-all. Nothing like what I was used to in my heyday. I remember one time when we were filming a segment for *Beyond Explanation* in Las Vegas. We were on location at a casino once owned by an organized-crime figure back in the 1960s. Supposedly, he killed several of his enemies and concealed their bodies in the building's foundation during the casino's construction. There had never been any proof, of course, so we'd brought a medium with us to attempt to make contact with the spirits of the victims. We were in the middle of shooting my intro to the piece when a little old grandmother from Tallahassee hit on a slot machine not ten feet from where I was standing. She screamed in joy, lights and sirens went off on the machine, and coins started flooding out of the damned thing and pouring onto the floor. When she noticed us, she thought we were there to document her triumph and insisted that I interview her on camera. She refused to listen when I attempted to explain to her why we were really there. Finally, I relented and asked her a few questions to placate her, and she departed with her winnings, satisfied that she was now the celebrity she thought she deserved to be. Well, the crew and I had a good laugh about it, of course, and then resumed film-ing. And wouldn't you know it? *Another* damned slot machine paid out and interrupted me yet again! And since I'd interviewed the grandmother, the gentleman who'd won this time insisted he get *his* turn on camera as well. By this time, my good humor was wearing more than a little thin, so—"

Trevor interrupted. "That's a great story, but before the women return, I'd like to get your professional opinion on what happened at Forgotten Lore last night."

Carrington scowled with displeasure at having his monologue cut short, but he put on a smile as he turned to Trevor. "I'm not sure what you mean."

"You know, your opinion as a paranormal investigator."

Carrington looked at Trevor a moment and then laughed. "My boy, I have been investigating strange phenomena since before you were born, and if there's one thing I've learned in that time, it's that the principle of Occam's razor usually holds true. The simplest explanation is almost always the most likely one. So my professional opinion is that last night, poor Tonya had the unfortunate luck to encounter a lunatic with a strong throwing arm. Nothing more. Now, if you'll excuse me, gentlemen, I think I'll get a coffee after all."

Carrington got up from the table and headed over to speak with the barista.

"He seems more than a bit cynical," Drew said.

"I thought you'd approve. Better that than too gullible, right?"

"I suppose." But there was a difference between being objective and being snide, and Drew thought Carrington came down more on the latter side.

"It looks like we won't have to worry about Carrington trying to horn in on us, which is good."

Drew frowned. "I'm not sure what you mean."

"There's obviously some kind of correlation between Amber's nightmare and Tonya's murder. And from the way Jenn described the scene inside the store—all the books off the shelves, scattered everywhere around Tonya, covering her . . . Do you really think one person stood there throwing books at her? And that Tonya just remained motionless while her killer pelted her with them? The only reason she wouldn't have fled is if she hadn't been capable of getting away. Once the coroner's report is in, I'll bet it shows she was hit numerous times from multiple angles, just like in Amber's dream."

"There could have been more than one killer," Drew said. "Or someone could've struck Tonya from behind, knocked her out, and then hit her with books."

"But—"

Drew held up a hand to cut off his friend. "*But* I think the situation is strange enough to warrant looking into. Is that what you're talking about?"

Trevor smiled. "You read my mind, pal."

Drew glanced in the direction of the restrooms. "Carrington may not have any interest in interfering with our investigation, but I don't think we can say the same about Erin."

"Jenn? Are you OK?"

Amber resisted the urge to knock on the stall door. If Jenn hadn't heard her words, she certainly wouldn't hear her knocking. As soon as the three women had entered the restroom, Jenn had gone into the stall—the only one—closed the door, and locked it. She had been in there for several minutes, silent the entire time. Amber was afraid she was crying softly, face buried in a wad of toilet tissue to sop up tears and muffle the sound.

Amber gave in and rapped a knuckle against the metal door three times.

"Jenn? Honey?"

No response.

Erin stood leaning against the sink counter, arms crossed over her chest. "I get that a girl needs her privacy," she said, her voice raised so Jenn could hear. "But you can't stay in there all day. Other people have to pee, you know."

Amber whirled to face Erin. "Leave her alone! You have no idea what she's been through!"

Erin raised an eyebrow. "And you do?"

Amber fixed her with a cold, direct stare. "As a matter of fact, yes."

Erin met Amber's gaze for a three count, finally breaking eye contact and looking down at the floor.

"*That's my girl.*"

The voice startled Amber, not the least because it seemed to be coming from inside her head. A mirror hung on the wall behind the sink, and reflected in it Amber could see the back of Erin's head and, to the right of it, her own face. But although no one stood next to her in the restroom, there was another face in the mirror. A pale, scarred ruin of a face.

Greg Daniels smiled, shiny-tight lip flesh cracking as it stretched back to reveal soot-blackened teeth.

"Miss me?"

FOUR

Amber didn't scream, but it was a near thing.

"Something wrong?"

She blinked. Greg was gone.

"No," she told Erin, surprised at how calm she sounded. "I'm fine." She returned to Jenn's stall door, doing her best not to think about what she had just seen. If she was lucky, it had been a hallucination. If not . . .

She rapped on the door again. "Jenn? We can take you home if you want. Or if you think you need something to calm your nerves, we can take you to see a doctor." She had only recently weaned herself from the numerous prescription drugs she had been on, and she didn't like the idea of pushing someone else toward a bottle of "Mother's little helpers." But given what Jenn had been through, she could probably use the pharmaceutical industry's assistance.

As before, Jenn didn't reply, but the lock *snicked,* and the door opened. Jenn came out, a wadded-up mass of toilet tissue clutched in her hand. Her eyes were red and still glistened with tears.

Once Erin saw her, she dropped her arms to her side and stepped forward. "Hey, about that 'other people have to pee' crack? I'm sorry. I . . . don't handle emotionally difficult situations well."

Amber was surprised. Maybe Erin wasn't such a jerk after all.

"That's OK," Jenn said. She used the tissue wad to blow her nose and then tossed it into the trash. She gave Amber a weak smile. "Thanks for offering to help. I'm glad that Trevor has a friend like you. Honestly, I don't know what to do now. I can't stand the idea of going home and being by myself, and while it's tempting to take a pill and escape reality for a while—*very* tempting—it's only a temporary solution. Reality will still be here when I wake up, you know?"

Amber knew exactly what she meant.

"Maybe you should try to stay busy," Erin offered. "I admit, I'm already prone to be a workaholic, but doing something—anything—helps keep my mind occupied when there's stuff I don't want to think about."

"I can't go back to the bookstore," Jenn said. "I don't know if I'll *ever* want to go back!" She thought for a moment. "I was supposed to sell books at Esotericon today. Maybe I can still do that."

"Are you sure you're up to it?" Amber asked. "I mean, given the topic of the conference, there'll be a lot of . . ." She paused. She didn't want to mention the word *death*. "A lot of dark imagery around."

"True," Jenn said, "but I'm used to that kind of thing. On the plus side, there will be a lot of people there, and the only thing they'll want to talk with me about is books."

"All right," Amber said. "If you really think it'll help. But if it gets to be too much for you, promise me that you'll let Trevor, Drew, or me know. We'll be at the conference, and we'll be happy to take you home."

"I promise."

Jenn and Erin started to leave, but Amber held back. When Jenn and Erin looked at her questioningly, she said, "Some of us really do have to pee," which made the other women laugh. When they were gone, instead of entering the stall, she walked back to the counter and gazed into the mirror.

Greg was there once again, standing next to her. Only now, instead of his burn-scarred visage, he looked like a handsome man in his early thirties with short black hair, dressed in a dark blue mock turtleneck. Amber knew it wasn't his real face, but then, considering that he was dead, he no longer had *any* kind of face, did he?

"Greetings from the Great Beyond." In the mirror, Greg's mouth moved, but Amber heard his words in her head.

"You're real. I can feel it."

"Surreal might be a more appropriate word, but yes. How are you and Drew doing? Still getting along? Is the sex everything you dreamed it would be? Do you call out his name when you climax, or do you just let out a shriek of ecstasy? Inquiring minds want to know!"

Her skin crawled, not so much because of what he said—although that was disgusting enough—but because of the leering tone in his voice. She kept her own voice even as she replied. "You found a way to communicate between the worlds of the living and the dead just to prove how big an asshole you can be?"

Greg smirked. *"No, but it's a nice side benefit. I'm here to tell you to watch yourself. There are nasty things in this town, and you've drawn their attention. All three of you have. If you're not careful, you'll find yourself over here on the other side of the mirror."* He smiled, displaying teeth black with soot. *"With me."*

She frowned. "How do I know you're really Greg and not just something pretending to be him?"

"I'm not Greg. At least, not only. When I died—sacrificing myself to save you, Drew, and Trevor, I might add—I carried the Darkness that had possessed me over to the Other Side with me."

"You did save us, but considering that it was you who endangered us in the first place . . ."

"Don't pick nits, Amber. Once we were on this side of the mirror, the Darkness and I merged. We'd been together too long to remain separate. It's a permanent part of me now—or I'm a permanent part of it. I'm not sure which."

"So I can't trust you."

He shrugged. *"That's for you to decide. I didn't have to reach out to you like this, you know. I could've just remained on the sidelines and watched you die."*

"And not taunt me? What would be the fun in that?"

"True." Greg's smile widened into a grin, and his eyes became pools of swirling black. *"I'll be in touch. Big wet kisses to Drew and Trevor."*

Then he was gone.

Amber stared at her lone reflection in the mirror for several moments before turning and leaving the restroom. As she opened the door, she thought she heard a soft chuckling in her mind, but she told herself it was just her imagination. She didn't believe it.

Amber tried to keep her expression neutral as she approached the table, but Drew raised his eyebrows and cocked his head, as if to ask if something was bothering her. She smiled and put her hand on his shoulder. He might not be psychic, but he was the next best thing.

She leaned down and whispered in his ear. "Tell you later."

He nodded, and everyone got up and headed for the door. Trevor remained close to Jenn but not *too* close. Amber knew he didn't want to seem to be hovering over her, even if that was exactly what he felt compelled to do. She wondered if Tonya's death, as tragic as it was, might prove to be the catalyst that would spark a renewed relationship between them. It was obvious they still cared about each other, but whether those feelings would deepen into love once more was impossible to say. For Trevor's sake, she hoped so. He was a good guy, and he deserved to be happy—as happy as she and Drew were.

She smiled at Drew and took his hand as they stepped out of Burial Grounds and onto the street.

Once they were all standing on the sidewalk, Trevor turned to Jenn. "I'm not sure going to the conference is such a good idea for you."

"I think it's just what I need." She glanced in the direction of

Forgotten Lore. The police cars and the paramedic van were still parked outside, and Jenn turned her back so she wouldn't have to look at them. She looked at Drew. "You're a psychologist. What's your opinion?"

Drew answered, but even though Amber was listening, she couldn't concentrate on his words. She felt a strange prickly sensation on the back of her neck, as if someone was watching her. She turned toward the bookstore and saw two people standing on the sidewalk slightly apart from the rest of the crowd. She didn't recognize the raven-haired woman in the long black dress. Amber assumed she was in costume for Dead Days, but there was something about her that seemed wrong. She stood too still, almost as if she were a frozen image, like a photograph or a painting instead of a real person. And although she was only half a block away, Amber had trouble seeing her clearly. The harder she tried to focus on the woman's face, the more indistinct her features became. But as disturbing as the woman was, she was nothing compared with the man standing next to her.

At first, she didn't believe it was him. It was easier for her to accept that a dead friend had spoken to her through a mirror than it was to accept that Mitch Sagers stood on a sidewalk in Exeter, staring at her, a woman in black at his side. It just didn't make any sense. What was he doing there? It couldn't be him. It had to be someone else, someone who just looked like him. But then she remembered what Greg had told her.

There are nasty things in this town, and you've drawn their attention.

An ice-water surge of panic raced through her, and her hand clenched tightly on Drew's. She couldn't imagine too many things nastier than Mitch.

"What's wrong?" Drew's voice was filled with concern.

Amber tried to answer, but she couldn't manage to draw in a breath. Mitch stared at her for a long moment, his gaze blank and unreadable. Then the woman in black took him by the arm, and together they turned and disappeared into the crowd.

"Amber?"

Drew stepped around in front of her, and as soon as he filled her vision, her trance broke. She pulled in a gasping breath of air, threw herself into his arms, and began crying.

Amber had looked surprised to see him. No, more than that: she had looked *afraid*. Mitch smiled with grim satisfaction. It was a good first step toward getting back the respect she owed him. But he still had more he wanted to do—much more.

Which was why he was so confused to be walking away from her right then. And away from that wimp of a new boyfriend she had. He could snap that asshole in two like a pencil without even trying. The more he thought about it, the more walking in the other direction might seem to Amber as if he were running away, as if he were the one afraid of a confrontation. It was a sign of weakness, and if his daddy were there right then, he would pound the shit out of him for it.

Mitch started to turn around, but the Dark Lady's cold grip tightened on his arm, stopping him. He grimaced in pain. Damn, but she was stronger than she looked!

"It's better this way. Give the fear time to grow within her. Meanwhile, there's something I'd like you to do for me."

He wasn't the kind to take orders from anyone, let alone a woman. But he listened as she whispered her plans to him in a voice like a midnight wind blowing across an empty field. And when she was finished, he thought, *What the hell? Sounds like fun.*

They continued walking down the street, the Dark Lady's whispers growing ever more sinister as they went.

Connie Flaxman gripped her steering wheel tightly as the strains of Mozart's *Symphony No. 40 in G Minor* wafted through her Mercedes. Mozart usually soothed her, but this day all it did was set her teeth on edge. She stabbed out a finger to turn off the CD, and the resulting silence came as a relief.

She couldn't believe she was doing this. She had left her house in Lincoln Park at five that morning, after a night of tossing and turning and getting almost no sleep. And now there she was, several hours later, getting ready to take the highway exit for Exeter, Indiana. As she drew close, she was tempted to press down on the accelerator and roar past it. She could find another exit, turn around, get back on the highway, and start heading home to Chicago. If she drove straight through, she could be home by early afternoon. She would have wasted half a day, but that was better than wasting the whole day, right?

She almost did it. But in the end, she lifted her foot off the gas, hit the turn signal, and pulled off the highway.

She had made her feelings quite clear to Drew when he had told her he planned to attend the so-called conference going on there that weekend. He had listened to her politely and said that he understood her viewpoint and that while he agreed that Esotericon wasn't the usual sort of conference he attended, he had made a commitment to a couple of friends to be there, and he wasn't going to let them down. And then he had given her one of *those* smiles—the warm, self-deprecating kind that always made a warm flush come over her—and said, "Besides, what's wrong with going outside your comfort zone once in a while?"

She had acted stern and disapproving, but she had granted his leave request. How could she not? He was a model employee, beloved by both patients and staff. All she would have gained by turning him down was to make herself look like even more of a coldhearted bitch than people already thought her to be.

As she entered the "Most Haunted Town in America," she drove slowly so she could look around and get a feel for the place. Small-town Americana, for the most part, with a quaint old-fashioned business district downtown. It might have been a nice place to spend an afternoon antiquing, if it hadn't been for two things: the childish names of many of the businesses—such as Diner of the Living Dead and Howl at the Moon Saloon—and the throng of fools walking the streets decked out in Halloween costumes. To make it worse, most of them seemed to be adults, at least biologically speaking. Psychologically was a different matter.

She had anticipated this, of course. A quick Internet search the day before had brought her to the town's Web site, and she had read up on its history and its current tourist trade. But she'd had no idea it would be *this* cheesy. More than that, the town seemed tasteless and ghoulish to her. According to the Web site, Exeter was located on the banks of the Mossapeak River, and in the early twentieth century, there was a devastating flood. Hundreds of people were killed, and most of the townsfolk who survived moved away soon after. Some remained to rebuild, and while it was a slow process, Exeter was eventually reborn. An inspiring enough story, she supposed—the phoenix rising from the ashes and all that. But as the years passed, residents began reporting incidents of ghostly visitations and the like. Ridiculous, of course, and undoubtedly tied to repressed feelings about rebuilding the town on the site of what was, symbolically at least, a mass grave. But to turn around and use the tragedy of the flood as a marketing ploy to bring in tourist dollars was nothing short of reprehensible. In all her years as a practicing psychologist, she had run across worse examples of human callousness but not many.

Satisfied that she had seen enough, she ended her little tour and headed for the hotel where Esotericon—and wasn't *that* a too-cutesy name?—was to be held. She had programmed the location into her car's GPS, and she reached the hotel without any problem. Once there, she parked, turned off the engine, and then sat, unsure what to do next.

When she had set out way too early that morning, she had told herself she was going there to check on an employee who was making a very questionable career move. After all, as Drew's supervisor, it was her job to make sure he maintained the highest professional standards in his work. Admittedly, driving all the way from Chicago on a Saturday was a bit above and beyond, but then, she had always been something of an overachiever. And she had been concerned about Drew lately. Over the last couple of months, his behavior had changed, although in some ways for the better. He had always been personable and caring, but only up to a point. It was more than just maintaining professional distance. It was as if he hadn't been able to bring himself to get too close to people. But that wall had come down, and he had begun interacting more with his colleagues at work, forging deeper relationships with them. With everyone but her, it seemed.

But there had been some distressing changes, too. He was willing to explore what he called "alternative explanations" for his patients' problems. He hadn't gone all woo-woo New Age on her, but he was definitely more broad-minded than he had been—and not in a good way. She'd had several conversations with him in which she had told him she was concerned that his new "perspective" might negatively affect the quality of his work. He had, of course, listened with respect, validated her concerns, and told her that he would continue to provide the very best service to his patients of which he was capable.

So she had come to Esotericon to see just how far down the rabbit hole Drew had fallen. And if he was no longer capable of functioning on a professional level as a psychologist, she would have no choice but to terminate his employment. That was the *only* reason she was there. Not because she suspected that one of the two friends he was presenting with was the woman he spoke about so often at work, the one he had been dating for the last couple of months, and who Connie suspected was the reason for his newfound emotional depth. And she most definitely wasn't there because she hoped to get a look at this woman for herself and see just what it took to capture Drew's heart—and perhaps gain some insight into how she might accomplish that goal for herself.

She looked at herself in the rearview mirror.

"You are so full of shit," she said.

She checked her makeup, did a quick touch-up, and then, satisfied, got out of the car and began heading for the hotel's entrance.

Drew, Amber, Trevor, and Jenn were in the Exhibition Hall. Trevor and Carrington were scheduled to sign books soon, but Carrington was nowhere in sight. When they had arrived at the hotel, Carrington had said he needed to "make an offering to the porcelain gods" and headed off in search of a restroom. That had been fifteen minutes ago, and no one had seen him since. Erin had taken his disappearance in stride. "He's either in the bar having a drink, or he's outside smoking. I'll go find him." In the meantime, Drew, Amber, and Trevor intended to help Jenn get set up for the signing. At the other end of the hall, a crowd had gathered around a table, where a pair of well-known paranormal investigators who had their own popular cable television show were signing autographs. When Jenn saw Trevor staring at them, she insisted he go over and introduce himself.

"Don't worry about me," she told him. "Amber and Drew will still be here."

"I know," Trevor said. "But I'd rather . . ."

Drew caught his eye and shook his head slightly. Trevor picked up on Drew's signal, and although he might not have understood the reason, he knew Drew wanted him to leave the book-signing table for a couple of minutes.

"All right," he said, a reluctant tone in his voice. "Maybe I can get them to give me a blurb for my book about the Lowry House. But I'll be back soon."

He gave Drew and Amber a parting look, as if to say, *Take good care of her,* and then he headed off. When he was out of earshot, Jenn said, "He's a sweetheart, but he can be a mother hen sometimes. It's hard for me to try to take my mind off what happened with him always standing at my elbow radiating concern, you know?"

Drew did know, which was why he had wanted Trevor to go away for a bit: to give Jenn the space she needed.

Esotericon's Exhibition Hall had been set up in the hotel's ballroom, a large, clean space, if a bit overdue for remodeling, with faded maroon carpet and tacky faux-crystal chandeliers overhead. Tables and booths lined the walls, with two more rows of exhibitor space running through the center of the room. Some booths featured sophisticated equipment that paranormal investigators could use to bring a scientific approach to their inquiries—full-spectrum camcorders and cameras, EMF detectors, night-vision scopes, infrared thermal scanners, air ion counters, motion detectors, and more. Other vendors took a more old-school approach, selling Ouija boards and tarot cards of various makes and designs, along with crystal balls and homemade charms. A number of regional ghost-hunting groups manned information booths, while several psychics sat at tables, ready to divine futures for twenty-five dollars.

An interesting mix of people wandered through the hall, inspecting the wares on display. Some wouldn't have been out of place at any professional academic conference—well groomed and nicely dressed but with a bookish air to them. Others were more casual in style, wearing jeans and T-shirts with slogans such as "Paranormal Investigators Do It with Spirit." There was a contingent of pierced, tattooed, black-garbed Goths, along with a handful of costumed conference goers who looked more than ready for the night's big celebration. Ghosts, vampires, and zombies were the most popular outfits for this crowd, although there were some Ghostbusters with homemade proton packs and—for reasons Drew didn't pretend to understand—several *Harry Potter* characters.

Trevor and Carrington had been assigned a single long table, and Jenn went to work arranging Trevor's books first. She had several cardboard boxes of books sitting on the floor behind the tabletop. Amber pulled books out of the boxes and handed them to Jenn, who placed them on the table. She had already erected a sign on an easel announcing that Arthur Carrington and Trevor Ward would be signing books that morning. There was still a half-hour to go, but people carrying books kept walking past the table, looking at the sign, and glancing at their watches. Drew saw that most of the books they carried had been written by Carrington, but he was pleased to see a few of Trevor's represented, too.

"I was surprised to hear you express such strong disbelief in the supernatural back at the coffee shop," Drew said to Jenn as she worked. "Trevor told us you originally contacted him to tell him about the increase in paranormal activity in town."

"I might've fibbed a bit," she admitted as she straightened a row of *Insidious Inns*. "Not about the incidents. Over the last few weeks, reports of strange encounters *have* increased. But then, they usually do this time of year. The tourist population surges, and everyone has Dead Days on the mind, you know? Imaginations start to kick into high gear, and soon people are seeing ghosts around every corner. But even so, this year, the reports have been . . . different. More bizarre. I thought Trevor would be interested in them and he might get another book out of it, or at least an article. I thought . . ." She trailed off as she placed a stack of *Taverns of Terror* on the tabletop and put a single display copy in front on a plastic stand.

"You thought maybe Trevor would come to visit," Amber said.

Jenn nodded. "It had been a while since I'd seen him. I . . . missed him."

Drew had been keeping a close eye on Jenn. Her hands trembled as she worked, and her voice quavered now and then, but overall, she seemed to be holding up remarkably well. He would continue to watch her, though. Severe trauma like the kind she had experienced wasn't something you could get over in an hour or two.

Erin returned then, Carrington in tow.

"My apologies," he said, sounding anything but apologetic. "I seem to have lost track of the time."

"Lost track of how much you had to drink," Erin muttered.

Carrington ignored her. "I see you haven't set up my books yet, Jenn. How much longer do you need? Another ten, fifteen minutes? Perhaps I'll wander around the hall for a bit until you—"

"No!" Erin said. She took hold of Carrington's arm, steered him around behind the table, and forced him to sit in one of the chairs. "You stay here until the signing starts. I intend to shoot footage of you interacting with fans, and I can't do that if you vanish again. Now, I'm going to call my crew and make sure they know what I want them to be filming today. I will be looking at you the entire time I'm on the phone, Arthur, so don't even try to lift your butt off the seat."

Carrington smiled at her. "Yes, Mommy."

She gave him a dirty look, pulled her cell phone out of her pocket, and made a call.

Jenn began setting up Carrington's books, and he started arguing with her about how they should be displayed. Jenn took it in stride, and Drew thought this might be a good time to speak with Amber alone. Something had happened at the coffee shop to disturb her, and he wanted to make sure she was all right.

He turned to Amber. "Trevor and Arthur could probably use some bottled water to sip while they sign."

"Good idea. Why don't you go get some while I finish helping Jenn set up?"

Drew leaned closer to Amber and whispered, "Erin and Arthur are here. Jenn will be all right for a few minutes. I want to talk with you—alone."

"I . . ." She glanced at Jenn.

Jenn smiled. "Go ahead. I'll be all right."

Carrington reached out and patted Jenn's hand. "We'll take good care of her, dear. Rest assured."

Amber looked doubtful, but she nodded, and she and Drew walked away from the signing table. Neither of them spoke as they headed for the Exhibition Hall's exit—there were too many people walking around and checking out the various booths—but as soon as they were out in the hall, Drew asked her how she was doing.

"What do you mean?"

He had the sense that she understood exactly what he meant, but she was stalling. Normally, he might drop the matter and allow her to tell him what was bothering her in her own time. But this was anything but a normal situation.

"About your dream paralleling Tonya's murder."

She looked almost relieved, as if she had expected him to bring up something else. Something worse. But what could be worse than someone's murder?

"I'm doing all right. I mean, don't get me wrong. It's damned eerie to have a nightmare like that come true. Or at least, kind of come true. I doubt the books actually flew around the room, like in my dream."

They kept walking until they reached the hotel's lobby. They continued past the check-in desk to the gift shop. Up front was a display featuring a variety of Exeter-themed souvenirs—refrigerator magnets, coffee mugs, T-shirts, hoodies, and ball caps—all tied to the town's reputation as a center of paranormal activity. Most of them featured a cartoonish ghost that evidently served as something of a mascot for the town. There was even a plush doll of the character, a smiling white blob of a thing that looked to Drew more like a friendly snowman than a fearsome creature from beyond the grave.

Amber picked up one of the toy ghosts and read its name off the tag.

"This is Hector the Specter . . ."

And at the same time, they both said, "From Exeter!" and laughed.

"I wonder who came up with such an awful name," Amber said as she put the toy back on the display table.

"People throughout the world deal with death by minimizing it somehow, either by making it seem cute and harmless or by turning it into an object of ridicule," Drew said. "A toy like this does both."

The food and drink were toward the back of the gift shop, and they headed for it. Drew grabbed a couple of bottled waters out of the cooler, and they took them to the register. The clerk—a middle-aged woman dressed like a zombie in a torn blouse stained with fake blood—rang up their purchase with a bored detachment that perfectly suited her costume.

As they walked out of the gift shop, Drew carrying the water bottles in a plastic shopping bag, he said, "They might've. The books, I mean. Flown around the room."

Amber gave him a suspicious look. "All right, who are you, and what have you done with Drew?"

He laughed. "I admit, my perspective on the world has shifted dramatically in the last couple of months. After what we experienced back home in Ash Creek, can you blame me?"

"No," Amber said in a subdued voice, as if she were remembering. "I can't." She paused, as if trying to decide whether to go on. Finally, she sighed and said, "At the coffee shop, when I went to the restroom with Jenn and Erin, I . . . saw Greg. In the mirror."

Drew listened as she told him what she had experienced. Despite what he had said a moment ago, his first instinct was to dismiss Greg's appearance as a product of stress. This was the first time after what had happened at their high-school reunion that Amber had been exposed to images and ideas relating to the paranormal—add that to her dream's bizarre similarity to Tonya's murder, and you had a perfect recipe for a stress-induced hallucination. But Drew had learned that there were "more things in heaven and earth," to quote Hamlet, and he forced himself to keep an open mind. Besides, if there was anyone who could find a way to taunt the living from the Other Side, it would be Greg Daniels.

"Let's assume for now that you did communicate with Greg." Before she could protest, he added, "I mean, that it really was him and not something else *masquerading* as him."

"I thought about that possibility, and I've been trying to forget it."

"Sorry, but when you're dealing with the paranormal, you have to explore alternative explanations. But like I said, let's say it was Greg. You said it felt like his . . . well, I suppose 'psychic presence' is as good a way as any to describe it, right?"

She nodded.

"So if it *was* him, it seems clear that he came to warn us. What do you think the 'nasty things' are that he told you about? Do you have any sense of what they might be?"

Just as she had earlier, she looked uncomfortable, as if she knew something but was reluctant to share it with him. He was going to press her to talk, but before he could say anything, his attention was drawn by the clacking of high heels as someone approached. Drew turned to see Connie Flaxman coming toward them, a wide smile on her face and ice in her gaze. His reaction was as heartfelt as it was succinct.

"Shit."

FIVE

"**Hello, Drew. Thought** I'd pop down here and see what this conference of yours is all about. You made it sound so *fascinating,* I just couldn't resist."

Amber had heard Drew talk about his supervisor on numerous occasions, but at none of those times had he ever described her—and now she knew why. Connie Flaxman wasn't just pretty; she was *gorgeous*. Silky blond shoulder-length hair, startlingly blue eyes, high cheekbones, full lips, and a porcelain-smooth complexion accentuated with precise but understated makeup. She was tall—almost as tall as Drew—and curvy in all the right places. Large breasts, narrow waist, flaring hips . . . and she affected an ice-queen persona that Amber knew drove some men crazy. She wore a long-sleeved white blouse, a gray skirt that was just a little too short, glossy black high heels that were just a little too high, and to top it all off, black-framed geek-chic glasses, the kind that drew attention to beauty by trying to conceal it. And then there was her voice. It was honey-smooth, strong and confident, containing a touch of mockery along with a velvet softness. It was the sort of voice that promised both reward and punishment in the same breath.

Before Drew could respond, Connie turned to Amber.

"And is this the special friend you've been telling everyone at work about?" She stuck out her hand with a sharp motion, almost as if she were thrusting a weapon at Amber. "I'm Dr. Flaxman, Drew's supervisor. But you can call me Connie."

Amber didn't miss the subtle stress she put on the word *doctor,* as if she were pointing out the difference in their education levels. The last thing she wanted to do was touch the woman's hand, but she put on a smile that she hoped didn't look too false and shook.

"Amber Lozier. Nice to meet you," she said. "Drew's told me a lot about you." *Except that you look like you should be on the cover of* Cosmo *instead of* Psychology Today, she thought.

Connie let out a ringing laugh that drew the attention of everyone in the vicinity—everyone who wasn't already staring at her, that is.

"I hope he wasn't complaining that I'm too hard on him! I do my best to be a firm but fair boss." She smiled at Drew, put a hand on his arm, and gave it a quick squeeze before letting go.

Amber knew what the woman was doing. She was trying to show that she had a prior claim on Drew, marking her territory as if she were an animal. It was a transparent ploy, but that didn't make it any less effective. Amber already feared that she wasn't a good enough partner for Drew, that she wasn't as smart as he was, didn't have anything even approaching a career, and hadn't accomplished anything in life worth speaking of. Normally, she was able to put aside these self-doubts, if not silence them altogether. But seeing Mitch had brought them back full force. Maybe she really wasn't the kind of woman Drew should be with, the kind of woman he deserved.

Drew looked from Amber to Connie and back again, his expression that of a small animal caught in the headlights of an onrushing semi.

"This is, uh, quite a surprise," he said. "Especially given how you reacted when I first told you about Esotericon."

"You know that old sexist cliché about how it's a woman's prerogative to change her mind?" Connie said. "I hate to admit it, but there's more than a kernel of truth there." She turned to Amber. "Isn't that right?"

Amber couldn't bring herself to respond, but Connie acted as if she didn't notice. She turned back to Drew.

"So this is the new world you're exploring." She glanced at a passing couple who were dressed as a vampire bride and groom. "How amusing. You must give me an orientation." She looked at Amber once again. "You don't mind me joining the fun, do you, dear?"

"Connie," Drew said, "I don't think—"

"Of course not," Amber said. "Drew, why don't you show her around? I'll take these to Trevor and Arthur." She took the bag holding the bottled water out of Drew's hand and, without another word, started heading down the hall toward the ballroom. She managed not to cry, but it was a near thing.

"What are you doing, Connie?"

She gave Drew what she hoped was an innocent look. "I told you. I became curious about this conference. If you're going to start changing your approach to therapy because of your new-found interest in"—she waved her hand as she searched for the right words—"alternative views of reality, then, as your supervisor, I need to be better informed about precisely what that means. For the sake of our patients, if nothing else."

He looked at her for a moment with those puppy-dog brown eyes of his. There was no warmth in his gaze, though. Only cold assessment.

"What sort of game are you playing?" he asked. Before she could answer, he said, "Never mind. It doesn't matter. If you really are here to attend the conference, I hope you find the sessions interesting. But if you're here for some other reason, I don't care what it is. Now, if you'll excuse me, I need to get back to my friends."

He headed down the hall after Amber. Connie watched him go, admiring the way his rear looked in those jeans. *That could've gone better,* she thought. Still, it hadn't been a total loss. Drew might be angry with her for running off his girlfriend, but during their brief conversation, she'd had a chance to take the woman's measure, and if *that* was her competition, she felt confident that she would win Drew's affections eventually. Maybe a couple of days of seeing her at the same conference as Amber would make Drew realize just how unsuitable the woman was for him—and what a far better match she would be.

It was clear what Drew saw in Amber. It was typical, really. Highly empathetic people like him—especially if they had devoted their lives to healing the mind—were often attracted to the emotionally wounded. She had seen it numerous times in her career, although, of course, it had never happened to her personally. She had far too much control for that. Such relationships were based on an uneven balance of power, and because of that, they were destined to fail sooner or later. Drew was a highly intelligent, sensible man. He would realize this before long and break it off with Amber. And if by being there this weekend, she could hurry that process along, so much the better.

She should find the registration table for Esotericon and officially register for the conference, but first things first. It had been a long drive from Chicago, and she needed to pee and apply fresh lipstick. She had noted the restrooms near the lobby when she had walked in, and she headed for them.

"This is so *cool!"*

"If you say so." Rach didn't look up from her phone. She was writing a status update for her Facebook page: "Bored beyond all human comprehension. All museums should be shut down and dynamited into rubble."

Donner—who once again was wearing his silly Ghostbuster uniform—looked at her with a pouty little-boy expression that was really creepy on a man his age.

"C'mon, Rachel. This exhibit might be kind of dry, but it's the

most important one in here. I mean, it tells how everything began!"
He broke off and then grinned. "Hey, I made a joke! *Dry*. Get it?"

"I told you, call me Rach." She pronounced it "Rash," as if she
were a kind of skin disease. She continued gazing down at her
phone. "And no, I don't get it."

"This exhibit is about the flood back in the 1920s. Hundreds of
people died, and the survivors almost abandoned the town. A flood
is *wet*, right? But I said the exhibit was *dry*. It's funny."

"Uh-huh." In addition to Facebooking, she was also texting a
former boyfriend who lived in Portland: "Snd ninjas to sve me! Cnt
take much more!!!!!"

Rach had wanted to sleep in until at least noon, but Donner had
pulled her out of bed at nine-thirty. If she'd had a straight razor, she
would have gleefully slit his throat for forcing her to get up. She
had asked him if the motel was on fire, because that was the only
reason she could conceive of for waking up so goddamned early.
But no, Donner had wanted to go to a museum—a *museum!*—
which opened at ten. She had been royally pissed, but when he
told her the place was called Beyond the Veil and it featured all
kinds of spooky-ass exhibits, she had calmed down a bit. So far, the
Dead Days celebration hadn't been as much fun as she had hoped,
and she was beginning to regret letting Donner talk her into coming. But if the museum had some really gross exhibits—like wax
figures of mutilated bodies with their guts hanging out—it might
be worth killing an hour or so there.

But Beyond the Veil had turned out to be depressingly mundane
so far. Worse than that, it was *educational*. There were exhibits on
the Spiritualist movement of the mid-1800s, famous psychic mediums throughout history, and people such as Harry Houdini and
James Randi who had made it their mission to expose paranormal
hoaxes. Most numerous of all were exhibits about ghosts—and not
scary-cool exhibits like the rooms in a Halloween haunted house,
where people in hockey masks jumped out of the shadows shriek-

ing and waving rubber knives at you. These exhibits featured supposedly true accounts of hauntings dating back to ancient times, and while there were some wax figures to illustrate the stories behind the hauntings, they were strictly PG-rated.

And this exhibit—atrociously titled "Rain of Terror"—was the dullest of the lot. It was all about the flood that had devastated the town almost a century ago, and it was made up almost entirely of photographs and text, along with a few personal effects recovered after the flood—moldy-looking children's toys, rusted jewelry, mud-encrusted bottles—displayed in glass cases. She thought the exhibit was the pinnacle of eye-gouging boredom, but Donner was really grooving on it.

"C'mon, Rachel. I mean *Rach*. The rest of the museum is cool and all, but this—this stuff really *happened,* you know?"

Rach had met Donner at a comic shop in Indianapolis. She had been checking out the adults-only manga for sale, Japanese comics that were heavy on sex and violence, when Donner approached her, a stack of graphic novels in his hands. He began chatting her up, nothing too creepy, just asking her about what manga she liked and all that, and at first, her answers were curt and dismissive. But Donner didn't give up, and after a few minutes, she found herself warming to his sarcastic sense of humor. It wasn't as dark and cutting as hers, but they clicked, and when he asked her out, she said OK, despite the difference in their ages.

They had been together almost three months, which was longer than Rach's relationships usually lasted, and she was starting to get bored. The longer they dated, the more obvious it became that any similarities they shared were outweighed by their differences. Donner might be older than she was, but he acted like a little boy much of the time. Like now, for instance. He looked as if he might stamp his foot and hold his breath if she didn't start showing some interest in the display.

Rach let out a heavy sigh to let Donner know she was put out at having to feign interest—not that he was perceptive enough to pick up on it—and she looked up from her phone and began reading the information placards accompanying the photos. And despite herself, the more she read, the more intrigued she became.

In the spring of 1923, a series of heavy rainstorms swept through Indiana. As bad as it was throughout the rest of the state, the deluge hit Exeter the hardest—and by the middle of May, the Mossapeak River—normally sedate and slow-running—had become a swollen, raging torrent. The townsfolk were nervous, and some were talking about evacuating, but the mayor called a town meeting and assured the good folk of Exeter that the worst of the rain was over and that the Mossapeak would soon begin to subside. Reassured, the townspeople returned to their homes.

That night, another storm hit, this one a veritable monster. It was as if the heavens cracked in two and released all the rain they had stored for the remainder of the year in a single awful night. The Mossapeak exploded over its banks, and water flooded the town. People tried to flee, and while some made it, most of them were pulled beneath the churning water and drowned. Those who survived did so by seeking higher ground, heading for second floors and attics, even climbing on top of their roofs if necessary. It took seventeen hours for the storm to blow itself out and the rain to dribble away to a gentle mist. It was another thirty-six hours before the floodwaters finally began to recede. When it was all over, two-thirds of Exeter's populace was dead, and most of the buildings had suffered such extreme damage that they were unsalvageable.

Black-and-white photos of the flood's aftermath covered the museum walls. Entire buildings had been swept away and reduced to kindling. Piles of lumber were scattered across a muddy landscape. Wagons and old-fashioned cars lay wherever they had come to rest after the water released them. Often, they were broken and incomplete, lying at odd angles and sometimes clustered together, as if they were surreal sculptures. The most disturbing pictures were of bodies lying in rows on the muddy ground, arms folded over their chests and eyes closed. Arranged that way by the survivors, Rach guessed. She was surprised they hadn't covered the bodies with sheets, but maybe they hadn't been able to salvage any—or maybe there had been too many bodies to cover them all.

There were more pictures: the town in various states of reconstruction, mediums and psychics coming in to investigate reports of ghostly manifestations, to exorcise earthbound spirits and guide them to the afterlife. But Rach didn't pay attention to those. She was too caught up in the story of the flood itself. She tried to imagine what it had been like for the survivors, clinging to one another as they huddled on the roofs of their homes and businesses, sheets of driving rain pounding down on them from a bruise-colored sky. Wild, chaotic currents flowing past, carrying broken branches, splintered lengths of lumber, barrels and boxes, the corpses of animals—cattle, sheep, pigs, chickens, dogs, cats—and, worst of all, the bodies of their friends and neighbors. Men, women, and children, young and old—the flood wouldn't have been choosy about its victims. And how many had been alive as they were swept along in the raging floodwaters, crying out for help, stretching their arms toward those they passed, moving too swiftly to be saved?

Despite the hard shell of cynicism she presented to the world—which wasn't an act; she really *was* that cynical—Rach felt an almost overwhelming sorrow for those who had lost their lives in the flood. Hard on the heels of that emotion came anger toward whatever moron had thought so little of the tragedy as to dub the display "Rain of Terror." Such a sensationalized name, not to mention that lame pun, dishonored the memory of all those who had died when the Mossapeak had overflowed its banks. She turned to Donner, intending to demand that they go find someone in charge—a manager or director or something—and complain about the display's name, but before she could speak, a blast of cold, wet wind struck her in the face and sent her stumbling backward in surprise. Her right foot slipped out from under her, and she fell hard on her ass. She landed at an angle and began sliding downward—her mind trying to understand how there could *be* an angle when the floor she had been standing on was level—and she rolled onto her stomach, hands scrabbling frantically to grab hold of something and stop her descent. The surface was hard and grainy beneath her fingers, but it was so slick with water that she couldn't get a handhold, and she picked up speed as she slid. She felt a sudden stomach-dropping sensation of space opening up beneath her, and then she was falling. Falling *where*, falling *how*—she was in a *museum*, for godsakes! And then she hit the water.

Cold bit into her flesh, sank its teeth deep into her bones, and she opened her mouth to cry out, but water rushed down her throat, choking off her voice before she could make a sound. She slipped beneath the surface, her vision clouded by the murky water, pressure roaring in her ears. Lungs heavy and chest burning, she began thrashing about, her arms and legs flailing spastically, as if her body was seeking something solid to grab hold of so it could climb out of the water. A distant, detached part of her mind wondered if this was how humans had learned to swim in the first place, climbing instincts kicking in whenever they found themselves in water over their heads. Those who didn't manage to keep their heads above the surface drowned. Those who did survived to pass on their genes, and several million years later, voilà! Hairless apes put pools in their backyards and spent vacations at the beach.

You're losing it! she warned herself. *Don't worry about how and why this is happening. Just get some air into your lungs, damn it!*

She forced her body to relax and kicked toward the surface. She felt the current pulling her sideways, but she continued kicking, and after what seemed like a lifetime, her head broke the surface. She drew in a gasp of the sweetest air she had ever breathed and did her best to tread water while she tried to figure out what was going on.

A storm raged around her. Wind and rain lashed her skin, and muddy brown water surrounded her. She was drifting with the current, floating past rooftops, most of which had people clinging to them for safety. That's what had happened to her, she realized. She'd fallen off a roof and into the water.

"Hey!" she called out to a family—a man, a woman, and two children—as she floated by. "Help me! Please!"

They just looked at her as the current pulled her away from them, and really, what else could they do? It wasn't as if they had a life preserver tethered to a rope to throw to her. She knew there had been no point in calling out to them for help, but she hadn't been able to stop herself.

How could this possibly be happening? It was as if she had fallen through a hole in time and had somehow ended up in Exeter in the middle of the famous flood. Suddenly, the museum's title for the exhibit, "Rain of Terror," no longer seemed so stupid.

She used to tease Donner about his fascination with the paranormal and his willingness to believe weird shit. If she somehow made it out of this, she vowed that she would never tease him again.

Something big and solid slammed into her side, knocking the air out of her lungs. She slipped beneath the surface and sucked in another mouthful of river before regaining control of her body and treading water again. She saw a large shape bobbing next to her and with horror realized it was the body of a horse. Something else struck her back, and when she turned her head, she saw it was a dead pig. She remembered the photo of all those bodies laid out in rows on the wet, muddy ground. Those bodies were there now, floating in the water with her. And if she couldn't keep treading water, she would end up drowned and laid out with them. She wondered if someone back in the present, examining the photo on the museum wall closely, would see that one of the bodies was that of a young woman dressed in black who looked more than a little out of place among Exeter's dead.

She knew she couldn't keep treading water forever, especially if she had to keep fighting the current. She needed to find something that floated to hold on to, preferably not the corpse of a large farm animal. A chunk of lumber or a big tree branch, maybe. If only she—

With the black clouds and driving rain, visibility was poor, and when Rach saw the shapes in the water in front of her—dozens upon dozens of them, smooth and rounded, some light, some dark—she couldn't make out what they were at first. But as the current bore her closer to them, she realized that they remained stationary, somehow resisting the floodwaters' flow. Almost as if they were waiting for her

When she was within ten feet, they lifted their heads out of the water, and Rach understood that what she had been looking at before were the backs of bodies, *human* bodies, that had been floating facedown. Men, woman, children, infants—all stared at her with milky-white eyes, their skin wrinkled and bluish-white, as if they had been in the water for a very long time. Then, as one, they smiled at her, revealing rows of sharp teeth like a shark's.

She screamed, spun around, and began swimming as hard as she could in the opposite direction. But the current was too strong, and it swept her into the townspeople's waiting arms.

"Rach? You OK?"

Donner was worried. Rach had been standing in front of the photo of the flood victims for several minutes. She hadn't moved in all that time, and what was even more surprising, she hadn't *said* anything. It was the longest period he had known her to remain silent—when she wasn't sleeping, that is. Maybe the exhibit had gotten to her, had broken through her ever-present veneer of cynicism. But there was something about the too-rigid way she stood, as if her joints were locked tight, that seemed wrong. His stomach twisted into a cold knot of anxiety, and he stepped toward her.

"Rach? Rachel?"

He reached out and put a trembling hand on her shoulder, which felt cold and strangely damp. He took hold of her other shoulder and gently turned her around to face him, pulse pounding in his ears. Her eyes were wide and staring, and for an awful instant, he thought she was dead. But then she opened her mouth and vomited a gout of brown water onto his chest. Her body went slack, as if she were a machine and someone had flicked her off switch, and she collapsed to the floor.

"Shit," Donner whispered. Water—river water, from the smell of it—dripped off the front of his coveralls, and a trickle of it still ran from the corner of Rach's mouth. Her eyes remained open, focused on nothing, and Donner was certain she was dead. How could this have happened? She was a lot younger than he was and in good shape, too. It didn't seem—

"Turn around."

Donner jumped at the sound of the voice. He turned to see a man dressed in a brown flannel shirt, jeans, and work boots standing there, hands balled into fists at his sides, a cold, unreadable expression in his eyes.

"Do you work here? I didn't do anything to her, I swear! We need to get her to a hospital, call an ambulance—something!"

The man didn't reply. He just continued staring. For an instant, Donner thought he saw someone else standing next to the man—a woman wearing a long, old-fashioned black dress. But he blinked, and she was gone. He was seeing things, he figured, because of the shock of Rach collapsing.

The man still wasn't talking. At first, Donner had taken him to be a museum employee, perhaps drawn when he had shouted Rach's name. But the freak just kept standing there, silent, doing nothing. Donner didn't know what the hell his problem was, and he didn't care. Rach needed help. He pulled out his cell phone, intending to dial 911. But before he could enter the first number, the man finally spoke.

"I wouldn't do that, Drew."

Now it was Donner's turn to stare.

"Um . . . who?"

Mitch was filled with cold fury. Not because this sonofabitch had killed Amber but because he'd done it before Mitch had got his chance to teach her a lesson. Amber had been so proud when she had told him she was dating a psychologist. "A real great guy," she had said. Looked like her real great guy had turned out to have one hell of a temper. Mitch wondered what she had done to piss Drew off so much that he had killed her right there in the museum. Come to think of it, no matter how angry Drew had been, wouldn't he have waited to do the deed until they were somewhere private, where there weren't any witnesses? He didn't know much about the man, but he didn't seem like the type of guy who would suddenly snap and fly into a homicidal rage.

In fact, the woman lying on the floor didn't resemble Amber all that much now that he took a closer look. And the man didn't look as much like Drew as he had a second ago. He was shorter, fatter, and dressed in some kind of uniform.

Mitch felt a cold hand clasp his, and then the Dark Lady leaned close to his ear and whispered. Her voice sounded like rustling leaves, her breath as frigid as January wind on his flesh.

"Hesitation is a sign of weakness."

Rage welled strong within him, burying his doubts, and he clearly saw Amber lying on the floor, Drew standing next to her, cell phone in hand.

"I wouldn't do that, Drew."

The man mumbled something in reply, but Mitch paid no attention. He ran forward, locked his hands around Drew's throat, and began to squeeze.

Drew fought back. He tried to pry Mitch's hands off his throat, and when he couldn't break his grip, he pounded his fists against Mitch's forearms and then the sides of his head. Mitch ignored the pain, such as it was. Drew might have looked in shape, but his blows lacked any real strength. What a fucking wimp!

Drew's face reddened, then purpled, and then his knees gave out on him, and he slumped to the floor. Mitch followed him down, maintaining his grip. He was squeezing so hard he thought he could feel the man's neck bones beneath his hands. In the movies, tough guys could break someone's neck simply by giving the head a single savage twist. Cool as that always looked, he had figured it was Hollywood bullshit. But now, feeling Drew's bones like this, he understood just how fragile a neck could be, and he believed that it wouldn't take a lot to snap it. All he would have to do was—

Drew's body went slack, breaking Mitch's train of thought. He examined the man's swollen face, his open, bulging eyes, and realized it was too late for him to try to break his neck. Oh, well. Maybe next time.

He released his grip, and Drew fell to the floor, only a couple of feet from where Amber was lying. He stood up and regarded their still forms. He expected to feel something—exhilaration at having broken one of society's greatest taboos, satisfaction at showing Drew what a real man could do, a sense of justice at knowing that Amber had gotten what she deserved, even if he hadn't been the one to give it to her. But the truth was, he didn't feel much of anything, and that lack of emotional payoff made him feel cheated.

His vision blurred for an instant, and when it cleared, the two bodies lying on the museum floor no longer resembled Amber and Drew. Instead, they were two strangers: a young girl in a black minidress and an older guy dressed like a sanitation worker or something. Before Mitch could question what was happening, the Dark Lady whispered to him again in her autumn-leaf voice.

"We need to leave before anyone comes and sees what we have done."

She wrapped fingers of ice around his hand and led him away from the bodies. He accompanied her without resistance, trying to understand what had just happened.

"I wanted to send another message, and I needed to see how far you would go for me. Your former girlfriend has a strong spirit, stronger than she realizes. Where others are blind, she can see. She may prove a threat to me—she and her friends. Stay with me, help me take care of them, and when this night is done, we will both have what we most desire."

Mitch still wasn't sure how much he liked the idea of taking orders from a woman, but so far, the Dark Lady hadn't steered him wrong.

As they walked through the museum lobby and out into the daylight, he asked, "All right, what next?"

"I think it's time you and Amber had a reunion."

SIX

"Thank you very much. I hope you enjoy it."

Trevor slid the copy of *Insidious Inns* across the table. The woman who had bought it—early twenties, thick glasses, blond hair almost white and tied in a ponytail—picked it up and added it to the stack she carried. All of her other books were ones Arthur Carrington had written.

"Thanks. I figured I'd get you to sign for me first since Arthur's line is so long."

Trevor resisted sighing. "I've noticed."

The woman smiled, then went off to take a place at the end of Carrington's line with the rest of his fans, of which there were currently several dozen—and those were just the ones whose books he hadn't signed yet. He'd already signed close to fifty, Trevor figured. Counting this last book, he had signed only eleven. Honestly, though, he had done better than he feared he might, considering that Carrington had been at this a lot longer than he had.

He wondered where Amber and Drew were. After bringing bottled water for both Carrington and him, Amber had left the Exhibition Hall. She hadn't said anything, but Trevor had been able to tell that something had upset her. A few minutes later, Drew had returned and looked around—presumably for Amber—and when he didn't see her, he left, too. That had been a while ago, and Trevor hadn't seen either one of them since. He hoped the lovebirds weren't having a fight, but he supposed it was inevitable. All of the experts said that it was normal and healthy for people in a relationship to fight from time to time. They were both good-hearted, intelligent people, and they loved each other very much. Whatever was going on, they would work it out. He hoped.

Jenn stood behind the table between Trevor and Carrington, in case they needed her to supply more books. Erin stood off to the side, filming the signing with her hand camera. Carrington was in his element, chatting with fans, posing for pictures, telling amusing anecdotes. As much as Trevor disliked Carrington's less-than-scientific approach to paranormal investigation, he had to admit the man oozed charm and knew how to work a crowd. If Trevor could pick up a few pointers from him, he might sell more books.

Jenn leaned down close and spoke softly. "Jealous?"

Trevor pretended to be hurt by her question. "Me? I'm a professional!" He paused for effect. "Of course I'm jealous!"

She laughed, as he had hoped. It was good to see her smile after what she had been through. Since he had no other readers waiting for his signature, he figured this might be a good time to press Jenn for some information. But he knew he had to do so carefully, so as not to upset her any further.

"If I remember right, the Forgotten Lore building is one of the structures that made it through the flood intact."

"More or less," she said. "It's been refurbished so many times over the years, I'm not sure how much of the original building is left. A number of the buildings in the downtown business district are at least partially preflood. The museum is one. And there's a farm outside town. Erin could tell you better than I could."

"Why is that?"

"She researched which buildings in town date from before the flood, whether in whole or in part. She wanted to film them for her documentary. That's the main reason she shot some footage in the bookstore."

A devastating tragedy like the flood could create a major disruption in the psychospiritual plane, resulting in a nexus for all manner of paranormal manifestations. It was the most common theory behind Exeter's reputation as a hotbed of ghostly activity and, in Trevor's opinion, the most likely. The fact that the building that housed Jenn's store dated from before the flood might be significant, too. It could account for why such a powerful manifestation had taken place there the night before. The stronger a place's tie to past tragedy, the stronger the manifestation. Still, a manifestation powerful enough to hurl books around a room via psychokinetic force was in a whole different category from a few phantom footsteps in the night or a couple of unexplained cold spots.

"Did you ever have any incidents of objects moving on their own at the store? Books that ended up shelved in different places from where you remember putting them? Pens or papers left on a desk that ended up on the floor or in the trash?"

Jenn's expression hardened. "Trevor, a woman died in my store last night. I can't say we were friends, exactly, but I won't have you exploiting her death just so you can play ghost hunter!"

Her voice had risen as she spoke those last words, and Carrington— along with a number of his fans still waiting in line—turned to look at them. Carrington cocked an eyebrow, and Trevor muttered, "Sorry."

Carrington gave him a nod and turned his attention to the fan next in line. Trevor noticed that Erin had stopped filming for the moment and was looking at Jenn and him thoughtfully. That wasn't a good sign. The last thing Trevor wanted was for Erin to get the idea of refocusing her documentary on Tonya's death. Jenn didn't need to have the woman following her around with a camera, hounding her. But then, wasn't that what she thought *he* was doing? Using Tonya's death as an opportunity to indulge his interest in the paranormal—and maybe get another book out of it?

"Jenn, I sent you an electronic copy of the book I'm working on. The one about the Lowry House. Did you read it?"

She still looked angry, but she answered. "Yes."

"What did you think about it?"

She stared at him. "This is a strange time to ask for feedback on your writing."

"Humor me."

She looked at him another moment and then shrugged. "Honestly, it reads more like fiction than anything. I mean, I understand that you want to increase your book sales, and it's a great read, but . . ."

"But you don't think the things I wrote about actually happened."

Jenn looked uncomfortable. "I knew about your missing memories, of course, and that Drew and Amber were involved in whatever happened to you three back in high school. But as for the rest of it . . . I guess the kindest thing I can say is that you used a lot of artistic license."

Trevor smiled. "You mean I lied."

Jenn cocked her head to the side in puzzlement. It was a gesture Trevor was intimately familiar with, and he was surprised at how much he had missed seeing her do it. "You seem awfully calm for a man who's just been accused of fraud."

"I know this is hard for you to believe, Jenn. Hell, it would be hard for anyone to believe who didn't live through it. But every word in that book is true. Ask Drew and Amber when they come back. They'll confirm it. And it's because of those experiences that I'm asking you questions now. Not because I care about getting material for another book. But because something bad happened last night, and I want to make sure it doesn't happen again."

She still looked doubtful, and Trevor didn't blame her. If their positions had been reversed, he would have felt the same.

"Let me ask you this question. Have I ever lied to you?"

She smiled. "No. But just because you believe something doesn't make it true. You could be crazy, you know."

Trevor laughed. "What can I say? Sanity is overrated! Look, if there's even the remotest possibility that something paranormal *did* happen in your store last night, and it resulted in Tonya's death, you would want to do something about it, wouldn't you?"

Jenn thought for a moment. "Yes, I would." She took a deep breath and sighed. "All right. But this doesn't mean I believe in ghosts or anything."

Trevor smiled. "Duly noted." He and Jenn continued talking while Carrington signed books and Erin kept filming. Trevor had the impression that Erin had her camera trained on the two of them most of the time, but he hoped he was wrong.

Amber stood on the sidewalk outside the hotel, watching people in costume stroll by. The hotel was on the outskirts of town, not all that close to the main business district where the bulk of the Dead Days festivities were taking place, but there were plenty of people attending the conference, and it seemed quite a few of them didn't want to wait for the big parade that night to don their Halloween finery. Amber had loved Halloween when she was a kid, and each year, she would wear the spookiest costume she could think of. Her favorite had been the year she had trick-or-treated as the witch from "Hansel and Gretel." She had carried a small plastic cauldron with a tiny bit of dry ice in it to make it look as if it were bubbling and a rubber hand reaching out as if someone—perhaps one of the children from the story—was being cooked. More than a few adults at the houses where she had stopped had given her strange looks, and their reactions were just as sweet as all the candy she got that year.

But she had lost her taste for Halloween after what had happened at the Lowry House when they were teenagers, and although the three of them had put that experience behind them for the most part, she didn't think she would ever fully enjoy the holiday again. Drew would probably have said that dressing up as ghosts and monsters was psychologically healthy, that it helped people learn to accept the darker side of their nature. But the act of cloaking oneself in the trappings of darkness seemed sinister to Amber. Most people thought creatures of the night were nothing more than fables to frighten children, but she knew better. Monsters were real. And if what Greg had told her was true—assuming, of course, that she hadn't merely hallucinated talking with him—there was something bad in Exeter. Whatever it was, it had killed Tonya last night, and Amber doubted that it would stop at one death. Darkness possessed an endless hunger, and no matter how often it fed, it could never be satisfied.

She turned her mind away from such thoughts. Since the events at the high-school reunion a couple of months earlier, she had been reading up on psychic and spiritual phenomena. Never again did she want to face something like what they had confronted in the Lowry House without being prepared—or at least as prepared as it was possible to be. A number of the sources she had consulted agreed that dwelling too much on negative thoughts could attract dark forces to you, calling out to them like a beacon. Amber had no idea if that was true, but given Greg's warning—not to mention her dream the night before—she figured it was better to be safe than sorry.

She wished she hadn't reacted so poorly to the unexpected appearance of Drew's boss. Sure, she was intimidating as hell—a gorgeous, highly educated woman with a strong personality. But Amber knew that Drew loved her, and he had never given her any reason to feel insecure. If she felt that she didn't measure up to *Dr.* Flaxman, it came out of her own insecurities, nowhere else. Because she had been upset, she had left before telling Drew about seeing Mitch—or at least seeing someone who looked a hell of lot like him. Drew knew about him in general, but she had never told him the whole story. She was too ashamed to share all the details with him. Besides, he was so sensitive and caring that she was afraid that knowing the full truth would only hurt him. Not because he would be jealous but because he couldn't stand the thought of how much her time with Mitch had hurt her. But as difficult as it was, she knew she had to tell Drew that she had seen Mitch. Or thought she had. Not only because she wanted to be completely honest with Drew but also because of what Greg had told her.

"There are nasty things in this town, and you've drawn their attention."

Things, plural. Greg's warning didn't have to be about supernatural entities, or at least not *only* about them. Maybe Mitch was one of those things Greg had been talking about. He could be pretty damned nasty when he—

Her thoughts froze as she saw him walking down the sidewalk toward her. Any doubts she had about having seen him outside the coffee shop vanished. It was him.

"Hello, Amber," Mitch said as he drew near. "Been a while."

She wanted to turn, run back into the hotel, and go find Drew or Trevor. If nothing else, she could go to the lobby. Even if Mitch followed her inside the hotel, she would feel safer there, as long as others were around. But she forced herself to stay where she was and even managed an approximation of a smile.

"What are you doing here?" The question came out more bluntly than she had wanted, but Mitch didn't seem to notice.

"I came for the Dead Days celebration. I come every year. How about you?"

He appeared relaxed. He smiled easily, his tone was friendly enough, and there was none of the usual forcefulness in his manner. Mitch liked to dominate other people. No, he *needed* to, and he attempted to do it from the very first moment he interacted with someone. Especially women. Amber didn't sense any of that now, but even so, there was something not right about how he was acting. The words he spoke came out fast and clipped, as if he were too eager to recite a memorized speech. And his eyes were flat and devoid of expression, like the painted-on eyes of a mannequin. When Amber looked into them, she felt a chill ripple down her back. Even at his most abusive, Mitch had never had eyes that looked so empty, so dead.

Instead of answering his question, she said, "I didn't know you were into this kind of thing."

"Sure. Halloween has always been my favorite holiday, and the people around here know how to do it right. It's a hell of a party. How's Drew?"

Mitch's abrupt change of topic took Amber by surprise. He barely paused between sentences, speaking so fast that his words ran together. He continued without waiting for a reply.

"I assume he's here somewhere, isn't he? Dead Days isn't exactly my idea of a romantic weekend getaway, but hey, whatever floats your boat, right?"

Mitch stepped forward—not far, just a couple of inches, but it was enough to make Amber feel threatened. She wanted to step back and maintain distance between them, but she remained where she was. She didn't want him to see that she was afraid. She felt like a mouse cornered by a cat; if she tried to flee, she would be pounced on. The only way to stay safe, at least for the moment, was to keep still.

"He's inside at the conference, helping out in the Exhibition Hall," she said. It was a guess. In truth, she had no idea what Drew was doing. "Would you like to meet him? I'd be happy to introduce you."

A corner of Mitch's mouth lifted in an expression that wasn't quite a smirk. She had the feeling that he knew exactly what she was trying to do: find a way to get him to accompany her inside, where she would feel safe. Or safer, anyway.

His eyes darted to the left for an instant, and his head turned slightly in that direction, almost as if he were listening to something. But Amber heard nothing.

"Maybe later," he said. "After we've had a chance to catch up a little."

She looked to his left, and although the sidewalk there was empty, she sensed a presence, as if someone were looking directly at her. She squinted and concentrated on the spot. At first, she saw nothing, but then a hazy image appeared, there and not there at the same time, as if she were seeing it through only one eye while the other still saw only empty space. She saw the outline of a dark figure, more a suggestion than a solid form, like a shadow that existed independently of anyone casting it. The figure was large enough to be that of an adult, and while there was nothing specific to suggest it, Amber nevertheless had the impression that it was female.

Then it was gone. No, that wasn't true. The figure might not be visible any longer, but it was still there, still watching her. She could *feel* it.

"I'm sorry, Mitch, but I really should get back inside. Drew's probably looking for me. We're supposed to present a session at the conference later, and we need to get ready."

She started to go, but Mitch snagged hold of her wrist and stopped her. His grip was firm but not painful. Not yet.

"No shit? What sort of presentation?"

Amber was through messing around. "Let go of me."

He tightened his grip, just enough so Amber could feel the pressure, but it still didn't hurt, not quite. He leaned close and spoke softly. His breath reeked of greasy food and stale coffee.

"I have a new friend I'd like you to meet. Let's go somewhere quiet, and I'll introduce you to her."

He increased the pressure of his grip as he spoke, until Amber thought the bones in her wrist might shatter like glass. He was too physically powerful for her to fight, so she drew in a breath, intending to scream as loudly as she possibly could.

"Amber! There you are! I've been looking all over this damn hotel for you!"

Mitch let up on the pressure, but he didn't release her wrist.

Amber looked over her shoulder to see Connie Flaxman approaching. The woman was smiling warmly, as if she and Amber were old friends instead of rivals for Drew's affections.

Connie walked up to Amber without so much as looking at Mitch. She did glance at the empty space next to him—the space where Amber sensed the mysterious presence—but then she refocused her attention on Amber. Connie put her arms around her and gave her a big hug. As she did, Amber felt Mitch finally let go of her wrist. But she was so surprised by the other woman's sudden display of affection that she almost didn't notice. Amber returned the hug in an awkward, halfhearted way.

When Connie drew back, she said, "I just want to say how sorry I am for the *inexcusable* way I treated you earlier. I was jealous, plain and simple. It's obvious how much Drew cares for you. You're a very lucky woman."

Amber had no idea how to respond. "Uh . . . thanks?"

"Believe it or not, I really *am* interested in learning more about this fascinating"—she waved her hand in the air as she searched for the words she wanted—"*field of study* that you and Drew are involved in. If you don't mind, I think I'll stick around for a while and see what the conference has to offer. Is that OK?"

"Sure." Amber didn't know if she believed that Connie's sudden change of heart was sincere, and right then, she didn't care. She was too grateful for the distraction the woman had provided.

"I'm afraid I'm not officially signed up for the conference yet," Connie said. "Would you mind showing me where the registration table is?"

Amber smiled. "I'd be happy to." She turned to Mitch, and her smile fell away. "See you later."

She regretted her choice of parting words a moment later when, as she accompanied Connie toward the hotel entrance, she heard Mitch murmur, "Count on it."

Mitch watched Amber depart with the blonde. She was gorgeous as hell, and normally, he would have felt a stirring of lust at the sight of her shapely, toned ass moving away from him. But right then, all he felt was frustrated fury at having to let Amber go.

"I could still take her," he said. It wouldn't be difficult. He could run over, grab her, and carry her back to his car. He was parked close by. Any witnesses would think it was a Dead Days prank of some kind, and by the time they realized otherwise, he would be gone. If Amber gave him any trouble, a good crack on the jaw would settle her down. Same for the blonde. If she tried to interfere, he would hit her, too, although it would be a damn shame to mark that beautiful face.

"Be patient. You'll have another chance."

The two women had almost reached the hotel entrance. If he was going to make an attempt to grab Amber, it would have to be now.

"What if I don't want to wait?"

A couple walking gave him an odd look, but he ignored them. Let them think he was talking to himself. He had killed a man that day, and he could kill them, too, if he wanted. He could kill anybody. He was officially a badass now, and he held the power of life and death in his hands.

"Death? You think you understand death?"

Darkness rushed in to surround him. It was cold, far colder than anything he had ever experienced before. It was a cold that came equally from without and within, and it gnawed at both his flesh and his spirit with ice-needle teeth. Pain suffused his entire being, so intense that he forgot about anything else. His name, even his very identity, was lost, obliterated by agony. He opened his mouth and tried to scream, but nothing emerged. The darkness that had claimed him muffled all sound, denying him even the meager release that screaming could provide. He tried to weep, but he felt darkness press against his eyes, arctic cold sealing his tear ducts shut, the cold so intense that it felt as if his eyes had been seared by an open flame.

He couldn't cry, couldn't scream, couldn't think . . . all he knew was darkness, cold, and pain.

"Hey, are you all right? Do you need help?"

He was looking at a smooth grayish-white surface only inches from his face. For a moment, he didn't know where he was or even *who* he was. But then he realized he was looking at a section of sidewalk, and he understood that he had fallen to his hands and knees. The sidewalk wasn't in front of him; it was beneath him. He glanced up at the person who had spoken to him, a teenage kid dressed in a black robe, white-and-black skull makeup on his face.

Irony's a bitch, he thought.

"I'm all right." He rose to his feet, shaky but steady enough. He forced himself to smile at the would-be Samaritan. "Guess I had a little too much fun last night, you know?"

The kid—he couldn't have been more than eighteen—backed off a step, and Mitch wondered what he saw in his smile that made him want to retreat.

"Yeah. OK. No problem." The not-so-grim reaper turned and hurried off toward the hotel entrance. He didn't look back.

"Be patient," the Dark Lady whispered.

This time, Mitch kept his mouth shut.

Drew checked his watch. There was only fifteen minutes left in Trevor and Carrington's joint book signing. After that, they were scheduled to make their presentation on the Lowry House. He had gone around the hotel several times looking for Amber, but he hadn't found her. He had tried calling and texting her but without any response. Sometimes she forgot to turn her cell on, and he hoped that was the case this time. But he was afraid that she had been so upset by Connie's unexpected arrival that she didn't want to talk with him. They didn't have a room in the hotel for her to go to, and since Trevor had driven them there, he doubted she had left the building. Unless she had called a cab. Would she have done that? Was she upset enough to direct the driver to take her back to the bed-and-breakfast, where she would pack up, get into her car, and head back to Ohio? While Amber's self-confidence had grown over the last couple of months, it was still a fragile thing, and dreaming about Tonya's murder—then having that dream come true—was enough to make anyone feel emotionally unsettled. And then to have Connie appear and begin playing mind games with her . . .

He felt like such an idiot. He'd had no idea that Connie had any romantic interest in him, although in retrospect, it made sense. Her coldness toward him both professionally and personally was a classic sign of denial, an attempt to mask emotions that made her feel uncomfortable. He supposed that on some level, he should be flattered, but he wasn't. He was angry at Connie for her impulsive decision to attend the conference in some misguided attempt to get closer to him. Not because it complicated his life—although it did, immeasurably—but because it hurt Amber. While his search for her hadn't been successful, at least he hadn't seen Connie, either. If he was lucky, she had realized that her plan had back-fired, and she had chosen to leave the conference and go back to Chicago. They would have to sit down and talk when he returned to work on Monday, but at least for the rest of the weekend, he could—

His thoughts came to a screeching halt as he saw Amber approach the book-signing table, Connie at her side—and they were both smiling.

Trevor and Carrington still had fans waiting in line for them to sign books. Trevor paused while signing as he noticed Connie approach, and he gave Drew a questioning look, as if to say, *Where did Amber find her?*

"Hey, there, sweetie," Amber said as they drew near. She stopped and gave him a quick kiss on the cheek. "You ready to give our presentation?"

"Amber was telling me all about it," Connie said. "Do you mind if I sit in and listen?" When Drew hesitated, she smiled. "No need to be anxious. Don't think of me as your boss this weekend. Just think of me as"—her smile widened—"an old friend."

He glanced at Amber to see what she thought, and she gave him a smile and nodded.

"Sure," he said, bewildered. "Why not?"

"**. . . and in** the end, we were left with a single, perhaps ultimately unanswerable question. Do we choose evil, or does it choose us?"

The screen behind the panel table displayed two photos side-by-side: teenage Trevor, Drew, and Amber standing in front of the Lowry House and a high-school yearbook picture of a smiling Greg Daniels.

Drew put his hand over the microphone in front of him and whispered, "I didn't know you were a philosopher."

"Don't tease," Amber said to Drew. She sat between her two friends, and she leaned over to Trevor and softly said, "I like the way you ended. Very dramatic—and a nice tribute to Greg."

"Thanks."

Trevor allowed the images to linger for a moment before running his finger across the screen of his laptop and ending the PowerPoint presentation. The audience applauded, and the conference worker who had been assigned to help with the presentations turned on the lights in the back of the room.

The presentation room was one of the smaller ones in the hotel, but all of the seats were filled, and several people stood in the back. Carrington and Erin sat in the front row, alongside Jenn and Connie.

Trevor hadn't had a chance to do more than say hi to Drew's boss before the presentation began, but he was looking forward to talking with her afterward. Drew had made her sound like a dragon lady, cold and dictatorial. Maybe she was, but Trevor didn't care. She was perhaps the single most beautiful woman he had ever met, and he found the contrast between her physical appearance and her personality fascinating. Not that he was hoping to start anything with her. Not only was she way out of his league, but returning to Exeter and seeing Jenn again had stirred up old feelings for her—feelings that had been a lot closer to the surface than he had realized.

Before this session had begun, he had told Jenn that he would understand if she wanted to skip it. Listening to a talk about ghosts and death might be emotionally difficult for her right then. But she had told him she would be all right, and true to her word, she looked OK.

He had been surprised that Carrington and Erin had attended the presentation. Trevor figured Carrington would rather have headed straight for the hotel bar after their joint book signing was over, and since the incident with the Lowry House had no connection to Exeter, Trevor couldn't see that the session had any bearing on Erin's documentary. But Erin had urged Carrington to attend with her. Maybe she was using the presentation as an excuse to babysit him. Or maybe she really was interested in learning about what Drew, Amber, and he had been through. But Erin struck him as an eye-on-the-prize kind of person, one who didn't do anything without a specific purpose in mind. He wondered what it might be. Whatever it was, he doubted he would like it.

"Thank you very much," Trevor said as the applause began to die down. "We'll take questions now."

Hands went up, more than he expected. A good sign. If people responded enthusiastically today, it boded well for the book's eventual release. He scanned the audience—a mix of scholars, academics, and costumed enthusiasts—and chose a person at random. He pointed to a middle-aged man with a bushy walrus mustache. He wore a rumpled gray suit, no tie, running shoes, and a black ball cap with the words "Miskatonic University" on it. The hat was a nice touch, Trevor thought, if maybe a bit too cute.

The man rose to his feet and spoke. "You spin a fascinating story, Mr. Ward, but you must admit, it strains credulity. The experiences you relate are almost entirely subjective and therefore impossible to substantiate. One might almost accuse you of fabricating the whole thing."

Trevor tried to keep his tone civil. "I'm sorry, I didn't catch your name."

"Brian Pratt." He said it with a small smile, as if he expected Trevor to recognize it.

Trevor did. Amber must have noticed the recognition on his face, for she whispered into his ear. "Who's that?"

"He's a professional skeptic whose specialty is debunking what he sees as bogus paranormal experiences." Trevor had read all of the man's books, and while he could be derisive toward those whom he viewed as either gullible fools or manipulative hoaxers, in general, Trevor found the man's approach to the paranormal to be rational and scientific. He hadn't seen Pratt listed as one of Esotericon's presenters, but he wasn't surprised. Pratt had a reputation for guerrilla confrontations, showing up unannounced so the targets of his skeptical inquiry wouldn't have time to prepare to counter his verbal assault on them. It was his favorite tactic, as he had related in his books on numerous occasions.

Carrington must have recognized Pratt, too, for he turned in his seat and shot the man a venomous glare. Pratt acknowledged Carrington with a smile and a nod.

Before Trevor could respond to Pratt's accusation, Amber stood up. "Trevor wouldn't lie—he's a professional journalist!"

"He wouldn't be the first so-called professional who made up a story for profit," Pratt said.

There were more than a few murmurs of agreement from the audience. Trevor was surprised, but he knew he shouldn't have been. Their experience at the Lowry House *had* been unbelievable. Hell, he had lived through it, and even he had a hard time believing some of it.

"But I was there!" Amber said. "So was Drew. We can verify everything Trevor says." She gestured to Drew. "He's a respected psychologist. Do you think he'd be here, speaking in public about all this, if it wasn't true?"

Up to this point in the presentation, Trevor had done the bulk of the speaking, although Amber and Drew had interjected points here and there. But now the audience turned its full attention to Drew, and Trevor wondered what he would say—especially with his boss sitting in the front row. Trevor wasn't worried that he would deny the events they had experienced. Drew was an honest man, and besides, he would never betray a friend like that. But Trevor feared he might soft-pedal what had happened, make the events seem less extreme and more open to interpretation.

Drew motioned for Amber to sit, and she did so, looking a trifle embarrassed at her outburst.

"The three of us are fully aware of how unbelievable our claims sound, and we grant that most of our evidence is subjective at best. But it's all true, every word. All we can do is tell people our story and let them react however they will."

"Even at the cost of your professional credibility?" Pratt asked.

Trevor glanced at Connie, but her face remained expressionless.

"Yes," Drew said.

Trevor had never loved the man more than he did at that moment. He smiled.

"Anyone else have questions?" he asked.

Pratt asked nothing more, and he left as soon as the Q&A session was over. Trevor was grateful. The last thing he wanted to do was get into a heated conversation with the man. But a number of other people did want to talk afterward, so Trevor, Amber, and Drew came out from behind the table and walked into the midst of the remaining audience to answer questions personally. Members of a local ghost-hunting group asked Trevor for tips on how to publish a book about the cases they had investigated. While he answered their questions, he eavesdropped on Amber's and Drew's conversations. Amber was talking with an elderly woman who claimed that the spirit of her dead twin sister visited her at night to chat, which was OK, except that she kept the woman up all night, and she was always exhausted. Drew was listening to a well-dressed, portly man in his thirties who was prematurely bald. The man was intently telling Drew his theories for conducting therapy sessions for earthbound spirits in order to help them deal with whatever unresolved emotional issues were keeping them from moving on to the next plane of existence.

Carrington and Erin stood off to the side away from the crowd, talking quietly, with almost a conspiratorial air, and Trevor wondered what they were up to. Erin's cell phone rang, and she broke off her conversation with Carrington to answer it. She listened for a moment and then shouted, "No fucking way!"

When everyone in the room turned to look at her, she disconnected and placed another call. Carrington looked at her questioningly, but she ignored him as she waited for whomever she was calling to answer.

"Do you have an agent?"

Trevor had forgotten all about the local ghost hunters. He gave them one of his cards, told them to e-mail him with any more questions they had, and excused himself. Jenn was still sitting in the front row, chatting with Connie. The woman sure seemed friendlier than Drew had made her out to be. Maybe she was one of those people who were more casual and relaxed when they weren't at work. He figured this would be a good time to go over and introduce himself to her—but he would have to make sure not to look *too* interested in her, since Jenn was there. But as he started to walk over, Erin finished her latest call, disconnected, and came rushing over, Carrington in tow. Excitement rolled off of her in waves, and Trevor knew something big was up.

"I just called my film crew and told them to get their asses over to the museum," she said.

"Let me guess," he said. "There's been another death."

Her excitement ebbed a bit. "Two, actually. How did you know?"

Trevor glanced at Drew and Amber and smiled grimly. "We've traveled down this road before."

SEVEN

"I don't see why you felt the need to invite them along. I'm perfectly capable of investigating the scene all by myself, you know. After all, I've been at this game longer than those three have been alive."

Carrington stared out the passenger window of Erin's Beetle. Actually, *sulked* was more like it, she thought. He could be such a prima donna sometimes.

"Having other investigators along will create a stronger sense of place," she said. "Dead Days and Esotericon are both going on right now. It's the busiest time of the year for Exeter, and the place is crawling with professional and amateur paranormal investigators. Besides that, I'm going for an elder-statesman kind of thing here. You're the seasoned investigator mentoring the next generation, that kind of thing." These were all lies, of course, created on the spot, but she had to admit that her faux reasons for asking Drew, Amber, and Trevor to accompany them sounded good.

"Not *too* elder of a statesman, I hope." He turned to face forward, and if he didn't sound especially happy, he at least sounded somewhat mollified. "But it might work."

I'm so glad my star approves, she thought wryly. When she had originally e-mailed Carrington and asked him to be in her documentary, she had only read his Wikipedia entry and a third of one of his books. If she'd had any idea what a pain in the ass he would turn out to be, she never would have contacted him. Still, she had to admit he *was* good on camera. He exuded a natural, if somewhat cheesy, charm mixed with a gravitas that worked well for the subject matter. Kind of like a combination of Boris Karloff and Peter O'Toole.

She glanced into the rearview mirror and saw that Trevor's Prius was still right on her tail. Trevor drove, Jenn sat next to him in the front passenger seat, and Drew, Amber, and the new woman . . . what was her name? Connie. They all sat in the back. Erin still wasn't clear on just who Connie was or why she had asked to ride along to the museum. She was gorgeous, the kind of woman whose very existence made other women feel inadequate. She wondered how Amber was taking the addition of Connie to their field trip. If Erin had been in Amber's place and a woman like Connie was hanging around *her* boyfriend, she wouldn't have been happy at all. In her experience, all men had roving eyes—and roving eyes all too easily led to roving hands. And a woman like Connie was hard to compete with. Well, that was Amber's problem, not hers. She had a movie to make.

She was surprised that Jenn had decided to come along. The woman seemed to be having a hell of a time dealing with the murder of her employee, and Erin figured the last thing she would want to do was visit another crime scene. Maybe it was a moth-to-the-flame kind of thing. Or maybe she figured the killings were linked, and she wanted to help find her employee's murderer and bring him or her to justice.

Erin broke off her musings. It was time to get to work. She pulled out her cell phone and called Ray, but when he didn't answer after the first few rings, she thought he was going to ignore her call. He had a tendency to do that, especially when she shifted into what he called her "micro-micro-manager mode." But just as she expected his phone to go to voice mail, he picked up.

"Don't freak. We're here," he said before she could speak. "All of us."

"Good. You got your equipment set up?"

"Working on it with all due speed, my liege."

"We'll be there in a couple of minutes. Make sure you get a shot of us pulling up and getting out of the car. And we've brought some friends along. Make sure you film them, too."

"Friends?" Ray asked, but she disconnected without answering. She didn't want to waste any more time talking. She wasn't worried that he would be offended by her hanging up on him. Her crew knew what she was like when she was working.

As she slipped her cell phone back into her jeans pocket, Carrington asked, "Do we have access to the murder scene this time?"

"I'll work on that when we get there." Her source in the police department—a dispatcher who didn't mind supplementing what she viewed as her too-meager paycheck—had called to tell her about the deaths at the museum, just as she had called about the one at the bookstore the night before. But that was the extent of Erin's influence with the local authorities. She hadn't been able to get past Chief Hoffman that morning to film inside the bookstore, but she really wanted to persuade him to let them film in the museum. The setting was just too visually perfect. She supposed she could always use some footage they had already shot of the museum, maybe add some new footage later, once the crime scene was cleaned up and the museum reopened to the public. But it would be so much better—so much more *real*—if she could shoot while the scene was still an active one.

She checked the rearview one more time, as if she were afraid that Trevor and the others might change their minds and drive off. But of course, they were still there.

She had lied to Carrington about her motivation for inviting them to join in the investigation of the crime scene—assuming that they could do more than stand on the sidewalk and shoot footage of Carrington talking at the camera this time. But she wasn't actually certain why she *had* asked them to come along. It was mostly instinct, she supposed, along with curiosity. They weren't like other paranormal investigators she had met, and they certainly weren't like Carrington. They were serious about the paranormal but in a different way from others. They were more matter-of-fact about it, as if they didn't merely believe it but had actually experienced it. That impression had been strengthened by attending their presentation on the Lowry House. Their story was hard to believe, damned hard, but if it was true, then maybe they would be able to get at the truth of what was happening in the town. And if so, she was determined to capture it all on film.

She grinned. *Just try to hide your secrets from me, Exeter!* she thought. *I'll find them out, every one, and show them to the whole world!*

A sudden gust of wind slammed into the driver's side of the Beetle, causing the VW to swerve to the right. Erin thought the car was going to jump the curb and hit a large oak tree at the edge of someone's yard, and adrenaline shot through her system. She yanked the steering wheel to the left. The Beetle's tires squealed as it fishtailed, but then Erin managed to get the car under control again and straightened their course.

Carrington scowled at her. "I realize you're in a hurry, my dear, but getting us killed on the way to the museum isn't going to get your film made any faster."

"Sorry," she mumbled, and she eased her foot off the gas pedal and drove five miles under the speed limit the rest of the way.

The scene was a repeat of that morning at Forgotten Lore. Several police cars were parked outside the museum, along with a paramedic vehicle and several news vans. Reporters—the same ones Amber had seen that morning—stood on the sidewalk, gripping microphones and talking into cameras with almost feverish urgency. From the expressions on their faces, they were even more excited than they had been earlier, and Amber wondered what it would be like to have a job where you looked forward to something terrible happening, where you lived for others' deaths. But what gave her the right to criticize? Hadn't they come for the same reason?

"I feel like a ghoul," she said.

Drew took her hand and gave it a squeeze. "Erin and Carrington might be primarily interested in making a film, but we've come to help if we can. There's nothing ghoulish about that."

Before Amber could respond, Jenn said, "I don't know if I can do this. I thought I could, but now that we're here, I'm—I'm not so sure." She trembled, and her face was pale.

Amber reached over the seat and put a hand on her shoulder. Jenn started at her touch but then relaxed a bit.

"It's all right," Amber said. "You can stay in the car if you want. Right, Trevor?"

"Of course." He spotted a parking place and slipped the Prius into it. Once parked, he turned off the engine, but he left the keys in the ignition. He turned to Jenn. "I'll leave the keys so you can play the radio if you want. Will you be all right by yourself? I'll be happy to stay if you—"

She smiled and patted his hand. "It's sweet of you to offer, but I'll be fine. I'm not sure I believe everything about what happened at the Lowry House"—she glanced quickly back at Amber and Drew in the backseat—"but if there's anything you can do to find out what's happening, and maybe even stop it, I want you to do it."

Amber admired Jenn's bravery. She knew how difficult it was to deal with trauma, especially when the paranormal was involved. It changed your whole view of reality, made you feel as if you didn't know what the rules were anymore—or if there even *were* any rules.

Amber was sitting in the middle of the backseat between Drew and Connie. Just because the woman had started being nice to her didn't mean she was going to let her cozy up to Drew.

He leaned forward so he could speak with Connie. "If you wouldn't mind, perhaps you could stay with Jenn."

Maybe he thought that Connie, as a psychologist, would be able to take care of Jenn if she lost control of her emotions. Or maybe he simply wanted to keep Connie and Amber apart, which would be fine with Amber. Besides, she wasn't sure she believed the woman's reason for coming with them to the museum. "What better way to learn about what you do than to tag along on an actual investigation?" she had said. But something about it had sounded false to Amber, as if Connie had an ulterior motive for wanting to be included. At first, she had thought it might be because Connie wanted to stay close to Drew, but that didn't feel right. The longer she was in the woman's presence, the more she bothered her, and not because Amber saw her as a rival for Drew. There was something else going on, but she couldn't figure out what it was. A lot of it had to do with the way she spoke.

"I think I'd be more useful if I went with you. I *am* a trained observer and an expert in human behavior, you know." Connie smiled. "Of course, so are you, Drew, but it can't hurt to have another shrink along to serve as an extra set of eyes, can it?"

There it was again. This time, it was the use of the word *shrink*. It didn't seem like the way Connie would speak. Evidently, Drew felt the same way, for his brow furrowed as he gave Connie an appraising look.

"It's all right," Jenn said. "Honestly. And if she can help you three in any way, I want her to go. For Tonya's sake." Her voice quavered when she spoke Tonya's name, and for a second, Amber feared she would break down crying. But Jenn managed to keep a rein on her emotions, although Amber doubted it was easy for her.

Trevor checked with Jenn one more time to make sure she would be OK, she assured him that she would be, and then the four of them got out of the car and started walking toward the museum. Erin and Carrington were already there, but instead of shooting footage herself with her handheld camera, three other people were taking care of filming while Erin stood off to the side, presumably directing, although it looked as if she was just standing and watching. One of her crew operated a camera and one a boom mic, while the other was busy dabbing makeup on Carrington's face. The cameraman—a skinny, black-bearded guy wearing a *Teen Titans* T-shirt—was shooting the crowd that had gathered on the street near the museum. Amber remembered a story she had once read in which the crowd that gathered around accidents was made up of the same people every time. It had been a spooky story, and it was an even spookier idea, especially now. Because the crowd sure seemed like the same people who had gathered outside the bookstore that morning. Some in costume, some not, and the news reporters were definitely the same. It was probably just her imagination, but after what she, Drew, and Trevor had experienced at the Lowry House, she knew that just because an idea seemed too strange to be real, that didn't mean it wasn't. She wondered if, on some level, she would always mistrust reality, always wonder if things weren't really as they appeared on the surface. Maybe, she decided, but that wasn't necessarily bad, considering some of the things that lurked beneath the thin veneer of what most people thought of as reality. Better to be a little paranoid and alive than too trusting and dead.

And speaking of paranoid, she scanned the crowd to see if Mitch was there. He had always been controlling, but the vibes he had given off outside the hotel earlier had raised all sorts of alarm bells for Amber. Something had happened to change him, to deepen his anger and bring it closer to the surface. She was more frightened of him now than she ever had been before. She saw no sign of him, though, and more important, she didn't sense his presence. Trevor believed that she was psychically sensitive, and while she knew that her dreams sometimes provided insights she couldn't get through rational means—as with her nightmare about Tonya's murder—she wasn't ready to believe that she possessed true psychic powers. Still, she was relieved not to feel Mitch anywhere close by.

She was also glad that she didn't catch any glimpses of the shadowy figure she had seen standing next to Mitch outside the hotel. She hoped that sighting had been a result of her imagination, too, but she feared otherwise. She really needed a chance to talk to Drew about Mitch and to tell both him and Trevor about the apparition she had seen. But she could hardly do it now, especially with Connie in tow. She supposed she could try to put up with Connie for Drew, if for no other reason than to make his life at work easier. But she didn't have to like it.

The Beyond the Veil Museum, like Jenn's bookstore, was housed in an older building. Two buildings, actually, connected by an additional section that been constructed between them over the years. The property was enclosed by a black wrought-iron fence, and each building was two stories high and painted a dark purple with black shutters and a black roof, like a cartoon version of a haunted manor. This effect was compounded by the mechanical skeletons erected in the museum's front yard. They stood in various poses near headstones engraved with names such as Mr. and Mrs. Kreep (dressed as a bride and groom), Prof. N. O. Boddy (in a tweed jacket with elbow patches), and Dee Ceased (in a cheerleader outfit complete with curly blond wig). The Digger Brothers both held shovels, but while one was digging down from the surface, the other was digging his way up out of the ground. The skeletons—plastic bones yellowed and clothes faded from long exposure to the elements— moved with slow, whirring motions, jaws clacking in arrhythmic cadence. The tableau was supposed to make the museum appear to be a fun tourist destination, but considering what had happened within its walls that day, Amber found the skeletons more disturbing than cute.

"Couldn't they have turned those things off?" she said.

"I think they're amusing," Connie said. When everyone looked at her, she added, "In a morbid way, of course."

Amber exchanged glances with Drew, and he responded with a little shrug. They made their way through the crowd until they reached Carrington, Erin, and her crew. The boom-mic operator was a petite girl in her early twenties whose short hair had been dyed a garish blue more suitable for an anime character, and the makeup artist was an older woman in her thirties with long, flowing hair that had gone prematurely white. Like the cameraman, they were dressed in T-shirts and jeans, and both women wore flip-flops despite the cool weather.

The cameraman turned to look at the four of them as they approached. "I assume these are the friends you mentioned, my queen."

"Shut up, Raymond," Erin snapped. She pulled out her cell phone and ignored them while she made a call.

He turned his attention back to Amber and the others. "She's in a foul mood because the chief won't let us inside. I'm Ray Somers. That's Sarah Brooks, and she's Pattie Jordan." He nodded to the mic operator and the makeup woman, who both smiled in greeting.

"As you can see, our stalwart camera monkey has a bit of a mouth on him," Carrington said. "But he's right about Erin. The chief didn't even come out to talk to her this time. He turned her down over the phone." Pattie dabbed at his nose with a makeup sponge, and he brushed her hand away, scowling. "That's enough! You make my skin look any more orange, and everyone will think I'm a jack-o'-lantern."

Pattie gave him an irritated look and then looked at Amber and the others. She turned toward Erin and asked, "Should I make them up, too?"

Erin was still on the phone, evidently waiting for someone to pick up, since she wasn't talking yet. She waved Pattie's question away without answering it.

Pattie looked at Sarah. "What do you think?"

"Don't ask me, sweetie. If I've learned anything working with Erin, it's that there's no way to guess what she wants. Ever."

Pattie sighed. "True that."

There was something about the tone in Sarah's voice as she said "sweetie" that made Amber think the younger woman used it not as a generic term of endearment for a coworker but rather as a person speaking casually to her lover.

"Shit!" Erin shoved her cell phone back into her pocket. "Now he won't even answer!"

Amber assumed she was talking about the chief.

"When you spoke with him earlier, did you tell him *I* was here?" Carrington asked.

Erin shot him a withering look. "I hate to break this to you, Arthur, but you're only a legend in your own mind."

Ray smirked, and Sarah and Pattie looked as if they were trying very hard not to smile. Carrington, however, did not look amused.

"I suppose we'll have to shoot some interior footage later," Erin said. She turned to Amber and the others. "Sorry I had you guys come here for nothing. I even had Arthur bring his ghost-hunting equipment." She gestured to a pair of metal cases resting on the sidewalk next to the fence. "I thought you might be able to use it inside, and we'd see what sort of readings you'd get."

"What kind of equipment?" Trevor asked. He sounded as excited as a kid on Christmas morning.

"Top of the line, of course," Carrington said. "Would you like to see?"

"You know it!"

Carrington led Trevor over to the cases. He turned one onto its side and opened it, and Trevor became even more excited as Carrington began showing him the contents.

"Do you really think you'll be able to find out something if you go inside?" It was Jenn. They turned to see that she had joined them. Her eyes were red from crying, but she seemed in control of her emotions at the moment.

Amber looked at Drew. He appeared uncomfortable, and she

knew why. He didn't want to promise something they couldn't deliver. She turned back to Jenn.

"You were at our presentation," she said. "Everything we said was true. We did it once, and we can do it again." She hoped.

Jenn looked at her for a long moment, as if she were searching Amber's eyes for any hint of deception or overconfidence. Finally, she nodded. She took out her cell phone and made a call.

"Peter? It's Jenn. I'm standing on the sidewalk outside the museum. I have some friends here with me, and I think they might be able to help."

I'm not sure about this." Chief Hoffman looked them up and down, and from the expression on his face, it was clear he wasn't impressed with what he saw.

At least the man had allowed them to enter the museum, Drew thought. That was something. And he had permitted Erin and her crew to set up their equipment so they could film their conversation with him.

They had gathered in Beyond the Veil's lobby. From what the chief had already told them, he had done the initial questioning of the staff, and they, along with the museumgoers who had discovered the bodies and everyone else who had been inside the museum when the murders took place, had been taken to the staff offices, where they were being questioned further by the police. The medical examiner had finished his on-site inspection of the bodies, and they'd been bagged and were on their way to the county morgue.

"If the media get wind that I let you do a psychic investigation in here, I'll probably lose my job."

"In Exeter?" Jenn said. "If anything, it'll end up getting you a raise. Peter, you know me. Just because I run a bookstore that specializes in the paranormal doesn't mean I believe in it. But I know *you* do—at least a little."

The chief looked embarrassed, but he didn't explain.

"If I, a confirmed skeptic, believe that these people are the real thing, isn't that reason enough to give them a chance? Besides, what can it hurt?"

"My reputation. My credibility. My self-respect . . ." The chief sighed. "All right. Leave no stone unturned, I suppose. I'd rather have you come back later, but if I say that, you'll probably just tell me that the psychic impressions are strongest when they're fresh."

"As a matter of fact—" Trevor began, but Jenn shushed him with a look.

As the chief continued, his voice took on an official tone. "Here's the deal. I can't allow you to disturb the crime scene, so you won't be able to enter the room where the murders occurred. And I can't let you talk to any of the witnesses we're still questioning. I've got a couple of officers searching the museum for evidence. Don't get in their way. And if you find anything—anything at all—that you think might be evidence, don't touch it. Call me, and I'll have one of my people check it out. I'll expect a full report once you're finished. Clear?"

Drew, Amber, and Trevor nodded. He was surprised to see Connie nodding, too. Carrington stepped forward then.

"Don't worry, Chief. I intend to personally oversee the entire investigation, and I assure you that the highest standards of professionalism will be observed at all times."

"I wasn't aware that this investigation had an *overseer,*" Trevor said.

Carrington gave him a smile. "My tools, my rules."

Trevor made a face, but he gave no further protest.

The chief looked at Jenn. "Are you sure you're up for this? You've been through a lot today. Maybe it would be better if you waited outside."

"You're sweet to worry about me, but I'll be OK. If it gets to be too much for me, though, I promise I'll leave."

A look passed between the two of them, and Drew realized

they had a closer relationship than he'd initially thought. He didn't think it was romantic in any way, but it was more than friendship. A father-daughter thing, perhaps.

"You'd better." The chief turned to Erin. "You can film in here, but I don't want you sensationalizing the murders, out of respect for the victims' families. If you do, I'll bring you up on charges of interfering with a police investigation, and I'll confiscate your film as evidence. And before you make any promises, Jenn will tell me if you go back on your word. Right?"

"Sure, Peter," Jenn said.

Erin didn't look offended by the chief's words. "No worries. I'm trying to make a documentary about the paranormal, not a true-crime film."

Drew didn't believe Erin. Whatever her original intentions for her film were, she seemed too driven a person to let an opportunity pass her by, especially when it could lead to her film getting stronger advance buzz and perhaps wider distribution. A film about a town that celebrated the paranormal was one thing. But a film about a town that celebrated the paranormal *and* where a series of mysterious, sinister murders had taken place? That was quite another.

"And make sure your crew is careful," the chief added. "I don't want any more accidents happening."

"Accidents?" Trevor said.

Erin looked suddenly uncomfortable, but she ignored the question. "Will do," she said to the chief.

Drew, Amber, and Trevor shot quick glances at one another. There was a story there, one they would have to look into later.

"What can you tell us about the murders, Chief?" Trevor asked. He removed a pen and a small notebook from his jacket pocket, opened it, and prepared to take notes. "Any information you can give us will help."

"None of this better get out to the media," he said. "If it does—"

"Yes, yes," Connie said, sounding impatient. "The full wrath of the law will come crashing down upon us like God's sledgehammer. We get it."

Drew looked at her, but she steadily avoided his gaze. Something strange was going on with her. He had known her to have a sharp tongue from time to time, but that normally manifested in a blunt directness that some people found offensive. But he had never known her to be such a . . . well, such a smartass.

The chief scowled at her, but he didn't respond to her comment. "The deceased were Donner Cummings, forty-two, and Rachel Hartwell, twenty-eight. Both lived in Indianapolis. Based on how they were dressed, we assume they were tourists in town for Dead Days."

Trevor opened his mouth, but before he could say anything, Carrington jumped in.

"And precisely how were they dressed, Chief?" he asked. He gave Trevor a smug smile that said, *See? I* am *in charge*.

"Cummings was dressed as a Ghostbuster. You know, like in the movies. Hartwell dressed like a typical Goth kid."

Trevor was busy writing that down, so Drew asked the next question. "How did they die?"

"According to the medical examiner, Cummings was strangled. As for Hartwell . . ." Chief Hoffman hesitated. "The ME said that it looked like she'd drowned. But there was no water at the scene, except for a bit that appeared to have leaked out of her mouth. There's nowhere in the museum where she could've come into contact with enough water to drown her, except a restroom, I suppose. But that doesn't seem likely."

Drew glanced at Jenn. She was trembling, and she held her hand to her stomach, as if she were feeling nauseated. Trevor was too busy writing to notice, but Amber walked over to her and took the woman's hand. Jenn gave her a grateful look and held on to Amber as if she were a lifeline. Drew loved how sensitive Amber was to the emotional environment around her, and not for the first time, he thought what a terrific therapist she would make.

"Were there any witnesses?" he asked.

"None. No one saw or heard anything, even though there were a number of people visiting the museum at the time."

"Interesting," Carrington said. "A psychic cloak, perhaps?"

Trevor looked up from his notebook, surprise on his face. "Could be," he said.

"Security cameras?" Drew asked.

"There are a few," Chief Hoffman said. "But this place isn't an art museum filled with valuable treasures, so there aren't cameras in every room. There's one here in the lobby"—he pointed to a shiny reflective dome on the ceiling that hid the camera in question—"and one in the gift shop."

"Both places where money is kept," Trevor said.

The chief nodded. "There are three more, installed in random locations in the museum. There is none in the room where the murders occurred."

"But one of the cameras must've picked up *something* useful," Amber said. "Images of the two victims entering the museum, if nothing else."

"The security footage is worthless. Nothing but electronic distortion," Connie said. She looked around at everyone then, as if she had momentarily forgotten them. "At least, that's the kind of thing I've heard happens in these sorts of situations."

The chief looked at her, eyes narrowing in reappraisal.

Great, Drew thought. *The last thing we need is for him to start suspecting Connie of something.*

But all the chief said was, "That's right."

"If I could get a copy of the footage, I might be able to do something with it," Trevor said. "I have several programs on my laptop designed to filter out electronic video distortion." He looked at Carrington. "You're not the only one with cool toys, you know."

Carrington inclined his head in acknowledgment.

"I'm not comfortable with making a copy of possible evidence," the chief said. "I'll have to think about it."

Trevor looked disappointed, but he didn't protest. Instead, he said, "In what room did the murders take place?"

"On the first floor of this building, toward the rear. There's an emergency exit back there. There's an alarm on the door that's set to go off if it's opened, but it was never tripped. Whoever committed the murders didn't escape that way. Not unless they disabled the alarm somehow. But we've found no evidence of that."

"Thanks, but what I meant was what's *in* the room?" Trevor said. "What sort of exhibit?"

The chief frowned. "I don't see how that matters, but it's an exhibit about the flood. The one that nearly wiped out the town in the 1920s. There are photos, objects that were recovered after the waters receded, that kind of thing."

Trevor and Carrington exchanged a look.

"Interesting that the woman would have drowned in that particular room," Carrington said.

"It sure is." Trevor scribbled something in his notebook. He continued writing as he asked his next question. "Is there any history of ghostly manifestations in the museum? Or any violent incidents that took place here over the years?"

"Not that I'm aware of," the chief said. He looked to Jenn. "Anything you know about?"

She thought for a moment and shook her head.

"All right, then," the chief said. "Anything else? If not, I have work to do."

Drew, Trevor, and Amber exchanged glances and shook their heads.

"I think that's all for now, Chief," Carrington said. "We appreciate your cooperation."

"I'm so very glad." The chief gave them a last look, as if he were silently warning them to be on their best behavior, like a dad who was about to turn over his house reluctantly to the kids so they could have a party. Then he turned and headed toward the museum offices.

"I'm surprised he let us in," Amber said after the chief had departed. "He doesn't seem too thrilled to have us here."

Drew turned to Jenn. "During the conversation, you indicated that he was a believer in the paranormal."

Jenn looked at Erin. "You'd better not put this in your movie."

Erin crossed her heart and held up her hand in a Girl Scout salute. Drew doubted the sincerity of the gesture, but it must have been enough for Jenn, because she continued.

"His wife passed away a couple of years ago. He comes into the store and buys books on ghosts and the afterlife. We talk sometimes. He told me he's not interested in trying to contact her spirit or anything. He misses her a great deal, and reading books like that makes him feel closer to her, as if she's not really gone, you know? They give him hope that maybe they'll be reunited one day."

Drew better understood Jenn's relationship with the chief now. Not father-daughter so much as confessor-confidante.

"*If* they can find each other," Connie said. "The afterlife is a damn big place. You think it's challenging to find the proverbial needle in a haystack? Try finding one in a *galaxy* of haystacks." She paused. "Uh, I mean, that's what I imagine it would be like."

Drew puzzled over Connie's latest odd comment. Maybe she was simply trying to participate in her own way, but she was coming across as more than a little strange. He had never known her to give any thought whatsoever to spiritual topics. Then again, maybe that was a side of herself that she usually kept hidden. It wouldn't be surprising. Many people viewed their spirituality as private. Still, it didn't seem right to Drew. Something else was going on with her, but he didn't know what, and it bugged him.

Carrington clapped his hands together and rubbed them vigorously. "Well, then. Shall we get started?"

"Dibs on the EMF detector!" Trevor said. He tucked his pen and notebook into his jacket pocket and hurried over to Carrington's equipment cases. Carrington followed him, and the two began arguing over who was going to get to use what.

While Erin got her crew ready to go mobile, Drew went over to Amber and Jenn. Connie stood alone, sweeping her gaze slowly around the lobby as if she were looking for something, but Drew had no idea what it might be.

Amber was still holding on to Jenn's hand, but the woman seemed better now.

"Thank you for talking to the chief," Drew said. "He wouldn't have allowed us to enter if not for you. You've done more than your share to help us, and you've been through a great deal today. If you want to wait here in the lobby until we're finished . . ."

"I'd rather come with you, if you don't mind. I've lived in Exeter for a long time, and you might need a native guide." Her smile, while a bit shaky, seemed genuine.

She was a strong person, and Drew thought that strength would serve her well as she worked to come to terms with her employee's murder in the days ahead. He hoped that she wasn't risking worse trauma by staying with them, but given the way things had gone so far, he feared that hope would be in vain.

Amber looked at Jenn. "Excuse me. I need to talk to Trevor for a minute."

"Sure." Jenn let go of her hand, and Amber walked over to the equipment cases, where Trevor and Carrington were still arguing. Drew suspected what Amber was up to, and after speaking to Trevor for a few seconds, she returned. A moment later, Trevor walked over, carrying an EMF detector. He looked a little embarrassed.

"Sorry I got carried away," he said, holding up the detector for emphasis. "A boy and his toys. Jenn, do you think you can help me work this thing? I've never used one before, and Carrington's going to be busy doing his thing for the camera." He smiled. "You were always more mechanically inclined than me. Remember that time I tried to fix your disposal?"

She laughed. "It took me forever to scrub the food stains off the ceiling!"

Trevor led Jenn off to the side to show her the EMF detector, and Drew turned to Amber.

"Playing matchmaker?" he asked in a quiet voice so the others wouldn't overhear.

"She needs him," Amber said just as quietly. "Almost as much as he needs her."

Yep, Drew thought. *She'd definitely make a great therapist.*

"All right," Erin said in a take-charge voice. Now that the chief was gone, Drew figured she no longer felt the need to feign deference to his authority. "My crew's ready to roll."

"Time to go to work," Amber said.

Connie walked over to join them. She smiled, a strange gleam in her eye. "Lights, camera, action," she said.

EIGHT

"Getting anything?" Jenn asked.

"Not really," Trevor said. EMF detectors were designed to measure variances in electromagnetic fields, and they were standard equipment for ghost hunters. The devices were calibrated to ignore the mild EMF emissions given off by human bodies and detect the energy fluctuations commonly associated with hauntings. While some of the readings they had gotten so far were suggestive of ghostly activity, they were hardly definitive.

"You sound disappointed."

"I guess I am, a bit. After our experience at the Lowry House, I suppose I expected . . . I don't know. *More*."

"Like bizarre manifestations of long-dead serial killers and Revolutionary War–era werewolves?"

He smiled. "Something like that. So you really did read the book."

She nodded. "Like I said before, it's hard to believe that you guys experienced all that stuff." She held up a hand before he could protest. "But let's say you did. What I don't understand is why you're here *now*. I mean, if *I* had experienced anything as terrifying as what you wrote about, I wouldn't want to come within a hundred miles of any place that was even rumored to be haunted. I never really understood why you were so into the paranormal. I thought maybe it was kind of like a hobby, like it is with most of my customers, you know? I mean, I knew you believed in it, but to keep investigating after what you went through . . . I'd think you'd almost have to be obsessed." She turned to look at him, a concerned expression on her face. "Sorry. *Obsess* is probably too strong a word. I'm not trying to criticize you. I'm just trying to understand."

"It's OK," Trevor said.

It had been forty minutes since they had started investigating, and so far, they didn't have much to show for their time. Drew read information about the exhibits as they moved through the museum, while Amber examined the actual displays, touching anything that wasn't kept behind glass. It seemed to Trevor that she did so unconsciously, as if she were instinctively trying to get a read on the psychic atmosphere in the museum.

For a while, Carrington had carried an infrared thermal scanner, searching for cold spots, but he hadn't had any more luck getting hits on his device than Trevor had, so he gave up on it. He handed the scanner over to Sarah to carry, and now he held an audio recorder. Every few minutes, he would ask a question aloud. "Are you here?" "What do you want?" "Do you wish to send us a message?" He would pause to give any spirits that might be listening a chance to respond, and then he would ask another question. He was trying to capture EVP, electronic voice phenomena. The idea was that ghosts could psychically imprint their voices directly onto electronic devices, and their words could be heard during playback.

Erin was pleased when Carrington switched over to audio recording. "Makes for better footage," she had said. She and her crew kept busy filming the investigation. They spent a good portion of their time focusing on Carrington, but Erin had them shoot footage of Trevor and the others, too, something Carrington was clearly displeased with, but he kept his complaints about not being the absolute center of attention at all times to a minimum.

Connie trailed along with the group, seeming content to watch everyone with an amused smile, although from time to time, she would frown and cock her head to the side, as if she were listening to something that none of the rest of them could hear.

"In a way, what happened at the Lowry House made me even

more determined to investigate the paranormal," Trevor said. "It's the same for Drew and Amber. None of us is eager to repeat what we went through—who would be?—but once you know that Darkness is real and that it can reach out from the Other Side and hurt people, you can't stand by and do nothing anymore. At least, we can't."

Jenn looked at him for a moment. "You've changed. You're more confident, more focused."

"More mature?"

She smiled. "I don't know if I'd go that far."

He smiled back and continued scanning for EMF energy.

The group took its time getting to the room where the murders had taken place—or as near to the room as the chief wanted them to go. Yellow police tape had been stretched across the entrance to the room, and a pair of crime-scene techs were still busy processing the scene. The bodies had been removed, and instead of chalk outlines indicating their positions, the techs had set up small plastic markers with numbers on them and were taking photographs. The markers were probably more efficient and less damaging to the crime scene than chalk lines, but Trevor thought they lacked the morbid melodrama of the classic approach.

They all couldn't stand in the doorway at the same time—one of the downsides to investigating the paranormal en masse, Trevor thought—so they took turns. Jenn might have steeled her nerves to enter the museum with them, but she wasn't up to actually viewing the scene where the deaths happened. She hung back, and Trevor stayed with her and let the others take the first look. Carrington stepped up to the tape right away, naturally, and he made a show of leaning forward, as if he were a master detective scanning the room for clues. Erin made sure her crew filmed the action, such as it was.

Carrington stretched his arm over the tape to get his recorder as far into the room as he could. "Is there a presence here?" he said loudly. Then, after a pause, "Are you responsible for the deaths that occurred here?"

While Carrington did his thing, Drew, Amber, and Connie came over to join Trevor and Jenn.

"Jenn, what can you tell us about the exhibit in there?" Drew asked.

"Peter pretty much covered it. It's all about the flood and its effect on the town. It's really more of a historical exhibit than anything else."

"It does talk a bit about the ghost sightings in the years following the flood and how spiritualists and mediums were drawn by reports of paranormal activity," Trevor said. "But Jenn's right. The exhibit's primary focus is on the flood."

"Did the town have a reputation for strange occurrences before the flood?" Amber asked.

"No more than any other town," Trevor said.

"So the murders took place in the one room dedicated to the death of old Exeter and the town's rebirth as a nexus of psycho-spiritual energy," Connie said. "I doubt that's a coincidence. I wonder if whatever is responsible for the murders was trying to send a message by committing them here."

Trevor exchanged glances with Drew and Amber. For someone who supposedly had zero interest in the paranormal before that day, Connie was picking up things fast. Maybe too fast.

"What sort of message?" Amber said.

"'I'm here' would be the simplest one, wouldn't it?" Connie said. "To us, death is the worst thing that can happen, but to something who's already dead, maybe not so much. Such a being might not even see murder as a form of aggression, merely as a way of introducing itself."

"Interesting insight," Drew said with a slight frown, as if he wasn't quite sure what to make of what Connie had said.

She smiled. "I didn't go to psychology school just to have a fancy diploma to hang on the wall."

"It could be a warning of some kind," Trevor said. "Or maybe retaliation for some transgression. Folklore around the world is filled with stories of dark forces that attack and kill people for some kind of wrong they did, whether real or perceived. Like in just about every episode of *Tales from the Crypt*."

"Now, *there's* a scholarly source," Connie said. "But the principle is sound enough."

"We need to know more about the victims," Drew said. "Who they are and what they did in town before coming here. If we can retrace their steps, we might—" Drew broke off and looked past Trevor's shoulder.

Trevor turned to see what had caught Drew's attention. Erin was watching them, a smug smile on her face. Ray had his camera trained on them, and Sarah held the mic out to pick up their conversation. Carrington was still asking questions of any ghosts that might be lingering about and pausing to give them a chance to speak, without any idea that Erin and her crew were no longer filming him.

"Don't stop on our account," Erin said. "That was good stuff."

Carrington turned then and saw what was happening.

"Are you having a discussion about the scene without me? Not very collegial of you." He turned off his audio recorder and came over to join them.

"My turn," Trevor said.

He walked over to the room's entrance and, like Carrington before him, held out the EMF detector as far as he could without breaking the police tape. The readings were a little higher but nothing to get excited about. Sarah had put Carrington's infrared thermal scanner down on the floor, and Trevor picked it up and scanned the room with it. The IR scanner sent out a thermal beam to check for unusually cold or hot spots, which might indicate a ghostly presence. This was a high-end model, one of the MX Ranger series, with a built-in laser pointer to help aim the thermal beam more precisely. Trevor had never used an IR scanner before. As a struggling freelance writer, he had never been able to afford one. As much fun as it was to use the device, it would have been even more fun if it picked up anything. But aside from the crime-scene techs, there were no significant temperature variances in the room.

Trevor figured the presence of the techs made it impossible to get any clear readings, so he lowered the scanner and examined the room the old-fashioned way: with his eyes. The techs, a man and a woman, shot him dirty looks, as if they thought he was some kind of crime-scene voyeur, but evidently, the chief had informed them that Trevor and the others would be coming, because they didn't say anything and soon returned to their work. There was nothing of note to see in the room, no bloodstains or anything like that, and he didn't feel any sense of foreboding. No chills down the back, no feeling that unseen eyes were watching him. He was considering asking Amber to join him to see what she might be able to pick up from the scene, when Connie walked over.

"You made the right move coming over here as soon as Carrington joined the conversation," she said. "The man has an ego almost as big as his mouth. Right now, he's regaling the others about a case he investigated twenty years ago that has absolutely no bearing on what happened here."

Trevor saw that Erin and her crew were filming Carrington's monologue. "At least he'll give Erin some footage for her film. I didn't get anything with either the EMF detector or the IR scanner."

Connie shrugged. "So? Even if you had, it wouldn't have told you anything you don't already know. Something supernatural occurred here, and it resulted in the deaths of two people."

"I thought you didn't believe in the paranormal."

She flashed a smile that could have been on a magazine cover. "Let's just say I'm doing my best to keep an open mind. There is something about the murders that I find curious."

"Oh?"

"The woman died in a way that seems impossible. She drowned in a room that contains no water, and there was no water on the outside of her body or on her clothes. *And* this happened in a room dedicated to the Exeter flood. Very mysterious and darkly poetic, wouldn't you say?"

"I suppose."

"But the man was strangled to death. A very mundane way to die, with no sense of style at all. It's almost as if they were killed by two different forces: one spiritual, one physical."

Trevor hadn't thought of that, but now that Connie had pointed it out to him, he had to admit that her observation made a lot of sense, even if he wasn't sure where it might ultimately lead.

On impulse, he asked, "What's your game, Connie? You're way too knowledgeable about this kind of stuff for someone who up to now has had no interest in the supernatural. And don't try to tell me you're some kind of savant with instinctive insight into the paranormal."

"I *do* like games, Trevor, I must admit. But I'm not playing any now . . . at least, none that isn't necessary. I only want to help. After all"—Connie's supermodel smile took on a sly edge—"that's the reason I traveled so far to get here."

The next room they went to was dedicated to malign female spirits in folklore, such as the Irish banshee, the Welsh Hag of the Mist, the English Black Annis, the Scottish Cailleach, the Indonesian Pontianak, the Dominican Soucouyant, and others. Trevor had visited the museum before, back when he had been dating Jenn, but this exhibit was new to him. Any other time, he would have stopped to check it out, but he had better things to do right then than learn about some obscure supernatural folklore. That was why God had invented Wikipedia.

Drew, however, had stopped before a painting of a pale-skinned, dark-haired woman garbed in a black dress.

"The Dark Lady," he read from the placard next to the painting. "Looks like she's a local version of the myth. According to this, she predates the flood, but her appearances increased dramatically after it. Unlike the other spirits in this exhibit, her manifestation doesn't seem to be linked to death or disaster. As spirits go, she seems fairly benign."

Amber stared at the painting for a long moment before whispering, "It's her."

Drew frowned. "What do you mean?"

Carrington was standing before the banshee's picture, going on about a trip to Ireland he had made to investigate reports of a headless ghost haunting a castle. Erin had her crew dutifully filming him, but when she saw Amber staring at the painting of the Dark Lady, she shushed Carrington and motioned for Ray to turn the camera on Amber, and Sarah moved the boom mic to pick up her voice. Carrington scowled, but he didn't protest.

Trevor left Jenn and hurried over to join Amber and Drew.

"I've seen her twice today," Amber said. She glanced at Ray, noticed that he was filming them, and frowned slightly but kept talking. "The first time was in front of the coffee shop, and the second time was outside the hotel before our presentation. At least, I think it was her the second time. Her form was less distinct then, like a smear of shadow. I almost had the sense that she was trying to hide from me, but it was her. I *felt* it."

"What did she do?" Trevor asked. He was aware that the camera was trained on them, but this was the first lead they'd had so far, and he was too excited to care.

"Nothing," Amber said. "She only watched me, but she did so intensely, as if she were trying to . . . I don't know, take my measure, I guess." She paused. "And there's . . . something else."

Her tone changed. She sounded almost embarrassed now. No, Trevor thought, it was more than that. She sounded ashamed.

Drew picked up on her emotional shift, and he reached out to take her hand. "Whatever it is, you know you can tell us." He looked at Trevor. "Maybe it would be best if you could give us some privacy."

Trevor tried to hide his surprise. He understood that the dynamic among the three of them had changed since Amber and Drew had become a couple, and he didn't expect them to include him in every conversation they had, by any means. But for Drew to ask him to leave when Amber was about to reveal something that might be important to the investigation . . . well, it hurt.

He struggled to put his feelings aside and was about to leave when Amber said, "It's OK, Drew. She was with me outside the hotel."

She? Trevor glanced over his shoulder and saw that Connie had joined them. He hadn't been aware that the woman had followed him over. He was relieved that Drew and Amber hadn't wanted to send him away, but he was irritated with Connie for insinuating herself into their conversation without being invited. Before today, neither Amber nor he had met her, and now she was acting as if she were an intimate member of their group. She might be attractive as hell, but beauty only went so far, and she was beginning to piss him off.

Connie didn't appear to feel awkward at all about intruding. Quite the opposite. She seemed relaxed and comfortable, as if she felt she belonged there. But if Amber wasn't going to protest, Trevor decided he wouldn't, either. At least, not this time.

Amber continued. "Both times I saw the apparition, she wasn't alone. She was with a man. A living man, not a ghost, and . . . I know him. We dated for a short time about a year ago. He's . . . not a nice person."

She hadn't said much. "He's . . . not a nice person." Only five words, but they spoke volumes. Trevor felt as if he had been punched in the gut. Amber was his friend, and he loved her dearly, and the thought of anyone being *not nice* to her filled him with rage. And if this revelation hit him that hard, how much worse was it for Drew? He looked to his friend and saw that his expression was blank. Anyone who didn't know him might think that he felt nothing about Amber's confession, but Trevor knew better. Drew was struggling to control his emotions, not because he was reluctant to display them but because he didn't want them to get in the way. He would deal with his feelings later, but right now, he needed to focus on Amber.

"Do you want to leave and go somewhere to talk?" Drew asked.

She smiled and put her hand on his chest. "We can talk later. Right now, we have work to do."

"Some things are more important than work," Drew said.

"Three people are dead. What could be more important than that? We can't afford to get distracted, not if we hope to prevent any more deaths. Whatever we're up against here, it's bad. Remember the warning Greg gave me."

Trevor wasn't sure he had heard right. "You mean Greg, as in our *deceased* friend Greg?"

Amber turned to him. "I haven't had a chance to fill you in. We haven't had much alone time lately." She nodded toward Erin and her crew.

Up to this point, Connie hadn't spoken, but now she said, "You boys don't have to worry about Amber. She's a lot stronger than either of you think." She said this with conviction, almost as if she felt she knew Amber better than either Drew or Trevor did.

Some people think they know everything once there's a PhD after their name, Trevor thought.

Amber told Trevor about seeing Greg's spirit in the restroom of Burial Grounds.

"Who would've thought that Greg would end up haunting toilets?" Trevor said. "More than a bit of a comedown for a guy who was once a lord of Darkness, don't you think?"

Connie gave him a strange look that he couldn't interpret, but she didn't say anything.

Trevor went on. "So Greg tweeted at us from the Great Beyond to warn us about some vague threat in Exeter. Why do ghosts always give cryptic warnings? Why can't they just come right out and say, 'Your house is built over an ancient Indian burial site. You might want to think about relocating'?"

"Maybe because the Other Side is a complicated place," Connie said. "You know how when American tourists visit other countries, the people who live there ask if they know so-and-so from East Nowhere, Idaho, as if all Americans are best friends? It's because they don't really grasp just how big America is. Maybe it's like that in this case. Maybe your friend didn't give a more specific warning because he couldn't."

Trevor had to admit that she had a good point. "Maybe. Or maybe Greg is playing games with us. He's been known to do that. Or worse, maybe he's responsible for the murders."

"He did tell you that he carried the Darkness that had possessed him to the Other Side," Drew said, "and that he'd merged with it."

"If that's true, then maybe he only wants us to think he's helping us," Trevor said. "Maybe he's been biding his time for the last couple of months, waiting for a chance to get revenge."

Connie let out a derisive snort. "You watch too many bad horror movies."

"I believe he's sincere," Amber said. "He didn't have to admit that the Darkness was still a part of him. If he intended to manipulate us, why would he plant doubt about himself in our minds?"

"Games within games," Trevor said. "It's a classic 'lull them into a false sense of security' ploy. By sowing doubt, he appears to be confessing everything to us. Paradoxically, because we doubt him, we end up trusting him more."

Drew thought about that for a moment. "Your reasoning is psychologically sound. Unfortunately, there's no way to determine the truth for ourselves. And that's assuming the spirit that appeared to Amber was even Greg in the first place. It could have been something else masquerading as him."

Amber shook her head. "It was him. I'm sure of it."

"Fine," Trevor said. "But that doesn't mean we can trust him."

Amber sighed. "No, I suppose it doesn't."

Connie looked irritated, although Trevor couldn't understand why. She opened her mouth to say something, but before she could speak, Carrington said, "I think you should all hear this."

They all turned their attention to Carrington. He walked into the center of the room but without his usual air of showmanship. He looked shaken, and when he held up his digital audio recorder, Trevor could see that the man's hand was trembling.

"While you were talking, I decided to play back the audio and see if we caught any EVP." Without further explanation, he activated the recorder.

At first, there was silence, and then Carrington's voice issued from the tiny speaker.

"Are you there?" No response. *"What do you want?"* Again, nothing. *"Do you wish to send us a message?"*

Silence for a few seconds, this time followed by a second voice—a woman's.

"Stop," she whispered. And then, louder, *"Stop!"*

Trevor had heard EVP before—had even picked up some himself once or twice—but he had never heard any this clear and distinct. It sounded as if the woman had been speaking directly into the recorder.

"That was a woman's voice," he said. "Do you suppose it belonged to the Dark Lady?"

Before anyone could respond, he felt a sudden chill, as if a light coating of frost had settled over his body. At first, he thought the sensation was a reaction to listening to the eerie voice, but then he realized that what he was feeling was an actual drop in temperature.

He was still holding the IR scanner, and he raised it, intending to scan for cold spots in the room. But before he could activate the device, cracking sounds filled the air. Tiny fissures shot through the floor, walls, and ceiling, as if the museum was experiencing a mild earthquake. It was over in seconds, and when the noise died away, the entire room was covered with a single word formed from fissures etched into its surfaces. Some of the words were large, some small, but they all said the same thing.

STOP.

"Message received," Connie said.

"I can't believe we got that on video!" Erin said. "That was absolutely a-fucking-mazing!"

"I wouldn't get excited just yet," Trevor said. "Remember, the chief confirmed that the video from the security camera was ruined by electronic interference. The same thing could have happened here."

"Who cares if it did?" Erin said. "As a matter of fact, it'll be even better if the footage *is* distorted. If viewers see the letters forming, they'll just put it down to special effects. But to hear that spooky voice, see our reaction to it, then see the video cut out, and when it comes back, the audience sees that it's covered with the word *Stop* . . . that is one-hundred-percent pure gold! You know that old theater adage, 'Less is more.' In this case, not only is less *way* more mysterious and dramatic, it's also more believable. It allows people to use their imaginations, makes them wonder, could it be real? That's what people love most about the paranormal, playing the what-if game."

They stood on the sidewalk outside the museum. The police cars were still there, although their lights had been turned off. A small crowd of rubberneckers still stuck around, but they numbered considerably fewer than before. As soon as Trevor and the others had exited the museum, the two news reporters had swooped in on them like starving birds of prey. Carrington had been only too happy to oblige them both with interviews, and he stood off to the side with them now, blabbing away at their cameras. Ray, Sarah, and Pattie had followed, shooting video of Carrington being interviewed. The whole thing struck Trevor as more than a bit surreal, one camera operator filming two others, like some media version of an *ouroboros* devouring its own tail. Erin left her crew to it and stood talking with the rest of them.

Everyone had reacted differently to the psychokinetic event they had witnessed. Drew and Amber didn't exactly take it in stride, but they had experienced far worse things in the Lowry House. Connie didn't seem scared, just thoughtful. Erin was giddy with excitement, although her crew seemed less thrilled. It looked to Trevor as if they were concentrating extra hard on their work so they could avoid thinking about what they had seen. Carrington had appeared disturbed at the time of the event, but he had quickly recovered and now affected an I-knew-it-all-along air.

Jenn was the one Trevor was most worried about.

She looked shell-shocked, her face slack and expressionless, displaying what Drew would have called flat affect. Despite the fact that she owned a bookstore called Forgotten Lore and lived in a town whose prime industry was paranormal-themed tourism, she didn't believe in the supernatural on any level, not even in a religious sense. Jenn was clearly having difficulty dealing with the experience, unlike Connie, who seemed to be having no problem readjusting her worldview to include the existence of the paranormal. Add this to the trauma of Jenn's employee being killed the night before, perhaps by the same supernatural force whose power she had just witnessed, and it was no wonder she looked almost catatonic.

Trevor took hold of her elbow and gently steered her away from the others so they could talk in private. She allowed him to lead her without comment, her gaze distant, as if she were looking at a point far away.

Trevor turned to the others to tell them that he wanted to leave, but he stopped when he saw Amber looking back at the museum, Drew on one side, Connie on the other. The three of them were talking, but Trevor couldn't make out what they were saying. He wanted to join them, but he didn't want to abandon Jenn.

When she saw where he was looking, she smiled. "I'll be all right. Go see what's up with them."

Trevor flashed her a grateful smile and hurried over to join his friends.

"Sorry I'm late. I didn't get the memo that you guys were going to hold a meeting."

"I was just wondering about the buildings that house the museum," Amber said. "How old do you think they are?"

"We didn't spend much time in the lobby," Trevor said. "If we had, you might've seen the placard that tells about the history of the buildings. Both date from before the flood. They needed extensive repairs, of course, but much of the original structure is intact. It's the same for a lot of the buildings downtown. The townspeople who stayed to rebuild were determined to save as many of the original buildings as they could, especially here in downtown. It was important to them to keep the heart of Exeter alive."

"So the building where Jenn's bookstore is also predates the flood?" Amber asked.

"That's right," Trevor said. "Why? Do you think that's important?"

She shrugged. "I don't know, but it *feels* like it might be."

"We'll have to file that away for later discussion," Drew said. He glanced in Jenn's direction. "I think it would be best if we got her away from here as soon as possible."

"I suggested we could go back to the hotel," Trevor said.

"I'd rather she go somewhere that doesn't constantly remind

her of death, but I doubt anywhere in town fits that qualification right now. Once we get her to the hotel, we can see if she has any friends or relatives she can stay with, preferably someone who lives outside of town."

Trevor didn't want Jenn to pack up and leave, but that was just his own selfishness talking. If it would be better for her to get out of Exeter for a time, then that's what she should do.

"Any thought about what the Dark Lady's message might mean?" Connie asked.

"One word isn't much to go on," Drew said.

"Yeah," Trevor agreed. "At least in Amityville, they got two words: 'Get out.'"

"And that's a clear enough message when you've recently moved into a house," Amber said. "But 'Stop' could mean any number of things."

"I wish ghosts would learn to write simple declarative sentences containing specific details," Trevor said. "It would make things so much easier for us poor mortals."

"You try sending a message from one plane of existence to another," Connie said. "It's like trying to throw a paper airplane from the earth to the moon. You're lucky if even the tiniest portion of your message gets through."

Trevor bristled at the woman's know-it-all tone. "You don't need to lecture me about the paranormal. I've been researching and writing about it my entire professional life."

"I don't mean to denigrate your credentials," she said, "but I'm not aware of any universities that hand out degrees in ghostology."

"My degree's in journalism, and when it comes to the paranormal, I know what the hell I'm talking about, because I've seen shit that would make you pee your panties."

Connie smiled. "What makes you think I wear any?"

Drew stepped in then. "Bickering like this isn't helpful. Let's get Jenn settled in at the hotel, and then we can plan our next move."

"By *we*," Trevor said, "I assume you mean the three of us." He gave Connie a pointed look.

"Don't think you can leave me out now," Connie said, almost smirking. "I'm having way too much fun."

NINE

"And that's the last I saw of him until today."

Amber fell silent after that, and everyone sat quietly as they digested what she had told them. After getting Jenn settled in her room, the others had gathered in the hotel bar. Drew, Amber, Trevor, and Connie had taken a table in the back, while Carrington sat at the bar itself, drinking Scotch and regaling the bartender with tales of his exploits. Erin and her crew had gone up to her room to go over the footage they had shot, but not before Erin had made the others promise they wouldn't leave the hotel without informing her.

When Amber began to tell them about Mitch, Drew asked Connie to give the three of them some privacy, but Amber said that it was OK with her if Connie stayed. "She's a psychologist," Amber said. "I'm sure she's heard the same story a hundred times." Drew wasn't comfortable with Connie being privy to such an intimate conversation, though. It was different with Trevor. He was like a brother to both Drew and Amber, but Connie was Drew's supervisor, and while they were colleagues, he didn't consider her a friend. To make matters even more confusing, today she had admitted to being attracted to him. And while she seemed to have adjusted to the fact that he didn't return her romantic feelings, having her sit there while the woman he *did* love told her tale of abuse was, not to put too fine a point on it, damned weird. But it was Amber's choice, and since she didn't mind that Connie stayed, Drew didn't object. From the scowls Trevor had directed Connie's way as Amber spoke, it was clear that he was even less happy about her presence than Drew was, but he didn't say anything, either.

An instrumental version of "Misty" played on the bar's sound system, the song's overdone sentimentality almost seeming like an ironic commentary on Amber's story.

"I assume this was the gentleman you were speaking to outside the hotel." Connie made a face. "He seemed like a real charmer." She nodded toward Drew. "Kudos to you for realizing you could do better."

Drew would have preferred to steer the conversation away from Mitch. He understood why Amber hadn't told him about the man, but he couldn't help feeling—or perhaps *fearing* was a better word—that the reason she had been reluctant to tell him about Mitch was that she didn't fully trust him yet. They were close as teenagers, but after high school, they hadn't seen each other for fifteen years. They had been dating for a couple of months, but as strong as their bond had grown, it was only natural that she should still be hesitant to share certain things with him. But knowing this didn't make him feel any better.

"Quite a coincidence that Mitch should turn up the same time as the murders start," Trevor said. "Not to mention that both times Amber saw him, he was in the presence of the Dark Lady. And those are the *only* times Amber has seen her."

"It really *could* be a coincidence," Drew said. "But I have to admit, I was thinking along the same lines you were."

Trevor looked at Amber. "Did you ever have any strange experiences with Mitch?" His face immediately reddened. "I, uh, I mean . . . shit!"

Amber smiled. "Don't worry. I know what you mean. There was never any hint of paranormal activity in his presence. But back then, I was so depressed and on so many meds that it felt as if my head was stuffed with wet cotton all the time. It's hard to be psychically aware when it's all you can do to function from day to day."

"And just because the Dark Lady appeared next to Mitch, that doesn't mean there's any link between them," Drew said. "Perhaps she was drawn to him for some reason."

"The museum organizers did put information about her in the same room as the banshee and those other spirits," Trevor said. "I suppose she could turn out to be a harbinger of ill fortune after all. Maybe she was attracted to Mitch simply because he's bad news."

"She wouldn't be the first woman to go for the bad-boy type," Connie said.

Amber gave her a look that said she wasn't funny, but Connie just smiled back sweetly.

"Greg did say there were bad *things* in town," Drew said. "Perhaps he was referring to both Mitch and the Dark Lady."

"Exeter is the Most Haunted Town in America, remember?" Trevor said. "It's supposed to be crawling with ghosts. There could be any number of bad things here."

"Whatever the things are, Greg told me we had 'drawn their attention,'" Amber said. "But he didn't say how we'd done it."

"Before we go any further, let me just say that it was damned rude of Greg to dead-dial you from the afterlife and leave Drew and me out," Trevor said.

"If you had been in the women's restroom at the time, I'm sure he would've been happy to say hi," Connie said. "But I thought you suspected your former friend of having a hand in these killings."

"I *do* suspect him," Trevor said. "He killed two people—that we know of—and he would've killed a lot more if we hadn't stopped him."

"You said he was possessed by some sort of evil force," Connie said. "Maybe he wasn't completely in control of his actions. And from what I understand, he *did* help save your lives in the end."

"True," Trevor said. "But he told Amber that the Darkness was still a part of him. By his own admission, he can't be trusted."

"I suppose you're right," Connie said. She fell silent after that, her manner subdued.

Drew didn't understand her reaction, but he didn't have time to worry about it now.

"The chief said the man who died at the museum had been strangled. As awful as it is, it's an ordinary way to die. Nothing necessarily paranormal about it."

"You think . . ." Amber paused, swallowed, started over. "You think Mitch did it? But why?"

"I have no idea what his motivation might've been," Drew said. "But it's clear he has anger issues and is capable of violence."

"Yes," Amber said, "but murder? I don't know if he's capable of going that far."

"Given the right circumstances, any human being is capable of going that far," Connie said.

She sounded so certain, Drew thought, as if she spoke from experience.

"Are we supposed to believe that Mitch also somehow drowned the woman in the museum?" Trevor said. "And that he rigged the security cameras to fail so he could commit his murders unseen?"

"Seems unlikely, doesn't it?" Drew said.

"He's part of this, though," Amber said. "Somehow. I can—"

"Feel it," Connie said.

Amber looked at her defiantly. "That's right."

"For what it's worth, I agree."

"You do?" Amber said, surprised.

Connie nodded. "The question is how he's connected—and how deeply."

"We should tell the chief about him," Drew said. "Jenn said he was open to the possibility of paranormal explanations for events. He may be skeptical, but there have been three deaths in his town in less than twenty-four hours, *and* they've occurred during the most important tourist event of the year. He'll at least be interested in bringing Mitch in for questioning."

"Drew and I can go talk with the chief," Amber said.

"You don't have to," Drew said. "I can—"

"I need to go. I'm the one who can testify to how violent Mitch can be." She turned to Trevor. "Are you going to come with us?"

"I think I should try to learn as much about the Dark Lady as I can," he said. "I'll talk to Jenn, see how much she knows. Maybe I'll do a Web search and see what turns up."

"You're forgetting about another source that's much closer at the moment," Connie said. She pointed toward the bar where Carrington sat. He downed the last of his Scotch and ordered another.

"Him? He won't be any help," Trevor said. "He's a showman, not a serious researcher."

"I used to read his books when I was a teenager. He might not be much of a scientist, but he knew how to tell a hell of a story. He may know a lot more about Exeter's history than you think." She paused. "Sometimes we have to accept people for what they are, not what we want them to be."

Trevor scowled. "I thought you claimed to have no interest in the paranormal."

She shrugged. "What can I say? It was an adolescent phase."

"I'll give the chief a call," Drew said.

Trevor sighed. "I suppose I'll go over and see what Carrington has to say."

"Mind if I go with?" Connie asked him. "I used to be something of a fan. Plus, I'm good at getting people to talk to me. Comes with the job, you know."

Drew doubted that Trevor liked the idea of Connie horning in on his conversation with Carrington, but her experience as a psychologist might come in handy. If nothing else, maybe she could keep Carrington focused so he didn't run off on tangents every few minutes.

"Sure," Trevor said. "Glad to have the help."

Connie smiled. "You're a lousy liar, but I appreciate you letting me tag along."

"One more thing," Drew said. "Let's not tell Erin. I think we might get more out of Carrington and the chief if they don't have a camera pointed at their faces."

"You know she'll complain when she discovers we left her out," Amber said.

"Let her," Trevor said. "At first, I was thrilled that she wanted to include us in her documentary. More publicity for my new book, right? But she and her crew are starting to get in the way. It's better if we can investigate on our own."

"Good luck with that," Connie said. "Erin strikes me as the kind of person who doesn't let go once she sinks her teeth into something. At least, not without tearing off a mouthful of flesh first."

Drew looked at Connie, once more struck by how odd she had been acting.

"Problem, Drew?" she asked.

"It's nothing. I've just never known you to use such . . . colorful language before."

Her smile turned into a grin. "What can I say? I'm just chock-full of surprises."

Erin grinned as she watched the footage from the museum play on her laptop screen.

"Here it comes . . . get ready for it."

She sat at the desk in her hotel room, computer open in front of her, her crew standing behind her. As they watched, the word *Stop* appeared as if by magic on every surface in the room. The image flickered once or twice and at one point blurred out entirely, but otherwise there was no interference. The footage couldn't have been more perfect. Clear enough to be seen but not so clear all the way through that it looked as if they had used special effects.

"I was hoping that watching it on the small screen would make it less terrifying," Pattie said. "But it doesn't. It's just as bad."

"Sure is!" Sarah leaned against Pattie, and the older woman put her arm around her.

"I'm still too stunned to be scared," Ray said. "I mean, I filmed the whole damned thing, and I'm still not sure I believe it."

"Well, *I* believe it," Sarah said. "And I don't want to ever experience anything like that again!"

The footage ended, and although Erin was tempted to play it over, she didn't. The last thing she wanted was for any of her crew to get so spooked that they quit. It wasn't as if they would be walking out on a big paycheck if they left. As little as she could afford to pay them, they were almost working for free. Since she hadn't been able to use money to motivate them, she'd had to find other ways. She'd told them that the film would be good exposure and a great addition to their résumés. It might even win some awards at festivals, get picked up for broadcast on a cable network, eventually see a DVD release . . . It could end up being a stepping-stone to bigger and better things for all of them. But she knew none of that bullshit would work on them right now. It might later, once they'd had a few days for their nerves to settle down, but she couldn't give them any time off. This was the last weekend for Dead Days, and the big parade was that night. She needed them to keep working.

"You know what we've got here, right? This is the best footage of an actual paranormal event that's ever been captured. We're going to make history! This footage will be spread all over the Internet. People will debate whether or not it's real and, if it is real, what that means. We may have found the first definitive proof of life after death!"

"People will just say we faked it," Ray said.

"Some will, sure," Erin said. "But specialists will examine the footage, and they won't be able to find any evidence that it was faked, because it wasn't. We'll be famous! And afterward, we'll be able to write our own tickets. Any kind of job you want, you'll get. Writing, directing, producing . . . it'll be your choice."

She hoped she wasn't laying it on too thick, but she truly did believe this film was going to change their lives.

"Maybe you and Carrington will get famous," Pattie said. "Or in his case, more famous. But we're just the crew." She sounded skeptical, but it was clear from her tone that she was tempted by the scenario Erin was painting for them, and she wanted it to be true.

"Your average Joe and Jill on the street may not think much about the people behind the cameras," Erin said, "but industry professionals know better. Of course, it'll be up to us to make the most out of the opportunities we'll get, but they'll come, believe me."

Her crew was silent for a few moments after that, and Erin knew they were all imagining the possibilities. One thing you could always count on about people who worked in the arts: they were all dreamers. And the easiest way to manipulate them was to steer their imaginations in the direction you wanted them to go.

"But if there really are ghosts in this town, do we want to disturb them any further?" Sarah said. "I mean, people have *died*, Erin! None of us wants to be next."

"When you find a hornets' nest, the last thing you should do is stick your hand in and shake it around," Ray said. "You're just asking to get stung—a lot."

"And it's not just those three who died in the last day," Pattie said. "Don't forget Alex."

Erin closed the laptop more forcibly than she needed to. "That was different. What happened to him was an accident. And we all agreed to keep working on the film because that was what he would've wanted."

"That was before these latest deaths happened," Ray said. "Yeah, at first, it seemed like Alex died accidentally. But now . . . well, let's just say I'm open to alternative explanations."

Erin examined her crew's faces. Each of them was scared, Sarah more than the other two. She looked as if she were fighting to hold back tears. Erin knew that she needed to try another approach if she didn't want her crew walking out on her in the next few minutes.

"Look, we're almost done with this shoot. We're scheduled to film at the college this afternoon and then tonight during the parade. After that, it's a wrap. If anything else comes up—"

"Like another murder?" Pattie asked.

Erin ignored her. "If anything else comes up, I'll shoot it myself. All right?"

Her crew looked at one another, silently conferring. She honestly didn't know which way they were going to decide until Ray let out a long sigh.

"What the hell. It's just a tiny college and a rinky-dink parade. What can happen?"

Erin smiled. *A lot,* she hoped. And with any luck, they would get it all on film.

Mitch sat in his Impala, listening to a hard-rock station on the radio. It was funny. He should have been hungry for lunch by now. He glanced at the dashboard clock and saw that it was well after noon. Hell, he hadn't had any breakfast that morning—he should be *starving.* But he didn't have any appetite at all. In fact, his stomach felt a little upset. All he'd had to eat the day before was fast food, so he figured that was the problem. That junk had got his whole system out of whack. He would make sure to eat a decent meal the next time he was hungry, and that should fix him right up.

He was parked behind a Mexican restaurant several blocks from the hotel where Esotericon was happening. He had his windows down, and the greasy-spicy food smells drifting in made him feel even queasier. He rolled his windows up, but that only trapped the food smells in the car with him. He concentrated on breathing through his mouth, and that helped.

He didn't know where the Dark Lady was. She came and went as she pleased, without so much as hello or good-bye. One moment she was there, the next she wasn't. Wasn't that just like a woman? Not that he was sure she *was* a woman. Oh, she looked like one . . . at least, he thought so. He had trouble looking at her directly. Every time he tried, his gaze slid away from her, as if his eyes refused to view her image. Or maybe he simply didn't want to look at her too closely for too long, afraid he might see past her veneer to what lay beneath. Her voice sounded like a woman's, and she gave off a distinctly feminine energy, but he couldn't help feeling that it all was a disguise, a costume no different from the Halloween outfits worn by the idiots thronging the streets.

You're afraid.

It was his father's voice.

Mitch wanted to deny it, but he didn't bother. Daddy always knew when he was lying.

Fear makes you weak. And no son of mine is going to be a weakling.

A memory rose from the depths of his mind. He was nine and playing in his first Little League baseball game. His team was the Pirates, and they were playing the Braves. His daddy was sitting in the stands with the other parents. His mom had stayed home. Daddy didn't like it when she went out in public, said he wasn't going to have other men staring at her like a whore, even if she was one. Mitch wasn't sure what a whore was, but he knew it wasn't good by the way his mom cringed whenever Daddy called her that.

Not much happened in the first inning. Mitch played left field, and no one hit the ball toward him, and he didn't get to bat. The Braves didn't score, and neither did the Pirates. The second inning came, and the Braves were up. The first batter grounded out, and the second hit a pop-up foul that the catcher nabbed, making another out. The third batter stepped up to the plate, swung at the first pitch, and missed. He connected with the second, a good, solid hit, and his ball sailed straight out into left field, right toward Mitch. Adrenaline surged through his body. He didn't have to run far to get under the ball, and when he was in position, he raised his glove, squinted his eyes against the bright sunlight, and waited for the ball to fall into his hand.

It should have been easy. The ball floated down toward him as gently as a soap bubble, seeming to move so slowly that he thought he could reach out with his bare hand and simply pluck it out of the air. But as the ball came closer, his excitement gave way to a sick, fluttery feeling in his stomach. He remembered playing catch with his daddy in the backyard one time the summer before. It had been one of the few times he could recall Daddy spending time with him—he was usually too busy watching TV or building something in his basement woodshop and downing copious amounts of beer in the process. So it had been a special afternoon for Mitch. They had thrown the ball back and forth a few times to warm up, nothing too hard, and then Daddy had decided to start making Mitch work. He's thrown fast balls, curve balls, sliders . . . Daddy had played on the high-school baseball team, and he was still pretty good. Mitch hadn't caught every throw, but he'd caught most of them, and while his daddy hadn't praised him, he hadn't criticized, and to Mitch, that was just as good.

Then Daddy had decided to throw some high balls. Mitch had caught the first two easily enough, and without thinking, he'd grinned at his daddy and said something he'd heard older boys say when they played ball around the neighborhood.

"Is that all you got?"

It was nothing, just a bit of playful banter, but Daddy's expression had darkened.

"You think you're so smart, you little fucker? Try and catch this!"

Mitch had been afraid his daddy would fire off a fast ball straight at him, but instead he'd thrown the ball almost straight up, and it had flown much higher than any of the others, higher than Mitch thought possible. It had seemed to dwindle to a black speck against the blue sky, and Mitch had wondered if he would ever be big enough and strong enough to hurl a ball so high.

"Catch it, or I'll bust your ass." Daddy had said this softly, but Mitch had no trouble hearing it or believing it. Then Daddy had stepped back to give Mitch room to go after the ball.

He had stood frozen for a moment—but only a moment—before getting his ass in gear. He'd run forward, keeping his eyes on the ball, glove held at the ready. The ball, already descending, had seemed to come down so much faster than it had gone up, and Mitch had imagined that instead of a baseball, he was trying to catch a meteor that was rocketing to earth, trailing a tail of burning fire behind.

He had got into position, eyes still on the ball, glove up and ready, and his father's words had whispered through his mind. *Catch it, or I'll bust your ass.* Mitch knew that Daddy had been talking about more than a spanking—much more.

The ball had hurtled toward him, and at the last instant, he'd squeezed his eyes shut and gritted his teeth.

The ball had slammed into the left side of his head and mashed his ear before bouncing off and landing in the grass. Bright light had exploded behind his eyes, and pain had roared through his nerves like wildfire. The impact had caused his knees to buckle, and he'd fallen onto his side, sobbing. Tentatively, he had reached up to touch his ear and found it swollen and hot. He had feared he would feel blood gushing from his ear canal, but the only moisture he'd felt was a bit of sweat.

"That was pathetic. *You're* pathetic."

Mitch had looked up to see his father silhouetted against the sky like some dark giant.

The promised ass-beating had begun soon after that.

So, months later, when Mitch stood in left field, watching a ball come down toward him, he froze. This ball didn't hit him, but he almost wished it had. It fell to the ground less than two feet away from him, bounced a couple of times, then rolled to a stop.

A collective moan of disappointment came from the crowd. Mitch's coach shouted for him to pick up the ball and throw it to second, but Mitch didn't move. All he could do was focus on his father, who was sitting in the stands right behind the dugout, glaring at him from behind the chain-link backstop.

The ass-beating he got later that night was worse than any he had ever experienced at his father's hands before. The next morning, he was in the emergency room at the hospital, his mother trying to explain to the doctor how her son had come by three cracked ribs, a dislocated shoulder, and two broken fingers. "Skateboarding accident" was the excuse the doctor had finally accepted. At least, that's what he had written down on the chart. Whether he believed it was a different matter.

And now there he was, thinking of the Dark Lady, hearing his father's voice again. *You're afraid of her, just like you were afraid of that ball. She's just a woman.*

"No, she's not," Mitch mumbled. "I don't think she's *just* anything."

Whatever she is, you're her bitch, and it makes me sick!

"I am not." He sounded like a pouty little boy, and he hated it.

She snaps her fingers, and you come running to her like a dog. Not a real dog, either. One of those tiny yipping things that are always trembling and squirting pee on the floor when they get excited.

"Stop it."

You killed a man for her, for Christ's sake!

"I . . . was being strong."

Bullshit! You kill someone because they wronged you somehow and they got it coming, that's being strong. Killing someone because some-one else wants you to, that's being a puppet. I didn't raise you to be anyone's toy, now, did I, Mitch?

"No, sir."

You drove all the way to this pesthole of a town so you could get that little bitch alone and teach her a few well-deserved lessons. You didn't come here to be the servant for . . . for whatever the hell she is. Did you?

"No."

All right, then. So what the hell are you going to do about it?

Before he could answer, a dark smudge appeared in the air on the passenger seat next to him. The Dark Lady had returned.

He gripped the steering wheel tightly and kept his gaze focused forward. The temperature inside the car dropped swiftly, causing tiny veins of frost to appear on the inside windows.

"Where were you?" He was afraid to talk to her, let alone demand to know what she had been up to during her absence, but Daddy wanted him to be strong, to show this bitch who was really in charge around here.

He kept his gaze trained on the Dumpster behind the restaurant. An employee came out the back door, bulging white plastic garbage bags dangling from his hands by thin red loops. The employee—Hispanic from the look of him—didn't so much as glance at Mitch's car as he tossed the trash into the Dumpster and headed back inside the restaurant.

The Dark Lady said nothing the entire time the man was outside, but Mitch knew she had heard his question. He could feel anger radiating off her in waves, but she didn't speak until they were alone again.

"I returned to the museum to leave a message."

What the hell was she talking about? The two of them had already left a message, hadn't they? And a goddamned big one, too—a pair of dead bodies sprawled on the museum floor.

"You got what you wanted. Now it's my turn. I want Amber, and you promised you'd help me get her. I'm tired of waiting."

No matter how much vehemence he put into his voice, he knew she wouldn't take him seriously if he continued looking out the windshield. So he forced himself to turn toward her, but try as he might, he couldn't meet her gaze full on. The best he could do was look past her and out the passenger-side window.

The cold within the Impala intensified, and frost spread across the interior of all the windows, the white crystals making soft crackling sounds as they appeared. The Dark Lady didn't respond to his words right away, and he had the terrible feeling that challenging her wasn't the smartest thing he had ever done.

"You keep hearing your father's voice telling you that you're weak. Would you like to know what being weak really feels like?"

Before Mitch could answer—and he most assuredly would have answered no—fingers of ice gripped his head and forced him to look into the obsidian eyes and marble face of the Dark Lady. He started to scream, but as he opened his mouth, she lunged forward and fastened her lips to his. He screamed anyway, but their lips were stuck tightly together, almost as if their flesh had merged, and his scream was muffled. He tried to pull away, but her grip was like iron, and she held him fast. Her tongue slithered forward, a thick length of meat as soft and sinuous as a snake. It filled his mouth, touched the back of his throat gently, almost hesitantly, as if exploring. And then—after pausing the merest instant—it began sliding down. Panic surged through him as the tongue seemed to swell within his throat, blocking his airway. He placed his hands against the Dark Lady's chest and tried to push her away, but he found her body as hard and immovable as a stone wall. He tried clawing at her cheeks and gouging her eyes, but his nails found no purchase anywhere on her flesh. Lungs burning for air, he grabbed double handfuls of her long black hair and tried to yank her head away from him. But no matter how hard he pulled, he couldn't budge her.

Down, down, down the tongue wriggled—how long could the goddamned thing possibly be?—and still farther down it went. His throat spasmed as he gagged around the meat-snake, but although his body desperately tried to expel the alien invader, the tongue continued its slow downward slide into the depths of his body.

By the time the tongue reached his stomach, his vision had gone gray, he tingled all over, and his lungs felt like empty, shriveled sacks inside him. He stared into the Dark Lady's glossy black eyes, looking for any hint of pity or mercy, but all he saw was endless, absolute darkness. And then he knew nothing else.

How long he dwelled within that darkness, he couldn't have said, but after a while, the black gave way to white, and he realized he was looking at the ice-covered interior of his car once again. The Dark Lady sat in the passenger seat, hands folded almost demurely in her lap, her mouth closed. He drew in a deep, gasping breath and then began to sob.

"Your father's voice is a lie. Just a trick of your mind. But I am real, and if you defy me again, I'll send you back into the dark and leave you there forever. Do you understand?"

Mitch couldn't bring himself to speak. He wiped his eyes and nodded once.

"Good. Now, drive back to the hotel. We have work to do there."

Tears still trickling down his cheeks, Mitch reached out with trembling fingers and turned the key in the ignition. He turned the heater on high, switched it to defrost, put the car in gear, and slowly pulled away from the curb. After a few moments, the windshield was clear, and the interior of the Impala was warm and toasty. But Mitch continued to tremble.

TEN

"I think I can safely say that if it wasn't for you, I never would've gone into journalism as a career field, and I certainly wouldn't have made a specialty out of writing about the paranormal."

Carrington inclined his head in a brief nod. "That's kind of you to say, Trevor."

Trevor was impressed despite himself. Carrington was working on his fourth Scotch, and so far, he showed no signs of being drunk. He had ordered a Samuel Adams and had barely touched it, while Connie had gotten a shot of whiskey, downed it immediately, and then ordered another. Trevor sat on Carrington's left, Connie on his right. Given how beautiful Connie was, Trevor had expected Carrington's attention to be almost solely focused on her—there were plenty of other men in the bar, and more than a few women, who couldn't take their eyes off her—but he paid no special attention to her. He sat hunched over the bar, holding on to his Scotch and staring straight ahead, as if deep in thought. He would answer whenever either of them spoke to him, but Trevor had the sense that he only half heard them. Trevor had tried flattery in the hope that it would draw Carrington out, but the man had barely acknowledged his words. Trevor was a bit surprised to find himself hurt by Carrington's lackluster reaction. Despite the situation, what Trevor had told him was true. Carrington had been something of a hero to him once upon a time, and it wasn't an easy thing to admit to your hero how much he had influenced you, only to have him barely react to your words.

"You seem subdued, Arthur," Connie said. "Is something bothering you?"

He didn't answer right away. He took a sip of his Scotch, set the glass down on the counter gently, and continued staring ahead. Trevor thought he wasn't going to say anything, but then he began talking in a soft voice.

"What we saw today . . ." He trailed off, shook his head, and started over. "When I first began as a paranormal researcher, I hoped to open people's minds to the possibilities that there was more to existence than what our five senses could perceive. To help them see that there was magic and wonder in the world, that death wasn't an ending but rather a transition. That we are all caterpillars on a journey to becoming butterflies." He let out a small, bitter laugh. "Sounds sickeningly naïve now, doesn't it? But what can I say? It was the sixties. As the years went by and my books began selling, I began making more and more personal appearances. Doing readings, signing books. People would come up to me and tell me how much they enjoyed reading my books. I soon realized that few of them were interested in the scientific or metaphysical aspects of my work. Instead, they read them to be scared. I remember how one woman put it to me: 'I love it when I read your books and I get that deliciously creepy feeling like I have to keep looking over my shoulder.' That was the day I realized that despite my lofty ambitions, what I had become was nothing more than an entertainer.

"Perhaps I should have retired and sought out a new career, but my books were selling well, and then I got the offer to do the television show. The money was tempting, and I tried to rationalize it by telling myself that even if people tuned in only to be entertained, the subject matter would still stimulate their imaginations and broaden their minds. And if we didn't adhere to rigorous standards of scientific investigation . . . well, in the end, it *was* just entertainment, wasn't it? And now, here I am, a long way from the idealistic young man who set out to change the world in his own small way. I've become an actor playing a parody of the man he used to be, interested only in getting a paycheck, which he'll spend as soon as possible at the nearest bar."

Trevor wanted to say something to comfort Carrington, but when he opened his mouth to speak, Connie shook her head. Trevor remained silent, and after another sip of Scotch, Carrington continued.

"I thought the murders were nothing more than a coincidence that Erin intended to exploit for the benefit of her film. I was sorry those people lost their lives, but by suggesting that their murders had something to do with Exeter's reputation for paranormal activity, Erin would draw a lot of attention to the film—and to me. I could see myself giving numerous interviews, being booked for dozens of personal appearances, and of course, getting a contract to write a new book. Who knows? I might even get a new TV show out of it."

"But then you went with us to the museum," Trevor said.

"Yes. I've seen some things during my career that I'd be hard-pressed to explain. But I've never seen anything like *that*. The way those words appeared all at once . . ." He finished the rest of his Scotch in a single gulp. He started to signal the bartender for another, glanced at Trevor, and then waved the bartender away. "The weird thing is, there's something naggingly familiar about the event, as if I'd heard of something similar happening once, but I can't recall any details." He gave Trevor a weary smile. "Perhaps I've had one too many, eh? At any rate, after today, I'm considerably less enthused about completing Erin's film. And it certainly doesn't help that we shot at both locations yesterday. To think I might have been standing in the same spot where someone later lost his or her life." He sighed. "That cannot be good for my karma."

"Wait a minute," Trevor said. "You filmed at both locations yesterday? The bookstore *and* the museum?"

"Yes, and in that order." He frowned. "Why?"

"Interesting that Erin failed to mention that little factoid to us," Connie said.

"Isn't it?" Trevor turned his attention back to Carrington. "Did any of you experience anything strange at either location yesterday? Temperature variances, a feeling you were being watched, psycho-kinetic activity . . ."

"I may not be the most professional paranormal investigator who ever lived, but I know what signs to look for, Trevor. But to answer your question, no, there was nothing out of the ordinary."

"Did you see the Dark Lady?" Connie asked. "You wouldn't have recognized her as such, of course, but she might have been pres-ent at either location, watching. She could've been on the sidewalk outside the bookstore or perhaps posing as merely another museum-goer. She might've appeared normal enough to you, but your sub-conscious would've sensed there was something wrong with her."

Trevor had just been about to raise the issue of the Dark Lady when Connie beat him to it. Earlier, she had claimed to have no expertise with the paranormal, but once again, her actions belied those words. Maybe she was simply an intelligent person who picked up on things fast, and she *had* read Carrington's books when she was a teenager, or so she said. But his instincts told him that something else was going on. He didn't want to confront her about his suspicions, not now that they had finally got Carrington talking. And he wanted to wait until he had a chance to confer with Drew and Amber.

Carrington considered Connie's question for a moment. "If she was there, I didn't notice her. I suppose we could ask Erin to go through the footage we shot yesterday and see if it captured her image."

"It's worth a try, I suppose," Trevor said. "But remember what happened to the security video at the museum. If you did catch the Dark Lady on film, the footage is probably ruined."

They fell into a silence for a few moments after that. Trevor sipped his beer while he thought, and Connie finished off her second whiskey and ordered a third. Carrington didn't order another drink. He just sat quietly, until at length he began speaking again.

"The story you told at your session today. It was the truth, wasn't it?"

"Every word," Trevor said.

"Part of me is jealous of what you and your friends experienced. But another part of me—a much larger part, I think—is grateful that I've never gone through anything like that. I'm not sure I could've handled it." He smiled. "My grip on reality is fragile enough as it is."

"I hate to be the one to point this out," Connie said, "but you're going through a similar experience right now."

Carrington laughed. "I suppose I am—and I haven't lost my marbles yet, have I?"

Connie's smile had an edge to it. "The day's still young."

"Indeed. And I, unfortunately, am not. So . . . what do we have so far? Erin films at two locations on Friday, and afterward murders occur at those same locations within the span of twenty-four hours. What's the connection?"

"I would think it's obvious," Connie said.

"The filming itself," Trevor said.

"That hadn't occurred to me." Carrington frowned. "But if that's the case, then the message we received at the museum, the word *Stop* . . ."

"Could mean the Dark Lady wants Erin to stop filming," Trevor said.

"Or it could mean she intends to stop Erin herself," Connie said. "By whatever means necessary."

Carrington's eyes widened. "If that's true, I wonder if Alex's death is part of this, too. We all thought it was an accident, but now . . ."

"Who's Alex?" Trevor said.

"Erin's production assistant. He died last week while scouting a location for the film."

Trevor and Connie exchanged glances.

"Tell us about it," Trevor said.

"I appreciate your coming here to meet us, Chief," Drew said.

Amber thought Chief Hoffman looked as if he had been awake for days. His eyes seemed to have receded into their sockets since she had last seen him, and the flesh beneath was puffy and discolored. He radiated a deep weariness that was as much mental as physical.

"I'd have met you outside the gates of hell if it meant getting away from those reporters for a while. I'm used to media types asking me questions about Dead Days every year, and Ms. Gilman interviewed me for her movie the other day. But standing in front of cameras and trying to sound like I know what I'm doing as reporters grill me about murder investigations that are just starting . . . I'm just a small-time police chief of a tourist town, you know? I don't exactly have a lot of experience in that kind of thing."

The three of them sat in a conversation pit off to the side of the front lobby, Amber and Drew on a couch, the chief in a well-padded armchair next to them. A steady stream of people walked by, mostly attendees of Esotericon, but no one paid them any attention. Normally, the chief's uniform might have drawn at least a few glances, but given that half the conference goers wore costumes of one sort or another, a law-enforcement uniform looked unremarkable by comparison.

"How's Jenn doing?" the chief asked. "I know she's taking Tonya's death hard."

"She's resting right now," Drew said. "Later, she plans to go back to selling books in the Exhibition Hall."

"On the phone, you said you were a psychologist. Do you think it's a good idea for Jenn to try to work today?" the chief asked.

"If it helps her cope, then yes. Sometimes keeping busy is the best way to work through the initial shock of a trauma. But of course, it depends on the person."

"Jenn's a hard worker, no doubt about that. She's always in that shop of hers, day and night. She's a good person, too. Gave me someone to talk to after my wife passed. If it wasn't for her . . ." He trailed off. "I hope she'll be OK, that's all."

"I think she will," Drew said. "In time."

The chief nodded. "So, you said you wanted to tell me what you learned at the museum. I'm willing to listen, but despite what Jenn may have told you about my, uh, personal reading habits, I'm skeptical when it comes to ghosts and psychic stuff. Just so you know."

"We did experience something strange at the museum," Drew said, "but that's not the main reason we wanted to talk to you." He glanced at Amber.

Amber knew it was important to tell the chief about Mitch. Not that she believed he had strangled that man in the museum, but she didn't disbelieve it, either. The fact that she thought it was even possible that Mitch could have done it was reason enough to tell the chief. But now that the time had come, she was hesitant. It had been hard enough telling Drew and Trevor, but to tell a stranger . . . She imagined the way he might look at her afterward as he tried to picture the things Mitch had done to her. She didn't know if she could stand to have anyone look at her like that. But if there was even a chance that Mitch was connected to these murders, she had to tell the chief. She couldn't stand by and remain silent while more people died.

She told her story as succinctly as possible, Drew holding her hand the entire time. When she was finished, Drew gave her hand a squeeze to tell her she had done a good job, and she smiled a thank you to him.

The chief took a small notepad and pen out of his shirt pocket and asked Amber to tell him everything she could about Mitch: his full name, physical details, place of residence, make and model of his vehicle, place of employment, and anything else she could remember. She did her best, and when she could remember no more, the chief asked them to excuse him a minute while he called the information in to his office. He pulled out his cell phone, called the station, and read information off his notepad to one of his deputies. When he was finished, he disconnected and tucked his phone back into his pants pocket.

"Thanks for the information. We'll check to see if there's any kind of record on him, and we'll bring him in for questioning."

"If you can find him," Drew said. "With the Dead Days festival in full swing, you've got hundreds more people in town than usual."

"Thousands, actually," the chief said. "And most of them are in costume, which makes it a little hard to track down a specific individual. But my entire department will be working throughout the day, and a lot of the local businesses hire extra security. My people will spread the word, and with any luck, I'll be having a heart-to-heart chat with Mr. Sagers before the night's over. You have anything else for me? If not, I've got a pair of murder investigations to oversee."

"As Drew said, we experienced something out of the ordinary at the museum." Amber told the chief how she had recognized the painting of the Dark Lady and about the bizarre appearance of the word *Stop* in the floor, walls, and ceiling that followed. When she was finished, she said, "I understand you might be skeptical, but is there anything you can tell us about the Dark Lady?"

"I don't really see how this will help, but I guess I can spare a couple more minutes. I've lived in Exeter all my life, and the Dark Lady is a town fixture. Kind of an unofficial mascot in some ways, I suppose, though not as family-friendly as Hector the Specter. All the kids in town grow up hearing stories about the Dark Lady—

how she likes to creep into the rooms of naughty children at night and scare them, how she eats the souls of kids who are especially bad. Nothing special, really. Just our version of the bogeyman, you know?"

"The information about her at the museum said that witnesses have seen her apparition numerous times since the flood," Drew said.

"I've never seen her myself, but the police department gets reports from time to time. I don't know what people expect us to do about it. Track her down, arrest her, and toss her into a cell with ghost-proof bars?" He paused and frowned. "Now that I think of it, we *have* received more sighting reports than usual recently."

Amber glanced at Drew, excited. Then she turned back to the chief. "When did the sightings start to increase?"

"Hard to say off the top of my head. A year ago, maybe? Yeah, that's right. The first one came in less than a week after last year's Dead Days celebration ended. I remember because I thought that if she'd shown up earlier, no one would've noticed. They would've just thought she was another person in a creepy costume. Hell, do you know how many people—both women *and* men—dress up like her every year?"

"Did anything happen at Dead Days last year that might've served as a catalyst for the sightings?" Drew asked. "Some sort of tragedy, maybe?"

"Nothing that I know of. The Chamber of Commerce estimated that we had a record number of tourists last year, though it looks like we may be in the running to beat that total this year. But that's all."

"There were no murders or mysterious deaths over the last year?" Amber asked. "Before Tonya, I mean."

"No. Just a few drunk drivers wrapping their vehicles around telephone poles. There *was* that kid who died out at the Reilly Farm last week, but that was an accident. He was poking around in the barn when a rusty old hay elevator fell on him. There were No Trespassing signs posted all around the property, but the kid ignored them. Guess he was too eager to get some good footage."

Amber and Drew looked at each other.

"What do you mean?" she said.

"He was one of the people making the documentary about Exeter. Ms. Gilman sent him to take some film of locations where they might shoot later. Scouting, she called it. I don't know why she even bothered with the Reilly Farm. Nothing much ever happened out there. A few reports of horses neighing in the night even though the farm's deserted, but that's about it. I guess a run-down, abandoned farm looks spooky on film. I suppose she'll have a marketing hook now, though. You know how movie people are. 'A crew member died under mysterious circumstances during the making of this film.'" He sighed. "Well, that's all the time I've got to give you. Thanks for the information, Ms. Lozier, Dr. Pearson. I'll let you know what happens."

The chief stood, but before he could depart, Amber said, "One more thing."

He frowned. "Make it fast, please."

"There have been three murders so far. Don't you think it might be a good idea if you canceled the rest of the Dead Days festivities? Just as a precaution?"

Chief Hoffman looked at her as if she were crazy. "You think this is the movie *Jaws,* and I'm the chief who should close the beaches because there's a killer shark in the water? Right now, I don't have any proof that the murders at the bookstore and the museum are connected. Hell, I don't have any proof of *anything* yet. All I've got are three dead bodies and a hell of a lot of questions. And that's not enough to shut down the town's biggest moneymaking event of the year."

The chief gave them a parting nod, then turned and walked out the hotel's front entrance.

Amber looked at Drew. "He's not the chief from *Jaws*. He's the mayor who wants to keep the beaches open."

"You can't blame him," Drew said. "As he said, we don't have any solid proof. Besides, even if he canceled the parade, a lot of tourists booked hotel rooms for the weekend. They'd be disappointed that the parade wasn't happening, but they wouldn't leave town any earlier because of it. They'd just start their parties earlier."

"I suppose you're right. But I don't like it. Things are going to get worse—a *lot* worse—if we don't do something soon."

Drew sighed. "I figured you were going to say something like that."

"Hey, everyone."
As Jenn approached their table, Trevor got up and pulled over a chair for her. Amber thought the gesture was sweet. She had never known Trevor to make a fuss over anyone like this. It was a side of him she had never seen before, and she liked it. He waited until Jenn sat down before retaking his own seat.

"How are you doing?" Drew asked.

Jenn shrugged. "As well as can be expected, I suppose. I think I slept some. I'm not sure. If I did, at least I didn't have any nightmares. None I can remember, anyway." She attempted a smile and managed a passable imitation of one.

Her eyes were still half-lidded from sleep, her face pale and puffy. But she seemed awake and alert. Amber thought she was holding up well, considering the circumstances.

"Can I get you something?" Trevor asked. "Water? Coffee?"

"Nothing right now, thanks." Her smile was more genuine this time. "So, what have you four been up to?"

"Asking questions and comparing answers," Trevor said.

"And unfortunately, the answers are just leading to more questions," Drew said.

"As usual," Amber added.

"Where's Arthur?" Jenn asked.

"He was here until a few minutes ago," Amber said. "He decided to go wander through the Exhibition Hall, talk to some more fans, and sign a few more autographs."

"Speaking of Arthur, he said that Erin filmed a segment at your store yesterday," Trevor said.

"That's right."

"Did anything unusual happen?" Drew asked.

"What, you mean unusual as in paranormal? No. She just asked me some questions. What I think about living in Exeter, what sort of customers I get, stuff like that. She filmed me serving some customers, interviewed a few, and shot some footage of Arthur chatting with them. She also shot close-ups of a few book covers—and before you ask, Trevor, I made sure she filmed yours as well as Arthur's. But that was it."

"Was your assistant there at the time?" Connie asked.

"Yes, Tonya was working then. Why?"

Connie looked thoughtful, but she didn't reply.

"Did you ever experience anything strange in the bookstore?" Amber asked.

"Given the kind of customers that Forgotten Lore attracts, of course I have," Jenn said. "But no, not in the way you mean."

"How about any previous owners of the building?" Drew said. "Did they ever report any strange occurrences?"

"Not that I'm aware of." She thought for a moment. "When I bought the place, the real estate agent told me that it was supposed to have been haunted a long time ago, but a spiritualist had been brought in to 'cleanse' the building. I didn't pay her story any attention. A lot of people around here believe in ghosts. Some of them like the idea that the building they're about to buy is haunted, especially if they're running a business and can use that to attract customers, but some want nothing to do with ghosts. I figured the real estate agent had pegged me for the latter type and was just feeding me a line to get me to make an offer on the property."

"If her story was true, it sounds as if whoever it was didn't do a very good job of cleansing," Trevor said. "At least, based on what happened last night."

"Maybe," Connie said. "Or maybe the building had been cleared of supernatural entities for a time, but new ones moved in. It's like spraying for termites. If you don't do it regularly, you risk a new infestation."

Amber was getting used to Connie's unexpected insight into paranormal matters, but she could tell that it still bothered Drew and Trevor. The two shared a quick glance after Connie's latest observation, and Amber knew it was only a matter of time until the three of them would need to address the matter. She supposed she should have been more bothered than she was about Connie, but the more time she spent in the woman's presence, the more comfortable she was around her. She wasn't sure why, but having her be a part of the team felt right, and that was enough for now.

"Why the focus on Erin's film?" Jenn asked. "Do you think it has something to do with the murders?"

Before any of them could answer, Erin said, "It's not polite to talk about people when they're not present."

The five of them turned to see Erin standing next to their table, hands on her hips and a scowl on her face.

"Did I hear right? Do you really believe that my film pissed off some ghost, and she's now going on a murderous rampage through town?"

"Something like that," Trevor said.

"That's ridiculous! We've been filming in town all week. We've shot footage in a dozen different locations. It's a coincidence that the murders happened in two of the places where we filmed. That's all."

"Two of the places where you filmed *yesterday*," Trevor said.

"And the murders happened in the same order you filmed in," Drew said.

"That doesn't mean anything," Erin said.

"And then there was Alex," Connie said. "Arthur told us he died last week while scouting a location for you."

"That was an *accident*," Erin said. "Tragic as it was, there was nothing weird about it. No flying books, no lungs filled with river water."

"What about the message that appeared while you were filming at the museum today?" Amber asked. "'Stop.'"

Erin frowned. "Are you suggesting the message was for me? That the ghost or whatever it is wants me to stop making my film?"

"It's a theory," Drew said.

"Well, it's a dumb theory," Erin said. "If some ghost wants me to quit making my movie, the easiest way would be to kill *me*, not kill other people in places where I filmed."

They all looked at her for a moment.

"She has a point," Connie said. "That's how I'd do it—*if* I were a murderous ghost, that is."

"Look, I understand that you're all just trying to figure out what's going on," Erin said. "You want to prevent more deaths from happening. I get that, and I'm totally with you. But the best way to do that is to keep investigating. My crew and I are scheduled to film at Tri-County Community College this afternoon. It was built on the site where a prison stood for almost fifty years before the flood. And every Dead Days, they have a festival for students. They have ghost tours, a costume contest, a horror-film marathon in the student union, and a haunted maze set up in the library. A lot of prisoners died during the flood. The guards didn't bother letting them out of their cells, and they drowned. The college is supposed to have more ghost sightings than any other location in town. It's a perfect place for you guys to do your thing."

"And our thing would be . . ." Drew said.

Erin made a vague gesture. "You know. Checking out the psychic vibes in the area, seeing if you can contact any spirits. That kind of stuff."

"Stuff that makes for great footage, you mean," Amber said.

"Duh," Erin said, smiling. "Of *course,* I want to get cool shots for my movie, but that doesn't mean I don't want to help you guys figure out what's going on, too. I'm a firm believer in win-win scenarios."

"No murders have occurred at the college," Connie said. "At least, not yet. It would be quite a coup if you and your crew were present during a killing, wouldn't it? You could record every gory detail, and your film would go from a minor-league documentary that almost no one would see to a movie notorious the world over. I imagine that would do a great deal to boost your career."

Erin glared at Connie, but she didn't respond. Her silence was response enough.

Then she said, "Look, I'm going to track down Arthur, and then my crew and I are heading over to the college, with or without you. You can't stop me. What are you going to do? Call the chief and tell him that you're worried I'm going to stir up a bunch of murderous spooks? He'll just hang up on you. Since I'm going to do this, you might as well come along. If something bad *does* happen, at least you'll be there to try to deal with it."

"And you'll be there to film it all," Amber said.

Erin grinned. "Like I said, I believe in win-win scenarios."

Mitch had parked his Impala close enough to the hotel entrance so he could keep an eye on it but not so close that he would be easily spotted. There was a dull throbbing at the base of his skull, and although he tried to ignore it, it was really starting to bug him. Maybe his headache was from not getting much sleep last night and sitting upright in his car when he had slept. Maybe it was because he still hadn't had anything to eat.

Maybe it's because you let a damned ghost-bitch mess with your head, his father's voice said.

Mitch paid his father's voice no mind. It wasn't real. More to the point, *she* didn't like it when he listened to his father's voice. He didn't want to be punished again. Until today, he had thought his father's punishments would be the worst he would ever experience. He had been wrong.

He was watching the hotel entrance when Amber walked out. Drew was with her, as was that chunky guy, the sexy babe, the old guy, the black chick, and three other people he didn't recognize. But from the equipment they carried, he guessed they were the black chick's film crew. The black chick and the old guy got into a VW Bug, the film crew climbed into a van, and Amber and the others got into a Prius. *What a pussy car,* he thought.

He started his Impala.

"What are you doing?"

"Getting ready to follow them."

"Turn it off."

Despite what she had done to him earlier, he hesitated, his hand still on the key. "But Amber—"

She reached over and placed her hand over his. Cold so intense it burned sank into his flesh and penetrated his bones. He gritted his teeth and turned off the engine. She kept her hand where it was a few seconds longer before removing it. Mitch's hand still burned, and he massaged it with his other one, trying to work feeling back into it.

"You'll get your chance at Amber, don't worry. But right now, there's something else I need you to do."

The Dark Lady gave Mitch his instructions, and he listened very carefully.

"Thank you. Enjoy the rest of the conference."

Jenn handed the book—a tome relating "true" accounts of vampirism throughout history—to a teenage girl wearing a black gown, a long black wig, black lipstick, and black false nails. The girl smiled as she took the book and left with her boyfriend, a skinny kid with a peach-fuzz goatee who wore a Ramones T-shirt and looked bored as hell. Jenn envied them. She would give anything to be wandering through the Exhibition Hall, talking, laughing, and checking out the various booths, with her biggest problem being how much money she could afford to spend buying useless junk.

The day before, her life had been chugging along just fine. The store had been busier than usual thanks to the Dead Days crowd, and Tonya had been manning the fort while she had been there at the hotel, helping to get the Exhibition Hall ready to open. She had gone back to the store in the early afternoon to answer some questions on-camera for Erin, which had been a nice break in the routine, but otherwise it had been business as usual. She had been looking forward to seeing Trevor again, and she had been curious to meet Drew and Amber, especially after reading about them in Trevor's new book. And had she been hoping to see if there were any sparks still left between them? Maybe.

But then Tonya had died, followed by those two poor people in the museum. Oh, and don't forget that crew member of Erin's who had died the week before. That made a grand total of four people dead . . . so far.

But as bad as that was, what freaked her out the most was seeing the word *Stop* appear as if by magic, etched in the surface of the museum room over and over, as if carved by dozens of unseen hands. Until that moment, the supernatural had been nothing more to her than a pastime, a game of what-if to play in her imagination. She read nonfiction books on the paranormal the same way other people read novels. She enjoyed imagining that the stories were true while she read them, but once she put the book down, the game was over.

But that afternoon, she had lived one of those stories. Hell, she was *still* living it. And as much as she wanted to believe that it had been some kind of elaborate Dead Days prank, she knew it wasn't. The supernatural was real. And that meant the world wasn't the way she thought it was. If something like what she had seen in the museum could happen, then *anything* could happen. She wasn't naïve. She knew the world wasn't a safe place. But until that day, she hadn't known just how unsafe it was. It was bad enough that you had to protect yourself from other human beings who might hurt you, whether on purpose or by accident, and of course, there was always the possibility of death from injury or disease. But now she knew that there were worse things in the world than all that— much worse—and there was nothing you could do to guard against them. If a supernatural force could carve a word into wood, what could stop it from boring a hole through your heart or brain, killing you instantly? You would drop dead without ever knowing what hit you. And it could happen at any moment, without warning.

When Trevor and the others had decided to accompany Erin to the college, Jenn had begged off, claiming that she would rather remain at the hotel and sell books at the Forgotten Lore booth, as she had originally planned to do that day. She had said it would be comforting to do something normal, that it would help to take her mind off Tonya's death. At first, Trevor had been reluctant to let her stay, but Drew had said it was a good idea, and Trevor had relented. He had offered to stay with her, but she had insisted that he go with the others. If something . . . bad . . . happened at the college, his friends would need him. Besides, how could she pretend that things were normal if he was hanging around? She could tell that her last excuse—although true enough—had hurt his feelings a bit, but he had said he understood and left, not before promising that he would call to check on her and making her promise to call him if she needed anything.

She had given him a quick kiss to reassure him that everything was OK, and he had been so surprised that he had departed without further argument. She smiled. Trevor liked to talk, but she had always known how to shut him up.

But the real reason she hadn't gone with them to the college was simple. She was afraid.

She didn't think she could take witnessing another paranormal event. It felt as if she was barely keeping it together as it was. If anything else happened, she feared she might lose it altogether. She had called a cousin of hers who lived in Evansville. Noelle was going to come get her the next day and take her away from Exeter. She planned to stay with Noelle while she adjusted to everything that had happened. She thought she might even sell the bookstore and move out of Exeter for good. After this weekend, the idea of continuing to live in the "Most Haunted Town in America" no longer appealed.

She pulled herself out of her dark thoughts when a man approached her booth. She was grateful to have another customer to distract her, and she flashed him a welcoming smile.

"Looking for anything in particular?" she asked.

The man stared at her with eyes as flat and dead as a doll's.

"As a matter of fact, I am," he said, his voice toneless. Then he slowly smiled, and a dark glint came into his gaze. "My name's Mitch. And I'm looking for you."

ELEVEN

Drew noted how Amber kept glancing around as they walked.

"Keeping an eye out for Mitch?" he asked.

She looked at him and smiled. "Like you aren't? On the surface, you may be an educated, rational, modern man, but underneath, you're still a caveman protecting his mate."

Drew grinned. "Ugh. Me no comment."

They were in Tri-County Community College's library. The building had two stories, with an open-air atrium that rose all the way to a skylight in the ceiling. Erin's crew was setting up near the circulation desk on the first floor, where the library's director stood chatting with Connie while waiting to be interviewed. Not far away, Trevor was taking readings with the EMF detector, while Carrington tried to capture EVP with the digital audio recorder. Erin stood equidistant between them, filming first one, then the other, with her handheld camera, as if she couldn't decide which man was more important to focus on.

Drew and Amber had decided to take a walk through the library to see what, if anything, she might be able to sense about the place. Currently, they stood next to the second-floor railing, gazing down at the scene below. In the middle of the atrium was a landscaped area filled with flowers and green plants of various kinds, and next to it was a small lounge area where students could buy coffee and pastries, sit at a table, and chat or watch whatever was playing on the flat-screen TV. Rows of computer stations took up the rest of the main floor, and Drew wondered if the library had any physical books at all and, if so, where they were kept.

"Looks more like a student center than a library," Amber said, echoing his thoughts.

"I guess if you want students to register for classes these days, you have to up the fun factor," he said.

"Well, it certainly looks like they take their fun seriously here."

The library had been transformed for Dead Days. The staff members were dressed in old-fashioned black suits or dresses, making them resemble Victorian-era undertakers. Most of the students wore costumes, and while a few of their outfits were whimsical—one couple was dressed as a plug and a socket—most were ghoulish in theme: monsters, ghosts, zombies, masked slashers, and the like. *The Rocky Horror Picture Show* was playing on the flat-screen, and the students in the lounge area were laughing and singing along with the lyrics. Erin had told them that there was a maze of some kind there, but so far, Drew hadn't seen it. Maybe it was farther back on the first floor, where it couldn't be seen from above.

"I wish Erin hadn't insisted on coming here," Amber said.

"Do you sense something?" Only a couple of months ago, Drew would have dismissed the notion of paranormal abilities as nonsense. Now here he was, asking his lover if she was picking up anything on her psychic radar, as if it were the most normal thing in the world. Life could be pretty damned strange sometimes.

"You know how it is in August, when the air is so humid and heavy it feels like a weight pressing down on you? It's felt like that to me ever since we set foot on this campus. I don't have any trouble believing this place was built on the site of an old prison and that a lot of people died here. I'm worried that the college is a can of gasoline, and Erin's a match."

She shuddered, and Drew put his arm around her shoulder.

"Erin was right when she said we couldn't stop her. It's not like we could've taken out a supernatural restraining order on her."

Amber smiled. "I suppose not. I just don't understand why someone who knows that dark forces exist—and that they're responsible for the deaths of four people—would knowingly provoke those forces."

"Ego," Drew said. "Erin believes she's stronger than any supernatural entity, and she intends to prove it by documenting proof of paranormal activity for the world to see."

"And get famous in the process," Amber added.

Drew nodded. "It's also possible that on some level, she is deeply terrified of the supernatural, and because of that, she's driven to confront it. Some people flee what they fear, some attempt to face it and overcome it, and some are compelled to rush headlong toward it, regardless of the consequences. They can't help themselves. Erin may be expressing a death wish."

Amber frowned. "Isn't that the title of an old movie about a vigilante who hunts criminals in New York?"

Drew smiled. "Yes, but it refers to one of Freud's theories. He postulated that all living things have an innate desire to return to the inanimate. In other words, the purpose of all life is to die."

"That's a cheerful thought." She fell silent for a moment before continuing. "Drew, I'm sorry I didn't tell you about Mitch before. I guess I was just too ashamed."

He still had his arm around her, and he tightened his grip to give her a hug. "I understand, but as far as I'm concerned, you have nothing to be ashamed of."

Amber slipped her arm around his waist. "I love you, Drew Pearson."

"I love you, too."

They turned toward each other then, embraced, and kissed.

"Isn't that sweet?"

They broke apart and turned to see Connie standing there, a mocking grin on her face.

"Erin's ready to start filming her interview with the library director. I thought you'd want to be there . . . that is, unless the two of you have something better to do?" She gave them a teasing smile, then turned and headed toward the stairs.

"You work for a very strange woman," Amber said.

Drew sighed. "Tell me about it."

The land the college is built on has a unique history," Erin said. "Can you tell us a little about it?"

The library director, a scarecrow of a man dressed in a black suit and wearing a large top hat, seemed nervous at the prospect of being filmed. He glanced at Ray or, more precisely, at the camera he was holding, and then he eyed Sarah's boom mic with suspicion, almost as if it were a snake that might attack him any moment.

"Uh . . . where do I look? At you or the camera?"

Erin's smile was a bit strained as she answered. "At me. Just pretend the rest of my crew isn't here."

Drew figured that the crowd of students and staff that had gathered to watch the filming wasn't helping the director's nerves any. And neither were Trevor and Carrington. Trevor continued scanning the area with the EMF detector, while Carrington was using the infrared thermal scanner. From what Drew understood, the latter device could be used both in light and in the dark, but he didn't see how it could get a decent reading with so many people gathered around. Wouldn't their combined heat signatures interfere with the scanner?

Unlike everyone else, Connie paid no attention to the director and Erin's crew. She glanced right and left, looked up, down, backward, and forward, her head continuously moving, as if she were searching for something. No, Drew thought, more as if she were *scanning* for something, using her senses the same way Trevor and Carrington used technology. It was a ridiculous thought. As long as he had known her, she had never demonstrated intuitive insight, let alone the kind of uncanny perception that might be considered psychic. She was a straightforward, logical, and, above all, unimaginative thinker. At least, she had been before now. People could change. Drew sincerely believed that, or he wouldn't have become a psychologist. But in his experience, people didn't make radical changes within the space of a few hours. So how could he explain Connie's atypical behavior? Perhaps she was simply doing her best to adjust to the situation she found herself caught up in. Or perhaps she was feigning interest in the investigation in order to get closer to him. Just because she had appeared to make nice with Amber, that didn't mean that Connie still didn't consider her a competitor. Or maybe there was a different reason, one far more sinister in nature. A lot of strange things had happened since they had come to Exeter. Maybe the change in Connie's personality wasn't so much situational as supernatural. It was a far-fetched idea, to say the least, and his suspicions could very well be a product of his imagination. After all, he was only human, and it was only natural to become a bit paranoid when dealing with malevolent otherworldly forces. But it was precisely because they *were* dealing with such forces that he decided to keep a close eye on Connie from then on. If she had been tainted by Darkness, as they suspected Mitch had been, they needed to be on their guard.

The director started to answer Erin's question, coughed a couple of times, and asked one of his staff for a bottle of water from the snack bar. Everyone waited while the water was fetched, and the director took a long drink before capping the bottle and setting it down on the circulation counter.

"OK," he said, "I'm ready."

He didn't look ready to Drew. He looked more as if he might throw up any moment. But Erin nodded and repeated her question.

The director cleared his throat and began speaking. "Exeter State Prison used to stand on what are now the campus grounds. In fact, this very library supposedly rests on the site where the prison gallows once stood. The prison was damaged during the flood in the 1920s, and the buildings were demolished afterward. The land remained empty for a number of years until construction began on the college in the late 1950s."

The director relaxed the more he spoke, and Erin was clearly relieved. "What happened to the prisoners during the flood?" she asked.

"The least dangerous ones were released by the guards. But the worst ones—the murderers, rapists, and the like—were left behind. The prison staff didn't have the manpower to guard so many men, and the warden didn't want to risk unleashing such violent offenders on society. Not a very humanitarian choice, but the floodwaters rose quickly back then, and there was little time. The prison staff vacated the buildings, and when the waters flooded the prison, those left behind were trapped in their cells and drowned."

"How awful," Erin said, although her pleased expression told how she really felt.

"Afterward, the land was reputed to be cursed, which was why it remained vacant for so long. Eventually, people forgot about the curse, or at least, they didn't take the rumors seriously anymore, and plans were made for constructing the college."

"But it wasn't long before people began reporting paranormal activity on campus," Erin said.

"True. Over the years, students, faculty, and staff have reported stories of invisible hands touching them, sinister laughter coming from nowhere, the sound of footsteps echoing when no one is present, doors slamming shut, elevators working on their own . . . In fact, there have been so many reports over the years that during Dead Days, we conduct ghost tours around campus."

"So, like the rest of the town, the college has embraced its reputation for the paranormal."

"Yes, especially during the Dead Days celebration. It's all in good fun, of course, but it does present educational opportunities, too. Many professors present units on the history of the town—the flood and the prison in particular—and the science faculty discuss the scientific method and compare it with the pseudoscientific approach of the psychics and mediums who flocked to the town after the flood." He glanced at Trevor and Carrington. "Uh, no offense."

Ray swung his camera around to capture any reactions Trevor or Carrington might have, but neither man seemed to be paying attention.

"EMF readings are rising," Trevor said. "Fast." He looked up at Drew. "This isn't good."

"It's getting colder," Amber said. "Can't you feel it?"

Drew did. It felt as if someone had turned the air conditioning up full blast, except that there was no breeze.

"Well, I'm not picking anything up on this," Carrington said. He lowered the infrared thermal scanner and smacked it on the side. "Then again, maybe I'm not operating the damned thing correctly. I never did read the instructions."

Connie was gazing toward the skylight. "Point it upward," she said.

Carrington frowned at her, but he did as she suggested. And when he peered into the device's visual display, he gasped. "There are cold spots—dozens of them—circling above us. I've never seen anything like it!"

"We need to get these people out of here," Amber said. "Now."

Drew had no idea what was happening, but he didn't hesitate. "Listen up, everyone! We need to evacuate the library immediately!"

The director looked at Erin. "I'm confused. Is this some sort of improv?"

Erin paid him no further attention. "Point the camera up!" she shouted at Ray.

The students and staff looked at one another, unsure what was happening and what, if anything, to do about it. Several students thought it was a joke and began laughing. One of them called out, "We're all gonna die!"

Connie sighed. "I really wish you hadn't said that."

One instant the air above them was empty, and the next it was filled with circling shapes. They were human—or at least human-like—all wearing long-sleeved gray shirts and gray pants, although their feet were bare. From their basic physical forms, Drew assumed they were male, but given the state of their bodies, it was difficult to know for sure. Their skin had sloughed away in numerous places, revealing bleached bone, and what skin remained was blanched, swollen, and wrinkled. They moved slowly through the air, arms stroking and legs kicking as if they were swimming.

"It's the prisoners!" Amber said. "The ones who drowned!"

The students and staff just stared at the apparitions circling like ghostly sharks through the air above them. But then one of the students let out a whoop, another yelled, "Awesome!" and everyone began to applaud.

"They think it's some kind of special effect," Drew said. "A Dead Days surprise."

"It's going to be a surprise, all right," Connie said. "A nasty, bloody one if we don't get these idiots out of here!"

Erin was grinning like a kid on Christmas Day. "Don't you miss a single second of this, Ray!"

Ray had his camera pointed toward the floating specters, but he didn't look happy about it. "Erin, this is *way* more intense than some words scratched into walls!"

"Don't I know it!"

"I don't mean that in a good way," he said. "I mean it in an I-hope-we-all-don't-die way!"

Sarah and Pattie also looked scared. Sarah still had hold of the boom mic, but she didn't seem to know where to direct it. Her eyes kept darting back and forth as the ghosts swam through the air above. Pattie stood close to her, one hand on Sarah's shoulder, looking upward with wide eyes, lips moving silently. Drew wondered if she was saying a prayer.

Carrington stepped forward. "There's no need to panic!" he said in a loud, authoritative voice. "These apparitions have no physical substance, and therefore they cannot hurt you!"

"Tell that to Tonya and those two people in the museum," Trevor said, but Carrington ignored him.

A young woman in the crowd who was dressed as the Bride of Frankenstein, complete with towering hairdo, stretched her hand above her head as one of the ghosts swam near.

"This is so cool!" she said. "I wonder how they—"

One of the prisoners swam down toward her and wrapped fingers that were half bone and half rotting flesh around the woman's wrist. His eyes bulged from their sockets, and his wrinkled worm lips were pulled back to reveal a mouthful of jagged yellow teeth. There was hunger in his gaze, and he grinned in savage delight as he swam upward, pulling the screaming woman off her feet and into the air along with him.

Erin clapped her hands together and actually jumped up and down in excitement. Ray shouted, "Fuck me!" but continued filming. Sarah dropped the boom mic and turned, sobbing, toward Pattie. The older woman embraced her lover but could not take her eyes off the spectacle of the girl being carried aloft by a grinning corpse.

Without thinking, Drew ran forward and jumped, making a grab for the girl's legs. He missed the left one but managed to get his fingers around her right ankle. As he started to fall, his arm jerked, and for an instant, he feared that the ghost was strong enough to carry both of them aloft. But then he plummeted to the floor, dragging the girl down with him. He landed hard on his right side, pain flaring in his chest. He had bruised a rib or two for sure, maybe even broken them. But he wasn't concerned about himself; he was worried about the girl. She had hit the floor pretty hard, too, and she might need medical attention.

He pushed himself up to a sitting position, breathing shallowly to keep his ribs from hurting any more than they already did. And if he had broken any, the last thing he needed right then was to puncture a lung. The girl was lying facedown on the floor, and in her Bride of Frankenstein costume, she looked as if this were the ending scene of a horror movie, in which the Bride had been slain and would return to the grave to await resurrection in a sequel. The girl lay completely still, and Drew couldn't tell if she was breathing. He scooted forward, intending to check her pulse, but he caught a flash of movement out of the corner of his eye. He turned to see a ghost swimming through the air toward him. He thought it might be the same one that had tried to abduct the girl, but he couldn't be sure, and he supposed it really didn't matter. One murderous apparition could kill him as easily as another. And if the ghosts possessed enough physical reality to grab hold of a person and pull her into the air, they surely were solid enough to kill someone.

Drew steeled himself to meet the specter's attack, although he had no idea how to fight the damned thing. But as the airborne corpse came toward him, bone-claws reaching out, eager to find purchase in his flesh, Connie stepped forward, raised her foot, and kicked, slamming the point of her shoe into the ghost's head. The heel broke through the creature's skull and sank into its rotten brain. Watery black goo dribbled forth from the wound, and while the ghost appeared to suffer no pain from the blow, it veered off its attack and swam upward, taking Connie's shoe with it. As her shoe popped off, she almost lost her balance, but she hopped a couple of times in place and managed to keep from falling over.

"I didn't know high heels could be so useful," she said as she watched the ghost ascend.

Amber rushed to Drew's side and helped him to his feet. "Are you all right?" she asked.

"I'll live," he said. The right side of his chest felt as if it were on fire, but he didn't think he was in need of immediate medical attention. Besides, he had more important things to worry about right then than a couple of bruised ribs.

Connie kicked off her remaining shoe and helped the Bride of Frankenstein to stand. The girl looked as if she'd had the breath knocked out of her, and she would probably have some hellacious bruising the next day, but she appeared well enough. Assuming the ghost that had tried to carry her away didn't make another try for her.

The ghosts—a dozen or more—swarmed the library atrium, moving through the air with eerie, silent grace as they targeted people. Some tried to grab hold of their victims and lift them into the air, while others fell upon them, clawing and biting. Those who were attacked screamed in pain and fear, and the rest of the crowd— who up to this point had been standing around, unsure what was happening—finally figured out that they were in danger and ran for the exits, shouting and sobbing.

"Keep running!" Trevor shouted. "Get as far away from the library as you can!"

"That means you, too, missy." Connie gave the Bride a push, and she staggered off in the direction of an exit. Connie turned to Trevor. "You figure the manifestation is confined to this location?"

He nodded. "It has to be the Dark Lady's doing. She's here somewhere. If we can find her—" Trevor broke off as a ghost swooped down and made a grab for him. He ducked, but the flying corpse managed to snag a handful of his hair before it arced up and away. He cried out as the ghost tore the hair from his scalp and swam off, waving the strands around as if they were a trophy.

Trevor swore and clapped a hand to the small bloody patch of skin on his head. "That's dirty pool! I have little enough hair left as it is!"

Two other ghosts came toward them. One was long and lean, a flesh-covered skeleton in a gray prison uniform, while the other was short and squat, eye sockets empty, skin covered with fissures as if it were molting. They glided through the air like sharks on the hunt, and Drew wondered if, like sharks, they were drawn by the scent of Trevor's blood.

"Chairs!" he shouted, and Trevor nodded. The four of them ran to the snack area, and Drew and Trevor each grabbed one of the hard black plastic chairs and raised them as the ghosts approached.

"Get behind us!" he told Amber and Connie.

"As if," Amber said. She grabbed a chair, and so did Connie.

The skeleton ghost swooped in first, making for Trevor. Trevor swung his makeshift weapon at the creature and struck a solid blow to its head. The apparitions might be spirits, but Drew was gratified to see that they possessed enough physical substance to hit. Teeth flew from the skeleton's mouth, and Drew watched in fascination as they faded to nothing, as if they couldn't maintain their existence without a connection to the ghost's body. In response, the skeleton veered off, although Drew doubted that Trevor's blow had done it any real harm.

The eyeless one moved in next. It headed for Amber, but Drew stepped in front of it, raised his chair high, and brought it crashing down on the ghost's head. The impact sent jolts of pain up Drew's arms, and fiery pain flared anew in his ribs. The eyeless ghost hit the floor, and Amber and Connie stepped forward and began pounding it with their chairs. The ghost thrashed and struggled to rise, but the women didn't let up. They hit it over and over again, each blow knocking off chunks of bloodless white flesh that quickly faded away. The women kept at it, meat sliding off the creature's bones as if off a well-cooked chicken. Soon the main body of the ghost began to fade, and it was gone.

Panting for breath, skin slick with sweat, Amber and Connie put their chairs down and gulped air.

"That was hard-core!" Trevor said.

Drew agreed, but before he could say anything, the skeleton ghost swung back around for a second attack.

This time, all four of them battered it into nonexistence.

They had a breather after that, and Drew took a moment to survey the scene.

Erin continued standing where she was, watching the chaos around her with glee. She appeared unaware that she was in danger, or at least unconcerned. Drew wondered if her apparent lack of fear was because she was a filmmaker. She was so used to being in control and observing events without being a participant that she couldn't conceive that she might actually get hurt. The library director had already fled, but he hadn't gotten halfway to the exit before a ghost had brought him down. The man lay on the floor screaming, while the animated corpse crouched over him, clawing him like a wild animal.

Pattie and Sarah knelt together to make themselves smaller targets, arms wrapped around each other. Sarah was sobbing, her face buried against Pattie's chest, and the older woman leaned her head against her partner's, eyes squeezed shut as if she expected death to find them at any moment, and she didn't want to see it coming. Ray had backed up against the circulation counter to brace himself as he continued filming. Drew assumed that the act of viewing the scene through the distancing lens of a camera helped him keep the worst of his fear at bay, but if their theory was right, and the Dark Lady was angered by Erin making a documentary about Exeter, Ray was making himself a prime target by continuing to film.

Carrington made no attempt to flee. He stood watching the chaos, appearing fascinated and terrified in equal measure.

"Trevor, you said the Dark Lady is causing this," Drew said.

"She has to be. She's like . . . well, like Erin. She's the director. The other ghosts do what she tells them."

"He's right," Amber said. "I can feel her somewhere close. She's the center of all this."

"More than that, she's the power source," Connie said. "She's channeling the energy that's making this manifestation possible."

Drew didn't ask how Connie knew this. Right then, he didn't care. They had to do something to stop the prison ghosts before someone got killed. Most of the crowd had managed to reach the exits and escape the building, but a half-dozen people—not counting Carrington, Erin, and the film crew—still remained. Some were running from pursuing ghosts, but others, like the poor library director, were fighting for their lives as gray-clad corpses ravaged them with tooth and claw. Drew wanted to run over and pull the ghosts off them, but he forced himself to remain where he was. There were too many ghosts and too few of them, and he knew that if they attempted to help those being attacked, they would end up being attacked themselves. If they really wanted to help the victims, the best thing they could do was cut the ghosts off from their power source: the Dark Lady.

Another pair of ghosts made a run at them then, but the specters broke off their attack when confronted by the chair-wielding humans. It seemed the creatures weren't entirely mindless, Drew thought.

"I think we may need to add chairs to our ghost-hunting arsenal," Trevor said. "These things work better than a crucifix dipped in holy water!"

"We have to find the Dark Lady and stop this," Trevor said. "She has to be around here somewhere."

"I'm sure she is," Trevor said. "But she's hiding. We won't be able to find her unless she wants us to."

"That may be true for most people," Connie said. "But the Dark Lady can't hide from Amber. Not if she's really looking."

"All right, that's it," Trevor said. "You may be a good psychologist, but what makes you think you're an expert in—"

"Hush," Amber said, cutting him off. "I need to concentrate."

Trevor shut up. He glared at Connie, but she just smiled at him.

Amber closed her eyes and lowered her head, almost as if she were praying. The rest of them lifted their chairs and stood guard over her.

The ghosts continued to attack in silence, and the library echoed with the cries of their victims. So far, the vicious spirits had left Erin alone—something Drew found remarkable if, as they had theorized, her film was what had drawn the Dark Lady's ire. But the ghosts had no reluctance when it came to attacking her crew. Three of them circled Sarah and Pattie, mouths twisted into rictus grins as they snatched at the women's clothes and clawed their exposed skin. Carrington ran over, grabbed the boom mic that Sarah had dropped, and began wielding it like a club at the ghosts. The mic rod was made of light plastic, and it bounced off the specters without doing any damage. Although no sound escaped the creatures' mouths as Carrington lashed out at them with his makeshift weapon, Drew had the impression that the damned things were laughing.

Ray looked as if he couldn't decide whether to keep filming or not. He would start to lower the camera and then start filming again. From the man's expression, Drew thought he might be in shock and operating on automatic. He continued filming because the act of doing his job gave him something normal to focus on in the midst of all the madness.

Amber raised her head and opened her eyes. "That way." Without waiting for a response from anyone, she began walking away from the circulation desk, deeper into the library.

Drew felt guilty about leaving Erin and the others to fend off the prison ghosts on their own. But if the Dark Lady was at the center of this disturbance, finding and stopping her was the best way to help them. Besides, he knew he could never stand by and let Amber walk into danger without him.

Drew, Trevor, and Connie carried their chairs as they walked, in case any ghosts should attempt to attack them again. He imagined their group looked more than a bit ridiculous walking around armed with furniture, but makeshift weapons were better than no weapons at all. Ridiculous-looking or not, he did feel a strong sense of rightness about what they were doing. This was the way it should be: the four of them, Connie included, striding forth to confront the darkness that plagued the town. Why it should feel right for Connie to be a part of it, Drew had no idea, but it did.

As they walked, everyone but Amber kept glancing back. Drew expected to see gray-clad ghosts swimming through the air toward them, teeth bared, bleached-white fingers reaching for them. But it appeared that they no longer held any interest for the ghosts. The apparitions remained in the general vicinity of the circulation desk, attacking those few who hadn't managed to flee. Were the creatures somehow confined to that spot, or was there another reason they weren't pursuing them? Somehow Drew doubted it was because they were armed with deadly ghost-repelling chairs.

They continued past the snack area—on the TV screen, Riff Raff was singing about time being fleeting—and more rows of computer desks until they finally reached the book stacks. There were far fewer books than Drew expected, and that they were kept way in the back of the ground floor like that spoke of just how little the print medium was valued these days. He wondered how many students there had actually read a physical book in the last year or, for that matter, had even touched one.

At least, the book stacks served a useful function during Dead Days. They had been turned into a haunted maze, with black partitions set up at regular intervals to create walls. There was a single open entrance, above which was a cardboard sign painted to look like gray stone, the words "Abandon All Hope Ye Who Enter Here" written on it in jagged black letters. From there, they could see lights strobing within, and they could hear ominous music playing, funereal tones punctuated by eerie sound effects: mad cackling, crashing thunder, creaking doors, rattling chains, and yowling cats.

They put their chairs down and regarded the maze entrance.

"Don't tell me she's in *there*," Trevor said.

"Sorry," Amber said. "But she is. Or at least, something powerful is."

"Maybe she has a sense of humor," Connie said.

"Maybe it's a trap," Drew said.

Connie looked at him as if he had just stated the incredibly obvious. "Well, of course it is. Why else do you think the ghosts broke off their attack once we started heading this way? The Dark Lady wants us to go inside."

"And what makes you think that?" Trevor demanded.

She shrugged. "It's what I'd do."

"It makes sense," Drew said. "The question is, do we go in anyway?"

From behind them came the cries of people scared and in pain.

"We have to," Amber said.

And without any further discussion, the four of them entered the maze.

TWELVE

Ray wanted to run. He wanted it so bad that it felt as if every cell in his body was screaming for him to drop his camera and race for the exit. And once he was outside—in the open air and sunlight, where the world made sense and grinning ghouls didn't fly through the fucking air and try to kill you—he would keep running, as fast and as far as he could. And who knows? Once he started really running, once he hit his goddamned *stride,* he might never stop.

But he didn't run. Instead, he kept filming. Oh, he lowered his camera once or twice, as if he *intended* to drop it and get the hell out of Dodge, but he shouldered it again and resumed recording. He didn't keep filming because he was dedicated to his job. He liked being a cameraman, maybe even loved it, but not more than he loved his own life. No way. And he sure as hell didn't do it for Erin, even though he knew it was exactly what she wanted. He was sick of working for that bitch, and now she had gotten him, Sarah, and Pattie into a mess of shit, just like she had poor Alex. She had brought them there hoping that something like this would happen, and it would be a miracle if they all didn't end up laid out on a mortician's slab.

The reason he kept filming was simple: he couldn't stop.

Maybe he was too scared to stop, or maybe he was mesmerized by the bizarre spectacle he was witnessing. Maybe he hoped that if he kept filming, he would capture evidence that this wasn't real—see thin wires attached to the "ghosts," holding them aloft, or maybe even see distortion in their images indicating that they were holograms of some kind. Although what a small-town community college would be doing with that kind of technology, he couldn't say.

Or maybe there was no reason. Maybe he continued to film simply because he did.

Whatever the reason, or lack thereof, one thing was certain: he was an idiot for sticking around. Not only was there an excellent chance that he would be joining the ranks of the previously living any moment, but he probably wasn't getting any usable footage. The museum security camera hadn't been able to capture images of the murders that had taken place there, and after checking his footage of the multiple manifestations of the word *Stop* he'd taken at the scene, he had discovered it was filled with electronic distortion, rendering it only partially usable. If these ghosts were real—and although he wished like hell they weren't, deep down he knew they were—whatever kind of energy they emitted was likely ruining this footage, too. Still, he kept going.

There was no real thought to his filming. He didn't worry about camera angles or framing shots or even if the lens was in focus. He just pointed his camera one way, then another, and then another. There was so much going on that it really didn't matter which way he faced. His camera always picked up something.

At first, he had been grateful that the ghosts made no sound, although their silence was creepy as hell. But as the attack continued, he found himself wishing otherwise. If the ghosts had laughed, shouted, roared, *anything*, it would have helped to drown out the screams of the people they savaged. A number of students, faculty, and staff had managed to escape, although many of them had suffered tooth and claw wounds as they fled. But a half-dozen or so remained behind, and the ghosts toyed with them like cats with small rodents.

Sarah and Pattie knelt together on the ground, holding each other for both physical and emotional support. Several ghosts circled them, clawed hands tearing at their clothes and scratching furrows in their flesh. The women cried out in pain as the specters tormented them, but they didn't attempt to fight back—maybe because they were too scared or maybe because the absolute insanity of what was happening had overwhelmed their minds to the point where it had tripped their mental circuit breakers, leaving them incapable of resisting. He felt like a rat bastard for just standing and filming as the ghosts assaulted them, but he couldn't make himself stop.

It seemed that Carrington was made of sterner stuff, or maybe his years as a paranormal investigator made it easier for him to accept what was happening, although Ray doubted the man had ever experienced anything this intense before. Carrington picked up Sarah's boom mic and began pounding the ghosts with it, like a skinny, gray-bearded Conan the Barbarian. Not that his heroic efforts did much good. The ghosts continued clawing at Sarah and Pattie, and one of them, evidently irritated by Carrington's attempt to drive them off, broke away from the pack. It circled around and headed for Carrington, swollen white features contorted into a mask of unreasoning hate. The boom mic was bent and looked as if it might fall apart any second, but Carrington held it out before him and prepared to meet the ghost's charge as if the fragile piece of equipment were Excalibur itself. Up to that point, Ray hadn't thought much of the older man. He had seen him as nothing more than a boozy charlatan, and an over-the-hill one at that. But now, seeing him attempt to defend Sarah and Pattie, Ray realized that there was a lot more to the man than he had originally thought, and he felt shamed by his own inability to act.

Carrington swung as the ghost drew near, and the boom mic smashed into the side of the creature's face. The impact snapped the mic pole in two and created a wound over the ghost's right temple from which a watery black substance spurted forth. The injury didn't slow the specter's approach, and when it reached Carrington, it lashed out with a vicious backhand strike. Carrington's head snapped back, and he flew backward a dozen feet. He landed hard, slid to a stop, and didn't move. Ray didn't know if he was alive or dead, but given that he had suffered such a powerful blow, Ray feared the worst.

From the first moment the ghosts had appeared, they had left Erin alone, as if she stood in the eye of a hurricane. Like Ray, she had simply watched the madness happening around her, but, unlike him, she hadn't seemed so much frozen by fear as captivated by delight. Not only hadn't she made a move to help Sarah and Pattie, but it appeared she didn't realize, or didn't care, how terrified they were. He knew what was happening. Just as he was distancing himself from the horror around him by viewing it through a camera lens, she was imagining everything playing out on a screen, considering how she would edit the footage for maximum effect. But when Carrington hit the floor less than ten feet from where she stood, she turned to look at him. Seeing him lying there motionless, the smile left her face, and her delight was replaced with confusion and, he thought, a dawning awareness that what she was witnessing was, in fact, real.

One of the ghosts tired of toying with Sarah and Pattie, and it grabbed hold of Sarah from behind and sank its teeth into her shoulder. She let out a high-pitched shriek of pain, and although she thrashed and tried to dislodge herself from her spectral attacker, the ghost held on tight, and her shirt darkened with blood. Pattie yelled and pounded her fists against the ghost's head, tears of rage and fear streaming down her cheeks, but the horrible thing ignored her and continued gnawing on Sarah, biting its way through her shirt and getting down to the meat.

Ray made no conscious decision to start walking toward Sarah and Pattie. He became aware that he was doing so only because the image of the two women grew larger in his lens, even though he hadn't zoomed in on them. He continued walking, ghosts swimming through the air around him, their dead eyes focusing on him with raw hunger. One scratched a trail of bloody lines down his left cheek as it passed, licking its fingers with a mottled gray tongue as it moved off. Another took a good-size bite out of his left ear and gulped down the grisly morsel as if it were a delicious sweet treat. He felt the pain of his injuries, but it was muted and distant, something unimportant that he would deal with later. He continued walking, filming all the while, until he stood behind the ghost that was tearing into Sarah's shoulder. Still not thinking, his body moving on automatic, Ray raised his camera and brought it smashing down on top of the ghost's head so hard that its skull popped like a rotten melon. Black goo exploded, splattering Sarah and mixing with the blood streaming down her back. The ghost stopped moving, released its grip on Sarah, and started to fall to the floor. But before it could hit, its form faded away, like a shadow vanishing at sunlight's touch.

Sarah fell sobbing into Pattie's arms, and Ray dropped the camera, broken and coated with black gore, to the floor. He should have felt something—satisfied that he had helped prevent Sarah from being injured further, gratified that he'd overcome whatever emotional inertia had kept him from acting, smug that he had done something to help while Erin just stood there. But he felt nothing. Not even when the other ghosts that had been harassing Sarah and Pattie turned away from them and came at him.

There were three of them. Two grabbed his arms, while the third sank its fingers into his shoulders. There was more pain, but he barely registered it. *You're in shock,* he thought. *That's what's wrong with you.* It was so simple, so obvious, he wondered why it hadn't occurred to him before. The unholy trio began swimming upward, carrying him aloft with them. He didn't see the point in struggling as they ascended, and he relaxed and enjoyed the view. The ghosts carried him all the way to the top of the atrium, held him there for a moment, and then let him go.

As he watched the floor rush up to meet him, his only regret was that he wasn't holding his camera. This would have made for some kickass footage.

"I can't believe you three talked me into this," Drew said.

Trevor directed the beam of his flashlight toward the line of trees on the other side of the river. The Clearwater wasn't very wide at this point, but even so, the beam wasn't strong enough to illuminate the far bank.

"You were outvoted," Trevor said. "Fair and square."

The early-spring night air felt cool on his skin. Too cool. He was glad he had worn his black suede jacket, but then, he always wore it, except during the height of summer. Drew sometimes teased him about how often he wore the jacket, saying things like "Do you wear it in the shower? Do you keep it on when you sleep, like it's a security blanket?" But Trevor thought the jacket made him look cool . . . well, cooler than he looked without it, anyway. He had even worn it during picture day a few weeks ago, and his mother had had a fit when he brought the proofs home from school.

Some people just didn't know class when they saw it.

"It's a nice night for a walk by the river," Amber said. "Even if it is a bit chilly."

Trevor wondered if Drew would pick up on the hint this time. Amber had been nuts for him ever since the three of them had met in science class the previous fall. Even Trevor—who had never had a girlfriend even though he was a junior in high school—knew that Amber was using the cool air as an excuse and that she really wanted Drew to put his arm around her. But while Drew was one of the most perceptive people he knew, especially when it came to the way people thought and felt, he was clueless when it came to recognizing Amber's feelings for him.

"I suppose," Drew said. He shone his flashlight on the trees on their side of the bank. More to have something to do, Trevor guessed, than because he believed he would see anything interesting.

The riverbank wasn't wide enough for the four of them to walk side-by-side, especially now. It had rained quite a bit over the last couple of weeks, and the Clearwater was higher than any of them had ever seen it. There had been some talk around town that the river might flood, but it hadn't rained for the last few days, and . . . Trevor allowed the line of thought to trail away. Something nagged at his mind, something to do with the idea of flooding. Not this river, though. Another. But no matter how hard he tried to drag the thought to the forefront of his consciousness, it remained out of reach, and he decided not to worry about it. Whatever the idea was, if it was important enough, it would come to him eventually.

Trevor walked behind Drew and Amber. Even though he couldn't see her face, he didn't need to in order to imagine her crestfallen expression at Drew's once again failing to catch her hint. He had seen it often enough.

"If you're cold, you can borrow my jacket, Amber. I don't need it."

Greg was fourth in line—which, as far as Trevor was concerned, was exactly where he belonged. Greg was a tagalong who had invited himself to be a part of their group, and while neither Trevor nor Drew liked him very much, they tolerated him because of Amber. She felt sorry for Greg, who was even lower in the high-school pecking order than Trevor, and she didn't see any harm in allowing him to accompany them on their investigations.

Greg pushed his way past Trevor, already in the process of shucking off his jacket. Trevor wasn't exactly a skinny guy, but Greg was heavier, and since there wasn't much room on the bank, Greg bumped into him as he went by, knocking him off balance. He staggered and windmilled his arms to keep from falling into the river. Considering how high and fast the water was flowing, along with the fact that he wasn't the strongest of swimmers, taking a dip right then wouldn't merely be embarrassing. It would be danger-ous, maybe even fatal.

But he managed to regain his balance and keep from plunging into the river—barely.

"Damn it, Greg! Watch where you're going!"

But Greg ignored him. He reached Amber, finished removing his jacket, and held it out to her.

"Here! Go ahead. Like I said, I don't need it."

Greg only had on a thin T-shirt underneath his jacket, while Amber wore the oversize Ohio State sweatshirt that was on perma-nent loan from her dad. But Greg had such a pathetically obvious crush on Amber that Trevor wouldn't have been surprised if he had offered to take off all his clothes and give them to her.

Trevor doubted that Amber wanted to take Greg's jacket. For one thing, it would be huge on her. For another, Greg had an unpleas-ant body odor that reminded Trevor of freshly sliced Swiss cheese. But Amber smiled, took Greg's jacket, and slipped it on.

"Thanks," she said.

Amber smiled at Greg, and Drew—who was no longer examin-ing the trees but watching the two of them—frowned.

Trevor knew that Amber had accepted Greg's offer out of sim-ple kindness, but had she also done so in order to make Drew jealous? If so, he didn't blame her. Drew deserved to have his chain yanked a little bit. Maybe it would wake him up and get him to . . .

It was Trevor's turn to frown then. There was something about that thought that bothered him. Something to do with *wake up*. The words kept echoing in his mind, and they seemed important somehow, almost as if his subconscious was trying to send him a message. But if so, he had no idea what it might be. What the hell was wrong with him? It was as if his brain were stuck in low gear.

"I just don't see the point in this," Drew said. "Investigating reports of ghosts is one thing. But this . . ." He paused as if searching for the right words. "This is just silly."

"People have been telling stories about the Gork for a long time," Trevor said. "Since way before we were born."

"That doesn't make the stories true," Drew pointed out.

"My uncle said he saw the Gork once," Greg said. "He and some of his friends were down here drinking when they weren't much older than us. My uncle said they heard the Gork call out from the woods, and its cry sounded like a cross between a howl and a shriek."

"Hearing is not the same as seeing," Drew said. "What your uncle heard was probably one of his friends who snuck off to play a joke on everyone else."

The Gork was Ash Creek's version of Bigfoot, a bestial giant rumored to live in the woods near the Clearwater River. Despite all the tales, no one had ever come forward with solid evidence—no photos, no plaster casts of footprints, no bits of coarse fur snagged on branches. But that didn't deter Trevor. Someone had to be the first to find proof, right? Why shouldn't it be them?

"There *have* been reports of similar creatures from all around the world," Amber said. "Hundreds, maybe thousands of them. If such creatures do exist, why can't there be one living here?"

"I can think of lots of reasons," Drew said. "There would need to be a large enough population for them to breed, which would make it almost impossible for them to stay hidden. No one's ever found any remains of a dead one. As big as they're supposed to be, you'd think they'd leave large piles of poop lying around, but no one's even found that much."

Amber giggled. "That's gross!"

"That's because they're *smart,* Drew," Trevor said. He was starting to get irritated now. Drew could carry the skeptic thing too far sometimes. "They know we outnumber them, so they purposely hide from us, and they make sure not to leave any evidence of their presence."

"If that's true, then if the Gork *is* real, it won't have any trouble hiding from four high-school kids searching for it with flashlights."

"Four kids who are also making a lot of noise," Greg said. "Well, two, technically."

Trevor started to reply to Drew, but he realized he didn't have a counterargument. Maybe they could have planned out this investigation more thoroughly.

"Well, we're here now," Amber said, "so we might as well look around for a while." She smiled at Greg. "Quietly."

Drew scowled at Trevor, and Trevor scowled right back. But neither of them was the type to hold a grudge for long, and eventually, Drew sighed. "OK, why not? But let's at least kill the flashlights."

"Yeah. Good idea," Trevor said. They switched off their flashlights and stood on the bank, listening while they waited for their eyes to adjust to the darkness.

Not that there was much to hear besides the river, as swollen and fast-moving as it was. There was a slight breeze blowing, and Trevor could see the tree branches above them sway gently, silhouetted against the night sky. But he couldn't hear their leaves rustle. In fact, as loud as the river was—the nearly *flood*-stage river, his mind nagged—someone could be walking along the bank right behind them, and they wouldn't hear whoever it was approach. Whoever or *whatever,* Trevor thought.

The skin on the back of his neck began to tingle, and he had the sensation that someone was watching them. A thrill of adrenaline rushed through him, and he turned around to make sure nothing was there.

But something was.

A huge black shape loomed on the riverbank behind them less than ten yards away. Although the sky was clear, the moon was only a thin crescent and provided little light to see by. Trevor couldn't make out any facial features, but he could tell that the shape had broad shoulders, almost no neck, and a head that was narrower at the crown than at the base. The smell hit him then, a nauseating combination of wet dog and skunk so powerful it made his gorge rise. Acid burned the back of his throat and seared his nasal passages, and only a major effort of will kept him from vomiting. He could hear the thing's breathing even over the sound of rushing river water. Heavy and low, it was a sound that spoke of size, mass, and strength. There was an undertone to the breathing, a soft rumble that verged on a growl. It was an angry sound . . . or a hungry one.

Trevor felt as if his blood had turned to ice water, and his own breath seized in his chest. When he was little, he had seen a commercial on TV for asthma medicine. A kid about his age had been running around on a playground with his friends when his eyes bulged and his face turned red. The kid's mother, who had been sitting on a nearby bench and reading, rushed over with an inhaler. The kid was all right after a few blasts of medicine, and besides, it was just a commercial. It wasn't as if the kid had been in any real danger. But ever since then, Trevor had had a fear of experiencing an asthma attack, even though he had never shown the slightest sign of having the condition. Now, standing there on the bank of the Clearwater, confronted with a massive shadowy form that smelled more rank than an entire zoo full of animals, he found himself living his worst fear, for he was too scared to breathe.

This isn't right, he thought. *When I turned around to look, nothing was there. After that, we spent an hour or so walking up and down the riverbank, but we never saw or heard anything.*

They certainly hadn't seen the Gork. But here it was, as big as life and terrifying as all hell—and it shouldn't be.

He frowned and willed his lungs to relax. He took a breath—a shallow one, but it would do—and said, "Something weird is going on here."

The others, perhaps alerted by the same atavistic instinct as Trevor, had turned around and were staring at the Gork.

"That may be the greatest understatement in the history of the human race," Greg said.

He sounded just as frightened as Trevor. But while it was true that part of him was more scared than he had ever been in his life, another part of him was confused by what was happening. The whole thing didn't make any sense, he was sure of it, but he didn't know why.

"This isn't real," Amber said.

And there it was, three simple words that encapsulated what Trevor was feeling.

The Gork growled, the sound loud even over the rushing river, and it took a second for Trevor to realize that the creature had spoken a word.

"Stop."

As if the word was a trigger, a series of images flashed through his mind. It began with adult versions of Amber, Drew, and him having breakfast around a dining-room table, and it ended with the three of them, accompanied by a gorgeous blond woman, passing through the entrance to an amateur spook-house maze.

He remembered, and as soon as he did, the four of them were no longer teenagers but returned to their adult selves, although they remained standing on the bank of the Clearwater.

"This is a hallucination," Trevor said. "An illusory scenario cooked up by the Dark Lady." He raised his voice to make sure the Gork could hear him. "Nice try, but the next time you decide to shanghai people's minds, do it to someone who hasn't experienced it before. We've been there, done that, and, in my case, wrote the book on it."

Connie stepped closer and leaned over so her lips were near his ear. As she spoke, she kept her gaze fixed on the Gork.

"While I admire your bravado, I'd advise you not to piss her off.

She may be a spirit, and this may not be technically real, but that doesn't mean she can't harm us. Remember how that bookstore clerk was killed."

Trevor was about to reply when a thought struck him. "Hey, what happened to Greg? He was here a second ago."

"Just part of the illusion," Connie said. "I was here with you the whole time."

There was something in her tone, a teasing, mocking quality that was so familiar . . . Trevor pushed the thought aside and filed it away for later. Right then, they had bigger simians to fry.

Drew and Amber joined them.

"Connie's right," Drew said. "And here on the psychic plane, she can attack our minds directly."

"I can feel her reaching out to us," Amber said. "Probing our minds, checking our defenses, looking for weak spots."

"Can you block her?" Drew asked.

"I've . . . never done anything like that before. But I'll try." She closed her eyes and furrowed her brow. She grimaced as her concentration deepened, and her body began to shake.

Drew reached out to steady her, or perhaps just lend her strength, but Trevor stopped him.

"Don't. Physical contact could distract her."

Drew looked unhappy about it, but he did as Trevor suggested.

Trevor didn't know whether the Gork was the Dark Lady in disguise or just a puppet she had created to act as her avatar, but either way, it seemed clear that it was the focal point of her power in this mental landscape. At first, the creature didn't react to Amber's attempt to block the Dark Lady's psychic probes. But soon its breathing became more rapid and labored, as if it was exerting itself, although all it was doing was standing there. Then it took a single lumbering step forward, the movement clearly an effort, as if the Gork were pushing against an unseen force.

Amber gasped and took a step backward, as if she had been shoved. Her eyes sprang open in surprise, but she closed them again, stepped back to where she had been standing, and resumed concentrating.

The Gork growled, the sound rumbling forth from deep in its massive chest. It stirred a primitive fear in Trevor, rousing an ancestral memory of what it felt like to be the prey of something much larger, faster, and deadlier than a human could ever be. Trevor felt small and weak, and he was torn between two equally strong but opposing desires: to flee the scene or to stand frozen and hope the Gork would pass him by.

The creature raised its massive hands, thick fingers ending in unapelike talons. It took another step forward, moving more easily this time. Amber sucked in a hissing breath of air, as if she had just taken a punch to the stomach, but she held her ground. Standing this close to Amber, Trevor could make out her features well enough, and he saw a dark line roll down from one nostril and slide over her lips. She was bleeding.

"It's not working," Drew said. "She's slowing it down, but she can't stop it. Not by herself."

"Maybe we can pool our psychic resources, like we did in the Lowry House," Trevor said.

The Gork growled again, louder this time, and took another step forward. Amber let out a soft cry of pain and doubled over. Drew couldn't hold back any longer. He put his arm around Amber's shoulders and helped her to stand upright again.

The Gork was so large that in three steps, it had crossed two-thirds of the distance between them. Another step, and they would be within reach of those wicked-looking claws. Now that the creature was closer, Trevor should have been able to make out more details, get a better sense of what its facial features and body structure were like. But it still appeared to be a shape carved from shadow, a thing of darkness that only resembled a living creature in the crudest way. A silhouette brought to life and made three-dimensional.

The Dark Lady created this scenario from our memories of the night we searched for the Gork, Trevor thought. She had gotten the physical details of the setting—river, bank, trees, sky—correct, but since none of them had ever seen the Gork, all she'd had to work with was whatever vague images of the creature existed in their imaginations. And really, what was a monster to a kid but a big scary thing that came at you from out of the darkness? In that sense, the Dark Lady's version of the Gork was the perfect monster, just detailed enough to be terrifying but not so detailed that it became too real. Something that was real could be understood, could be fought. But how could you fight a shadow?

"We need to do something fast," Connie said. "Otherwise, we're going to end up Gork chow."

Blood was streaming from both of Amber's nostrils now, and she was trembling so hard it looked as if she were having a seizure. If it wasn't for Drew propping her up, Trevor thought she might have collapsed to the ground.

"I'm open to suggestions," he said.

"Don't look at me. You're the expert on the paranormal." Connie paused. "Although I will point out that it was awfully careless of the Dark Lady to create a scenario with a river on the verge of flooding, considering how she likely died."

At first, he didn't know what Connie was getting at, but then it came to him. Ghosts were often bound to the physical plane of existence by the circumstances of their deaths, a specific location or method of demise. It was part of what gave them their power, but it could be used against them, too.

He turned to Drew. "I've got a riddle for you. What's the best way to traumatize a drowning victim?"

Drew thought for a moment and then grinned. "Drown them again."

"The Gork is definitely a double-wide," Connie said. "At least. It's going to take all four of us to do this—and it's not going to be fun."

"Can you help us?" Drew asked Amber.

Eyes squeezed shut, jaw clamped tight, body shaking, she nevertheless managed a nod. "Just . . . say . . . when."

"When!" Trevor shouted.

Amber opened her eyes, and the four of them rushed toward the Gork. Now that she was no longer trying to hold the creature back, it stumbled forward, off balance, which gave them the edge they needed. They hit the Gork as a group, coming in from the creature's left and shoving it toward the water. Trevor expected it to be like hitting a brick wall covered with foul-smelling fur, but the Gork's body was as cold as ice, and it gave a little with the impact, almost as if it were made of rubber.

The creature let out an ear-splitting howl, the sound both angry and afraid. It tipped over the edge of the riverbank and hung there, fighting to regain its balance. For a moment, Trevor feared the creature wasn't going to go in, but then Amber stabbed her hand toward it, palm up and fingers splayed as if she were pushing air. The Gork flew backward several feet, and then, still howling, it plunged into the water with a tremendous splash. A small wave rushed toward them, and Trevor steeled himself for the sensation of being hit by cold river water. But the sensation never came.

Instead, his vision blurred, and he felt a few seconds of dizziness. When his vision cleared and his vertigo faded, he saw that the four of them were standing in an aisle between two bookshelves. Fake white webbing and black plastic spiders had been hung from the books, and life-size plastic skulls had been placed at intervals on the shelves. Spooky sound effects echoed around them, and light pulsed from strobes mounted on top of the shelves.

"We did it," Trevor said, grinning.

"We couldn't have defeated her that easily," Drew said. "Could we?"

Connie shook her head. "Not a chance. At best, we irritated her, like a bee stinging a lion. She'll try to get us again."

Trevor turned to Connie. "All right, whatever's going on with you, spill it. How did you gain your sudden insight into the supernatural?"

Before Connie could respond, Drew said, "I should think it's obvious. Her knowledge of the paranormal, her altered speech patterns, her smartass attitude . . . none of them fits the Connie Flaxman I know. That's because she's not Connie."

Trevor and Amber looked at Drew and then at Connie, comprehension dawning on their faces.

"Miss me?" Greg said.

THIRTEEN

"Can you loosen the ropes? They're cutting off my circulation."

Jenn sat tied to a wooden chair at her breakfast nook. Mitch was sitting on the couch, feet propped up on the coffee table, watching a movie on her DVR player. *When Harry Met Sally.* She thought it a strange choice for a creep like him, but although he kept muttering, "Man, that's so fucking stupid!" he seemed to be enjoying the film well enough. Who would have thought a kidnapping skuzzball like him would be into romantic comedies? From the looks of him, she would have guessed he was more into torture porn, films like *Hostel, Saw,* and *Turistas.* Considering her profession, she supposed she should have known better than to judge a book by its cover.

She strained at the ropes binding her. Then again, she doubted that his choice of entertainment meant that there was a kind heart concealed beneath his crazy-bastard exterior.

"Please?" she added. Mitch had turned the chair around to face the couch before tying her up. At first, she had thought it was because he wanted to keep an eye on her, but he hadn't paid any attention to her since the movie started.

He didn't take his gaze from the screen as he answered. "Shut up. I'm trying to watch this."

"I'm not trying to get you to loosen the ropes so I can attempt to escape. My hands and feet are going numb."

It was true. While she would have loved to get the hell away from him, this wasn't a movie and she wasn't a kickass heroine.

Even if she got free from her bonds, what could she do? She didn't know martial arts, although given her Asian heritage, many people assumed she had at least a passing acquaintance with them. And while Mitch wasn't a bodybuilder or anything, she was certain he was stronger than she was. But all that aside, she wouldn't try to escape for the simple reason that she didn't have it in her to do violence. Right now, she wished to God she did, though. There was nothing she'd like better than to beat the crap out of the sonofabitch who was holding her captive in her own home. But thinking about it and doing it were two very different things.

He sprang off the couch so fast that he was standing in front of her before she realized it. He gripped her wrists and leaned forward, pressing his weight down on them. Pain shot up her forearms, and she felt the bones in her wrist grind together. He leaned in further, until his face was only inches from hers. She imagined lunging forward, fastening her teeth on his nose, and biting down as hard as she could. But she didn't. Instead, she wrinkled her own nose at the stink of his foul breath, and she turned her head to the side, as if in a futile attempt to hide from him. As if there was anywhere she could go.

"Let's get something clear between us." His voice was low and dangerous. "You think I want to sit on your couch and watch one of your stupid movies? There are more fun things I can think of to do with a good-looking woman like you. A lot more."

He leaned even closer and took a deep breath, inhaling her scent. He moistened his lips with his tongue, and for a moment, she feared he was going to try to kiss her or lick her skin. She couldn't decide which would be worse. But then he pulled back, although he didn't release her wrists.

"So keep your mouth shut and count yourself lucky."

"Why?" The question was out of her mouth before she realized it.

He frowned. "Because I said so, that's why!"

"No, I mean why are you leaving me alone? It sounds like you don't really want to. So why are you?"

She couldn't believe she was doing this. Mitch had as much as come right out and said that he wanted to rape her, and there she was asking him why he was holding back.

When he had first approached her in the Exhibition Hall and told her that he had come to get her because Trevor, Drew, and Amber were in trouble and needed help, she hadn't questioned him. So many strange things had happened that day already, and this was just one more. So she had followed Mitch outside, got into his car, and let him drive her away from the hotel.

During the drive, she had peppered him with questions, but he hadn't answered. He had driven without looking at her, as if she no longer existed as far as he was concerned. At one point, she had reached out to touch his arm, hoping to get his attention. It had been a gentle touch, but he whirled on her as if she had punched him, teeth bared, eyes blazing with anger.

The mask of rage before her was so unlike the kind, concerned man who had walked up to her in the Exhibition Hall that for a moment, she didn't believe what she was seeing. But then he spoke, and the coldness in his voice convinced her that his transformation was genuine.

"Shut the fuck up, and don't give me any trouble, or you'll be the second person I've killed today."

He faced forward again, and she shut up. And when he drove her to Forgotten Lore, parked in the alley behind the building, and told her to get out of the car, she did. She also unlocked the back door at his command and led him up the stairs to her living quarters above the store. At first, she had been relieved when he tied her to the chair—she had been expecting him to force her into the bedroom—but as the minutes dragged on, the fear had returned. She'd wanted to believe that if he tied her up, it was because he wanted to keep her alive. But a new thought had crept into her mind, a dark, nasty, skittering cockroach of a thought: maybe he was saving her for later.

Maybe he was building up an appetite.

Now, as he looked at her, expression unreadable, her heart thudded in her chest, and cold nausea churned in her stomach. She didn't want to goad him into hurting her, but she could no longer sit in silence, waiting to see what he would do.

He frowned as he considered her question. "Because it's what I'm supposed to do. Besides, you're not her."

"Not Amber."

He didn't respond, but she knew she was right.

"If you're not supposed to hurt me, why don't you let me go?" She doubted it would be so easy to get him to release her, but she had to try. Besides, he might go for it. He *was* crazy, after all.

He looked uncomfortable, as if he didn't want to talk about it. But he answered anyway. "If I do what she says, she'll give me Amber."

"She?" Jenn was confused. The only other woman involved in this mess that she knew of was Connie. Then it came to her. "You mean the Dark Lady?"

He said nothing, but his lowered gaze and subdued expression answered for him.

"She's like, what? Your boss?"

Mitch's hand lashed out, bright pain flared in her jaw, and an instant later, she found herself lying on the floor without any idea how she had gotten there. Had she blacked out, just for an instant? She thought she might have.

Mitch crouched down and leaned his face in close to hers. "I'm my own man. No one tells me what to do, least of all some freaky-ass ghost bitch. Got it?"

Her jaw throbbed, and the side of her head ached. She wondered if she had cracked her skull on the floor when the chair tipped over. When she didn't respond right away, he grabbed hold of her ear and gave it a sharp twist.

"Got it?"

Wincing, she nodded.

He gave her ear a last hard pinch before releasing it and standing. He looked down at her for a moment, as if considering. "I think I'll leave you lying there. You're still tied up nice and tight. Maybe you'll take a nap or something and let me watch my goddamned movie in peace."

He started back toward the couch, but halfway there, he stopped. Standing in the middle of the room was a black-garbed woman with long raven hair and marble-white skin. She was soaking wet, and rivulets of water ran off her and pooled on the floor around her pale feet. Mitch's back was turned toward Jenn, so she couldn't see his face, but from the way he froze at the sight of the Dark Lady, she knew he was terrified of the apparition.

She supposed she should have been afraid, too, but instead, she felt only awe.

I'm looking at a ghost, she thought. *An honest-to-God house-haunting, chain-rattling ghost.* Although why the Dark Lady was soaking wet from head to toe, she had no idea. Not that it mattered. Jenn knew that whatever happened after that moment, however long, or short, her life might be, she would never again doubt the existence of the paranormal. She hoped she would get a chance to tell Trevor. She could imagine how he would joke about it, using humor to try to take away some of the pain she had experienced.

She could almost hear him say, "If I'd known that all it would take to open your mind was getting kidnapped by a psycho, I'd have abducted you myself years ago." Despite the situation, the thought made her smile. It was a comfort to have Trevor there with her, even if only in spirit.

"I did like you said." Mitch's tone was defensive. "I brought her here, and I haven't touched her." He glanced over his shoulder at

Jenn lying on the floor. When he turned back to face the Dark Lady, his words tumbled out in a rush. "It was an accident! I didn't mean to hit her so hard! She—"

The Dark Lady became an ebony blur as she darted forward and fastened marble-white hands around Mitch's throat. He made a strained gurgling sound as his airway was cut off, and he reached up and grabbed the Dark Lady's wrists. He attempted to pull her hands away, but although he was physically larger than she, he couldn't break her grip.

"I told you: she is not to be harmed."

The Dark Lady didn't open her mouth as she spoke. Instead, Jenn heard her words in her mind, as if they were her own thoughts. The "voice" was a cold one, though, as harsh and unforgiving as a blast of winter wind.

Mitch tried to answer, but all he could get out was a few wet clicks. The Dark Lady maintained her grip on his throat a moment longer, and then she released him. He crumpled to his hands and knees, gasping for air.

The Dark Lady turned her attention to Jenn. Although the ghost made no move toward her, didn't so much as gesture, Jenn's chair gently righted itself.

"My apologies."

Not knowing how else to respond, Jenn nodded. She felt it best not to speak. The Dark Lady might not have shown any aggression toward her yet, but Jenn knew better than to think the ghost was benign. After all, if Trevor and his friends were right, she was the one who'd killed Tonya. Jenn feared that if she said the wrong thing, it would be her turn to feel those cold white hands encircling her neck.

The Dark Lady looked down at Mitch, and her impassive features became an expression of contempt. *"Get up."*

Mitch rose to his feet. His breathing was raspy, but otherwise he seemed OK.

Too bad, Jenn thought.

"Put a gag on her, and double-check her bonds to make sure she can't get loose. You and I have more work to do." She glanced at Jenn. *"When this is all over, if you still want her, you can have her, too."*

Mitch gave Jenn a grin that was full of dark promise. It scared her just as much as the Dark Lady did.

Maybe more.

Amber didn't think she had any more tears to shed, but when the medical examiner's people wheeled Ray's sheet-covered body away, more started falling. Drew had kept his arm around her ever since they had driven the Dark Lady from the library, and she was more grateful than ever for his support. Confronting a supernatural force was hard enough, but dealing with the aftermath of that force's attack was far worse. Especially when it resulted in the death of someone you knew.

"I've never understood why a ghost would want to kill a living person," Trevor said. "I mean, all that does is create another ghost."

"Once a soul is brought over into the afterworld, it's much easier to torment," Greg said. "Trying to harass someone across the dimensional boundary is like sending threatening e-mails to a person on the other side of the planet. There's only so much harm you can do. But once you've dragged a soul over to your side of the metaphysical fence, there's no end to the fun you can have with them."

"Thanks for *that* disturbing tidbit of information," Trevor said. "I was happier when you were pretending to be Connie."

On one level, Greg's revelation of his true identity hadn't come as a surprise to Amber. It explained "Connie's" odd behavior and the strange sense of familiarity that Amber had increasingly felt around the woman. But now that she knew the truth, she was experiencing what Drew would call cognitive dissonance. Hearing Greg's words coming out of Connie's mouth in Connie's voice was, simply put, wrong. But there was one thing she didn't understand.

"Why didn't I sense that you'd taken possession of Connie?" she asked.

Greg smiled with Connie's mouth. "You're talented, but you're new at the whole psychic thing. It wasn't difficult for me to block your perceptions."

Chief Hoffman and a number of his officers had arrived not long after Amber and the others had emerged from the maze. They were taking statements from various witnesses, and Hoffman himself was questioning Erin and Carrington over by the circulation desk. Pattie sat with Sarah by the snack bar while a paramedic tended to the latter's shoulder wound. Pattie held Sarah's hand, her own tears trickling down her face. Sarah winced as the paramedic cleaned her wound, but she didn't cry out in pain. Considering how bad it must have hurt, Amber thought that was something of a miracle. Amber and her friends stood in a small group between the snack bar and the circulation desk, right where the chief had asked them to stay until he could get around to speaking with them.

One of the paramedics, when she saw the blood staining Amber's blouse, had offered to take a look at her, but Amber had declined, saying it was only the result of a bloody nose and that since the bleeding had stopped, she was OK. In truth, she had no idea if she was OK or not. She had never engaged in psychic warfare before, had never considered that she could be capable of such a thing. That battling the Dark Lady had taken a toll on her was clear. She felt drained of energy, and it was a struggle to keep her eyes open. She wanted to crawl into bed and sleep for a month. But was it possible that her brain had suffered injury during the struggle? And if so, how bad? Was she in danger of having a stroke or an embolism? She wondered if Greg might know, but she didn't want to ask him in front of Drew. She decided to do her best not to worry about herself right then. They had more important things to deal with, like making sure the Dark Lady didn't claim any more victims.

Hoffman finished with Erin and Carrington and came walking over to them. *He looks so tired,* Amber thought.

"Hell of a thing, huh?" he said.

He sounded tired, too, as if he would rather be anywhere else in the world than there. She knew exactly how he felt.

Carrington walked past them as he headed over to Sarah and Pattie. Erin accompanied him until she reached Amber and the others, then she stopped to listen in as the chief questioned them. That the woman didn't go check on her wounded crew member first spoke volumes about what kind of person she was, Amber thought.

"To be honest, I'm not sure I want to talk to you folks," Hoffman said. "What I've heard so far is wild enough. I really don't want to hear whatever craziness you have to add."

"All you need to know is that a supernatural force is responsible for the killings in your town," Drew said. "We're going to do everything we can to stop it, but it would help if you didn't make it easier for the spirit to find more victims."

Hoffman sighed. "You're talking about canceling the parade, aren't you? If I tried to do that, the mayor would go ballistic, and the Chamber of Commerce would want to string me up from the nearest tree."

"Four people have died—" Trevor began.

"Six," Hoffman interrupted. "I just got a call a few minutes ago. The head librarian died before they could load him into the ambulance. And a student named Emily Fernandez died on the way to the hospital." He paused. "She was just eighteen."

"Don't forget Alex," Amber said. "He died last week, and we think the spirit is responsible for his death, too." She looked at Erin, but the woman said nothing.

"Seven people, then," Hoffman said.

"And there's all the people who were injured in this attack," Drew said. "Along with the physical wounds, they've suffered significant psychological trauma."

"And they're the lucky ones," Trevor said. "At least they're still alive."

"Ever heard the phrase 'shooting fish in a barrel'?" Greg said. "If you allow the parade to go on as scheduled, it will be a disaster."

"All right," Hoffman said wearily. "I'll talk to the mayor and see if I can persuade her to cancel the parade." He shook his head. "I don't understand it. If Exeter really is haunted—and right now, I can't deny that it is—why would a ghost suddenly become violent now, after all these years?"

"We have a theory," Drew said. "We believe the spirit feels threatened by Erin's documentary."

Erin looked uncomfortable, but she didn't say anything.

"Seriously?" Hoffman said. He looked at them all for a moment and then sighed. "I want you all to tell me something straight, no bullshit. Can you really stop this ghost or spirit or whatever the hell it is?"

Amber looked at her friends, and they in turn looked at her.

"We can damn well try," she said.

When Hoffman had finished with them, he moved off, took out his cell phone, and placed a call—to the mayor, Amber assumed. Erin finally went over to check on Sarah and Pattie. Carrington sat at the table next to them as the paramedic finished dressing Sarah's wound. The paramedic was talking to Sarah, but whatever he was saying, Sarah wasn't happy about it. Amber couldn't hear her words, but it was clear from the animated way she was speaking that she was upset. Pattie tried to soothe her, but Sarah wasn't having any of it.

Drew noticed, too. "Maybe I should go over and see if I can help," he said.

"Not right now," Trevor said. "We have a bigger problem to deal with. We've just learned that our friend has returned from the dead and possessed the body of your boss."

The three of them turned to look at Greg.

"Would it help if I told you that Connie gave me permission to borrow her body?" he said.

"Only if it's the truth," Drew said. "And even then, I'd be concerned about the potential psychic damage to Connie's mind."

Greg sighed. "I can see that this whole redemption thing is going to be awfully inconvenient sometimes. Very well. Connie did not give me permission, but I assure you, no harm will come to her as a result of serving as my meat suit. At least, not for a day or two. After that . . . well, let's just say that if I overstay my welcome, the effects on Connie won't be pleasant."

"Why did you do this?" Amber said. "You've stolen her body, forced yourself on her in a way even worse than rape. A rapist violates the body. You've violated her spirit."

"I could tell you that right and wrong aren't viewed the same way on the Other Side, and that would be true enough. But the simple fact is that my friends were in danger, and I had to do something to help. It's my responsibility. This"—he gestured at Connie's body—"was the only thing I *could* do."

"It was wrong," Amber said.

"Maybe," Greg allowed. "All right, yes, I suppose it was. But cut me some slack. I'm new to the whole good-guy thing."

"I hate to admit it," Trevor said, "but we can use his help. With his powers—"

"Before you head too far down that road, I no longer have any special abilities. I was able to possess Connie's body, and I'm more sensitive to the presence of paranormal energy than most humans, but that's all. The abilities I commanded while alive were the result of all of the dark power that I'd absorbed over the years. When I died, I carried that power with me to the Other Side, and I managed to shed most of it. I'm still 'tainted' by Darkness, for lack of a better way to explain it, but I no longer have the mojo I once did."

"So you're not going to be able to wave your hand and send the Dark Lady running home in tears," Trevor said. "Too bad. It would've saved us some work."

"While I appreciate your motives, Greg," Drew said, "I can't condone your stealing Connie's body and using it for your own purposes. By helping us with this investigation, you're placing Connie in danger. There's no risk to you; you're already dead. But if the Dark Lady attacks you, Connie's body could be seriously injured, and she could die. You're risking a life that doesn't belong to you."

"I might not be able to make the Dark Lady go poof just by wishing it, but I'm better psychically equipped to resist her than the rest of you." He smiled at Amber. "Not counting you, of course, my dear." He faced Drew once more. "But if you think there's no risk to me in going up against the Dark Lady, you're mistaken. The Other Side is far more complex than you can possibly imagine, and death—to coin a cliché—is only the beginning. Consider how vast this planet is, how diverse the forms of life that inhabit it. The Other Side is so much larger, and the beings that dwell there are equally as varied: everything that's ever died in the entire universe, things that never lived or only nearly lived, things that did live but shouldn't have, things that only partially lived . . . and that's not to mention the creatures that are native to the Other Side, some of which come to *this* world when they die. Just because I'm dead doesn't mean I'm immune from harm, Drew. Not by a long shot."

"Don't expect any sympathy from us," Amber said. "You made your choice. But Connie didn't have one."

"She's fine. I promise." Greg hesitated and then added, "For the moment."

"What does that mean?" Drew asked.

"The longer my stay, the more risk there is to Connie's mind, both physically and psychologically," Greg said. "For the first twenty-four hours or so, any damage done to her will be minimal. After that . . . well, for Connie's sake, let's hope we can exorcise the Dark Lady sooner rather than later."

"If we let you stay and help us, you have to promise that you'll leave Connie's body if it becomes too dangerous for her," Amber said.

"If *you* let me?" Greg smiled. "What makes you think any of you can stop me?"

Amber gave him a hard stare. "You saw what I did to the Dark Lady when we were in the maze. I don't know if I can push an invading ghost out of a person's body, but I can give it a good try."

Greg looked at her for a moment, and something dark and dangerous moved in his gaze. But then he gave her a genuinely affectionate smile. "It looks like our little girl is all grown up. Very well. If Connie's brains show signs of becoming scrambled, I promise I'll bail out. Good enough?"

Amber looked at the others. Drew and Trevor nodded. "All right," she said. "But from this point on, no lies and no tricks."

"Cross my heart and . . . you know."

"So what's our next move?" Amber asked. "Even if the chief manages to cancel the parade, there are still thousands of tourists in town, not to mention all the people who live here. And every one of them is in danger as long as the Dark Lady is active."

"We need to learn more about Erin's film," Drew said. "If her documentary was the catalyst for the Dark Lady becoming violent, maybe we can find something in the footage that will give us a clue to stopping her."

"We need to look at her background research, too," Trevor added. "And I've written several articles about Exeter over the years. I still have that research on my laptop. I'll go through it and see what I can turn up."

"Carrington may appear to be little more than a showman," Greg said, "but he's been around the paranormal block a few times. I wouldn't be surprised if he has more insight into this haunting than even he's aware of. We need to sit down with him for a nice, long chat."

"Maybe I can somehow make psychic contact with the Dark Lady," Amber said. "If so, perhaps she'll tell us what she wants."

"You want to perform a séance?" Trevor said. "That is so cool!"

"It sounds dangerous," Drew said. "We know the Dark Lady can attack on the psychic plane. If you open your mind to her, you could be taking a terrible risk."

"Drew's vastly understating the matter," Greg said. "The Dark Lady isn't some simple earthbound spirit you can ask a few questions of with a Ouija board. Trying to touch her mind directly would be the psychic equivalent of taking a high-voltage power line and touching the exposed end to your tongue. The result would be Very Bad."

Trevor frowned. "You sound as if you know more about the Dark Lady than you're letting on. If you're holding out on us . . ."

"It doesn't take a genius to see how powerful the Dark Lady is," Greg said. "She's clearly not your run-of-the-mill ghost, but other than that, I have no more idea of her true nature than you do." Greg appeared suddenly uncomfortable. "However . . ."

Amber didn't like the sound of this. "What?"

"I'm afraid I might know what stirred her up in the first place."

"Sure," Trevor said. "Erin's film."

"That may well be what's drawing her ire at the moment," Greg said, "but it's not what awakened her in the first place."

"What was it, then?" Drew said.

Greg smiled sheepishly. "Actually, it was me."

"I wish you'd let me take you to the hospital in Exeter."

The speed limit on the highway was seventy, but Pattie was doing close to eighty-five. Her Citation's engine sounded as if it were grinding itself to pieces, and the car shimmied as it hurtled down the road. *Shouldn't have put off getting the old gal's wheels aligned,* she thought.

Sarah sat next to her on the passenger seat. Her face was pale, and she winced every time the car hit a bump or a pothole. The paramedic had bandaged her shoulder wound, but she hadn't given Sarah any painkillers. All they had in the car was some ibuprofen, and although Sarah had dry-swallowed a handful in the college parking lot, Pattie doubted the pills had done much to relieve her pain.

"I'm more than happy to go to a hospital. In fact, right now, it's my most fervent desire in all the world. But I won't stay in that goddamned town another minute, and if that means I bleed to death, then so be it."

Pattie slammed her hand down on the steering wheel. "Don't talk like that! You are *not* going to die!"

Pattie had used her iPhone to connect to the Internet, find the closest town with another hospital, and look up directions. Richmond was forty-eight miles from Exeter, and at their current speed, Pattie estimated they would get there in about thirty-five minutes. The paramedic had done what she could for Sarah, but she wasn't a doctor. Pattie prayed that Sarah would make it.

Although she was furious with Sarah for refusing to go to the hospital in Exeter, she had to admit that if their roles were reversed, she would have done the same thing. When Erin had first hired them to work on her documentary, it sounded like a fun project. Neither she nor Sarah was a believer in the paranormal, but they weren't really skeptics, either. She supposed the best way to describe their attitude toward strange phenomena was open-minded but not gullible. The shoot had started off enjoyably enough, until Alex's accident. They hadn't known him before taking the gig, but he had been a good guy, and his death had hit them hard. But they hadn't considered quitting. They were both professionals, and Sarah especially was determined to build up her résumé. She hoped to use this project as a springboard to bigger and better things. Pattie was older and didn't have quite so much fire in the belly anymore. She was content to work on small films for even smaller paychecks, but she loved Sarah and was determined to support her dreams.

And Erin, master manipulator that she was, had given them the "We need to finish this film for Alex" speech, and they had bought it. Even Ray, who was the most cynical of the crew, had wanted to continue shooting as a way to honor Alex's memory.

God, poor Ray! When she thought about what happened to him . . . She hadn't seen him die, had been too busy trying to keep Sarah from bleeding out, but she had heard the terrible sound of him hitting the floor, and she had seen his body afterward—head burst like an overripe melon, neck snapped, arms and legs bent at sickening angles. Even Erin hadn't tried to persuade them to stay after that. When Pattie had told her they were leaving, she had only nodded. She hadn't said anything, not even good-bye.

"Fucking bitch," Sarah muttered.

Pattie didn't have to ask whom she was referring to.

Sarah went on. "I can understand her not wanting to quit after Alex died. His death seemed like an accident to all of us. But she should have called the project off as soon as that girl died in the bookstore. But no, all Erin could think about was the publicity her film would get. Like the girl's death was the best free marketing tool she could ever have hoped for. Then those two people died in the museum, and those freaky words appeared . . ." Sarah shuddered. "As soon as you know there's a killer ghost on the loose—and for some reason, she's pissed off because you're making a movie in her town—you call off the goddamned project!"

Pattie knew she was just venting. She was in pain and in shock, both physically and emotionally, and she was looking for someone, anyone, to blame for what had happened. Preferably someone living. It was a lot easier, and safer, to blame another human being than a malign otherworldly force that you couldn't understand.

Pattie knew she should keep her mouth shut. But when she was upset, she became hyperverbal, and despite her better judgment, she found herself saying, "We chose to stay. It's not like Erin held a gun to our heads."

Sarah glared at her. "Since when did you become such a big fan of Erin's? Do you have the hots for her or something?"

Shut up, shut up, shut up! Pattie warned herself. "Of course not! At this point, I hate the woman as much as you do! But I'm not going to blame her for a choice I made, and you shouldn't, either."

"She's closer to your age than I am. That's it, isn't it? I don't have enough life experience for you or some bullshit like that."

This was rapidly veering off into an old argument between them. Sarah was sometimes insecure in their relationship, especially when it came to their age difference. She was afraid she wasn't smart enough or hadn't experienced enough in life to hold Pattie's interest long-term, and no matter how often Pattie tried to reassure her, those doubts flared up from time to time.

Pattie wanted to tell her that she was being foolish, that it was hardly the best time to get into that issue again, and besides that, they had been together for four years. In that time, had she shown the slightest hint of being bored in their relationship? Had she ever so much as looked at another woman? Well, maybe *looked,* but had she ever actually done anything?

But instead, she took one hand off the steering wheel, reached across the seat, took Sarah's hand, and squeezed it hard. "I love you."

Sarah opened her mouth, and for a second, Pattie thought she would continue the argument. But she smiled and said, "I love you, too."

"Good," Pattie said, smiling. "Now that we've got that settled, let's—"

She broke off. Standing on the road in front of them was an

ivory-fleshed woman with long raven hair. They were going too fast to stop, and out of reflex, Pattie yanked the steering wheel hard to the right—at eighty-five miles per hour.

The laws of physics can be a real bitch sometimes, and when what was left of the Citation finally rolled to a stop, Pattie and Sarah no longer had to worry about getting to a hospital, for no doctor in the world could help them anymore.

FOURTEEN

Peter Hoffman was an Exeter native. Growing up in the "Most Haunted Town in America" had been fun when he was a kid, especially when the Dead Days festival came around. But by the time he was in high school, he had grown tired of living in a perpetual spook show, as so many Exeter teens did, and more than a little embarrassed by it. So after graduation, he took classes at Tri-County Community College for a year before moving to Indianapolis to enroll in the police academy. It wasn't so much that he wanted to be a big-city cop as that he just wanted to get the hell out of Exeter and never return. He was the youngest of four children, all of whom had moved out of town as soon as they could. His mom died of breast cancer when he was in junior high, and his dad remarried during Peter's first year of college and moved with his new wife to Florida. So it wasn't as if he had anything or anyone to tie him to Exeter.

And then he met Beth.

She had been working at a Steak and Shake in downtown Indy back then, and Peter ate there often, partly because it was the best he could afford but mostly so he could see her. She was a petite brunette with jet-black hair, full lips, bright blue eyes, and the most joyful smile he had ever seen. It took him two months to work up the courage to say hi to her, and when he did, she gave him that wonderful smile and said, "What took you so long?"

Six months later, they were married. Everything was great between them, except for one thing: Beth was fascinated by his hometown. She loved anything to do with the paranormal or the occult, and when she found out that he was from Exeter, she peppered him with questions about what it had been like to grow up there. "Was your house haunted? Did you ever see a real ghost? Do you know anyone who did? Is it really the most haunted town in the country? How do they know? I mean, it's not like they can take a ghost census or anything."

Her fascination with Exeter had almost driven him away, especially when he began to get the feeling that she was primarily interested in him because of his hometown. But he stuck it out, and eventually, Beth's interest in Exeter waned—that, or she figured out that it was bugging him—and her questions stopped. But when Halloween rolled around, she asked him to take her to Dead Days, and while he had been reluctant at first, he gave in and was surprised to find himself enjoying the festivities, truly enjoying them, for the first time since he was a kid. Dead Days was all new to Beth; she loved every second of it, and her enthusiasm was contagious. They returned to Dead Days the next year, and when Peter graduated from the academy and learned that a job had opened up in the Exeter police department, he made the mistake of mentioning it to Beth.

She urged him to apply, which he did, mostly to humor her. He got an interview, and before he knew it, he was offered a position. He didn't want to take it. But Beth had said, "Imagine how much fun our kids will have growing up there!" It was the "our kids" that did it. He took the job and moved back to the town he'd once wanted so desperately to escape. He told himself that whatever he did, he would never apply to be chief, but when the old chief retired, there really hadn't been anyone else who wanted the job— or could do it as well as him, for that matter—and so he had taken it. And he had been chief ever since.

It had been hard going the last few years since Beth had died from uterine cancer, but all told, it hadn't been a bad life. He still found Exeter irritating, but over the years, he had developed a grudging fondness for the town, and he even looked forward to Dead Days—not that he would ever admit it to anyone. But this year . . . Jesus Christ, what a mess! Seven people dead, and who knew how many more if he couldn't persuade Mayor Shinn to cancel the parade. When he had called her from the college library to talk to her about it, she had accused him of being drunk on the job and threatened to fire him. He couldn't blame her. If one of his people called him with a wild story about killer ghosts that swam through the air, he would have thought the same thing. He had persisted, though, stressing the number of people who had died so far. "Whatever the cause of their deaths," he had said, "it's clear something bad is going on here. Do you really want to fill the streets with hundreds of more potential victims tonight?"

That had given her pause but not for long. "Can you imagine the kind of shitstorm the media will stir up when they find out the Most Haunted Town in America canceled its annual Halloween parade because they were afraid they had a murderous ghost on the loose? Exeter will be the laughingstock of the country!"

He had continued trying, but the mayor's mind was made up. She disconnected, but not before telling him that if he wanted to keep his job, he wouldn't say another word about ghosts until Dead Days was over.

He turned his attention to getting the crime scene at the library squared away, and once he was satisfied that his people could handle things without him, he had gotten into his cruiser and headed off in search of the mayor. She was stubborn, and once she made up her mind, she didn't change it easily, but he hoped that if he spoke with her face-to-face, he could make her see how serious the situation was.

She wouldn't be in her office. Normally, she wouldn't be in on a Saturday anyway, but this was Dead Days. Throughout the week, she appeared at one event after another, sometimes giving speeches,

sometimes introducing speakers or performers, sometimes participating in apple-bobbing, face painting, or storytelling. No event
was too small, no activity too juvenile. She was indefatigable when
it came to hobnobbing with her constituents, especially during this
time of year, and she had told him on more than one occasion that
being highly visible during Dead Days was how she kept winning
elections. He had tried calling her several times to find out where
she was, but she hadn't picked up. Either she was too busy, or she
was ignoring his calls. He suspected the latter. If this had been a
weekday, he could have called her assistant and gotten her itiner-
ary, but no one was in the office on weekends, especially not this
weekend. So that meant he had to track her down.

Exeter wasn't big enough or dangerous enough for the mayor to
feel she needed a police escort when in public—and in general,
he agreed with her—so he couldn't just call his people and get her
location. He had called the department dispatcher and asked her
to tell the officers on patrol to call in if they spotted the mayor, but
he didn't expect to hear anything. He'd had to pull about half his
people off patrol to help out at the library, and while the town hired
extra security for Dead Days, they were locals who were paid minimum wage and generally not the sharpest knives in the drawer. His
plan was to head downtown, drive around, and see if he could spot
her. If that didn't work, he would head over to her house, park outside, and wait. She would return home to change into her costume
before the parade. She always rode on one of the floats, and every
year, she chose a different, more elaborate costume. The townspeople always looked forward to seeing their mayor reveal her latest
Halloween finery, and she kept her outfit a closely guarded secret.
Whatever it was, it would take her at least a couple of hours to get
ready, and he hoped he would be able to persuade her to cancel the
parade before she applied her first line of makeup. But that was a
last resort. The sooner he found her, the better.

He decided to start at Oakgrove Park. Every year, the town held a scarecrow-making contest there on the Saturday of Dead Days, and while the mayor wasn't one of the judges as far as he knew, she usually made an appearance at the event. He figured it would be a good first stop. Who knew? Maybe he would get lucky.

Oakgrove was in the midst of an upper-class suburban neighborhood, and as he approached the park entrance, he saw a man standing on the sidewalk. Peter had never seen the man before, he was sure of that, and yet there was a nagging familiarity about him, as if he should recognize him. The man was facing the street, and as Peter drove by, slowing to take a better look, he grinned and waved.

And that's when Peter remembered: he *had* seen the sonofabitch before, at least a picture of him. It was Mitch Sagers, the bastard who was stalking Ms. Lozier, the one she suspected might have committed one of the murders at the museum. After she had told Peter about Mitch, he had contacted the Ohio BMV and requested that a copy of Sagers's driver's license be sent to him. It arrived via e-mail shortly thereafter, and he'd had the photo copied, downloaded to his officers' phones, and printed out in hard copy as well. He had ordered his people, along with the temp security, to keep watch for Sagers, but after what had happened at the library, Peter had forgotten about the man. But there he was, standing on the sidewalk, taunting the chief of police as he drove by.

Cocky motherfucker, Peter thought. That, or he was batshit crazy. Probably a little of both.

He whipped his steering wheel to the right, parked his cruiser with the front passenger-side wheel up on the curb, and exited the vehicle without pausing to turn off the engine. He had his gun drawn before he spoke his first syllable.

"Mitch Sagers!"

The man didn't react, just stood there grinning like an idiot. He didn't seem concerned that a police officer was pointing a gun at him. More as if he thought it was amusing, as if Peter were nothing more than a child trying to act tough while holding a squirt gun.

"Put your hands on your head!" Peter ordered.

Sagers still didn't respond, but there was something about the way the man was standing, head slightly cocked to the left, a small furrow in his brow, that gave Peter the impression that he was listening to something only he could hear.

Peter started walking slowly toward him. "I told you to put your hands on your head!"

Sagers's gaze was fixed on him as he approached, but he remained relaxed and continued grinning. Peter had never seen anyone stay so cool when they had a gun trained on them, and he found it more than a little spooky. For an instant, Peter was tempted to forgo his training and put a bullet in Sagers, maybe one in the leg or the shoulder. Not enough to kill him but enough to take the starch out of him. Something told him that Sagers was that dangerous, although the man had done nothing to indicate that he was any sort of threat. Aside from allegedly strangling someone, that is. Peter stuck to his training and didn't fire, although his finger did tighten on the trigger.

He was about to order Sagers to lie facedown on the ground, but then the air to the man's left rippled, almost like waves of heat distortion rising off summer asphalt, and for an instant, Peter thought he saw a woman standing next to Sagers. Bone-white skin, raven-black hair, a dress as dark as night, eyes as empty and cold as the depths of space. But then the air rippled again, and she was gone— if she had ever been there in the first place.

Sagers turned and ran toward the park entrance. Peter almost squeezed off a shot, but he restrained himself. The scarecrow contest. Families, kids. He didn't want to start a panic or, God forbid, hit anyone with a stray bullet.

He should have run back to his car, got on the radio, and called for backup. But Sagers was already inside the park, with all of those innocent people, and Peter didn't want to give the sonofabitch the chance to hurt anyone else. Still holding on to his weapon, he ran into the park in pursuit.

The scarecrows were being constructed on one of the soccer fields. There were more people watching than building, most of them snacking on food they had bought at the concession stand—apple cider, hot chocolate, pumpkin muffins, skull-shaped candy, and caramel popcorn balls. Peter remembered how much Beth had loved the popcorn balls, always eating too many and complaining about how her stomach hurt afterward. Funny the things you missed when someone you loved died, and funny how you remembered them at the strangest times.

Luckily, Sagers wasn't running toward the soccer field. He was headed deeper into the park, and Peter followed. Past the playground and tennis courts, past the fenced-in field where folks could let their dogs loose to play. Peter wasn't like some cops, who let themselves go once they hit middle age. He tried to eat right and exercise, even if he didn't always manage to do so as regularly as he would have liked. In the academy, they taught you that your mind and body were two of your most important tools as a law-enforcement professional, and it was important to keep both of them fit. But even with his adrenaline pumping, Peter found himself becoming winded and slowing down.

Getting old, he told himself. Time was when he could have run down a suspect with no problem. Now, if he didn't pour on the gas, Sagers would get away.

Maybe I should've put a bullet in him after all, he thought.

There were woods at the back of the park, with a few hiking trails and a small stream where elementary-school science teachers would bring their students to gather water samples and collect tadpoles. Sagers plunged into the woods without stopping, and by the time Peter got there, he was sucking wind and trying to ignore the painful stitch in his side.

Definitely should've shot him.

He paused for a couple of seconds to catch his breath, not that it helped much, before heading into the woods. He knew there was a good chance that he could be walking into a trap, but that didn't matter. As far as he was concerned, *to serve and protect* was more than mere words. It was his job to put his ass on the line for the people of Exeter, and if that meant—

He saw the rock coming toward his face a split second before it connected. It was almost as big as Sagers's hand, and he was surprised the man could maintain hold of it. But when he slammed it into Peter's temple, there was no doubt that his grip was solid. Light bursts flared brightly behind Peter's eyes, followed by darkness.

He didn't remain unconscious for long. When he opened his eyes, he saw scattered blades of grass sticking up through bare, moist earth inches from his face, and he knew he was lying on the trail. He felt a sticky warmth on the side of his head that he figured was blood, and his skull pounded as if someone were taking a jackhammer to it from the inside.

Sagers stepped into his view. Peter's vision was blurry, but he could make out the man well enough. He was holding a different rock, much larger and heavier than the first, one that took him both hands to carry.

"My friend wants me to give you a message," he said. "The show must go on."

Sagers grinned as he stepped forward and lifted the rock over his head. The last thing Peter saw was the black-haired woman standing off to the side, smiling. *See you in a minute, Beth,* he thought.

Then Sagers brought the rock down.

"I came here about six months ago," Greg said. "It was early spring."

Trevor kept his eyes fastened on the road ahead of them. Greg—in Connie's body—sat on the passenger seat next to him. They were headed back to the conference hotel. Erin and Carrington following in Erin's VW. Trevor wasn't afraid to look at Greg, not exactly, although he supposed he should have been freaked out by the fact that his friend had returned from the dead. But he couldn't get used to hearing Greg speak with Connie's voice, and it didn't help that Connie's physical form remained as gorgeous as ever. He imagined that Drew would have a field day analyzing the Freudian underpinnings of his discomfort, but all Trevor knew was that looking at Greg squicked him out big-time.

"I had already come up with my plan to reunite the four of us at the Lowry House, and while I had plenty of psychospiritual energy at my command, I figured I could always use more, especially if I wanted to impress you. Creating psychic illusions takes a great deal of power, you know. Even more if you want your illusions to be able to have an impact on the material world."

Drew and Amber sat in the backseat. In the rearview mirror, Trevor saw Drew lean forward and turn toward Greg.

"That *impact* resulted in the deaths of two men."

Greg sighed. "You're never going to let up on that, are you? At any rate, I had known about Exeter for a number of years. While the Darkness within me sometimes guided me to sites of paranormal energy to absorb, other sites I found through my own research. I'd always meant to visit Exeter, but I'd never gotten around to it. The 'Most Haunted Town in America.' Honestly, it sounded like a slogan designed to lure in gullible tourists, and I didn't expect there to be any significant energy present in the town, but I decided it was time to at least look into it. And when I got here . . ."

"The Dark Lady was waiting for you," Amber said.

"Not exactly. But I could sense the town's power ten miles out. It was so strong that I had trouble concentrating while I was driving, and I nearly ran off the road a couple of times. For a nonpsychically gifted human, it would have been the equivalent of trying to drive into the face of a hurricane while suffering a migraine. But

I persevered and reached the town. Once I was there, the psychic pressure eased somewhat, and I parked in the main business district, got out of my car, and wandered around, scenting the spiritual air, so to speak. Now that I was in the midst of the town, I was better able to detect the nature of the power that dwelled there. As I said, it was strong—stronger than anything I had ever experienced before—and it was, if not sleeping, at least quiet. I was, as you might imagine, extremely excited by the prospect of gobbling down so much power, and I made my way to an alley between a pair of businesses, sat down with my back against a wall, closed my eyes, and reached out with my mind."

"I bet I can guess what happened next," Trevor said. "The town woke up."

"That it did," Greg said. "And it wasn't happy. It attacked me, and the pain I felt was beyond anything I thought possible. Both my body and my spirit were in agony. I tried to fight back, but it was useless. I was overwhelmed and blacked out. When I came to, I was behind the wheel of my Lexus, driving on a highway a hundred miles from Exeter."

"So it kicked your ass," Trevor said, not without some measure of satisfaction.

"Thoroughly," Greg said. He admitted this without hesitation or wounded pride.

"There's more to it than that, isn't there?" Amber said. "I can feel it."

Greg turned around in his seat and scowled at her. "It's one thing to explore the expanded range of your psychic abilities, dear heart, but it's quite another to use them as an excuse to be nosy."

"Greg . . ." she warned.

"Very well. I did plan to return to Exeter and try to absorb its energy again. But I knew I wouldn't be able to do the job on my own."

"You were going to take us with you," Drew said. "Once you'd managed to infect us with your Darkness, you'd have three partners to help you."

"Yes, although that wasn't the only reason I wanted to turn you," Greg said. "At the time, I truly believed I was offering you a great gift." He paused and then added, "And I was lonely."

"Spare us the sob story," Trevor said. "It's awfully convenient that you've returned to the land of the living to help us with a problem in the very town whose psychic energy you once coveted. Have you come back to find a way to capture that energy for yourself, maybe even use it to be reincarnated in a new physical form? Then you can pick right up where you left off, toying with people for your amusement and killing them when you get bored."

Greg leaned across the seat until his face—or, rather, Connie's face—was only inches from Trevor's. When he spoke, his voice was tight with anger. "At my current strength, I couldn't absorb the smallest iota of psychic energy if I wanted to. If I tried, the town would destroy me as easily as you would swat a fly. I'm here because I made a mess, and it's my responsibility to help clean it up. And because my friends are in danger."

He leaned back in his seat and turned to look out the passenger window. In a calmer voice, one tinged with sadness, he said, "I don't expect any of you to trust me. Why should you, after all the things I did? But what I've told you is the truth, and you can take it or leave it as you wish." He fell silent after that.

Trevor glanced over his shoulder at Drew and Amber. They looked just as confused as he felt. On one hand, Trevor couldn't imagine ever trusting Greg. He had tormented the three of them with nightmarish illusory scenarios as part of his scheme to "convert" them. And he was a murderer; there was no getting around that. But on the other hand, Trevor couldn't help feeling that Greg was being sincere. He caught Drew's eye, but Drew only gave him a shrug in return. It appeared that their resident psychologist didn't have any insight to offer. Trevor didn't blame him. Greg wasn't human anymore and probably hadn't been for a very long time. How could any of them truly understand his motives?

Maybe you don't need to understand. Maybe you just need to have a little faith in your friend.

He heard the words in Jenn's voice. She was a kind, forgiving person, very spiritual in her own way, even if she professed not to believe in any sort of unseen dimension of existence. It was exactly the sort of advice she would have given him if she had been there. Thinking of her made him wonder how she was doing. He hadn't spoken to her since they had left to accompany Erin and Carrington to the college. She had no idea that there had been another appearance by the Dark Lady and that Ray had died during the attack. Part of him wanted to spare her the news as long as possible, but part of him wondered if it might be better just to get it over with. But the truth was, more than anything else, he just really wanted to hear her voice. He went as far as reaching for his cell phone, but then he decided against calling. He would talk to her when they got back to the hotel. It wouldn't be much longer.

Despite the conversation they were going to have when he got back, he was looking forward to seeing Jenn. He wasn't sure exactly how he felt about their relationship—or if they even *had* a relationship. How could anyone sort out their emotions with so many terrible things happening? But maybe, just maybe, something good would come out of all of this awfulness in the end.

Provided, of course, they both managed to survive it.

When they reached the hotel, Amber, Drew, and Greg decided to head up to Erin's room, go over the research she had gathered on Exeter, and look at the footage she had shot so far. Trevor promised to join them once he checked on Jenn, and to his surprise, Carrington elected to accompany him. Trevor was irritated that Carrington was coming along—he would rather talk to Jenn alone—but before getting on the elevator, his friends gave him pointed looks that he figured were meant to remind him that Carrington might have some knowledge about Exeter that could prove useful. So Trevor gave Drew his laptop, which contained his own research on the town, told his friends he'd see them soon, and, as the elevator door slid shut, walked off in the direction of the Exhibition Hall, Carrington at his side.

He planned to pump Carrington for information as they walked, but as they made their way through the hotel, they were approached by numerous conference goers who wanted to ask the celebrity ghost hunter about the paranormal events rumored to have occurred at the college library. Trevor wasn't sure how word of what had happened had spread so fast—probably via Facebook and Twitter, he supposed—but it seemed as if everyone at the conference knew about it. Trevor expected to see Arthur Carrington, TV host, bestselling author, and attention junkie, make an appearance then. But each time someone asked, he merely mumbled that he was sorry, but he had no idea what they were talking about, and the people moved off, disappointed and embarrassed.

When Trevor gave him a questioning look after he sent away an attractive young redhead whose eyes gleamed with hero worship, Carrington simply said, "It's not a game anymore."

Trevor, who had come to the same realization during the investigation of the Lowry House, understood all too well. And so he restrained himself from asking Carrington any questions as they continued to the Exhibition Hall. He wanted to give the man some time to come to terms with his newfound feelings toward his profession before interrogating him.

Eventually, people stopped approaching them, perhaps because word had gotten around that Carrington didn't know anything about the library attack but more likely because the *haunted*—there was no better word for it—expression on the man's face warned everyone away.

They made it to the Exhibition Hall without any further trouble, but as they approached Jenn's table, they saw that she wasn't there. Trevor asked the people tending the nearby booths if they had seen Jenn recently, but no one had. Unfortunately, they couldn't remember exactly when she had left. The hall was bustling with conference attendees, and Trevor understood that the dealers had been too busy hawking their wares to pay attention to anyone's comings and goings. But it was clear that however long Jenn had been gone, it had been a while.

Trevor examined her table. There were still plenty of books displayed and available for sale, but there was no sign of her purse or jacket. Beneath her chair, he found a flat metal box. He pulled it out and placed it on the table.

"Her money box?" Carrington asked.

Trevor nodded. It wasn't locked, so he opened it. It was full of bills, coins, checks, and credit and debit receipts.

"Jenn's been a business owner too long to leave money lying around like this. If she had to take a break, she would have asked someone she knew and trusted to watch her table until she returned. If she couldn't find anyone, she'd take the box with her. But she'd never just walk off and forget about it."

He took out his cell and called Jenn's number. Her phone rang ten times before going to voice mail.

"Hi, you've reached Jenn Rinaldi, owner of Forgotten Lore Books. Business or personal, it's all good. Leave a message, and I'll get back to you ASAP."

Trevor waited for the beep and then started speaking. "Jenn, it's Trevor. We're back from the college, and I'm standing at your table in the Exhibition Hall. It looks like you've been gone for a while. When you get this, give me a call, and let me know what's up." He paused. "Hope you're OK." He said good-bye and disconnected.

"You sounded worried," Carrington said.

Trevor put his cell away, closed the money box, picked it up, and tucked it beneath his arm. He then came around from behind the table and joined Carrington.

"I am. Like I said, Jenn wouldn't run off and leave money lying around where anyone could steal it."

"Under normal circumstances, perhaps," Carrington said. "But this day has been anything but normal."

"True." Trevor thought for a moment. "Maybe she's in her room."

They went to the front desk. A clerk rang her room for them, but there was no answer. The two men moved away from the desk so they could speak in private.

"Maybe she unplugged the room phone so she could get some sleep?" Carrington ventured. "That could be why she didn't answer her cell, either."

"I suppose." Trevor was beginning to get worried. The longer they went without knowing what had happened to Jenn, the more his mind conjured all manner of dire possibilities. Normally, he might have chalked up his fears to his writer's imagination, but the Dark Lady was real, and so were all of the people she had killed.

Trevor continued. "She told me she's planning on staying with a cousin who lives in Evansville. I thought she wasn't supposed to get here until tomorrow, but maybe she arrived early and Jenn left with her. That doesn't explain why she didn't call or text me, though. Or why she didn't bother to check out of the hotel." He didn't want to admit it to Carrington, but the idea that she might have left without telling him hurt.

"As I said before, it's not a normal day. The poor girl suffered a great deal of trauma. We all have. There could be any number of reasons she might forget to contact you. She might be talking with her cousin as they drive, telling her everything that happened. Or she might have been so emotionally exhausted that she fell asleep as soon as she got into the car. And with everything else, checking out might've simply slipped her mind. She might have just wanted to get the hell out of this town as fast as she could. Can't say as I blame her for that."

Trevor had to admit that Carrington made some valid points, but they didn't make him feel any better.

They got into the elevator, disembarked on Jenn's floor, and went to her room. Trevor knocked several times and called her name, but she didn't answer.

He turned to Carrington. "We need to go back down to the front desk and get security to let us in."

"Trevor—"

"I agree that this is about as far away from an ordinary day as you can get. The Dark Lady has killed seven people so far. I hope to God that Jenn isn't the eighth, but I have to know. If she's in there . . ." Trevor trailed off, unable to complete the thought.

"All right. Let's go back to the desk."

As they headed toward the elevator, Trevor said, "And on the way, you can start telling me what you know about Exeter—and especially about the Dark Lady." He could feel his panic starting to build, and he hoped that listening to Carrington talk might help distract him from his fears. He told himself that he should hope for the best, but unfortunately, he knew better than to expect it.

FIFTEEN

Jenn was a book person. That's why she had started her business in the first place. But even after spending all day and a good portion of each evening surrounded by books, when she locked the door, turned over the closed sign, and headed upstairs for the night, what did she do to relax? She read. She was omnivorous and voracious, reading fiction and nonfiction, as much of it as she could get her hands on. She enjoyed movies well enough, although she didn't watch more than a half-dozen in a month. Even so, she recognized that she was living a scene from a suspense film, one so common as to be a cliché: the victim of a kidnapping, tied to a chair and left alone while her captor was out running some kind of nefarious errand, giving her a golden opportunity to escape.

If she remembered right, in those films, the captive never got away. Whoever it was, man or woman, struggled to get out of their bonds, and finally, after a great deal of effort, they managed to untie a knot, cut the rope, or break the chair, winning their freedom at last. They would make a run for it then, only to be stopped at the last second by their captor, who had just returned, dashing their hopes for escape.

And the characters in those films didn't have to deal with the fact that one of their captors was a ghost who could, presumably, reappear at any moment and who might be watching her right then, invisible and unseen. And even if the Dark Lady wasn't present, would she somehow know if Jenn tried to get free? Did ghosts have some sort of psychic alarm system? She tried to remember what she had learned about ghostly powers from all the books on the paranormal she had read over the years, but nothing came to her. Maybe it was because she was too frightened to think straight, but she had the feeling that she couldn't remember because no one had ever written about such things. Who knew enough about ghosts to write a field guide to them? Maybe Trevor could do the first. *Spooks, Specters, and Spirits: How to Identify, Classify, and Nullify the Predatory Dead* by Trevor Sloan. Not bad. She would be sure to suggest it to him the next time—

She broke off the thought. She was scared, and her mind was running wild. She needed to regain control of herself if she was to have any hope of getting away. And getting away was what she desired more than anything in the world. She remembered what the Dark Lady had told Mitch just before they left. *"When this is all over, if you still want her, you can have her, too."*

She had to escape. *Now,* while she had the chance, movie cliché or not.

She had no idea where her cell phone was. She had brought it with her in her purse when Mitch had tricked her into leaving the hotel, but she hadn't seen it since. Maybe it was still in his car. She had a land line though, and that phone was in the kitchen. If she couldn't get loose from the ropes, it might as well be on the moon. But if she *could* reach it, she could call 911 and Peter or one of his people would haul ass over there to help her. Better yet, she could hightail it out of there and make the call from somewhere, anywhere, else. Somewhere she would be safe. That was a plan she could get behind. A damned fine plan. But it all depended on whether she could get loose.

She tugged at the ropes that encircled her wrists and bound her to the chair back, strained at the ones binding her legs to those of the chair. But the knots were too tight, and Mitch had left her no slack. No escape that way. Mitch had gagged her before leaving, using strips of cloth torn from one of her favorite sheets, a cozy blue flannel one she loved to sleep under in wintertime. *Bastard*. The fabric was moist and gummy in her mouth, the taste faintly musty, as if it had been stored in the linen closet too long. If she could wiggle enough to get her mouth free of the gag, she could yell for help, scream at the top of her lungs. Sure, she was upstairs, but someone out on the street might . . .

Forget it. It was Dead Days. Even if someone outside did hear her scream, they would probably chalk it up to a sound effect on a spooky album or something similar. They wouldn't kick down the door, rush upstairs, find her tied up, free her, and help her get to safety before Mitch and the Dark Lady returned. So even if she could get the gag out—which was doubtful; Mitch had tied it pretty damned tight—it wouldn't help.

What did that leave her? Besides just sitting there and giving in to despair, that is.

Could she somehow break the chair? This wasn't Hollywood. Chairs weren't made to fall apart at the first blow. But then again, she wasn't tied to a chair made of cast iron, either. It was just wood, held together with screws and glue. How hard could it be to break?

Just tipping over wouldn't do it, she was sure about that. She'd knocked over chairs before, and they hadn't broken. When she was a child, she'd had a habit of leaning back in her chair, especially at dinnertime. It had driven her mother crazy. She had always worried that Jenn would fall backward while she was eating and the impact would cause whatever food she was chewing to lodge in her windpipe, choking her. Jenn had indeed fallen a couple of times, but despite her mother's fears, she had never choked. But she had never broken a chair, either. Of course, she had been smaller then, but she didn't think she massed enough now simply to break a chair by pushing herself backward. And with her legs tied, she would have to rock back and forth until she built up enough momentum to tip over backward. She wouldn't be able to fling herself backward with any significant force, though. And her hands were tied behind the chair.

If she did manage to tip herself over, she would land on her arms, which would not only be painful but would cushion the impact on the wood. She might break a wrist before she broke the chair.

She wasn't far from the wall, though. About three feet. If she could manage to lean forward and stand on her toes, she might be able to shuffle backward and get closer to the wall. And once she was within a foot of it, she could shove the chair back against it with as much force as she could muster. And if the first blow didn't break the chair, she could try again and again—assuming she could manage to avoid tipping over. Once she was on her side, she feared she would be as helpless as a turtle flipped onto its shell. But she figured that if she could keep her balance, there was a good chance that if the chair didn't break right away, it would land on all four of its legs. Then she could lean forward and try again.

She sat for a moment and ran through the plan in her head, visualizing it as completely as possible, testing it for flaws. But in the end, she knew that, good idea or not, she was going to go through with it. What choice did she have? And if she ended up breaking a couple of bones, so be it. A shattered wrist or a fractured elbow would be infinitely preferable to what Mitch would do to her when the Dark Lady finally let go of his leash.

She closed her eyes, took a deep breath to calm herself, and let it out slowly. Then she opened her eyes—

—and saw the Dark Lady standing before her.

Lips as white and bloodless as marble stretched into a smile.

"You're not going anywhere, Jenn. I still need you."

Behind her gag, Jenn let out a muffled cry of frustrated rage, and the Dark Lady's dead smile widened.

"We need to do something!" Trevor said. "And don't tell me we already are. Sitting around a hotel room reading through computer files isn't going to help us find Jenn!"

Amber had never seen Trevor so worked up before. But she

understood. She would have gone nuts if Drew had vanished. And while it was still possible that Jenn had left of her own accord, the fact that she'd gone without packing up anything—books, money box, overnight bag, clothes, toiletries—wasn't a good sign. Yes, she had been traumatized by the day's events, but she hadn't exhibited any signs of being that absentminded. And Amber couldn't imagine her leaving without letting Trevor know. They might not be a couple anymore, but she still had strong feelings for him. She wouldn't have departed without a word, leaving Trevor to worry about her.

"You've done everything you can," she said. "You've tried calling her a dozen times, both on her cell and at the store, and you've reported her disappearance to the police."

Amber, Drew, Trevor, Greg, and Carrington were camped out in Erin's room. Erin sat at the desk, her laptop open in front of her. Her face was drawn and expressionless, and she had said very little since they had arrived. It was obvious that she was taking Ray's death hard. Amber, Drew, and Greg sat on the bed closer to the window, while Carrington sat on the other bed, next to him a stack of manila folders filled with paper and Trevor's open laptop. As for Trevor, he paced the room with the wire-taut tension of a caged animal.

"And not to be too much of a downer," Greg said, "but if either the Dark Lady or Mitch got hold of Jenn, there's nothing you can do for her now, anyway."

Trevor stopped and spun around to glare at Greg. "If you weren't in someone else's—" He broke off and glanced around the room, as if just remembering that Carrington and Erin were there. "Well, if you *weren't,* I'd break your jaw right now."

"Lucky for me, eh?" Greg's tone was flippant, but something cold moved in his gaze, and Amber was reminded that while he might be trying to help them—and in the process find some measure of redemption for himself—he couldn't entirely be trusted.

"She's alive, Trevor," Amber said. "I can feel it."

Drew caught her eye and raised an eyebrow. She knew what

he was asking. Did she really have a psychic sense that Jenn was all right, or was she just trying to reassure Trevor? In truth, Amber wasn't certain herself. She didn't want to give Trevor false hope, but neither did she want him to lose all hope.

"Really?" he asked. The pleading tone in that one word nearly broke Amber's heart.

She looked deep inside herself before answering. "Yes," she said, and she meant it.

Trevor let out a long breath, and some of the tension left his body. He sat down on the bed next to Carrington. "All right. So . . . the Dark Lady." He looked down at his computer screen and began typing. "I saved all my research on Exeter in one file. Give me a second to call it up . . . There we go. Now I'll highlight the phrase *Dark Lady,* go through the document, and check every mention of her."

Several moments passed as Trevor skimmed the information.

"Not much here, I'm afraid. I did an article on the influx of ghostbreakers in the early days after the flood, and I mentioned the Dark Lady in it. She was one of the spirits they were hoping to exorcise. None of the attempts to get rid of her was successful, though, and she continued appearing periodically over the years. That's all I have."

"I believe I can add to that," Carrington said. "I did much of the research for Erin's film"—he patted the stack of folders on the bed next to him—"and I ran across a number of references to the Dark Lady. Enough that I tried to persuade Erin to feature her in the film."

"She wasn't very interesting," Erin said. Her voice was toneless, almost machinelike. "She'd show up, people would see her, she'd stand there for a few seconds, and then she would disappear. Not dramatic at all, and certainly not dangerous." She paused, then added more softly, "Not until now, anyway."

"Maybe she stepped up her game in hope of getting a bigger part in your magnum opus," Greg said.

Trevor stood up. "I've had just about enough—"

"Don't let *her* get to you," Amber said quickly, adding a subtle emphasis to the word *her*. While they had no need to keep Greg's identity secret from Carrington and Erin, they had agreed that things were complicated enough without telling them that one of their group was possessed by a formerly evil spirit.

Trevor glanced at Amber, nodded, and sat back down. He glared at Greg, who just smiled back, unconcerned.

"Do you have any information about the Dark Lady's first appearance?" Drew asked.

Before Carrington could answer, Greg said, "I'm not sure that's relevant. I told you my theory that the Dark Lady is in essence a mask for the accumulated spiritual energy of Exeter. If that's the case, then she's not an individual, and knowing details about her won't be of any help."

"If she is a mask, then there has to be reason the town not only chose her but continues to use her," Drew said. "The more we can learn about her, the more we'll learn about the collective entity you theorize is behind her mask."

"It's not a person, Drew," Greg said. "You can't psychoanalyze it."

"If a creature exhibits behavior, it can be understood," Drew said, "whatever its nature. And if this entity is using the Dark Lady as an avatar, her personality—her needs and desires—might shape its behavior."

"Besides," Trevor said, "a haunting needs some kind of focal point. A touchstone in our world. Something to link a spiritual being to this plane of existence and keep it here, right? If there was a real person who died and became the original Dark Lady, the details of her life, and death, might help us discover what that touchstone is. And once we know that—"

"We'll be able to sever the link keeping her here," Amber said. "And once the Dark Lady is gone—"

"The rest of the town's spirits might lose their collective identity and separate," Greg said. "Rendering them if not exactly harmless, then at least far less of a threat."

Erin looked at Carrington. "Do you have any idea what they're talking about?"

"I believe so. Most of it, anyway. They're saying that if we uncover the origin of the Dark Lady, we might find a way to stop her."

"OK, *that* I understand. So, what else do you have on her?"

"Not much more than what's written about her in the museum, I'm afraid," Carrington said. "I have a list of times and places where she was reported to manifest, but I'm sure it's not complete. In my experience, not everyone who witnesses a paranormal event is willing to talk about it. Even in a town such as Exeter." He pulled a piece of paper from one of the folders. "But here's what I have on her appearances." He handed it to Trevor, who quickly skimmed it.

"The earliest appearances are in the 1930s. Three of them. But there's nothing to indicate what order they occurred in."

"The sources where I got the information were sadly lacking in specifics," Carrington said.

"I don't see anything special about the locations. One was on a street corner, another in a vacant field, and the third was in an alley."

Trevor started to hand the list to Amber, but then, as if he'd thought better of it, he instead handed it to Greg, although reluctantly.

Greg scanned the list. "I agree. Nothing special here." He handed the list to Amber, and she and Drew looked it over.

The information meant nothing to Amber. She hoped that she might get a psychic hit from one of the locations, but they were just words on paper to her.

Drew looked at Carrington. "Do you have any information about the attempts to exorcise her spirit? Especially the first one?"

Carrington frowned. "I seem to remember something about

that." He searched through a couple of folders before finding what he was looking for. "Here it is." He read it over. "It took place at a local medium's home in 1942. A half-dozen spiritualists gathered to make contact with the Dark Lady, learn what bound her to the earthly plane, and try to help guide her to the afterlife. They managed to make contact and heard a single word issue from the air. *Stop*." His eyes widened. "Yes! I remember now! This is why the incident at the museum nagged at my mind so."

"The manifestation of the word would appear to suggest a connection between that attempt to exorcise her spirit and whatever has set her off this time," Drew said.

Amber frowned. "But I thought *Stop* meant she wanted Erin to quit making her film. How does exorcism equate with making a documentary?"

"People once believed that making an image of an individual was a way to capture the soul," Carrington said. "That's the basis for a great deal of magic. The image represents the thing it copies, allowing the spell caster to work his or her will upon it."

Trevor nodded. "And when photography was invented, some aboriginal cultures believed that a photo could capture a person's spirit."

"Seems a rather tenuous connection to me," Greg said. "But I suppose it's possible."

"But if that's the case, why not just kill Erin?" Amber asked. "We've talked about this before. She's the driving force behind the film. The simplest way to stop the film is to stop her. There has to be a reason the Dark Lady is attacking others instead of her."

"Maybe she wants to punish me," Erin said softly. "Maybe she wants me to feel responsible for the people she's killed."

"You're not," Drew said. "Whatever sort of entity the Dark Lady is, she makes her own choices. Even if she's essentially mindless, you're no more responsible for what she does than you would be responsible for the actions of a shark."

"But what if I pushed people into the water without knowing a hungry shark lurked beneath the surface? Even if I didn't mean for anyone to be hurt, they still died because of my actions."

"I'm a therapist," Drew said, "and that means I have all sorts of stock responses I can give to try to make you feel better. But the bottom line is that you can play all the what-if scenarios you want, but you'll never get an answer, because there isn't one. Once we make choices, they're done. It's what we do with the choices that lie ahead of us that's truly important. We have to focus on what we can do now to stop the Dark Lady—before she can hurt anyone else."

Erin looked at Drew for a moment, face expressionless. But finally, she managed a small smile and nodded.

Amber turned to Carrington. "Do you have the address where the exorcism was attempted?"

He shook his head. "The source I found said only 'home of a local medium.' It didn't even provide the person's name."

"Do you think that might be the focal point we're looking for?" Drew asked.

"It feels right," Amber said.

"If that's the case, then it would suggest that the Beyond the Veil Museum is the focal point," Drew said. "That's where the word *Stop* manifested this time. Perhaps the museum building was once the medium's home."

"But the museum isn't the first place the Dark Lady appeared this time," Trevor said. "That was at Jenn's store."

"No," Erin said. "It was several days earlier than that, out at the Reilly Farm, when Alex was shooting some location footage, remember? When he—" She broke off, unable to complete the sentence.

When he bought the farm, Greg mouthed. Amber was grateful that he hadn't said it aloud. She supposed even that meager sign of self-restraint was progress of a sort.

"Do you still have the footage?" Trevor asked.

Erin nodded. "But if you're thinking there's anything to be learned from it, you're going to be disappointed. Just before Alex is attacked, the footage becomes distorted, just like what happened to the security video from the museum."

"I know it will be difficult for you," Drew said, "but if you could show us the footage, it might prove useful. We might notice something about it that you missed."

"Chief Hoffman had me make him a copy, and he didn't learn anything from it," Erin said. She sighed. "But I have it on my laptop. Just let me bring it up."

She turned to her computer and began typing on the keyboard. The others gathered around behind her so they could better view the screen. The footage had been shot with a simple handheld camera, and Alex provided occasional commentary as he walked around the Reilly Farm. He had a warm, soothing voice that Amber thought would have been great for a late-night DJ. Since the footage was shot from his viewpoint, he wasn't visible in the frame, and she found it strange to know that she was witnessing the last moments of this man's life without having any idea what he looked like.

It had been a sunny fall afternoon, and honey-colored light gave the area a soft, gentle glow, the beautiful illumination a counterpoint to the abandoned farm. The fields had been left to go to seed, and the grass around the farmhouse and barn was waist high. The buildings themselves were in relatively good repair, however, and Amber figured the farm hadn't been deserted very long. Probably a casualty of the bad economy of the last few years. Alex didn't say much as he roamed the property, reserving his remarks for locations that he thought would work well in the film, such as the stately oak tree behind the farmhouse and the empty horse corral. Overall, he seemed underwhelmed by the farm as a possible location for filming.

"On a spook scale of one to ten, I'd rate this place a point five," he said. *"Maybe the barn will be more creepy. Let's take a look."*

He walked toward the barn—it was painted brown instead of the stereotypical red and had a corrugated metal roof. Amber wondered what it would sound like inside when it rained. It would probably sound like a million tiny hammers pounding overhead. It took some effort for Alex to slide open the large outer door, and the rollers creaked and groaned, as if they hadn't been asked to work in years and weren't too happy about it. It was dark inside, but enough sunlight filtered in to see by. Alex paused a moment at the entrance and panned the camera back and forth. The floor was concrete, and several pieces of farm equipment had been left behind by the owners: a rickety old manure spreader, an ancient riding mower that looked as if it were ninety-nine-percent rust, and an equally rust-eaten hay elevator standing propped up against the wall next to a horse stall.

"Nope. Still not scary." Alex stepped inside the barn.

Erin hadn't said anything up to this point, but now she spoke. "I had Alex check out the farm because of reports that people driving by hear horse noises coming from the barn, especially at night. Supposedly, the cries are so loud sometimes that they sound more like screams."

"Here, horsey-horsey-horsey." Alex followed this up by clicking his tongue several times, but if there were any spectral equines in the barn, they didn't respond.

"I don't know about this, Erin. Maybe if we add some sound effects of our own, some horses whinnying, and add a ghostly echo to it. Still, it seems lame to me. I suppose if we could track down some witnesses to interview, though . . ."

Alex continued walking through the barn as he talked, and he now passed near the hay elevator. It was a long, narrow metal machine with a hook-studded conveyer belt designed to grab hold of hay bales and transport them up to the loft. One of Amber's uncles had a farm, and when she was growing up, she would sometimes visit and help out with chores. She had used a hay elevator before, although never one so old that it looked as if it might fall apart any minute.

Then, without warning, the picture dissolved into waves of electronic distortion. The picture cleared after thirty seconds or so, but knowing what had happened to Alex during that interval made the time seem much longer. When the image returned, at first Amber wasn't certain what she was looking at. It was blue and white, with a criss-cross pattern. Then she realized that the camera was lying on the ground, on its side, the lens pointing at one of Alex's shoes. The criss-cross pattern was his shoelaces.

"The film continues like this for almost forty minutes," Erin said. "After that, his cell rings. It was me, calling to find out what was taking him so long. When he didn't answer, I got angry and drove there to find out what was going on. I . . . found him. But the battery on his camera ran down before I got there. I don't remember what I said and did when I saw him, but I'm glad it wasn't recorded. I don't think I could stand hearing it."

"What happened to him?" Amber asked.

"Chief Hoffman figured Alex bumped into the hay elevator, and it fell over, knocking him to the floor. He struck his head on the concrete, and . . . the chief said it probably happened so fast that Alex hadn't felt a thing. I wish I could believe that."

"I can see why you thought it was an accident at first," Drew said.

"And anyone would've chalked up the electronic distortion to the camera hitting the ground," Trevor said.

"No sign of the Dark Lady's favorite word anywhere?" Greg asked.

"No," Erin said. "If you don't mind, I'm going to turn this off. I can't watch it anymore." She reached for the keyboard, but Trevor stopped her.

"I want to try something real quick, if that's OK."

Erin hesitated, but then she nodded. She rose from her chair to give Trevor room to work. He popped a flash drive into her computer, downloaded a copy of Alex's footage, and removed the drive. He took it over to his computer, uploaded the file onto his machine, and ran it through one of his programs.

"What are you doing?" Erin asked.

"I imagine he's checking for EVP," Carrington said.

"Yep." When he was finished, Trevor hit Play.

They watched the footage again, but this time, after Alex was killed, there was a soft sound, almost like the sighing of a breeze. Trevor fiddled with the program a bit more and then replayed that section of film. This time, the sound, while still soft, was clearly audible.

"Stop."

That was it. Just the single word, no more.

Trevor stopped the playback.

"If we had any doubt that the Dark Lady was responsible for Alex's death, I think this clears it up."

"She started out small," Greg said. "Tipping over the hay elevator and imprinting the word onto the film instead of speaking it aloud. The latter is far more difficult for spirits to accomplish. It requires more energy to move air molecules in such a way as to simulate a speaking voice. She sent her message, and when it was ignored, she sent a second one by killing Tonya in the bookstore. The message was more dramatic this time—using psychokinetic force to hurl books at Tonya—and it required a far greater expenditure of power. When that message had no effect, she recruited a human ally to help her, and she tried again, killing two people at the museum. And when she still didn't get her message through, she decided to go big, resulting in the mass attack at the college and the psychic attack on us. Unfortunately, we still don't know for certain what she wants us to stop."

"Which means she'll send another message," Amber said, feeling a chill in the pit of her stomach at the thought. "An even bigger one."

Greg nodded. "And she'll do it soon. The more frustrated she becomes, the shorter the time interval between her messages. And by this point, I'm sure she's royally pissed."

"It's a good thing Chief Hoffman agreed that the parade should be canceled," Drew said. "Can you imagine what the Dark Lady might've— Amber? What's wrong?"

A horrible feeling had come over her, a cold, nauseating fear. It came on her so sudden and strong that for a moment, she feared she might vomit. But after a few seconds, she managed to get control of herself, and the sensation, while not vanishing entirely, became tolerable.

"It's the chief," she said. "I think something bad has happened to him . . . and something even worse is going to happen—soon."

"I'll see if I can reach him." Drew took out his phone and made a call.

Trevor looked at her, a frightened, pleading expression on his face. "Amber, I know you're still learning about your psychic abilities, but could you try to use them to find out where Jenn is? You said she's still alive, but if the Dark Lady plans to go nuclear with her next message, Jenn might not survive it."

"I don't know if I can, Trevor. Most of the time, I can't control it. It just comes and goes. But I'll try."

She closed her eyes and concentrated. She pictured Jenn in her mind, thought of how her voice sounded, how she moved, how it felt to be in her presence. She concentrated on Trevor, too, hoping that she might be able to zero in on Jenn if she could tap into the emotional connection between her and Trevor. She felt a hint of Jenn's presence, but it was distant, as if she were looking at the woman through the wrong end of binoculars.

She spoke without opening her eyes. "I can't tell where she is, but if feels like she can't move. Not much, anyway."

"Is she hurt?" Trevor asked.

"I don't think so. I don't get any sense of pain from her." Her brow furrowed as she concentrated harder. "Something's keeping me from getting too close to her. It's why I can't get a feeling for where she is. She could be in the next room or a thousand miles away." She opened her eyes. "I'm sorry."

Trevor forced a smile. "It's OK. You gave it your best shot, and at least I know she's alive and uninjured." And although he didn't say it, she didn't need psychic abilities to know what his next thought was: *But how long will she remain that way?*

"It's the Dark Lady," Greg said. "She's blocking you from connecting fully with Jenn."

While Amber had been trying to locate Jenn, Drew had been talking on the phone. Now he said, "Thank you," and disconnected.

"Chief Hoffman didn't answer, so I called the police station." He paused to take a deep breath and let it out before continuing. "He was killed this afternoon. It happened in the park. Someone . . . crushed his skull with a large rock."

"Oh, God!" The nausea returned with a vengeance, and Amber reflexively put her hands on her stomach, as if she might gain control of it that way. Drew sat down next to her on the bed and put his arms around her, and she leaned into his body gratefully.

"Sounds like Mitch's work," Greg said. "No style at all."

Erin's face went ashen, and she took out her cell phone and made a call.

Drew continued while she waited to be connected. "I asked the officer who answered if the parade was going to be canceled. He said that the mayor has cautioned the department to be on the alert tonight but that it was too late to stop it. It's almost time for it to start."

"Hello, Pattie? This is Erin. When you get this message, call or text me to let me know you and Sarah are all right, OK?" She waited a moment, in case Pattie might answer, Amber guessed, but then she disconnected.

"I hope they managed to get away," Erin said, but from the tone of her voice, Amber knew she doubted it. Amber wanted to reassure her, but she couldn't. She had a bad feeling about the two women. Real bad.

"We have to do something!" Trevor said. "Now!"

"Like what?" Greg asked. "Run out into the street and ask everyone gathered for the parade to calmly disperse because a crazed spirit is due to attack any minute?"

Carrington had been thoughtful for the last several moments, and now he said, "Trevor, you said you wrote an article about the people who came to Exeter not long after the flood to exorcise the spirits that were haunting the town."

"That's right."

"When you researched that article, you found no information on the attempt to exorcise the Dark Lady?"

"Not a single mention."

"I'm not surprised. I only found the one source, and as I said earlier, it was sadly lacking in specifics. But during your research, did you learn who the town's most prominent paranormalists were during that era?"

"Yeah, but . . . Wait, I get it! The account you read said that the mediums who came to town gathered at the home of someone local. It stands to reason that that someone would be one of the town's most . . ." He trailed off, a mixture of dawning realization and shock on his face. "Lucille Decker. They called her the Eye of Exeter because her psychic readings were supposed to be the best. People came from all over the country to consult her. Hell, from all over the world."

Carrington was nodding. "Yes, I remember her now. I'd forgotten her name, but who can forget a colorful title such as the Eye of Exeter?" He frowned. "Wasn't she the woman who founded the Beyond the Veil Museum?"

"So the museum *is* the focal point!" Greg said.

"No, it's not," Trevor said. "Lucille did start the museum, but back then, it was little more than her personal collection of memorabilia, and she kept it in her home. After she died, her collection, which had grown larger over the years, was moved to a new location. That's where the museum is now. But the place where she lived, and where the ceremony to exorcise the Dark Lady took place . . ."

It came to Amber then, all in a rush. "Was Jenn's bookstore," she said.

SIXTEEN

"There. Can you see OK?"

Jenn didn't answer Mitch. Not because she couldn't—he had removed her gag when he returned—but because she was too afraid. He was clearly crazy, and she didn't want to do or say anything that might set him off.

She was still bound to the chair, and he had moved her into the bedroom and sat her in front of a window that looked out over the street. He had drawn the curtains back to make sure she had an unobstructed view.

He grabbed hold of her left earlobe with his thumb and forefinger and gave it a hard twist.

She took in a hissing breath. *Damn, that hurt!* "Yes! I can see just fine!"

He held on to her earlobe a couple of seconds more before releasing it. He patted her on the shoulder.

"Good." He sat down on the foot of the bed.

The thought of him in her bedroom, let alone sitting on her bed, made her feel sick. When he had first picked her up, chair and all, and carried her in there, she had been afraid that he intended to rape her. She was relieved that he seemed to have a different agenda. For now, at least.

Outside it was dusk, and crowds of people lined both sides of the street. Most were in costume, and while some of the outfits weren't scary—a man dressed as Zorro, a woman garbed as the ubiquitous sexy nurse—most tended toward the macabre, and some were downright grotesque. Every year during Dead Days, there was a contingent of people who strove to outdo everyone else when it came to having the most bizarre, disgusting costume. She saw clawed and fanged creatures, distorted and misshapen figures, sinister demonic visages, and beings so malformed and surreal that they defied description. The bizarros had outdone themselves this year.

The street itself was empty, but she knew it wouldn't be for much longer. The parade would start soon.

She fantasized that someone in the crowd would look up, see her sitting there at her second-story bedroom window, and call the police. But she knew that would never happen. As dim as the light was outside, she doubted that anyone could see her, and even if they did, what would they see? Just a woman sitting in a chair, ready to watch the parade. They couldn't see that she was tied up, and she couldn't yell to attract attention, not with Mitch sitting close by. She would barely get out any sound before he shut her up, and she doubted that he would be gentle about it. She might as well stop dreaming about rescue and see what she could do to help herself.

"What are we supposed to be looking at, Mitch?" She turned her head to make sure he was looking at her face. She hated using his name, but she had read somewhere that when you were being held captive by someone, it was important to keep them from dehumanizing you. Using his name, facing him, saying *we* instead of *I* were all ways to keep him thinking of her as a person instead of an object. She hoped.

"Nothing yet," he said. "The show hasn't started."

"What show?" She didn't want to know, not really, but she needed to keep him talking. The more he talked, the greater the chance that he would begin to develop some measure of sympathy toward her.

"I don't know. She didn't tell me. But whatever she's going to do, you can bet it'll be pretty goddamned spectacular."

The Dark Lady had vanished not long after Mitch had returned, and Jenn had no idea where she had gone. To prepare for the "show," whatever it would be.

"Why is she doing this, Mitch? What does she want?"

He looked at her blankly for a moment, and she thought he hadn't heard her. She was about to ask again when he finally responded. "I don't know. She hasn't told me." He frowned. "It's funny, but I hadn't really thought about it before now. I suppose I don't care what she wants, just as long as I get what *I* want."

"Amber."

"She belongs with me. She just doesn't realize it yet, but she will." He smiled. "The Dark Lady promised me it'll happen. I just need to be patient a little longer."

"And you believe her?"

He frowned again but didn't reply.

She went on. "I don't know what she is, Mitch, but if she was human once, she isn't now. She's using you, making you do things you'd never have done on your own. Bad things. You've hurt people, Mitch. Killed them."

She was guessing about that last part, but Trevor and the others believed that Mitch had strangled the man in the museum, and if that was true, who else might he have harmed? When he didn't deny it, she knew her guess had been correct.

He looked confused now, uncertain. He glanced down at his hands, coiled them into fists, and then straightened his fingers, as if he were remembering the dark work he had done with them.

"I . . . did what I had to. It was what she needed me to do."

"What about what *you* need, Mitch?"

He frowned, not comprehending.

"Do you want to be her servant? Her *slave*? Do you want to be a killer?"

He thought for several moments, and then he grinned. "Why not? It's worked out pretty well for me so far."

"Try the police again."

"Trevor, I've called five times now," Drew said. "I can't get through."

"It's the same for all of us," Amber said. "Maybe they're all too busy with the parade."

"It's the Dark Lady," Greg said. "She's jamming our phones. She doesn't want anyone interfering with whatever she has planned."

Drew sat in the backseat of Trevor's car next to Amber. Greg was in the front passenger seat, and Trevor was driving. Given his emotional state, Drew wasn't certain that was a good idea. If he went any faster, they could end up in an accident, and then they might all become permanent additions to Exeter's ghostly population. Not the most attractive of prospects.

Erin and Carrington followed in her Volkswagen. Drew wasn't sure she should be driving, either. She was convinced that she was responsible for the Dark Lady's actions, which included the deaths of Alex and Ray and—perhaps—Pattie and Sarah. Her entire crew, men and women who would never have come to Exeter if she hadn't been making a film about the town. That level of guilt could affect a person in any number of ways, none of them good.

"But if Jenn's at the bookstore . . ." Trevor began.

"We don't know that for sure," Drew said. "Just because we suspect that's the locus of the Dark Lady's haunting doesn't mean Jenn's being held captive there."

"It's the most likely place," Greg said. "Jenn's lived there for years. Her spiritual energy is bound up with that of the building."

"You mean she's part of the locus?" Amber asked.

"Possibly," Greg said. "If so, that means there's a simple way to sever the Dark Lady's connection to this world."

"What's that?" Drew asked.

"Kill Jenn." Greg spoke these words without any emotion, as if he were merely suggesting that they stop by a drive-thru on the way over to pick up something to eat.

Trevor turned to look at Greg so swiftly that he jerked the steering wheel, causing the Prius to swerve and throwing Drew against Amber. Moving with a nonchalant, almost inhuman speed, Greg grabbed hold of the steering wheel and steadied the vehicle.

"Careful, Trevor. I'm not sure the three of you are ready to join me in the Great Beyond just yet."

Trevor got a solid grip on the wheel once more and looked forward, but when he spoke, his voice was tight with tension. "No one is going to hurt Jenn, not for any reason. Got it?"

"Of course. Just thinking aloud. I'd never *dream* of harming Jenn. As Norman's mother said, I'd never hurt a fly. Of course, the good news is that your girlfriend's connection to the Dark Lady makes her the safest person in town at the moment."

Trevor seemed mollified by that, and he kept driving, although he did ease up on the gas.

Drew and Amber exchanged glances. It seemed the tension was getting to all of them, even Greg, despite the aloof veneer he affected. Considering that they were racing to confront the Dark Lady without anything even remotely resembling a plan, Drew supposed it was only natural. But bickering among themselves would only distract them, and if they were to have any hope of stopping whatever fresh horror the Dark Lady had planned—and live to tell about it—they needed to stay focused.

"How close to the bookstore can we get?" Drew said. He rubbed his sore ribs. They didn't hurt as much as they had back at the library, but being thrown against Amber hadn't done them any good.

"If we're lucky, within a couple of blocks," Trevor said. "Forgotten Lore is right on the main parade route. Thousands of people gather to watch, and when the official parade is over, anyone in costume can take to the street and walk the route. Hundreds usually do. Because there are so many people on foot everywhere, the police block off all the streets leading to downtown. They'll reopen them after the parade."

"But it'll be too late by then," Amber said.

"Speak of the devil," Greg said.

A trio of wooden police barricades stretched across the street ahead of them, blocking the way. No one was standing guard.

"It appears the Exeter PD are trusting sorts," Greg said.

"It's the same every year," Trevor said. "Even after hiring additional security, the police are spread too thin to watch everywhere."

They were driving through the residential section of town close to the main business district. The sidewalks there were full of people in costume—adults, teenagers, children, toddlers—all heading toward the parade route. On the other side of the barricade, people walked down the middle of the street, most of them moving quickly so they wouldn't miss any of the fun. Trevor had the driver's-side window cracked, and the sound of drums and trumpets drifted into the car.

"That's the high-school band," Trevor said. "Sounds like they're still warming up. That's a good sign."

He slowed as they approached the barricade.

"What are you doing?" Greg asked. "This is an emergency, isn't it? Gun it, and break through the barrier!"

"There are too many people," Trevor said. "I can't—"

"Oh, for Oblivion's sake, that's why cars have horns!"

Greg wasn't wearing his seatbelt, and he slid close to the driver's seat, raised his left foot, and jammed Connie's shoe down onto Trevor's foot. Trevor swore as the Prius lunged forward. Amber let out a yelp of alarm and gripped Drew's leg.

"Better get to work with that horn," Greg said, sounding insufferably pleased with himself.

"Damn it, get off—shit!"

The barricades rushed toward them, and Trevor's only option

was to break through or swerve off the road, which would mean hitting pedestrians on the sidewalk. Drew knew which option he would take, and he told Amber to hold on.

Trevor laid on the horn, and people turned to look in their direction, alarmed. The Prius hit one of the wooden bars with a solid *thunk,* and chunks of wood went flying in different directions. Once the vehicle was through, Greg lifted his foot off Trevor's, and the Prius slowed. By this point, the people who had been walking in the street were now running like hell to get off of it, more than a few of them yelling in anger and flipping Trevor the bird. Greg waved as they drove past.

Drew turned around and saw that Erin and Carrington had followed. Carrington had his cell phone out, presumably trying to call one of them and ask what the hell they were doing, but none of their phones rang. The Dark Lady was still jamming their signals.

Even with Trevor honking the horn and Greg sticking his head out the window and shouting for people to get out of their way, they could only go so fast, and the crowd of pedestrians eventually became so thick that they had to slow to a crawl. People started kicking and hitting the Prius, and some hurled objects, mostly cardboard cups, plastic bottles, and cans. Soda, coffee, water, and beer splashed across Trevor's windshield, and he hit the wipers to clear it off.

"We keep up like this, and we'll start a riot," Drew said. The crowd was already revved up from the excitement of the night's event, and wearing costumes gave them a sense of anonymity, which in this situation could be dangerous. Massed together like this, their identities concealed, people would be tempted to act on the aggressive impulses that they normally kept under control.

"Drew's right," Amber said. "I can feel the anger building all around us, like a storm cloud ready to burst. Pull over and park, Trevor!"

"Pull over I can't do," he said. "Not enough room. Park, however . . ."

He braked to a stop in the middle of the street, put the car in park, and turned off the engine. Behind them, Erin did the same. Without a word, the four of them got out of the car. As soon as they did, a man with a shaved head came toward them. He was tall and full of bodybuilder muscle, and he wore a skintight skeleton outfit with skull makeup on his face. He looked damned intimidating, especially with his features contorted in rage.

"What the *fuck* do you morons think you're doing?" he demanded. "There are people *walking* here! And a lot of them are kids!"

Before anyone else could respond, Greg stepped forward. "It's my little girl! She left home without her inhaler, and I don't know where she is! If she has an attack . . . Have you seen her? She's twelve, thin, with long red hair braided into pigtails. She was dressed as a witch. Please, I have to find her!"

The man's anger drained out of him instantly. "Uh, no, I haven't. But there's bound to be some cops up ahead somewhere. Maybe they can help you."

"Thank you!" Greg said. "Thank you so much!"

Carrington and Erin joined them then, and Carrington stepped forward and put his arm around Greg. "It's all right, my dear. We'll find her."

The two of them turned away from the man and started walking.

"Pippi!" Greg called out. "Pippi, where are you!"

Drew, Amber, Trevor, and Erin followed close behind them. Some in the crowd still gave them dirty looks, but no one challenged them.

"Thank God there weren't any theater critics in the crowd," Trevor said.

"Jealous much?" Greg shot back.

They continued running down the street, weaving in and out of the crowd and ignoring the occasional shouts of "Slow down!

and "Where's the fire?" And from one kid, "No costumes? You suck!" After a few moments, they reached Sycamore Street and found the sidewalk in front of them jam-packed with costumed people standing shoulder to shoulder, waiting for the parade to start. From the looks of it, Trevor hadn't been exaggerating when he had said that thousands of spectators came to town for the parade.

Drew turned to Trevor. "Now what?"

"The bookstore is on the other side of the street, a block north," he said.

"You couldn't get us any closer?" Greg said.

"Sycamore Street's blocked off, remember?" Trevor said. "This is the best I could do. Now, let's try to get across before—"

A thunderous cheer went up from the crowd, someone blew a whistle, and the sounds of a marching band playing "Funeral March of a Marionette" filled the air.

"The parade starts," Trevor finished.

A moment later, the Exeter High School marching band began to file past. They were garbed in black uniforms, and they wore dark eye shadow and gray lipstick. Drew wondered if they wore that makeup all the time or just for the Dead Days parade. The latter, he hoped.

People cheered and clapped as the band marched by, and they were followed by the first float, a stereotypical haunted house, weathered and falling apart, with fake bats, ravens, and rats attached in various places. At the base of the float, a number of children stood waving at the crowd. Some of the kids were dressed as ghosts and some as witches, and standing at the top, on the roof of the house, grinning and waving for all she was worth, was an adult witch. But she was far from a generic one. She stood twelve feet tall, her long midnight-blue gown concealing the platform she was standing on, Drew guessed. Her skin was painted a light blue, and she held a crystalline staff with a dragon head on top. A steady stream of sparks shot forth from the dragon's mouth, to the crowd's delight.

"That's the mayor," Trevor said. "She always leads off the parade in one gaudy outfit or another."

"If gaudy is the goal, then I say mission accomplished," Greg said.

Drew craned his neck to see over the top of the crowd. Coming up behind the haunted-house float was an old-fashioned funeral carriage pulled by a horse. Men dressed in black suits and top hats walked on either side of the carriage, waving, and behind it came six solemn-faced men carrying a black coffin. There was plenty of space between the float and the carriage, probably to make sure the horse didn't get too nervous, Drew guessed.

"We can cross right after the house float is past," he said. "Let's get moving."

Drew grabbed hold of Amber's hand, and together they forced their way through the crowd on the sidewalk. Trevor, Greg, Carrington, and Erin followed, and although they earned more than a few curses—and a couple of elbows to the ribs—for their efforts, they managed to make it through and onto the street.

They started running, but they weren't more than a third of the way across when Drew saw a security guard break out of the crowd on the other side of the street and start toward them. Drew was trying to think of an excuse that would persuade the guard to let them pass, when the air around them shimmered and a strange feeling of vertigo overtook him. When it passed, the air cleared, and the man coming toward them no longer looked as he had a second before. In fact, he no longer looked like a man. He had become a distorted parody of a human, with some features and body parts grotesquely enlarged, while others were shrunken and withered. He came at them with a spastic, lurching stride, the best speed his twisted body could manage, and his eyes—one the size of a basketball, the other the size of a marble—were filled with rage.

Drew shot Amber a glance. "Is it real?"

"Real enough!" she said.

Drew nodded, stepped forward to meet the crooked man's charge, and swung a hard right hook at his malformed jaw. As a psychologist, Drew favored a more rational approach to solving problems, but sometimes you just had to punch a monster in the mouth. His fist connected quite solidly, and the pain that flared in his hand confirmed Amber's analysis. Whatever transformation had befallen the guard, he was definitely real. The crooked man staggered backward, but he didn't go down.

"Try not to be such a nice guy for a change." Greg stepped forward and delivered a savage kick to the crooked man's crotch. Breath whooshed out of his lungs, and he doubled over with a gurgling moan.

Before Drew could say anything about Greg's crude—if effective—tactic, he caught a flash of movement out of the corner of his eye. He turned toward it and saw that the black-suited men who accompanied the funeral carriage had become skeletons, bones bleached so white they almost glowed, the darkness within their eye hollows deep and endless. They moved with an eerie silent grace, their joints creaking softly as they came. The carriage driver had become a skeleton, too, as had the horse drawing the rig. The fleshless animal reared without making a sound, forelegs pistoning in the air, and when it came down on all fours again, it leaped forward, pulling the carriage after it.

Drew knew they couldn't fight their way out of this. There were just too many. He was about to yell that everyone should run, when Amber shouted, "Look!"

He turned to see that she pointed toward the haunted-house float. Except that now it wasn't a float; it was an actual dilapidated house sitting in the middle of the street. The children who had been standing at the base of the float had become actual ghosts and witches, although they remained kid-size. The ghosts looked like semitransparent shreds of white gauze clumped into vague approximations of human form, and the witches were wrinkle-faced dwarves with jagged teeth and long nails. They flew through the air, circling the house, the ghosts leaving trails of ectoplasm in their wake, the black-garbed witches cackling as they rode broomsticks fashioned from human spinal columns. But worst of all was the monstrous thing standing atop the house.

Like the children, the mayor had become her costume. She was still twelve feet tall, but now her body was in proportion to her height, and her dark blue gown was shredded, revealing that her torso blended with the roof shingles. She no longer was simply standing on the house. She had become one with it. Her arms and neck were now long and thin, almost sinuous like serpents. Her flesh was still blue, reminding Drew of some images he had seen of the Hindu death goddess Kali. Her mouth was filled with sharp silvery teeth resembling knife blades, and her solid-black eyes gleamed like polished obsidian. In her clawed hands, she held her staff, only now it was a gnarled hunk of wood formed from braided tree limbs, and the end of it burned bright with fire. The Witch Queen let out a hate-filled hiss and stabbed her staff toward them, releasing a blast of flame.

Drew yelled, "Run!" but he needn't have bothered. With skeletons advancing on one side and deadly fire shooting toward them on the other, no one needed encouragement to get the hell out of there as fast as possible. Drew glanced back over his shoulder and saw the flames engulf the skeletons and the bone horse, along with the crooked man who still hadn't recovered from Greg's attack. Fire wreathed their bodies, and they flailed about, shrieking and stumbling, before collapsing to the ground and lying still as they burned. Amber had said that these transformations were real, at least on some level, and he feared for the people who had been changed by the Dark Lady's power. Would the damage done to them in their new forms remain when they returned to normal?

The Witch Queen shrieked in frustration at missing her intended targets, and she unleashed a new blast of fire at them. This one missed, too, but it came close enough that Drew felt heat sear the back of his neck, leaving him with what felt like an instant sunburn there.

They were running toward the other side of the street in a blind panic, but when Drew saw what waited for them there, he shouted for the others to stop. The Dark Lady had done more than transform those participating in the parade. She had also changed the onlookers. A monstrous mob stood on the sidewalk, hundreds of creatures of every shape and size, all of them nightmarish versions of whatever costumes they had been wearing before their metamorphoses. One person's head had been replaced by a giant pus-weeping eyeball, while another looked as if he or she—it was impossible to tell—had been turned inside out, glistening organs revealed to the world. A rotted pumpkin-headed thing stood next to a clown with a long coiled spring of a neck, like a jack-in-the-box come to life. A boar-headed butcher complete with bloodstained apron and dripping red cleaver stood beside a couple who had been dressed in that perennial Halloween cliché, the tandem horse. They had become a hideous equine-human conglomeration, a two-headed thing with a jumble of human and animal parts. Even costumes that should have been benign—football players, cowboys, French maids, superheroes, fairy princesses, and the like—had become grotesque distortions of mottled flesh, fanged teeth, and clawed hands.

"She can't have this kind of power!" Trevor said. "It's not possible!"

"It's a trick," Greg said. "At least partly. The monstrous appearance of the people is an illusion created by the Dark Lady, but their aggression is quite real. If they manage to get hold of us, they'll tear us apart."

"You should all leave me," Erin said. "When they're busy with me, you can try to get to the bookstore."

"This is no time for suicide by possessed mob," Greg said, "no matter how guilt-ridden you feel. The best way to fight illusion is with illusion."

Drew thought of the burn on the back of his neck. If the Witch Queen's fire was an illusion, then he wasn't actually hurt. But he still felt as if he'd been burned. "If the possessed believe they're injured, they'll react as if they are. But any wounds they suffer will be merely psychosomatic."

While they talked, the creatures on the sidewalk stepped into the street and started toward them. They moved slowly at first, as if they were in a daze. Drew glanced backward and saw that the Witch Queen was looking around, seemingly confused. The skeletons—upright again and moving, although their clothes were aflame and their bones blackened—milled about uncertainly.

The Dark Lady is having trouble controlling them all, Drew thought. *She's spreading her power too thin. Good.* That gave them a chance to figure out a way to deal with the mess.

Trevor turned to Greg. "Illusion is your area of expertise. Can you do anything to help us?"

He shook his head. "Not as long as I'm in this body. Amber will have to do it."

"Me?" she said. "What can I do?"

"You're already shielding us from the Dark Lady's power, preventing us from being possessed," Greg said. "You're doing it instinctively. It helps that four of us have had experience resisting psychic assaults, but we couldn't do it without you."

"Tell me what to do," she said.

"There's a great deal of psychokinetic energy in the atmosphere right now," Greg said. "You need to tap into it and use it."

"But use it *how*?"

He shrugged. "It's up to you. You have to use your imagination."

She turned to Drew. "Help me."

He understood what she was asking. It was common for therapists to use guided visualization with their clients, although doing so would have been easier in the quiet confines of an office, as opposed to the middle of a street with a horde of possessed parade goers slowly advancing on them.

Drew took hold of Amber's hands and squeezed gently. "OK, close your eyes and concentrate on the sound of my voice. Take in a deep breath, hold it for a moment, then let it out slowly. Think of your mind as a pool of clear water, the surface still and calm. Take another breath, let it out. Now, picture the six of us. You, me, Trevor, Greg, Erin, and Arthur. We're in danger, but that's all right. We're protected from the Dark Lady's influence, and we have the ability to defend ourselves."

Amber did as he said, and her breathing became more relaxed as he spoke. At first, nothing happened, and Drew feared that she wouldn't be able to summon the concentration necessary for the task, but then Trevor said, "Whoa!" Drew turned to his friend and saw that he now held a sword, as did Greg, Carrington, and Erin. He let go of Amber's hands, and the moment he did so, a sword appeared in each of their hands as well.

"You couldn't have conjured up a few automatic weapons?" Greg said, giving his sword a few experimental swishes through the air.

"Stop complaining," Amber said, "and start moving."

"Sound advice," Carrington said. He raised his sword to his face in a salute. "'Once more unto the breach, dear friends.'"

And with that, the six of them began running down the street in the direction of Forgotten Lore. They stuck to the strip of street between the crowd on the sidewalk and the parade participants, hoping to avoid both.

As they ran, Drew looked at Amber. "Swords?"

She grinned. "When you said Arthur's name, it made me think of King Arthur. I guess my subconscious decided to whip up a bunch of Excaliburs for us."

As they passed the haunted house, child-size ghosts and witches came streaking through the air toward them. Drew knew they weren't really flying, that it was all part of the Dark Lady's illusion, just as he knew that hitting them with Amber's equally illusory swords wouldn't really hurt them. Still, he hesitated to swing his weapon at a witch who came flying toward him, cackling with mad glee. In reality, she was only a little girl, running toward him instead of flying, driven to attack by the mind-twisting power of the Dark Lady. She was as much a victim of the baleful spirit as the men and women she had killed, and he didn't want to hurt her. But when she was within range, he lashed out with his blade and struck her a solid blow to the side of her neck.

The witch screeched in pain, black blood spurted from the wound, and her spinal-column broom veered off to the left. She dipped toward the ground, smashed into the asphalt, bounced, rolled, and came to a stop, leaving a smear of black gore behind her. She lay still in a widening pool of blood.

He stood there shaking, ribs throbbing. *She's not dead,* he told himself. *She only thinks she is.* Once the Dark Lady released her grip on the girl's mind, she would return to normal and be restored to full health. He hoped. He had no more time for doubts then, for a ghost came at him, moaning like a midnight winter wind.

They hacked and slashed their way through the ghosts and witches, Drew doing his best not to think of them as boys and girls, and they were almost past the haunted house when the Witch Queen turned in their direction, let out a shriek of rage, aimed her staff, and released a blistering gout of flame.

Amber was right in the path of the fire blast, and although Drew took a panicked step forward, he knew he couldn't save her. As they had run and fought, space had opened up between them, and there was no way he could reach her before the flames. There wasn't even enough time to shout and warn her.

But Erin was standing right next to Amber, and she saw the flame blast coming. She slammed her shoulder into Amber and knocked her aside, just as the fire hit. Flames engulfed Erin, and she screamed in agony as her flesh blackened and sizzled. She dropped her sword and staggered around, still screaming, until Greg stepped forward and calmly rammed his swordpoint into her chest. She stiffened, her screaming stopped, and then she slipped off of Greg's blade and collapsed to the ground.

Trevor stepped toward Greg, sword raised. "You sonofabitch!" He swung, but Greg parried the blow easily.

"Relax. She's not dead. But she believed she was on fire, so the pain she felt was real. All I did by seeming to kill her was render her unconscious. It was a mercy." He glanced down at her still-burning form. "Believe me, I know."

Greg still wore Connie's face, but for an instant, Drew saw his actual visage, bald and burn-scarred, superimposed upon it. But the image faded, leaving him looking only like Connie again.

"Let's go before that bitch witch roasts the rest of us," Greg said. Without another word, he resumed running, and the others followed.

"Is Greg right?" Amber said to Drew as they ran. "Is Erin OK?"

He resisted glancing back over his shoulder at Erin's blackened, smoldering corpse. He wanted to reassure Amber, but he couldn't find the words, so they just kept running.

SEVENTEEN

Amber's right arm felt as heavy as lead, but it wasn't as heavy as her heart. She understood that they weren't really hurting anyone with their swords, that this was all an elaborate game of pretend, a psychological battle rather than a physical one. But it *felt* real. Every time her blade cut into an opponent's flesh, she felt the jolt run up her arm, saw blood spurt from the wound, heard the cries of pain. Real or not, she knew she would have nightmares about this for years to come.

The six of them—make that five—had reached Forgotten Lore. Everyone looked as exhausted as she felt: clothes splattered with blood, faces slick with sweat, lungs heaving, sword arms hanging limply at their sides. But the fight wasn't over yet. The high-school band was coming toward them, moving with halting, staggering steps. The kids had become emaciated, gray-fleshed corpses, with dark pools of shadow where their eyes had been. Their instruments had been transformed, too, becoming weapons—knives, axes, and hand scythes—fashioned from whatever material their instruments had been made from. Keys, valves, slides, and mouthpieces remained, indicating the weapons' musical origin, but rather than making the objects look ridiculous, their altered appearance rendered them sinister in the extreme.

Amber wondered how the band members would wield their strange weapons. They weren't really blades, after all; they only appeared that way. She assumed that the kids would use their instruments like clubs, beating their victims repeatedly until they died. It sounded like a very long and painful way to die, and she would prefer to avoid it if she could. They had their swords and could fight back, but there were too many kids, and they were too tired. Besides, their swords were illusory, but those instruments, despite their current appearance, were not. It would only be a matter of moments until they were overrun, and when they died, they would do so for real.

The five of them stood with their backs to the storefront so they could face the oncoming corpses. Amber looked over her shoulder and peered through the display window. If the Dark Lady was inside Forgotten Lore, she couldn't tell. The store was filled with an impenetrable darkness, the kind Amber imagined could only be found in the deepest ocean depths where no ray of light had ever touched.

Maybe we'd be safer staying out here, she thought.

Yellow crime-scene tape stretched across the door, and Amber wasn't surprised when Drew tried to open it and found it locked. He stepped back and tried kicking it open, but the door was made of thick, solid wood and refused to budge.

"I've got an idea," Trevor said. He walked up to the window, told everyone to stand back, and swung his sword at the glass. Amber knew what was going to happen, but she still gritted her teeth in anticipation of hearing the sound of glass shattering. But Trevor's blade passed through the glass without so much as leaving a scratch.

"What part of *illusion* don't you get, genius?" Greg said.

Then, as if Greg had said that the emperor had no clothes, all of their swords dissipated like mist.

"I'm sorry!" Amber said. "I must've lost my concentration."

Drew shook his head. "Seeing concrete evidence that the swords were illusory caused your subconscious mind to no longer believe in them. When that happened—"

"Poof," Greg said.

She turned to face the horde of teenage corpses staggering toward them, less than twenty feet away now. They only had a few moments left to do something before brass and woodwinds came bashing down on their skulls. Amber looked around, desperate to find something—

"The trashcan!" She pointed to a metal receptacle on the sidewalk nearby. It was painted white, and its domed lid had two black eyes to make it resemble a ghost. She figured the hinged flap was supposed to serve as the faux specter's mouth.

"That'll work!" Trevor ran over, grabbed hold of the trashcan, lifted it, and ran at the bookstore's window. He heaved the receptacle at the glass, and this time, it broke with an extremely satisfying shattering sound.

"It appears that the trashcan is mightier than the sword," Greg said.

"Amber, Greg, both of you get inside!" Drew said. "Arthur, Trevor, and I will follow."

Greg looked at her. "Do women have to put up with this macho nonsense a lot?"

She smiled. "You have no idea."

Amber went first, careful not to cut herself on the jagged shards that still jutted from the window frame. There had been a table display of books on the other side, but the trashcan had knocked the volumes to the floor. Enough light spilled in from outside that Amber could see that the books were Trevor's and Carrington's. As she set her foot on the floor, she accidentally bent back the front cover of one of Trevor's books, and she mentally apologized. Once she was all the way inside, Greg followed. A moment later, Carrington came through the broken window, followed by Trevor and then Drew. When Carrington saw his books on the floor, he reflexively bent down to pick them up, but then he straightened, as if he had thought better of it.

It was good to know that even the great Arthur Carrington could put aside his ego when there was a job to do, however hard he might have to struggle to do so.

Amber turned to look back out the window. The Marching Band of the Living Dead was still coming, and they showed no signs of stopping. If they didn't do something fast, the kids would soon be climbing in through the broken window. And once that happened, they would be trapped, with nowhere left to run.

"We need to find something to barricade the window!" Drew said, looking frantically around. But the light from the street only penetrated a few feet into the store. After that, only a solid wall of black was visible, and it was impossible to tell what lay beyond it.

"There's no time!" Carrington said. "They're almost here!"

Amber found herself strangely unconcerned about the band members' approach. Instead, she found her attention becoming even more focused on the wall of shadow. There was something compelling about it, something that seemed to be calling to her, urging her toward it.

"She's inside," Amber said, and as soon as the words left her mouth, she sensed that it was true.

"Then that's where we have to go," Greg said.

"What part of *trap* don't *you* understand?" Trevor said.

"I understand that if we stay here, we're dead." And with that, Greg calmly walked forward and was swallowed by darkness.

"It's easy for him to take a chance like that," Trevor grumbled. "He's already dead."

"He?" Carrington said. "Dead?"

"There's no time to explain," Amber said. She couldn't help giving him a quick smile. "And you're probably happier not knowing. Let's go." She took his hand, then reached out to take Drew's. "Ready?" she asked.

Drew smiled. "Let's see what's waiting for us this time."

Books were scattered all over the floor from when Tonya had

been killed, and they had to step carefully. Amber led the two men forward, and Trevor followed close behind.

"Whatever's in there," Trevor said, "I guarantee we're not going to like it."

The four of them entered the blackness.

Wind roared and swirled around her as rain slammed into her body like miniature spears of ice. She felt off balance, and her feet would have slid out from under her if she hadn't been holding on to Drew's and Carrington's hands. She heard Trevor swear, and she turned to see him lean forward, arms stretched out before him, as if he was trying to maintain his balance. He was sliding slowly backward, and that's when she realized that they were all standing on a slanted roof, rain-slick shingles beneath their feet.

Greg stood at the apex of the roof, straddling both sides with his bare feet—he had kicked off Connie's shoes when they had been running in the street—and he reached out to grab Trevor's hand and steady him. At first, she feared that Trevor would yank Greg toward him, and they would both go tumbling over the edge, but Greg was stronger than he looked. Or, rather, Connie's body was stronger than it looked, and Greg managed to maintain his position without losing hold of Trevor.

It took some doing, but the four of them joined Greg at the very top of the roof, and there they remained, clinging to one another for support.

Amber looked around. The rain and wind made it difficult to see, and she had to squint her eyes and shield them with a hand, but she was able to make out dozens of roofs around them, spreading outward in all directions. But roofs were all that was visible. The houses beneath them were concealed by high, fast-flowing floodwaters. She couldn't see anyone on the other roofs, though. The five of them appeared to be alone, and there was no Dark Lady in sight.

"Is this real?" Carrington asked. He had to almost shout to make himself heard over the wind and rain.

"More real than the monsters out in the street," Trevor said. "We entered the locus of the Dark Lady's haunting. This is where she's strongest."

"Remember the girl who died in the museum." Greg said. "Her lungs were filled with river water. Even an illusion can kill, if enough power is channeled into it."

"So don't go for a swim," Trevor said.

Drew turned his head back and forth, checking every direction. "If this truly is her locus, she should be here. So where is she?"

"Maybe Trevor was right," Carrington said. "Maybe this is a trap. A sort of pocket dimension where the Dark Lady has imprisoned us."

"I suppose it's possible," Greg said, although he sounded doubtful. "But . . ." He trailed off, his eyes widening as if he had just spotted something. "Oh, shit, that's not good."

"What?" Drew asked.

Greg pointed toward the water, and as Amber looked in that direction, she sensed a presence all around them. It was massive and angry, but most of all, it was *afraid*.

She saw forms gliding through the water just below the surface, dozens, hundreds of them, each roughly the size of a person. They were everywhere, as far as the eye could see, shadowy shapes without any individual features to distinguish one from another.

"Those are spirits of people who died in the flood," she said. "The Dark Lady gets her power from them."

"I get much more than that, my dear."

Amber spun around to see the Dark Lady standing next to her. The dead woman grinned, although her shadow-black eyes remained cold and unfeeling as she reached out and took hold of Amber's wrist. Her touch was so frigid it burned like fire, and Amber gasped in pain.

"I'd love to have a girl-to-girl chat with you, but I made a promise to a friend of mine."

The Dark Lady yanked Amber away from the others with unearthly strength and hurled her away from the roof. Amber spun through the air, and the last thing she heard before she hit the water—and joined the multitude of dark shapes swimming beneath the surface—was Drew shouting her name.

She woke up coughing, rolled over onto her side, and threw up a stream of river water. She was still retching when she realized that she was lying on a tiled floor in a lit room.

"It's about time that goddamned bitch kept her promise."

Mitch.

Feeling dizzy and sick, she pushed herself onto her feet and turned to face him. She didn't wonder how she had gotten there or even where "there" was. All that mattered was making sure he didn't get his hands on her.

"So that's what got you to serve her?" she asked. "She promised you could have me when it was all over?'

Mitch smiled. "Yep. Though truth to tell, I was beginning to wonder if she was planning on scamming me."

Amber's eyes darted from side to side as she took in her surroundings. They were in a small kitchen—a woman's, she guessed, based on the décor: butterfly and kitten magnets holding various coupons in place on the refrigerator, a calendar with nature scenes hanging on the wall, an oven mitt on the counter designed to look like the head of a cute, cartoonish cow. This had to be Jenn's place.

"Where is she?" she demanded.

"Jenn? Watching all the fun happening outside. Until a bit ago, that's what I was doing, too. That stunt with the swords was pretty impressive. I didn't know you could do stuff like that."

"You never knew me, Mitch. Not really."

He looked at her for a long moment, considering her words.

"Maybe not. But we're going to have lots of time to get better acquainted. In all kinds of ways." His smile widened. "Who knows? Maybe the Dark Lady will let me keep the Asian girl, too. What do you think? Some say three's a crowd, but it's also a number with magical significance, isn't it? You'd know better than me. You're into that kind of thing now."

She peered closely at Mitch. His eyes were too wide, his smile too close to a leer, and he gave off a manic energy that he seemed to be having trouble containing.

"What happened to you?" she asked. "The Mitch Sagers I knew might have been a controlling misogynist with anger issues, but he wasn't a killer. For all his faults, he was a man, not a monster."

He frowned, and Amber saw the confusion in his eyes. She hoped that she had managed to reach him, but then his gaze cleared, and when he spoke, his voice was cold and mocking. "Maybe *you* never really knew *me*," he said.

He came at her then, and without thinking, she extended her hand toward him, fingers curled as if she were gripping an unseen object. One instant her hand was empty, and the next it was holding a sword.

Mitch impaled himself on her blade, which was preternaturally sharp. His body stiffened, his face paled, and he took two more steps forward, sliding along the metal until the hilt was pressed against his chest. Blood darkened the front of his shirt, and his mouth opened and closed as if he was trying to say something, but only a whispering hiss of breath emerged. She wasn't certain, but she thought he said, "Sorry, Daddy."

The sword vanished, and Mitch collapsed to the kitchen floor like a puppet whose strings had been cut. She looked down at his body for several moments, trying to feel something but not really surprised that she didn't. She then went off in search of Jenn.

"Amber!"

Drew stepped forward as if he thought he might be able to catch hold of Amber and keep her from falling into the water. He started to slip on the rain-slick roof, but Trevor grabbed his arm to steady him. Drew watched as Amber plunged into the water and sank beneath the surface. He feared that the spirits of the flood victims would converge on her like hungry piranha attacking a hunk of raw meat, but they continued circling the rooftop. He watched for Amber to break the surface and draw in a gasping breath, but she didn't reappear.

Drew turned toward the Dark Lady, rage and fear roiling within him. "Bring her back! Now!"

The ghost looked at him with amusement, as if he were a precocious child who had just said something particularly charming. He was no more psychically sensitive than any normal human being, but this close to the Dark Lady, he could feel the power rolling off of her. Wave after wave of psychic energy, so strong that it took all of his willpower to continue facing her. He felt an atavistic fear at being in her presence, like a field mouse seeing a hawk swooping toward it, helpless to do anything but watch as death came gliding down on silent wings.

Drew knew his fear was well founded. With the power of all these spirits to draw on here in her locus, the Dark Lady was virtually a god. What could the four of them do against her, especially now, with Amber gone? She was the psychically strongest of all of them, which was why the Dark Lady had dealt with her first. But Drew wasn't about to give up, not as long as there was a chance that Amber was still alive. Just because it appeared that she had been lost to the floodwaters, that didn't make it so. It could have been an illusion, and despite Greg's warning that even illusions could kill if they were fueled by enough power, he had to believe that Amber possessed enough strength to resist the Dark Lady. He had to.

His voice was shaky as he spoke, but his words didn't falter. "Why are you doing this? What do you want?"

"I want it to stop."

Her voice was something felt as much as heard and seemed to come from everywhere and nowhere at once. It was in the wind and rain, in the sound of the water rushing past the roof and the rippling waves made by the swimming spirits.

"What?" Trevor said. "What do you want to stop?"

"You."

A chill fingered down Drew's spine upon hearing her speak that single word. Was she saying that she wanted them to die? It couldn't be that simple. The Dark Lady had been quiet for decades, and as far as they knew, she hadn't hurt anyone until the week before. If her only motivation was to kill, she'd had ample opportunity over the years. Why start now?

Trevor's thoughts must have been running along similar lines, for he turned to Greg. "You said you awakened her spirit six months ago, when you attempted to absorb her energy. Maybe it's *you* she wants to stop."

"I may have woken her up, but she harmed no one until recently. And she can't be reacting to my presence, because the first two murders took place before I contacted Amber," Greg said.

"Maybe she had a precognitive flash that you would return," Trevor said, although he didn't sound as if he believed it himself.

"A possibility. I suppose I could always try apologizing." He turned to the Dark Lady. "I'm very sorry that I disturbed your slumber. I promise I won't do it again. Can we return to reality now?"

She tilted her head to the side, a slightly bemused expression on her face, but otherwise didn't respond.

Greg shrugged. "I tried."

Carrington had been looking back and forth between Trevor and Greg as they had talked.

"What in the hell are you two going on about?" he asked.

"Long story," Trevor said. He turned to Drew. "Back to you, Doctor."

Drew decided to try a different approach. "Who are you?"

"I am the Dark Lady."

"You're appearing to us as the Dark Lady," Drew said. "But she's just a bit of local folklore. There's no evidence that she was ever a real person. In that case, what are you?"

She regarded him silently, a blank expression on her ivory face, as if she didn't understand his question.

Drew continued. "We know that your power comes from the spirits of those who drowned in the flood, but there's more to it than that. You *are* those spirits. They died together in a terrible disaster, and afterward their souls remained earthbound, but not as separate entities. They banded together, merged into a single collective consciousness, one that took on the form of the Dark Lady, a legend they were all familiar with." He gestured toward the shadowy shapes swimming around the rooftop. "That's who you truly are."

The Dark Lady frowned, but again, she didn't reply.

Trevor picked up the thread after that. "After the flood, spiritualists and mediums were drawn to Exeter. Maybe because of an increase in paranormal activity, maybe simply because a lot of people lost loved ones in the disaster and were desperate to make contact with them by any means possible. Whatever the reason, they came. And one day, a group of them decided to make contact with the Dark Lady and lay her spirit to rest. They tried to get rid of you. Send you away from your home. You were scared. You didn't want to go, so you lashed out and killed the psychic conducting the exorcism ceremony. And you said the word *Stop* to tell people to stop trying to make you leave."

The Dark Lady regarded him for a moment. *"This is our home. We lived here. We died here. It's where we belong."*

Drew was encouraged to hear the spirit refer to herself in the plural. The mask was beginning to come off. He continued speaking. "You were left alone for many years. People kept coming to

Exeter, drawn by its history and reputation for paranormal events, and many of them settled here. But no one attempted to send you away again."

"No one that we know of," Greg said. "That doesn't mean a psychically gifted person didn't drop dead from a heart attack now and again, raising no suspicion."

The Dark Lady smiled but made no comment.

Trevor turned to Greg. "Then you came to town and attempted to absorb the Dark Lady's power. I'd say that qualifies as trying to 'make her go away.'"

"And that put her on the alert," Greg said. "After I failed, she remained watchful, wary of anything that even resembled an attempt to drive her out."

"And she saw Erin's film as such an attempt," Carrington said. "But why? It wasn't as if we were conducting exorcism rites as part of the film."

The answer came to Drew then. "She wasn't afraid of the film itself. She was afraid of what people would do when they saw it." He turned toward the Dark Lady. "You feared that a new wave of psychic mediums would descend on Exeter, intrigued by the accounts reported in Erin's film. You feared that some of them might attempt to send you away. And if there were enough of them working together, you feared they might succeed."

"This is our home," the Dark Lady repeated.

"So she started killing people to . . . what?" Carrington said. "Scare us off? Get us to abandon the film and leave?"

"Yes," Drew said. "And she hoped you would spread the word to other filmmakers about how dangerous it was to shoot in Exeter, so that no one else would attempt to make a film. That's why she didn't simply kill Erin outright."

"Dearie, are you ever misguided," Greg said to the Dark Lady. "The way modern media work, the more horrific the story, the more drawn to it they are, like cats to a canary buffet. You'd have been better off lying low and letting them finish their film and leave."

"Of course she doesn't understand the media," Trevor said. "She's the collective spirit of hundreds of people who died almost a century ago."

"So this is all nothing but a huge misunderstanding," Carrington said. He turned to the Dark Lady. "All you have to do is release us, and it will be over. We will go away, and you'll be safe once more."

The Dark Lady frowned, as if she were considering his words. But then a cold smile stretched across her face. *"Yes, we will be safe. After tonight, we will be stronger. So strong that no one will ever be able to send us away."*

Drew didn't understand. But Greg did. "The parade! She didn't intend to use those people to stop us. She's going to turn them against one another, make them fight until they all die. And every new spirit that's released will join the Dark Lady's collective consciousness and add to her power."

Images flashed through Drew's mind, and he knew that the Dark Lady was showing them what was happening in the street outside the bookstore. People attacking one another, fighting with whatever weapons they could scrounge—hunks of wood and metal torn from parade floats, using their hands and teeth if they had nothing else. They still appeared monstrous, but that aspect was no longer as strong as it had been; it had become a semitransparent overlay, allowing the real people beneath the illusions to show through. But the expressions of animalistic hatred on their faces were just as horrible as any illusion, if not more so. Those possessed tore at one another with savage abandon, fighting on despite whatever wounds they had suffered themselves. Not everyone was caught up in the Dark Lady's spell, though. Some people ran instead of fighting, expressions of terror on their faces. Unfortunately, they were easily brought down by the possessed.

The vision faded, and once again, Drew stood on the rooftop, surrounded by wind and rain. "My God," he whispered. "All those people . . ."

From the expressions on the others' faces, Drew knew that they had witnessed the same horrific images. Trevor and Carrington looked just as shaken as he was, and even Greg appeared disturbed.

But when Greg spoke, he sounded calm. "You're spreading yourself awfully thin, honey. Your illusions aren't holding, and not everyone is dancing to your tune. And how much power is it taking to keep this part of the show running?" He gestured at their surroundings. "You're not going to be able to keep this up much longer."

The Dark Lady fixed him with a cold stare. *"It shall be long enough."*

"We have to do something!" Carrington said. "We can't just stand here and let those poor people die!"

Without waiting for any of them to respond, he started toward the Dark Lady. Her mouth twitched into a half-smile. She waited until he was within arm's reach, then she made a small gesture. Shingles came loose beneath Carrington's feet, causing him to slip. He fell, slid off the roof, and plunged into the water.

"Arthur!" Trevor shouted. He moved to the edge of the roof as fast as he could without losing his balance. Drew followed and grabbed hold of his hand for support. Trevor called out Carrington's name again, but there was no reply and no sign of him.

Greg turned to Drew. "If we're going to have any hope of stopping her, we have to do it now, while she's overextended and before she gains any more strength."

Trevor remained at the roof's edge, but he looked back over his shoulder at Greg. "You're a former evil mastermind. Don't you have any ideas?"

"Some," Greg said. "Unfortunately, I no longer possess the power to implement them. If we had—" He was interrupted by the sound of splashing water as something broke the surface near Trevor.

At first, Drew feared that one of the swimming specters had decided to attack, but then he saw who it was. "Amber!" he shouted.

She grabbed hold of the roof's edge and drew in a gasping breath. Trevor reached out to help her up, but another hand emerged from the water to take his. He pulled Jenn onto the roof and hugged her close.

Drew let go of Trevor's hand and moved to the edge to help Amber up, and they embraced. The relief he felt upon seeing her alive and unharmed was overwhelming. "I thought I'd lost you," he said softly.

She smiled. "You're not going to get rid of me that easily."

"People are dying," Greg said. "Reunions later, all right?"

"What does he mean?" Amber asked.

"The Dark Lady is causing everyone who gathered for the parade to fight. She hopes to harvest more spirits to add to her energy." He paused. "Did you see Mitch?"

She nodded. "I took care of him." She looked around. "Arthur?"

"He fell in."

"We didn't see him. I hope he'll be—"

She broke off as a swollen-fingered hand latched onto the roof's edge. It was followed by another, and another, and then faces came into view. Whitish-gray flesh, puffy and distorted features, milky film-coated eyes, and mouths filled with sharp teeth.

The four of them moved toward the top of the roof to join Greg as the flood victims slowly emerged from the water, crawling up the roof on all fours as if they were animals, teeth bared and eyes glistening.

"She recognizes Amber as the real threat," Greg said. "She's not messing around anymore."

Drew knew that they only had seconds before the undead creatures overwhelmed them. He thought furiously, running through everything they had learned about the Dark Lady. His mind latched onto their encounter with her in the college library, when she had used one of their memories to create an illusory scenario. She had masqueraded as the Gork, and they had bested her when they had realized what she feared.

"The water!" he said. "Remember what happened in the library?"

"But there's water all around," Trevor said. "Those damned ghouls are swimming around in it like it's nothing."

Speaking of ghouls, the fanged creatures were approaching from all sides now, and they were almost close enough to grab hold with their fat, water-swollen fingers. The Dark Lady watched as the creatures—which in truth were only another part of her—drew closer, a pleased smile on her ivory-fleshed face.

"This is water *she* controls," Greg said. "It holds no fear for her."

"Then we need water *we* control," Trevor said.

They all looked to Amber. "I'll try," she said. "But I can't do it alone." She turned to Jenn. "There's a reason she had Mitch kidnap you. She wanted to keep us away from each other. You're as much a part of her locus as the bookstore, and that means I can affect this place—affect *her*—through you." She held out her hand.

Jenn hesitated, but then she stepped away from Trevor and took hold of Amber's hand.

Amber closed her eyes and concentrated, and the Dark Lady stopped smiling. She gestured, and the flood victims scuttled forward, but they only moved a few inches before they froze. As one, they turned and looked in the same direction, suddenly wary, as if they were animals sensing danger.

From off in the distance came a deep sound, more felt than heard. It made Drew think of an approaching train. As the sound grew louder, the spirits of the flood victims whirled around and scuttled back to the water, leaping in and swiftly disappearing beneath the waves.

The Dark Lady also turned toward the sound, and her face contorted into a mask of sheer terror. They all looked toward the sound then—all except Amber, who continued holding on to Jenn's hand, her eyes closed—and saw a wall of solid water rushing at them, so massive it blocked out the sky. Drew couldn't see the top of it, and he wondered if it even had a top. It was as if an entire universe of water were rolling toward them, completely obliterating this one as it came.

"Surf's up," Trevor said in a hushed voice.

They could feel the vibrations in the shingles beneath their feet as the monster wave drew closer. Water surged in advance of the wave, and the level rose quickly up the roof, covering their feet and ankles, rising up their legs to their knees, thighs . . . The wind kicked up, and Drew knew that they were feeling the air that the wave pushed before it.

The Dark Lady stared at the gigantic wall of water as it bore down upon them. Tears rolled down her chalk-white cheeks, and she spoke a single word, one Drew couldn't hear over the water's roar, but he read her lips and was fairly sure that the word was *Please*. But did she mean *Please, no,* or was she perhaps asking for the release that she had resisted for so long? There was no way to know and no time left to wonder about it.

"Everyone grab hold of one another!" Drew shouted. "Before—"

But he was too late. The wave slammed into the rooftop and carried them all away into silence and darkness.

EIGHTEEN

Although it wasn't quite lunchtime, Trevor finished his Samuel Adams, went up to the bar, and ordered another. After the weekend they'd had, he figured he deserved it. He wished he hadn't quit smoking, though. He could really use a cigarette.

He returned to the table. Amber and Drew were holding hands, and while both of them had circles under their eyes from lack of sleep, they were smiling. It made a difference, having someone special to share the hard times with. He glanced at Jenn as he sat down beside her and couldn't help feeling a bit jealous at what Drew and Amber had together.

He started to take a sip of his beer, but everyone else was drinking soda. He felt suddenly self-conscious, so he put the beer down on the table without drinking from the bottle. He would pace himself this time.

No music played in the hotel bar. Maybe because it was still technically morning, at least for a few more minutes. But Trevor figured that after what the media were calling the "riot" the night before, the bartender felt silence was more appropriate. Trevor would have appreciated some music, though. It might help to take their minds off things, at least a little.

Jenn looked worse than either Drew or Amber. Her face was drawn, her eyes red and puffy as if she had been crying. He had offered to stay in her room the night before, just so she wouldn't have to be alone. She had thanked him but said she wanted to be alone. Trevor had told her he understood and tried not to view it as a rejection, but that morning, it still stung a little. From the look of her, she hadn't gotten any sleep at all, and if she had, he doubted that her dreams had been pleasant. His sure hadn't been.

"I'm sorry I'm not in the Exhibition Hall selling your books," Jenn said. She looked down at the tabletop as she spoke. "I'm just not up to working right now."

"No worries," Trevor said. He smiled. "Besides, it's not as if there are many people left to buy them."

A lot of the conference attendees had checked out of the hotel that morning and left town. Most of them had been in atten-dance at the parade, Trevor guessed, and that encounter with the paranormal had been too intense for even the most enthusiastic among them. They probably couldn't wait to get the hell out of Exeter.

He considered reaching over to take Jenn's hand, but she had been distant since the night before, and he was unsure how she would react. So he kept his hand to himself.

After Amber and Jenn had caused the gigantic wave to slam into the Dark Lady's rooftop, Trevor thought they had all died. The dark-ness had seemed to go on forever. But then they awoke in Jenn's store, soaked to the bone and lying on a floor covered with sodden books. A quick look through the shattered store window showed that the Dark Lady's spell had been broken and the parade goers were no longer attacking one another. Of the Dark Lady herself, there was no sign. Trevor had expected her to make a reappear-ance then, laughing maniacally because they had failed to defeat her. But she hadn't, and while he still wasn't one-hundred-percent confident that she was gone for good, he was beginning to feel cau-tiously optimistic.

He looked at Drew. "Have you heard anything from Connie?"

When they had woken in Forgotten Lore, Greg's spirit was gone from Connie's body. She had no memory of what had occurred while Greg was in control, and she was extremely confused and more than a little freaked out. Otherwise, she was seemingly no worse for the wear. Whether Amber's wave had forced Greg to vacate his host or he had left voluntarily because their work was done, Trevor didn't know. Greg was a pain in the ass, and he couldn't condone his hijacking someone else's body, but he was surprised to realize that he was going to miss the jerk—although he would never admit it to Drew and Amber.

"I feel sorry for her," Amber said. "One minute she's walking into a restroom, and the next it's almost twelve hours later, she's in some bookstore she's never seen before, and she's drenched with river water."

"I wonder if she'll check herself into her own hospital," Trevor said.

Drew smiled. "I doubt it. Knowing Connie, my guess is that she'll work hard to suppress the experience and act like it never happened. I won't be surprised if she doesn't mention it at all when I get back to work tomorrow."

"Work? If I were you, my boy, I'd take a week off—at least!" They turned to see Carrington walking toward their table, grinning as if he was in fine humor today. He didn't only look as if he had gotten a full night's sleep, but he looked refreshed and recharged, as if he had just returned from a restful vacation.

Erin, on the other hand, looked as bad as Jenn. Still, she managed a wan smile as she and Carrington joined them.

Carrington had been there in the bookstore when they had awakened, wet but not drowned. Erin had escaped injury during the riot, probably because she had been unconscious through most of it. Her body showed no signs of the burns she had suffered or the sword thrust she had taken to the chest. As Drew had predicted, the injuries had all been in her mind, and when the Dark Lady's spell was broken, Erin awoke, unhurt. Physically, at least. Psychologically was another matter, Trevor thought.

"A vacation *does* sound good right now," Amber said. "And it would give us time to pack up all my stuff. Not that I have all that much."

"Pack?" Trevor said. "Am I to take this as a sign that the two of you are going to quit hemming and hawing and move in together?"

Both Amber and Drew smiled.

"Yes," Amber said. "I'm going to move into Drew's place in Chicago and start looking for work. Who knows? Maybe I'll start taking classes at one of the colleges there, too."

"You could always hang out your shingle as a 'psychic advisor,'" Carrington said. "You are prodigiously talented in that area."

"Thanks, but I don't think I want to give up my amateur standing just yet. I don't know what field I might want to go into. I thought I might start by taking classes that I find interesting and see where they lead me."

"Good plan," Trevor said. "Just don't let Drew try to talk you into studying psychology. One headshrinker on our team is enough."

"In that case, she shouldn't go into journalism," Drew shot back. "One loud-mouthed writer on our team is enough."

Trevor grinned, picked up his beer, raised it to Drew in a mock toast, and took a sip.

"I'm just glad things weren't worse," Jenn said.

Erin turned toward her, showing some animation for the first time since she sat down.

"*Worse?* Ray, Sarah, and Pattie died yesterday, and so did Chief Hoffman. How could it possibly have been any worse?"

In the aftermath of all the chaos and confusion, it had taken a while for them to get hold of the police. But eventually, they had, and that's when they learned of Sarah's and Pattie's deaths.

Jenn's jaw muscles tightened, but she managed to remain calm. "I was thinking about all the people at the parade. Who knows how many would've died if the Dark Lady hadn't been stopped?"

They had defeated the Dark Lady, but not before a half-dozen additional people were killed in the street and dozens more had been injured.

Erin still looked upset, but she didn't argue any further. Trevor thought he understood. Ray, Sarah, and Pattie had been her crew, her friends, and she felt responsible for their deaths.

"I keep wondering if there was something we could've done to stop her sooner," Amber said. "If we had—"

"It's normal to feel that way," Drew said. "I've thought the same thing, and so has Trevor, I bet."

Trevor nodded, and Drew continued. "But the only one responsible for any of the deaths that happened—if the word *one* applies—is the Dark Lady. We need to be like Jenn and try to focus on all the lives we did save."

"There's one death she wasn't responsible for," Amber said.

"That wasn't your fault," Trevor said. "You were in the center of the Dark Lady's power. With all the psychokinetic energy flying around, you couldn't help tapping into it. It's what allowed you to manifest that gigantic wave—" He turned to Jenn. "With some help. It's what saved us all."

"It didn't save Mitch," she said softly.

Greg had told them that illusions could kill if they were charged with enough power. When Amber had manifested a sword and plunged it into Mitch's heart, the resultant energy discharge had caused him to suffer cardiac arrest. Unlike Erin, who had fallen to an illusory sword of far less power, he would never get up again. Trevor wasn't planning on shedding any tears for Mitch Sagers, but he wished he hadn't died, if only so his death wouldn't lie heavily on Amber's conscience.

Jenn reached across the table and took Amber's hand. "I know you didn't want to hurt him. You only wanted to stop him. But the things he planned to do to you—and me . . . The Dark Lady may have pushed him over the edge, but I can tell you this: she didn't have to push very hard. Trevor's right. You save us. Saved *me*. And I'll always be grateful."

Amber met Jenn's gaze, and the two women smiled at each other. Jenn squeezed Amber's hand once before letting go.

"Have you seen the video of last night?" Carrington asked. "It's absolutely chilling."

"How could we miss it?" Trevor said. "Seems like it's been playing nonstop on every TV channel and Internet news site in existence."

True to what they had told the Dark Lady, the media had descended in force on Exeter in the aftermath of the riot. The story was too juicy to ignore: mysterious deaths occurring in the Most Haunted Town in America, culminating in a full-on riot during a Halloween parade. Several local TV stations had been on hand during the action, in addition to parade goers who had escaped being caught in the Dark Lady's spell. Parade goers with video cameras and cell phones. Footage of the riot, both professional and amateur, had begun showing up on news stations and the Internet almost immediately. Much of the video had been distorted by electronic interference, but enough of it remained clear. Exeter had possessed a certain small amount of fame before, but after this, it would be forever infamous. If paranormal investigators and enthusiasts had been drawn to the town before, they would come in droves after this. The Dark Lady had created the very situation she had wanted to avoid. Trevor doubted that would be any comfort to those who had died and their loved ones, though.

"The images are horrible," Amber said. "Somehow it's even worse that none of the Dark Lady's illusions were recorded. Seeing ordinary people attack each other so savagely . . ." She trailed off.

"I'm a little ashamed to admit this," Trevor said, "but part of me is disappointed that the illusions didn't show up on film. If they had, then we finally would've had definitive proof of the existence of the supernatural."

"Certain open-minded individuals might believe such images," Carrington said, "along with those already predisposed to believe, of course. But most people would tell themselves it was all just special effects. A trick created by some computer program. They don't want to believe. They need to pretend they live in a sane, rational universe. If they knew that beings such as the Dark Lady existed among them, they would never feel safe again." He paused and then added, "I know I won't, not completely." Carrington turned to Erin. "I know it may be too early to ask this, my dear, but have you considered what you're going to do about your film?"

She glared at him. "Why? Afraid that all the fabulous footage we shot of you pontificating will go to waste?"

Carrington stiffened, but he managed to keep his tone even as he replied. "Believe it or not, after last night, I've rather lost my taste for the limelight. I was thinking about you. I would think continuing to work on the project would be extremely difficult for you after everything that's happened. But on the other hand, not finishing it might be just as difficult."

Erin continued glaring at him for a moment, but then she sighed, and the anger drained out of her. "You're right. The last thing I want to do now is make a film about ghosts. I don't care how much publicity it might get or how much it might advance my career. But I don't want to throw away all the work that Alex, Ray, Sarah, and Pattie did. I don't know what to do."

Drew looked thoughtful. "Maybe you could keep a lot of what you've already shot but change the focus of your film."

"What do you mean?" Erin said.

"Covering the town's reputation for paranormal activity is the obvious approach," Drew said. "But there's another story behind that, a story most people don't know about."

Amber smiled. "You're talking about the flood victims."

"That's a great idea!" Trevor said. "After last night, so many other people are going to report on Exeter, and that means your original approach will no longer be so original. Focusing on the flood victims will give your film a fresh slant."

"Plus, it would be a nice tribute to those who died in the flood," Amber said. "Who knows? It might even make them rest easier."

"And you can dedicate the film to the memory of your crew," Carrington said.

Erin thought about it for several moments, and then she slowly smiled. "It could work," she said. "And I think the gang would appreciate it."

"I'm sure they would," Carrington said. "I don't know if I'm the right person for that sort of film, but I'll be happy to help out in any way I can, either in front of or behind the camera."

"Thanks," Erin said, genuine gratitude in her voice.

"When will you find the time?" Trevor said to Carrington. "Won't you be too busy writing a book about what happened this weekend?" He didn't mean for it to come out as snotty as it sounded, but he didn't take his words back.

Carrington didn't appear offended, however. "I think that I'll leave the writing chores to you from now on. Despite how frightening it all was, and putting aside for the moment the terrible losses that occurred, this weekend I finally had the chance to experience the paranormal up close and personal." He smiled. "A little *too* close, I'm afraid. Still, I'm grateful to have had that experience. In many ways, it's the culmination of my career. But it also showed me that I've spent my entire adult life focusing on death. I think I'm going to try focusing on life for a change, while I still can."

Trevor smiled. "When I was a kid, you were a hero of mine, Arthur. When I grew up, though, I began to view you as a showman, a carnival barker of the paranormal shouting for people to hurry and see the freak show. But after this weekend . . . well, let's just say that as far as I'm concerned, you can bust a ghost with the best of them."

Carrington inclined his head. "Thank you, my friend."

"And if I do end up writing a book about this weekend, I hope you'll consider penning the introduction for it."

Carrington smiled. "It would be my honor."

The six of them talked for a while longer, but when Trevor suggested that they get some lunch, Carrington and Erin begged off. Despite his rested appearance, Carrington said that he was still tired and wanted to return to the bed-and-breakfast to rest, and Erin was his ride. They all exchanged contact information and promised to stay in touch, but Trevor wondered if they would. He knew what it was like to live with the memory of a traumatic experience, and sometimes the last thing you wanted was a reminder of it.

When Carrington and Erin had gone, Trevor said, "I got an e-mail from my editor this morning. She's really excited about the Lowry House book, and she's decided to put it on the fast track to publication. She's already working on scheduling a book tour, and she's come up with a cool publicity angle. She wants me to sign books in towns with paranormal sites that I can investigate." He grinned at Drew and Amber. "And she wants the two of you to come with me."

Drew and Amber looked at each other, silently conferring. Amber smiled and nodded, and Drew said, "I'll have to see what I can do about taking time off work, but why not? It could be fun."

"Excellent!" Trevor said. He turned to Jenn and asked, perhaps a bit too casually, "And you?"

"Huh? Oh, sorry. I was thinking that I need to go pack up my book table. They'll be closing the Exhibition Hall soon."

Trevor glanced at Drew and Amber, and they both gave him encouraging looks.

"How about I come along and help?" he said.

She gave him a small smile. "Sure, thanks."

He told himself that it wasn't a lack of enthusiasm he heard in her voice. It was just weariness.

They didn't speak at first as they walked through the hotel's hallways. The day before, the halls had been filled with conference attendees, many of them in costume. This day, there was hardly anyone around besides Trevor and Jenn, and those who were present wore street clothes.

"How are you doing?" Trevor finally asked.

Jenn didn't answer at first, and when she did, she didn't look at him. "I honestly don't know. I should feel all kinds of emotions, but I don't feel much of anything. I just feel numb."

"That's only to be expected," Trevor said. "After everything you went through—"

She did turn to look at him now. "But you went through it, too, and so did Drew and Amber. But none of you seem all that upset. The easy way you were talking . . . and you even joked a little."

"Believe me, we were shaken up by this experience, too. It's just that we've lived with the knowledge that the supernatural is real ever since we were teenagers. And then, after what happened at the Lowry House . . ."

"You get used to it?"

He shook his head. "No, but it helps you deal, you know?"

She gave him a blank look, and he knew she didn't understand. He decided to let the subject drop. She needed time to process her emotions, he told himself. She would be fine. Eventually.

Time to try again, he decided. "Would you like to come along? On the book tour, I mean."

They reached the Exhibition Hall and walked in. Half of the booths and tables were empty, and the remaining vendors were in the process of packing up.

"Why?" she asked. "I mean, I had nothing to do with the Lowry

House. Hell, until yesterday, I didn't believe things like that existed. Why would your publisher want me to come along?"

They reached Jenn's table. She walked behind it, picked up a cardboard box from the floor, set it on the tabletop, and began filling it with books. Trevor grabbed another box and began doing the same.

"The publisher doesn't want you to come," he said. "I do."

She stopped packing and turned to look at him. Her expression was unreadable, and Trevor, suddenly nervous, hurried to explain.

"I thought maybe it would be good for you to get out of town for a while. It might help you get some distance from what happened. And it would be great to have you along. You know, so we could spend more time together."

She smiled and reached out to touch his cheek gently. "Trevor . . ."

He forced a smile of his own. "Uh-oh. That doesn't sound good."

"It's sweet of you to ask, and under different circumstances, I think I would take you up on it. But you're part of what happened, and so are Amber and Drew. I don't know if I could stop thinking about this weekend if I came with you. How could I, with the three of you signing your book about the Lowry House and investigating spooky sites in the towns you visit? I would be living with the paranormal in one way or another every day."

"But things like last night aren't exactly common occurrences," he said.

"I used to think they couldn't occur at all. Can you promise me that something like that won't happen again?"

Trevor sighed. "No, I can't."

"That's what I thought." She lowered her hand from his cheek. "I'm going to clean up the mess in the bookstore and then put it up for sale, cheap. After that, I'm going to move away from Exeter. I don't know where I'll go yet. I have relatives in Alabama I haven't seen for a while. Maybe I'll visit them. But I don't really care where I end up, just as long as I get out of this town."

"I understand," Trevor said, working to keep the disappointment out of his voice.

"Now, listen to me closely, Trevor Ward. I am *not* saying I never want to see you again. I just need some time, OK? I fully expect you to call, text, and e-mail me from time to time. And you damned sure better 'like' all my status updates on Facebook. Understand?"

"Sure."

She gave him a long hug then, and he hugged her back, holding on to her as long as he could.

"How do you think it's going to go?" Drew asked.

"You're the psychologist," Amber said. "You tell me."

"*You're* the psychic."

She shrugged. "I don't know. But she didn't seem very warm toward Trevor, did she?"

"No, she didn't."

"Poor Trevor."

Drew nodded. "So how are you doing?"

Amber thought for a moment. "Good, I think. As good as can be expected, anyway."

"The more I think about accompanying Trevor on his book tour, the less sure I am that it's a good idea for us. For that matter, I'm not sure it's a good idea for him."

"Why?"

"Over the last few months, the three of us have had not one but two encounters with the supernatural. Both experiences were, to say the least, extreme. All three of us have been traumatized by these events to one extent or another, and if we were to continue investigating paranormal incidents, who's to say we won't encounter something else just as bad, if not worse? The psychological toll could be more than we can take."

"I admit it's not easy living with the things we've seen. But we have to focus on the people we've helped and the lives we've saved. That's what matters most in the end, right?"

Drew smiled. "Right."

Amber grinned. "Besides, regardless of whether the three of us should stop, do you really think we can?"

Drew didn't have an immediate answer for that, so Amber gave him a kiss and excused herself to go to the restroom. She went to the same one she had used the day before. Once inside, she checked to make sure she was alone, and then she stepped up to the sink and looked into the mirror.

"Hello, Greg."

His face—his true face, hairless and burn-scarred—smiled at her from behind the glass. *"Hi, sweetie. Long time no see."*

"I'm glad you're OK."

"Aside from being dead, I'm just peachy."

"When Connie woke up as herself again, I wasn't sure what happened to you. But I think I've figured it out. When the wave hit, it caught the Dark Lady off balance. As you'd pointed out, her power was already stretched thin, and when Jenn and I distracted her, you made your move. You left Connie's body, grabbed hold of the Dark Lady, and carried her with you over to the Other Side."

Greg grinned. *"Excellent deduction, Watson."*

"And when you took her, you took every spirit that was a part of her. All of them."

"Every ghost, specter, and spook in Exeter. It is now officially the Least Haunted Town in America. But you didn't come in here to verify your theory any more than you did to pee, did you?"

"I came to thank you—and to tell you that if you ever decide to help us again, we don't want you to possess anyone like you did Connie. All right?"

Greg made a pouty face. *"Party pooper."*

"But without you, we never would've been able to defeat the Dark Lady, so . . . thanks."

"You're welcome. And thank you for believing that I was sincere in my desire to help, even though you had every reason not to trust me. I have to say, I'm impressed by you, Amber. You've grown a great deal over the last couple of months, both personally and in power. But be careful. The stronger you become, the more dangers you'll be exposed to." His smile broadened. *"And the more temptations."*

An image flashed through her mind: the expression of stunned disbelief on Mitch's face as he impaled himself on her psychic sword.

"I'll be careful. Good-bye, Greg."

She turned to leave, but before she could go, he said, *"You'd better be. Because if you thought the Dark Lady was bad, wait until you see what's coming next."*

A chill grabbed hold of her at Greg's words, but she didn't look back as she walked out of the restroom, his laughter echoing in her ears.

Acknowledgments

All is only possible because my loving family. My wife, Kristen, my daughters Samantha, Haily, and Satori, and my twin sons Austin and Logan. You are the reason I wake every morning. You are all the reason I am where I am and I am who I am. You have all made my dreams possible and you walked this path beside me.

Jody Hotchkiss, thank you for everything. We changed the world all from a lunch meeting in CT. You had a vision and we had a dream.

—Jason

I'd like to thank my loving wife, Reanna, and my three amazing sons for their never-failing support of me in these various projects. My family and my good friends Mike, Chris, and Chris, for always sticking by me. Tim, of course, for weaving a better story than we ever could, and Jody for making it all happen. And to all those out there, still searching for answers to the unknown, your pioneering spirit is an inspiration to us all.

—Grant

As always, thanks to Jason and Grant for allowing me to play a small part in their paranormal adventures. Very special thanks to Larry Segriff and Emilia Pisani for picking up the ball and carrying it all the way for a touchdown.

—Tim